BILL OF THE DEAD

CARNAGE À TROIS

RICK GUALTIERI

ACKNOWLEDGEMENTS

A big shoutout of thanks to my awesome beta crew — Anthony, David, Kristi, Matt, Mark, Remy, Josh, Chris, Tom, and George. You guys helped me reengineer the inner workings of this book as well as ensuring I kept Gan as fun as she is dangerous.

PART I

PART I

1

TUNNEL OF BLOOD

I t's amazing the things I could fixate on as I ran for
my life.

Case in point, as I raced through the tunnels
beneath Manhattan, desperately trying to outrun the creatures chasing me, the one issue that kept coming up again
and again was how much it sucked not having a car.

My poor Toyota had gotten trashed by werewolves
about a week back, not exactly something I could admit to
my insurance company. It was much the same way I
couldn't just come out and casually tell ordinary people
that the reason I was in the sewers to begin with was
because daylight and vampires – of which I happened to
be one – didn't exactly mix.

The sewer tunnels had traditionally been a sort of
daytime haven for vamps. Sure, they stunk and were full
of shit, but they had the advantage of being dark, criss-
crossing the entirety of New York City, and lacking the
one thing that made being topside mostly unbearable –
the public.

My name's Bill Ryder and, even before my unfortunate
transformation into one of the undead, I was never what
you might call a people person. Right at that moment,

though, as the sound of skittering echoed in the tunnels behind me, I wouldn't have minded the safety of a crowd.

You're probably wondering what could frighten a vampire. After all, the legends say we're apex predators, the proverbial things that go bump in the night. Too bad a good chunk of that was just Hollywood bullshit.

Don't get me wrong. The older vamps got, the stronger we became. Safe to say, there were few things on Earth that could've stood up to a thousand-year-old vampire – had there been any left.

I wasn't a thousand, though. I was thirty, and I'd only been a vampire, again anyway, for maybe a month – roughly the same span of time since magic had returned to the world. Yeah, I could arm wrestle a powerlifter, leave an Olympic sprinter in the dust, and heal from most injuries in minutes. I even had a few extra perks, courtesy of being a special kind of vamp known as a Freewill. The problem was, cool as all of that could be, none of it equated to being unbeatable.

As my friend Sally, a former vamp herself, liked to remind me: the number one cause of permanent death among the undead was the dumbass belief that we were unstoppable.

You see, vamps and werewolves weren't the only monsters prowling the supernatural underworld that existed just outside the general public's radar – not by a long shot. And plenty of those other *things* could eat a young vampire for lunch.

Especially as of late.

The truth was, there seemed to be no shortage of freakish nasties crawling out of the woodwork. Primordial beasts, unknown even to scholars of the weird, had been popping up again after god-knows how long, thanks in part to the scales being reset.

The destruction of all magic five years ago – partly my fault, long story – had instantly banished, depowered, or outright destroyed many of the strange entities that had once ruled this world from behind the scenes. In the space of seconds, the mighty vampire nation was obliterated – nearly all the elders reduced to dust while young vamps like me simply became human again.

At the time it had seemed like a good deal.

But now magic was back and the balance that had existed in the supernatural world for millennia was gone, leaving behind a monster-sized vacuum to fill.

So, in a sense anyway, the things hot on my tail were karma given form, quite literally coming back to bite me in the ass.

Something leapt out at me as I reached a cross-tunnel. It was only due to my enhanced reflexes that I was able to stop in time, and only thanks to the slippery concrete that my feet slid out from beneath me, causing me to fall on my ass as the beast flew over my head.

Holy fuck!

Another perk of vampirism was excellent night vision, meaning I got more than a good enough look at the monstrosity to know to keep running, especially since its buddies weren't far behind.

As I scrambled to my feet, eyes wide with fear, I remembered a scene from *The Princess Bride* involving the so-called rodents of unusual size.

Mind you, calling it a giant rat was being generous as fuck. Its body was about five feet in length, around the size of a Great Dane, but that's where any semblance to Marmaduke ended. It had four pairs of spindly legs, a torso covered in greasy black fur, and a whiplike tail. It's freakishness was further cemented by a chitinous covering along its back that resembled nothing less than giant cock- roach wings.

I hadn't gotten a clear view of its face, but that was

okay. That's one nightmare I was happy to save for another day.

Or maybe not, as there came several high-pitched screeches from behind me. Reaching a relatively dry portion of the tunnel, because no way in hell did I want to slip again, I dared a glance back.

"Fuck me!"

I guess if I had to shit my pants, the sewer was the place to do it. Tempting as that was, though, I opted instead for running faster. That seemed the wiser choice.

I'd caught sight of two pairs of beady red eyes over a set of dripping mandible-like jaws. Had there been just the one, it would've been bad enough, but it seemed like the entire tunnel was full of them, charging after me from the ground, walls, and ceiling.

Worse, they were fast, but I guess that was to be expected. Eight legs trumped two in this rat race.

Goddamn! What the hell did you even call giant cockroach-spider-rats? Spiroats? Cockratters?

Ultimately, the only name that mattered was *dead meat*, as in what I'd be if they caught me. Call me crazy, but I didn't think these fucking monsters were after me because they were hoping to be Facebook friends.

Thulp!

Something splattered against the wall close by, a blob of sticky sludge. *Great! They have web shooters, too.* Or maybe not, as the wall immediately started sizzling.

Uh huh. Acid spitting cockratters. Just what I needed.

Fortunately, the proverbial light at the end of the tunnel was close. I was less than a short block away from the subbasement entrance beneath Sally's building, current HQ of the new and improved Village Coven.

Even so, it was going to be close.

Thulp!

Make that *really* close as two more of those acid blobs landed at my heels, just barely missing my shoes.

"Any thoughts on what these things are, Dr. ... um,

dude?" I asked my subconscious, stopping short of calling him Dr. Death. Ever since the weird-ass incident at the docks about a week back, in which I'd ended up tripping balls on leprechaun blood, that name had somehow felt wrong.

Mind you, now was probably not the time to worry about the feelings of the primal spirit I shared headspace with.

It was all for naught anyway. If the voice inside my head had any insight into these freaks, it was keeping that info to itself.

"Fine, be an asshole."

Thulp!

Something slammed into the back of my calf muscle, the sticky wetness turning to horrific pain a moment later as the substance ate through my pants leg and into my skin.

Fuuuuck!

It would've been enough to drop a normal person.

Thank goodness that didn't apply to me. Double thanks that I was terrified out of my fucking mind, the extra adrenalin keeping me moving even as I waited for my vamp healing to compensate.

There!

Fortunately, my leg managed to hold until I reached the ladder, buckling just as I grabbed onto it. That was okay. I still had three good limbs to spare.

I didn't dare look down to inspect the damage, the stench of burnt meat was more than enough. Instead, I focused on desperately pulling myself up toward the manhole cover above.

Please don't be locked!

That would be just my luck. Sally knew I was heading over. Yet the cover was still in place, telling me she'd either forgotten or had decided today would be a good day to fuck with me.

If so, the joke would be on her. She'd have to deal with

the coven all by herself while I was busy being digested by disgusting cockroach monsters.

As I neared the top, praying my wounded leg didn't pick that moment to fall off, I felt the metal rungs shudder from below.

Knowing I shouldn't look, but being far too scared to think rationally, I glanced down to see the first of the beasts had reached the ladder. Its spindly legs might be good for climbing walls, but the creepy-ass thing looked confused at the prospect of scaling rungs.

"Hah! Not so smart now, you roach motel motherfucker!"

Too bad its buddies were apparently bright enough to realize they didn't need to climb when they could simply pelt me with enough acid blobs to bring me down to their level.

I watched slack-jawed as a group of them opened their mouths wide, while even more came scuttling my way via the ceiling.

Jesus fucking Christ.

Just then there came the scrape of metal from above.

I turned back that way to see the manhole finally being dragged open. I resumed climbing, hoping I was fast enough to make it ... only to be stopped once again.

This time it wasn't the cockratters, though, so much as the shotgun pointing down at my face.

Uh oh.

2

COMING OUT OF THE CLOSET

"Here's an idea. Move if you want to keep your..."

That was all I heard before the deafening blast went off next to my noggin, likely shattering my eardrums.

Sally fired again, then waved me up, her frantic movements telling me I'd better haul ass. Well, either that or there was a handjob waiting for me.

Being that was unlikely, I dragged myself up the ladder without looking back, hoping she'd been able to scatter those things enough to buy me a second or two.

Sally was a far better shot than me, but it was no contest in the strength department these days. So, I grabbed the manhole cover and shoved it back in place while she worked the bolts to secure it shut.

We both stepped back just as there came a series of heavy thuds from below, enough to feel it through the soles of my sneakers. An acrid burning smell hit my nostrils along with it, the creatures trying their luck with their acid spit. Fortunately, the heavy iron cover seemed to be holding for now.

Several minutes passed as we waited, enough time for my hearing to return and my injured leg to start knitting back together. Thankfully, it seemed the cockratters had gotten the hint – not that I was planning to open up and check.

"Shall I assume you knew those things were down there, or did I do something to warrant a shotgun to the face?"

Sally smirked in return, her strange eyes – the irises and pupils both the same shade of green – twinkling. "Trust me. If you deserved a gun to the face, you'd be busy regrowing yours right now." She shook her head. "I came down earlier to unlock things, knowing you were on your way, but then closed it again real quick once I heard those things scurrying around. Fortunately for us both, you scream loud enough to hear you coming a mile away."

"That wasn't a scream. It was ... a battle cry."

She gestured toward her shoulder length tresses, currently raven black with green highlights. "Yeah, and my hair is naturally this color."

I opened my mouth to reply but stumbled before I could say anything, my leg still a mess. The wound had been ugly. If not for undead healing, I'd have likely ended the day debating between carbon fiber or aluminum replacements.

"You okay?" Sally asked.

"I will be. My pants on the other hand..."

"So long as they're covering the parts I don't want to see, it's all good. Save that stuff for Christy."

"Trying to." I glanced back at the manhole cover. "Any idea what those things were?"

"Yeah, more weird-ass shit we don't need ... unlike the stiff drink which I'm guessing we could both very much use right now."

I wasn't about to disagree.

"Are you sure you want to do this?" I asked about an hour later as we headed down the stairs from her fifth floor apartment, the excitement of the sewers finally fading. "I mean, what if it all goes...?"

"Tits up?" Sally replied, raising an eyebrow.

"I was gonna go with wrong."

"If it does, it does. Shit happens, Bill. That's a fact of life. Do you want to know the real difference between a good idea and a cataclysmically bad one?"

It was almost laughable how fast we could go from pants shitting terror to everyday business. But that quickly became the norm once someone was indoctrinated to the weird. "Sure."

"Good, because I was going to tell you anyway. There isn't any. All ideas are just that, ideas. Good or bad are determined in hindsight. The best idea in the world doesn't mean shit if you fuck it up."

"So you're saying we should forge ahead and not worry about it until such time as it bites us in the ass?"

"Exactly."

It was hard to argue with such impeccable logic as we headed downstairs to where the coven awaited us.

This was officially the first time Sally would be facing them since her little incident with Stewart – an unfortunate accident involving her new powers which had ended with him as a greasy smear on the wall.

Ever since, I'd been trying to talk the others off the ledge. They were all still too new to this life to understand how violently weird it could turn at a moment's notice. I hated to tell anyone they needed to become desensitized to that shit, but I'm not sure there was much choice if they wanted to survive without losing their minds.

I'd been debating how best to get everyone back on talking terms again when the simplest of solutions had dropped into my lap. One of the newbs had asked a question I didn't know the answer to. Sally, however, having once been a far more experienced vamp than I, could almost certainly provide some insight.

"You told these dipshits I was coming, right?" she

asked as we stepped out of the stairwell and onto the coven's floor.

"Shh. They can probably hear you."

"So?"

"So, I'm trying to fix things, not hurt their feelings."

"Hurt their feelings?" she replied extra loud. "They're vampires, not the fucking Care Bears."

"I know. I'm just trying to be ... nicer about it." We stopped in front of apartment 2A, the coven's unofficial common room, where I proceeded to rap on the door.

"What the hell are you doing?"

"Knocking."

"Oh, for fuck's sake. Get out of the way. You're embarrassing me."

She elbowed past and shoved the door open.

In the old Village Coven, it hadn't been uncommon to barge in and find vamps fucking each other's brains out atop piles of corpses. To say that things had changed was a bit of an understatement. The half dozen members I'd so far recruited were all seated on the couch, fully clothed, and doing nothing more nefarious than watching TV.

A new day had truly dawned.

All talk ceased as Sally stepped in, the only sound that of whatever banal sitcom they'd been watching.

To their credit, nobody bolted or attacked, but there were certainly plenty of deer in the headlights stares going on, broken only by Leslie, one of the new recruits, taking her eyes off us long enough to lower the volume.

"What's with the cutoffs?" she asked, eying my ruined jeans.

Not quite what I was expecting. "Um..."

Fortunately, Sally, never one for long hellos, jumped right in. "Your coven master asked me to come down here and..."

A thin, meek looking guy by the name of Craig raised his hand. "I'm not really comfortable with the word master."

Nods from the rest followed.

Oh boy.

I was immediately glad Sally hadn't brought a gun because I had a feeling every single vamp here would be eating a bullet to the face otherwise. But she apparently had a different take on things.

"Fine. Your coven *buddy* asked me to come down and speak to you. Call him whatever you want but remember he's in charge. And in a vampire coven that means he has the final say over whether you live or fucking die."

Okay, maybe not *that* different.

She stopped and took a deep breath. "But I'm not here to argue semantics. I've heard one of you had a question."

Jessica nodded, pushing her glasses up. She had such a strong Velma vibe going that I was surprised she didn't add "jinkies" to every sentence. "That was me. I wanted to know if it was possible to ... um, drink from someone without turning them into one of us."

"That's a good question..."

"Even if you'll hopefully never have to," I interrupted. "Remember, our number one goal is not to hurt anyone."

"Which is nice as far as pipe dreams go," Sally continued. "Bottom line is, you're vampires. You need blood to survive and it's the height of stupidity to think you'll never be in a situation where bottled blood is in short supply."

"I did pretty well ... for a while anyway."

"Exactly," she replied, turning her focus back toward the others. "Feeding isn't exactly an art form, but it does involve learning to control your powers." She paused for a moment, her demeanor changing from aggressive to the exact opposite. *What the?* "Without control, bad things can happen, even if you don't mean them to. I ... lost control last week and Stewart paid the price. I didn't mean for it to happen, but it's not something I can take back. I need to be better than that. We all do."

Wow.

Barely a week ago, Sally had emerged from her rocky

cocoon – the result of being zapped with a bolt of unearthly energy as we'd battled for our lives far underground. The strange metamorphosis had changed her in many ways, not the least of which was her body being rejuvenated back to her twenties, with an extra green flare to things. But that hadn't been all. She now possessed strange new powers that we didn't understand yet, powers which had inadvertently cost Stewart his life.

Even so, her apology had totally come out of left field. But perhaps that was for the best because her words felt genuine – and not just to me.

"Thank you," Leslie whispered.

Sally threw her a curt nod then said, "Getting back to the point, it takes time to build the control necessary to feed without turning. I think it was maybe four or five years before I could do it consistently."

"What did you do before then?" Bethany asked, her blue eyes opening wide beneath her pixie cut pink hairdo.

"Mostly crushed their skulls and set fire to the rest ... that sort of thing. Whatever worked."

So much for the touchy feely portion of our program.

"But you can start to build that control with a few simple exercises..."

"Wait," I interrupted. "How come you never told me any of this?"

She rolled her eyes. "Because I didn't expect you to make it four days, much less four years."

That led to a few chuckles at my expense, until Jessica said, "Hold on. If he's our coven ... leader, how come you can talk to him that way?"

Before I could even flash her a smile of gratitude, Sally replied, "Because I'm an outside consultant. The rules don't apply to me. Now, as I was saying..."

"Holy shit!" another of the guys, Oswald I think, cried.

"Relax. He's used to me saying stuff like..."

"Not that. Sorry, I meant on the TV."

I was about to tell him to shut it off and pay attention, when I realized I recognized the place on the screen.

Sally noticed it as well. "Turn that up."

"City officials have so far refused to comment, but some are claiming this video, which first surfaced on social media a few days ago, is proof positive that not only have the Strange Days returned, but that monsters now walk among us. We warn you in advance, what you are about to see may be disturbing to some viewers."

The video started innocently enough, someone filming a street in Midtown. Then it panned up to reveal a familiar view – a neglected chain link fence in the distance, and beyond it an abandoned pier and derelict warehouse.

"That's..."

"Falcon's place," Sally finished for me.

All at once, the air in front of the pier seemed to shimmer. In the next instant, the mundane imagery which had previously filled the screen was replaced with one of chaos. A purple energy dome appeared around the warehouse, for a moment anyway, before dissipating to nothingness. That was small beans, however, compared to the battle playing out around it.

It was a fight I knew all too well, being that we'd survived it barely a week ago. A flash of red from off to one side confirmed this. The only plus in our favor was that whoever had filmed it was too far away to capture Christy's face as she blasted a hole in the ground, sending several smaller figures flying.

The budding cinematographer apparently realized this, too, as they tried to zoom in, resulting in a still the newscast paused on – a blurry closeup of a glowing fish monster, a member of a race called the apkallu.

"It was me, wasn't it?" Sally asked as the news team continued to blather on, turning to a so-called expert to discuss the veracity of the film. "I caused that."

"Shit." There was no way the timing was a coincidence. Sally had been swarmed at one point during the battle, at least until the strange power inside her had activated, sending out a pulse of energy that had not only blown the shit out of the creatures closest her, but had shorted out the force dome protecting the warehouse owned by Matthias Falcon – wizard, millionaire, special consultant to the New York police, and the man single-handedly trying to bring porn-staches back in style.

What apparently none of us realized at the time, however, was that the pulse had apparently also frigged up the glamour surrounding the pier, the one keeping the world from seeing the weirdness going on inside.

And just our luck, one of the neighbors had been awake to capture it all.

I pulled out my phone and began scrolling through it. *Son of a...* Sure enough, thanks to the boost from the news, the video was now trending on Twitter and already had almost a million views on YouTube.

It wasn't the first time the weirdness of the world had been filmed, but it might've been the first time it had been allowed to go viral. In the past, such things had been quickly squashed by the powers that once were – the vampire nation, the Magi, et cetera. Almost all of the old vamps were dead, though. As for the other factions, they were either asleep at the switch or no longer gave a damn.

"What do we do?" Craig asked, panic edging into his voice. "You said they can't know about us, that they'd hunt us down and..."

"I know what I said," I replied, trying to figure this out before his anxiety became contagious. "But the situation has obviously changed. We..." *Come on, Bill, think!* "We ... need to get out in front of this."

"We do?" Sally asked, one eyebrow raised.

"Yeah. I think it's time we finally did it."

"Did what?"

"Let the world know that vampires exist. That we walk among them, but we're not their enemy. We need to tell them everything before they figure it out themselves, that way we control the narrative."

Sally inclined her head. "It sounds like you're talking about a..."

"Exactly. We need to hold a press conference."

"Are you serious?"

I let her question hang in the air for several seconds before replying. "Of course I'm not fucking serious! Are you crazy? You think I want to end up in a lab somewhere waiting to be dissected?"

Sally narrowed her eyes for a moment but then grinned. "Who am I to kink shame?"

Sadly, she was the only one who apparently found it amusing. Tough crowd.

"Um, excuse me," Leslie said, as a few nervous chuckles passed through the group. "Jokes aside, that still doesn't tell us what we're going to do about this."

"Sure it does," Sally said, throwing a nod my way that told me she had this. "We do absolutely fucking nothing."

"But..."

"It's not high res enough to ID anyone, and there's no way the NYPD is going to admit their golden boy Falcon was involved. So we lay low until it blows over, act like everything is hunky dory and..."

"And stay the fuck out of the sewers," I cut in.

"The sewers?" Jessica asked. "What does that...?"

I held up a hand, happy for the segue as my joke had obviously fallen flat. "I'm glad you asked because that brings us to our second agenda item of the evening — cockroach monsters and how to avoid them."

So much for being an effective coven master, leader, or even buddy.

3

A BITCH IN TIME

"Another few days and we'll be ready."

"Are you sure?" I asked into the phone, navigating the evening foot traffic back home, a pint of pig blood and some chicken empanadas in the bag by my side.

"Positive," Christy replied, sounding more cheerful than she had in days. "I have all the components that I need for the spell..."

"Including a thousand gold pieces worth of diamond dust?"

"What?"

"Sorry, gamer humor. Go on." Oh well, it was still better than watching my jokes fall flat during last week's coven meeting.

"I just want to spend a bit more time prepping Tina. She knows what needs to be done, but I..."

"You don't have to justify anything. I understand."

"Thanks, Bill." She let out a deep breath. "I just hope it works."

"I have full faith in the witches casting it."

"I'm glad one of us does. This type of blood magic is ... unusual, powerful. Like nothing I've ever done before."

"Are we talking human sacrifice here?"

"Nothing that drastic, fortunately. But even if it works, there's still the question of reaching Ed once we locate him. We don't know where Gan has him, or under what circumstances."

I nodded, despite her being unable to see me. It had been about two weeks since she'd discovered that new spell and we were all itching to see if it worked. "Yeah. Finding out that she's keeping him in, say, an undersea volcano lair doesn't help us much. But one step at a time. Right now this is the best shot we have."

"I know. I just want to get him back safe."

"Me, too. It'll be nice to have the old team back together. We might be a dysfunctional family, but we get shit done."

Another voice spoke up from the background. "Ooh. You said a bad word, Uncle Bill."

"Do you have me on speaker?"

"Sorry. I'm making her royal highness some chicken nuggets."

I couldn't help but laugh. Christy was all sorts of badass, but her daughter Tina was perhaps the most powerful witch to walk this Earth since the White Mother. Mind you, she was also only five. So if she wanted chicken nuggets, then chicken nuggets it was. "Tell her to put an IOU in the swear jar."

"Oh, she'll remember, believe me."

I had no doubt about that. My goddaughter was cute as a button, but she was mercenary as fuck when it came to her Disney fund – one of the few traits she'd inherited from her father.

Christy lowered her voice to a whisper. "By the way, I was thinking. After we get Ed back and things calm down a bit ... maybe we can finally do a little celebrating on our own."

That thought alone put a spring into my step. It was so awesome to have a girlfriend like her – someone I was good friends with, who truly understood me. Mind you, it would be even more awesome if we could get back to having sex. Sadly, the fates had conspired to cockblock us for several weeks now. Between trying to locate Ed, me becoming a vampire again, Christy's ex returning to life in the body of my ex, and all sorts of other weird-ass shit going on, there hadn't been much chance for any alone time.

And well, damnit, at this point even hearing her talk about chicken nuggets was enough to make my dick hard.

"Oh hey," she said, drawing my attention away from *little Dr. Death* before he decided to *vamp* out, "I got a text from Kelly earlier."

"Cool. Where's she been all this time?"

"Up north. She and Vincent had some things to work out. They should be back soon, though."

Which, knowing Kelly, probably meant they'd been doing a lot of boning and were finally exhausted enough to come home. Great, and we were right back to sad dicked Bill. Oh well. That's why they invented internet porn. "Good to hear it. It'll be nice to have them back."

"I'll say. Tina's got all the talent in the world, but I wouldn't mind having another adult witch to talk to again."

"I bet."

"Any plans for tonight?" she asked, changing the topic.

"Nothing major. Might go out and patrol a bit."

"Be careful," she said, turning serious. "I talked to Matthias yesterday and he said ... well, to be careful."

"We talking leprechauns, fish men, or something else?"

She paused before answering. "I got the impression it was kind of all the above."

Wonderful. Although I couldn't pretend it was surprising to hear. "Don't worry. I have no intention of playing hero."

"So you keep saying."

"And that's how I plan to keep it. What about you? Anything on your plate, aside from chicken nuggets?"

"The usual – battling the forces of evil."

That caught my attention. "Oh?"

She chuckled. "I have a Zoom call with the west coast marketing team."

"Ugh. I'd think I'd rather deal with those leprechauns."

"Me too." Christy paused, long enough for a comfortable silence to set in. "Okay, let me go finish dinner so I can get ready. Talk to you soon."

"Not soon enough. Love y... ly weather to go out on patrol." *Oh boy.*

"Huh? What was that?"

"I meant talk to you later, bye."

I quickly hung up, my eyes opening wide as I realized what I'd come this close to saying. The thing was, it hadn't been forced at all. It had just tried to come out on its own, as if it were the most natural thing in the world.

Holy crap.

Mere weeks ago, I'd been busying myself with thoughts about where our relationship might be headed. But I think a part of me was doing that for no other reason than I assumed that's what I *should* be thinking at this point. The truth, however, was that we were already far beyond that. Getting together with Christy had felt like the most natural thing in the world. Maybe that's because it was.

Despite us being forced to take a bit of a dating break due to things going crazy in our lives – including the threat of Gan, the three-hundred-year-old psycho who'd decided I was hers and hers alone – I think deep down in my subconscious I was doing the opposite, coming to terms with the fact that we were ... well, *right* together.

And now it was finally bubbling to the surface, demanding that I acknowledge it.

Talk about a complication none of us probably needed right now.

I stewed on that for several blocks, alternately embracing it, denying it, and trying to rationalize it, before realizing there was no fucking way I could process it at the moment.

So I instead did what I do best – pushed it to the back of my mind and tried to focus on stuff I could actually deal with. My thoughts turned back to the fight at the docks. We were now going on two weeks since it had gone down and, though the wounds I'd suffered were long gone, there was plenty left about it which continued to bother me.

As predicted, the zeal behind that video had died down pretty quickly. Thank goodness for the internet trolls who'd done their damnedest to debunk it, working furiously as if it were a new harem hentai that needed pirating.

Within a few days, the world had already moved on to its next obsession – some B-list celebrity endorsing a semen diet or something stupid like that.

That was the beauty of the human race, and part of the reason why the weird could cohabitate right next door to normalcy without anyone suspecting a thing. People had short attention spans.

Too bad ignoring something didn't make it any less real.

That was one crisis averted, but it didn't change the fact that we'd fought ancient fish monsters, troglodyte leprechauns, and brainwashed vampires. And more recently I'd found my ass running from freaky ass cockroach monsters in the sewers. In short, all signs pointed to things getting worse, not better.

Then there was the thing that haunted my thoughts in the wee hours of the morning when I was trying to sleep.

Near the end of the dock battle I'd ended up taking a

header into the Hudson. That itself was bad enough, but then I'd seen *something* in the water.

Heh, did I say stuff I could actually deal with?

The memory itself was terrifying enough to even counteract thoughts of sexing up Christy, if just barely. At the time, it had been easy to dismiss, being that I'd been high as fuck on leprechaun blood, but a part of me insisted it had been real – that I'd seen a massive sea beast living in the Hudson, as impossible as it was.

Unfortunately, being a vampire dating a witch and all, I was living proof that impossible was nothing more than a word.

I'd found myself conducting no small number of internet searches over the course of the last several days, seeking to prove it had all been in my mind, only to find that maybe wasn't the case. It wasn't much, just two recent photos, both blurry and inconclusive. One showed a massive shadow beneath the waters of the Hudson, the other a large wake with no apparent source. Unlike the dock fight video, neither had garnered any real buzz. However, they were enough to have me worried.

What the fuck could it mean?

And did it have anything to do with whatever Gan had unleashed upon this world – unwittingly or not – when she'd reopened the floodgates of magic, turning the spigot all the way up in the process.

Even crazier was why I was letting it bother me. Rescuing Ed was my priority. Beyond that, none of this was my problem – especially anything having to do with sea monsters. I was just a guy trying to live my life. Sure, I'd taken in some strays for the coven, but beyond that all I really wanted to do was spend time with my girl, get shit-faced with my friends, and mind my own fucking business.

That wasn't so much to ask for, was it?

"Oh, hey, Mr. Ryder!"

"Huh?" I looked up from collecting the mail to see Mike Walden heading my way. He was my newest tenant, having taken over the basement apartment after the Suarez family abruptly moved out.

Talk about a shit show. Mrs. Suarez had accidentally run into my roommates the week prior – Tom holding his sword and stinking of sewage and Glen minus his cat disguise. Needless to say, there'd been a bit of a freak out on her part at seeing a sentient ball of slime climbing the stairs. The only upside was the ink on the occupancy listing had barely been dry before I'd gotten a taker.

I tried not to smirk as Mike approached. His full name, the one he'd put on his lease, was Michael Hunter Walden, instantly bringing to mind every Mike Hunt joke I'd ever heard. He seemed like a nice enough guy, in that he didn't come across as a meth head, although it was painfully obvious he was new to the city. But whatever. Rent was rent – something I needed to remind my roomies not to fuck up for me again.

"What's up?" I greeted. "Oh, and it's just Bill."

"Not much. Just saying good evening, sir. I mean, Bill. And ... wondering if you maybe know of any good places to grab a burger around here."

"Sure. There's a Five Guys over on 7th, and the diner on 5th will actually serve them rare if you ask nicely ... um, assuming that's your thing."

"Thank you. I appreciate it."

I nodded before starting up the stairs.

"Oh, and Bill ... be careful."

That caught my attention, more so now than in years past. "Why?"

"Nothing really," he was quick to add. "Just saw some shady characters hanging around the neighborhood is all."

"Doesn't really narrow it down all that much."

I chuckled as I headed upstairs, remembering back to when I'd first moved here from New Jersey. It had all seemed so big and scary at the time, but it was just a place to live like anywhere else. He'd get with the program quickly enough – assuming nothing strange actually happened to send him screaming back to whence he came.

That was a big if these days, being that his upstairs neighbors included a vampire, a faith-imbued mystical warrior, and an eyeball laden blob of snot.

I swear, one of these days I needed to modify the rental application to add the interview questions from *Ghostbusters*.

None of that was important right then, though, compared to scarfing down some dinner. A plate of bloody Mexican food and a beer or two and then I could figure out how to spend my evening – be it out on patrol or working on my latest contract, some backend database programming for a local falafel chain.

Neither seemed particularly enticing as I opened the door to the top floor apartment and stepped inside, noting the lights were off. Though I didn't need them to see, I flipped them on out of habit before kicking the door shut.

I'd just set my bag down when my enhanced senses picked up the sound of movement from behind me.

Before I could turn around, however, a pair of exquisitely manicured hands wrapped around my midsection. I immediately tensed up when I felt the wonderful sensation of boobs pressing up against my backside.

Please don't be Tom.

A moment later, a pair of lips planted themselves gently on the side of my neck and started working their way down.

Ooh.

My crotch gave an excited twitch as I remembered what Christy had told me earlier. Guess she'd finished those chicken nuggets and had decided to apparate over for a quickie, as I'd been heavily hinting she do ever since her powers returned. If so, then I was more than happy to...

"I have missed you oh so much, my beloved," an entirely different voice said.

Oh crap...

And just like that, my dick wilted like a dead flower.

4

THANKS FOR THE MAMMARIES

G uess I should've listened to Mike's warning, because it sure as shit didn't get much shadier than Gan.

It would figure that weeks of speculation on where she was holed up, followed by intense preparation of a questionable spell meant to find her secret lair, would culminate in the creepy fucker just showing up out of the blue to cop a feel.

I *really* should've expected this would happen. Would have saved us a lot of prep work.

Oh well.

I pulled free from her embrace and spun – taking a wild swing in the hopes of hitting her stupid face – only to strike nothing but empty air, my momentum knocking me into the freaking refrigerator almost hard enough to upend it.

Unsurprisingly, Gan was already halfway across the living room by then, facing me in her full glory. When I'd first met her, the adopted daughter of Ögedei Khan, she'd been a three-hundred-year-old vampire forever trapped in the body of a twelve-year-old girl. It hadn't made for a good combo.

But then magic had gone poof. She should've as well.

By then, however, she was no longer a regular vampire. She'd been bitten by my friend Ed, the first of a new breed. It had changed something in her. Not only was she now able to withstand the sun but, unlike the other elder vamps, she hadn't withered to dust when magic fled this world. Instead, she'd become human – or something akin to it – the beast inside her going inert for five years, finally allowing her to age from a preteen terror into a lethal love-struck Lolita.

But now her powers were back in full, once again halting the clock but doing nothing for all the crazy still bottled up inside her.

Gan stood there now, her lithe form looking like she'd escaped from the cover of Teen Vogue. She put one hand on her hip in a manner that suggested she considered my attack to be little more than foreplay.

Oh God, I am never getting an erection ever again.

She let out a chuckle as I took a moment to right myself, her bright green eyes practically burrowing into my soul. "It is so good to see you can still make me laugh after all this time, my love."

I narrowed my eyes. "Well, you know what they say. If you gotta go, go with a smile." I launched myself at her, doing nothing but trashing our folding table because, as usual, Gan fought like the rest of the world was moving in slow motion.

"As enchanting as this is, Beloved, I'm here to..."

"Get your ass kicked?" I finished, writing checks with my mouth that I doubted my body could cash. "Because you sure as hell deserve it after what you did."

Her list of crimes was myriad. Not only was she a mass murderer several times over, but she'd orchestrated magic's return – putting us all in danger by making a deal with something powerful enough to kick open the doors to this world and reignite the Source again. Then, just to add insult to injury, she'd kidnapped Ed.

"I only did what was necessary," she replied, nimbly

dodging my next attack. "It is neither this world's destiny to remain locked from the multiverse, nor is it yours to while away your years in mediocrity."

"Maybe I like mediocrity! Um, you know what I mean."

Okay, this wasn't working. Not only was Gan my physical superior many times over, but she'd forgotten more about fighting than I ever cared to learn. I could chase her all day and still come up emptyhanded.

I needed to stop playing her game and use my own strengths to my advantage, which were ... um, coding database applications? Okay, forget that. I'm sure there was something *else* I could use.

Man, I really needed to buy a gun. If so, then maybe I could...

Use your surroundings, the voice in my head chimed in.

Wait! The living room. Dr. ... um whatever was right. This place was a shit hole, but it was *my* shit hole. I knew it like the back of my hand.

"I'm not here to fight, my love," she said, her eyes locked on me.

"Fine, then let's wrestle instead!" Okay, definitely a *poor* choice of words, but whatever. I once again launched myself at her, throwing my body length wise as if this were a WWE match and I was leaping off the top rope.

Gan tried to move, only to clip one of the end tables ... exactly as I'd hoped. It slowed her down just enough for me to plow into her, sending us both tumbling over the sofa and ending up with me on top.

"Hah! Gotcha you little ... mmmph."

She easily broke free of my grasp, wrapped her legs around me, then forced her tongue down my throat.

Gah! I'd once again played into her overly grabby hands. So much for a winning strategy.

She disengaged just long enough to say, "Using the environment to your advantage? Oh how it sets my loins afire."

"Fuck you, you psychotic..."

Her mouth enveloped mine again before I could finish, making me think it would be wise to avoid saying anything else that implied fucking.

Sadly, she had me right where she wanted me, quite literally. Even with my advantage in both position and leverage, she was able to overpower me as she continued drilling through the top of my mouth with her tongue.

Hell, I couldn't even make a Listerine crack since her breath was minty fresh. *Figures!*

click

What the? I turned my head to see she'd pulled out a cell phone and ... holy shit! Was she actually taking selfies? Talk about adding insult to injury.

Oh, fuck that noise.

I only had one recourse if I wanted to end this – something so vile the very thought of it made me want to puke in both our mouths.

As her tongue probed every square inch of my mouth, like an alien invader going hog wild with an abductee, I willed my fangs to extend.

This wasn't going to be pleasant, but the only way to fight her horny fire was with more fire.

Gan might've been a neo-vamp – my name for the new breed – but I was the legendary Freewill of the original vampire race. Stupid a title as that was, it came with some perks, not the least of which was the ability to borrow the strength of other vamps via way of their blood.

I clamped down onto her tongue and stared into her eyes, wanting her to know what was to come as I prepared to sink my teeth into...

So, of course it figured my roommates would pick that moment to return home, the front door opening to reveal Tom and a bloated, desiccated corgi that could only be Glen's latest disguise.

Fuck me!

Tom stood there a moment, gawking as I tried to pry myself off Gan.

"Not cool, dude. Christy's going to lose her shit."

"I..." Gan eased up just enough to let me catch my breath. "I'm not trying to bang her, you idiot. I'm trying to kick her ass."

"With your dick?"

"No!"

"Ooh, is this a battle?" Glen replied. "I need to go get my camera."

He began waddling past us toward his bedroom.

Idiots. I lived with fucking idiots.

At least Gan finally let me go, giving me a chance to scrabble away from her, feeling like I needed a good delousing. Goddamn, I really needed to start carrying pepper spray.

"Shining One," she said with a nod, standing up and straightening her dress. "Or should I say, new Shining One?"

Guess she'd clued in on the fact that it might be Sheila's body, but Tom was the current occupant.

"Oh shit, it's you!" Tom cried, finally taking a good look at her.

"Who else do you think would be trying to mouth fuck me like that?" I snapped.

"I don't know. A prostitute maybe."

If Gan took offense at the irony of being called a whore, she didn't show it. "The witch's former paramour returned in the Shining One's body. Fate, it would seem, possesses a sense of irony."

"What do you mean former?"

"Are you just going to take that shit?" I asked him. "Get her!"

"You get her, asshole. She's *your* girlfriend."

"No, she isn't."

31

"Indeed. I am his bride to be."

"Will you shut the fuck up with that?" I glanced back at Gan, noticing she was fiddling with her phone now. "Wait, what the hell are you doing?"

"Is it not obvious, my love? I'm uploading our photos to Instagram."

"What?!"

"For my six hundred thousand followers to enjoy."

"Six-hundred thousand..."

"Dude," Tom remarked. "That's a shitload more than..."

"Don't remind me." I turned my attention back to her. "Since when do you use social media?"

"Ever since," she replied, continuing to type, "I realized the modern world is fascinated by wealth, beauty, and love. As I possess all three, it's only natural that I should be an influencer."

Oh fuck. I'd thought she was bad when she was a love-struck twelve year old, but now she was morphing into some kind of ... Kardashian. All right, enough of this shit. I turned back toward Tom. "You're the Icon, she's a vampire. So ... do some Icon stuff."

"Um..."

"What? Are you afraid of her or something?"

"Well, yeah, kinda."

"I..." Okay, maybe I couldn't blame him for that one. The battle seemingly over for now, I took a moment to reflect on that.

Last time we'd seen Gan, she'd injected him with a concoction known as the blood of Baal, one of the few things that could counteract an Icon's powers, enigmatically calling it... "Wait ... why did you call it that?"

"Excuse me, my love?"

"You stabbed him with that needle and called it *your gift* to me."

Tom glared sidelong at me. "Thanks. Because I really needed to relive that moment."

Glen in the meanwhile slithered out of his room, minus the corgi body but with a digital camera nestled in a tendril of slime. "Is it over? Did I miss it?"

"It *was* indeed a gift," Gan replied, ignoring him, "because it allowed you to withdraw with honor. Staying would have surely resulted in the deaths of your allies. I wished to spare you that anguish, misguided as it might be."

"You..." *Grr!* She was right. Much as I didn't want to admit it, I would've kept going after her had she not done that — we all would've. Who knows what would have happened if we hadn't chosen to pull out when we did? As a result, we'd all walked away, even Sally, though I didn't know it at the time.

Fuck!

That didn't mean I was about to forgive and forget. "You took Ed."

"I had need of him."

"And because of you I'm this ... *thing* again," I added, flashing my eyes black.

"Technically that was Dave," Tom remarked.

"Do me a favor and stop trying to help."

Gan inclined her head. "Because of me, you are strong again. As are your friends."

"That's..." Okay, technically she was right. I was probably in the minority when it came to being unhappy about my powers being back. Hell, even Christy, with all her worries about Tina, had been very measured with her words whenever I'd broached the subject of anything we could've done differently down at The Source. In truth, I doubted I'd find many others who'd have opted to turn the power back off again.

Mind you, Ed was probably one of them. "Hold on. What do you mean *had need of him*, as in past tense?"

She dismissed my concerns with a wave of her hand. "The Progenitor has been well cared for, I can assure you. As for his usefulness, you needn't worry. His life is meaningful to you. Thus it is meaningful to me via the bond we share."

"We don't share a..."

Perhaps that is a thought worth rethinking, the voice in my head interrupted. He was right, too. The last thing I wanted to do was put Ed in more danger than he already was.

"What I meant is, where is he?"

"Allow me to speak my piece and I shall make that known, Beloved."

I glanced at Tom to gauge his opinion.

He shrugged in response. "You can always kick her ass later."

Yeah, I could ... maybe.

"Fine, but it had better be good." I gestured toward my roommate. "Want to grab us a couple of beers? I don't know about you, but I have a feeling I'm going to need one before this is over."

5

SPECIAL DELIVERY

Tom, Glen, and I sat on the couch, drinks in hand – or tendril – glaring at Gan as we waited to hear what she had to say.

Well, Tom and I were glaring anyway. Was hard to tell with Glen, being that the two dozen or so eyeballs in his gelatinous body were kinda looking every which way, but I figured I'd give him the benefit of the doubt.

Gan started by opening her pocketbook and pulling out a sheet of newsprint, which she unfolded and handed to me.

It was an obituary, the headline reading *City Mourns Death of Pandora's Light Founder*.

Below was a picture of Sally, or at least how she'd appeared about two months back, before her recent transformation.

I tossed it onto the coffee table. "So? Are you here to tell us you sent flowers?"

"No."

"I did," Glen announced. "I borrowed your credit card, Freewill. Tom said you wouldn't mind."

I turned to glare at my other roommate before getting back to the task at hand.

35

"Fine, then I'm going to assume you didn't stop by to offer your condolences. It was her idea, by the way. She figured it was easier to cut ties with the foundation rather than run it like some Howard Hughes recluse."

"I have no quarrel with your whore's methods."

"Good, then..."

"Merely her existence."

I narrowed my eyes. So that's what this was about. I should've fucking known. Sally's current *condition* was a result of her getting hit with a blast of power that had been meant for Gan, something promised in return for her fucking over the world.

"So this is about revenge?"

"If it was, I would have attempted it by now."

"What do you mean attempt?"

A pained look came over Gan's face, her mask dropping momentarily. "Do you have any idea what she has become, what her rebirth heralds?"

"What? Is she like a Capricorn or something?" Tom asked. "Because they tend to be assholes."

"You're a Capricorn, dipshit."

"See?"

I shook my head, turning my focus back toward Gan. "I doubt it heralds anything worse than if she hadn't pushed you out of the way."

"In that you are wrong, my love. I made a pact..."

"Let me guess, with something called the Great Beast?"

She nodded. "Yes. That is one of its names."

"So what, you sold us out to some asshole demigod?" Tom replied.

"To call the Beast a demigod is to call a dragon merely an oversized newt."

Can't say that gave me a warm and fuzzy feeling in the pit of my stomach.

There are ancient texts that make reference to creatures which are beyond even the gods of old.

Not now, Dr. Whoever the fuck you are.

"I wished for this world to be part of the multiverse again," Gan continued. "And yes, I desired my immortality back, the same way the Magi pined for their lost power. Alas, the Beast was one of the few entities powerful enough to respond to my plea. It took my entreaty as a sign that it was time for it to finally awaken after untold centuries. But that is where what you believe differs from reality."

"Oh? Do tell."

She met my gaze, her bright green eyes boring into mine like horny drill bits. "Tell me, my love, do you think so little of me to assume I would serve any master other than myself ... or you?"

I opened my mouth to reply, but her last two words caused me to get all tongue tied. *Fortunately*, Tom was there to fill in the blanks.

"I do."

Gan opted to ignore him, probably a good thing. "I was prepared to accept its covenant, yes, but not for the reasons you think. To be a herald of ... the Great Beast, as you have called it, is to be granted power that even one such as Lord Alexander would have considered daunting."

It made me remember back to how Sally had pulped Stewart so violently that his remains hadn't even gotten a chance to turn to ash.

"Let me guess. You planned to use this power so you could go off and rule this universe from beyond the grave."

"Or check into a psycho-ward," Tom added, reading me like a book. "Whichever comes first." He held up a hand. "Fuck that Lo Pan shit."

I high-fived him, then turned back to find Gan staring at us with one eyebrow raised. Huh. Guess she wasn't a John Carpenter fan.

"I planned to use its own power against it, to stop it from consuming this world."

"Likely story."

"Look me in the eyes and tell me if you see deception staring back."

Making eye contact with her was at the bottom of things I wanted to do, but I did so anyway – not that it did any good. She was utterly unreadable, the type of person who could probably fib all day while connected to a lie detector and never let it slip.

My gut, however, told me she wasn't. What would lying gain her? Besides, I knew her well enough to know there was one reason above all others. "Let me guess. You bow to no one." Before she could say anything, I added, "Except me. Yeah, I know the drill."

"Precisely, my love." She grinned. "That you are able to finish my thoughts tells me the time of our eternal union cannot be far off."

"No thanks. I still need to brush my teeth after our last union." I made a hurry up gesture. "Back to the point. What does any of this have to do with Sally?"

"That power now resides within her."

"Okay, so how do we use it to fuck over this Great Beast and get back to our regularly scheduled lives?"

She shook her head. "It's not that simple. She lacks the mental fortitude, the preparedness to undertake this with any notion of success. The Beast's power will overwhelm and consume her. Her shortsighted attempt to slight me has instead, I fear, put this world on a collision course with utter annihilation."

"Like we haven't been there before," Tom remarked.

"I'd prefer to not be there again, if it's all the same to you," Glen countered.

I held up a hand for them to hopefully shut the fuck up. "Okay, then how do we get it out of her ... and preferably not into you?"

"The covenant between myself and this entity has been fulfilled. Nothing more has been promised. As for the rest, is it not obvious?" Gan replied, causing my left eye to twitch. "She must be killed before she in turn kills us all."

I was neither surprised nor overly horrified by what Gan said. Call me desensitized, but death threats and vampires went together like peanut butter and bloody chocolate. Didn't mean I was going along with it, mind you.

"Not happening."

"There is no choice in this matter," she replied as if it were a mandate from heaven. "I only tell you this so you can prepare for whatever closure you might need. Your happiness matters to me after all."

"That's real big of you. But what if my happiness depends on Sally's survival?"

"Then you shall be disappointed, which will break my heart. But you will get over it eventually." She let out a sigh, as if she found her next words distasteful. "You should know I take no pleasure from this, my love. Contrary to what you may believe, I find your whore to have several agreeable traits."

"Such as?"

"She has befriended you."

Ask a stupid question.

"If it helps," she continued, "I have been investigating other means to stop this dire future, but at the moment I believe there will soon come a time when a hard choice needs to be made."

"What about just turning off the power again?" Tom asked. "I mean, you know where all those magic jizz pools are located. So go there and shut that shit down."

He had a point. Reigniting the Source and opening this world to magic again hadn't been enough for Gan. She and her Magi minions had done something to split its power – destroying the original for good, but creating thirteen new Sources scattered throughout the world – their location a mystery to the rest of us.

Gan was silent for several long moments as his question sank in.

"I'm gonna go out on a limb here," I said, "and assume you're willing to make every hard choice *but* that one."

It's not just her and you know it.

"Shut the fuck up."

"Nobody said anything," Tom replied. "Or are we back to voices in your head again? Because you know there's this thing called therapy right?"

"There's also this thing called my foot up your ass."

Sadly, Dr. Death, or this more thoughtful version of him, was right. Five years ago when we blew the shit out of The Source, it had been a move borne of desperation. There'd been little time to consider the ramifications of our actions in advance.

Some of us had been able to move on, true, but things had worked out a lot less wonderfully for many others. Hell, I'd seen firsthand the desperate lengths some had taken to get back what they'd lost.

Would we truly be doing anything more than resetting the clock if we turned things off again? How long would it be before the next group came up with an even crazier gambit to reopen the magical spigot?

The bigger question, though, was whether we – *I* – was willing to trade Sally's life for so many others.

Well, okay, that was an easy one. I wasn't vying for sainthood. Most people could go fuck themselves. Sue me for being a realist.

"I do not believe that would work," Gan said at last. "The Beast forced the doors open once. It could do so again. In fact, that would be even likelier now that its taste of this world has whet its hunger for conquest."

"I'm gonna lay that one squarely on your head."

She shrugged but didn't deny it. Ah, to have her lack of conscience. Life's gotta be so much easier when you don't give a single solitary shit about anyone else.

"Alas, I fear the only way to dissuade it is to deal it a suitable defeat but, in order to do so, we must..."

"I said it's not happening!" I brought my fist down onto the coffee table, hoping to intimidate her, but in actuality doing nothing more than ensuring we now needed a new one.

"I'll go get the IKEA catalog," Glen remarked, slithering off the couch.

"Um, yeah, you do that. As for you...," I locked eyes with Gan. "Don't touch Sally. Don't go near her. Don't even think bad thoughts about her. Because if you do, I swear I will spend all of eternity hunting you down."

A moment passed, making me wonder if my point had gotten through. Then she smiled, leered actually. *Oh fuck.* All I'd done was turn her on with the prospect of a never ending game of hide and seek. Goddamn, I really needed to remember who I was dealing with here.

At least Tom and Glen were around in case she tried to jump me again – probably to take pictures, knowing those two.

"As you wish," she said at last. "I will not act against her."

Wait, could it really be that easy? "Oh. Um, good then."

"*You* will be the one to end the threat she represents."

"What?! Now I know you're off your fucking rocker."

"Who else possibly could?"

"Anyone! Err, you know what I mean."

"This task must fall to you and you alone," she replied. "Destiny has marked you, my love."

"Don't start with that fate bullshit."

"You are also her friend. One of the few she trusts. Someone who can get close enough to deliver the final blow." She inclined her head, her eyes never leaving mine. "Do not think this to be a mere coincidence."

"No."

"You would choose her over the world?" Gan asked dispassionately.

"I ... would explore every avenue available before making that choice. End of discussion. Now if that's the only reason you're here..." *Aside from trying to win the Stanley Cup of tongue hockey.*

"It's not."

Oh God. Don't tell me she wanted to go for double overtime.

"I knew my words would be difficult for you to accept, my darling, so I came prepared to soothe your ire in whatever small way I can."

"She's talking about your dick, dude."

I threw Tom a glare that would've melted steel before focusing on Gan again. "You don't have anything that would *soothe my ire.*"

"Not even the Progenitor?"

Fuck! She'd gotten me so worked up over Sally that I'd completely forgotten about Ed. "Where is he?"

"Safe."

"That's nice, but I didn't fucking ask about Prince Adam. I swear if you..."

She waved off my anger. "I can see you need time to consider this. The end of days is still a ways off. I shall leave you to make whatever peace you can with what must happen."

"I already said it's not..."

"You do not have a choice. More importantly, the world doesn't." She reached into her bag again, pulled out a book, and placed it on the broken table between us.

I looked at it, realizing it was ... a Bible? The fuck? Had Gan become a Jehovah's Witness at some point when I wasn't paying attention?

If so, she really needed to work on her sales pitch. "I don't get it."

"There are few tomes left that speak of the Beast and that which it commands," she replied, a grin inching up the side of her mouth. "Ironic then, that one of the most read books of the mortal world would be among them. I dare say, those who wrote it must have been gifted with the glorious burden of sight."

"Which part?" Tom asked. "Because I'm partial to the chapter where the dude bangs his brother's wife then jacks off onto the ground." I turned and inclined my head at him. "What? It's like the original stepsister porn."

"The fuck is wrong with you?"

Gan raised an eyebrow. "Yes, destiny's choice for its new Shining One is interesting indeed. Regardless, the warnings of this book are clear ... for those with eyes open enough to see the subtext. Look to the seas first, then the skies, and finally the land itself. Once those events have been set in motion, the world will know..."

"The world can eat a dick," I snapped.

She shook her head, looking almost sad for a moment. "I was afraid you might say that."

"Specifically?" Tom replied. "About the world eating a dick?"

She opted to ignore him once again, turning instead to leave. "I do not wish to force your hand, but know I will if it becomes necessary."

"Good luck trying."

"You say you wouldn't trade her life for the world," Gan replied, opening the door. "But I will remind you, there are *others* in this world you care for as well."

Fuck! I knew it. "You leave Ed out of this."

Rather than answer, she headed for the stairs.

I debated going after her, but what good would it do? She'd already proven I had little chance of stopping her. Maybe I shouldn't have hesitated biting her when I had the chance – bad taste in my mouth or not.

"I'm serious, Gan," I cried as she disappeared from sight. "Ed's off limits."

"Yeah, that oughta do it," Tom said from behind me.

I flipped him the bird over my shoulder.

A few moments later, though, her voice floated back

up to us from below. "I was not speaking of the Progenitor, as I shall prove."

Prove? How?

There came no further answer other than silence. Well, that and the sound of her footsteps.

I walked out to the landing, knowing damned well she could hear me. "What did you mean by that?"

Whatever talking mood she'd been in, though, had apparently passed. After a few more seconds, I turned and stormed back into the apartment flustered, slamming the door behind me – albeit not hard enough to destroy it. We already had enough on our shopping list.

I stalked into the kitchen and grabbed another drink as I tried to make sense of all the crazy that had just taken a shit in the middle of my life.

"Okay, I think we need to set some ground rules here. Next time Gan shows up, we all work together to take her out. Sound good?"

Tom shrugged. "You're the one who was sucking face with her, dude."

"Not willingly."

"Likely story."

"Fuck you, Ranma ½."

"All I'm saying is you didn't exactly look like you were suffering."

"She's like five times stronger than me. What the fuck did you expect me to...?"

There came a knock at the door, interrupting my rant. I'd been so wound up, I hadn't heard anyone coming up the stairs.

Shit! "That's probably her again. Go get your sword."

"I think it's your *sword* she wants."

"Just fucking do it!"

"Let me grab my camera," Glen said.

Okay, my friends were useless. That meant it was up to me to get the bite on her and hopefully get lucky enough to finish this.

I yanked the door open, my fangs bared. "You're gonna wish you didn't come back here, you fucking..."

My voice trailed off as I realized it wasn't Gan after all.

"Well, I'm sure as fuck not going back to where I was," Ed replied, looking none too pleased. "Now are you gonna let me in, or do I need an engraved invitation?"

6

PROGENITOURING

"So ... that tracking spell you've been working on? Looks like we're not going to need it after all. Call me back when you can. I've got good news."

Left unsaid was what Gan had left dangling over our heads, but we could work on that as a group – me and my amigos together again.

I left the message on Christy's voicemail then hung up and rejoined my friends at the edge of the platform as we waited for the train to pull in.

There'd been no time to celebrate Ed's sudden reappearance, as we'd all realized we needed to get over to Sally's and warn her – something that sounded better to do in person, so as to hopefully keep her calm. Not to mention, knowing Gan, our lines were likely already tapped.

Thankfully, with rush hour over, there were relatively few people waiting, allowing us to talk in relative privacy.

"You're serious?" Ed was asking Tom. "It's actually you in there?"

"In the flesh, dude."

"Then what happened to Sheila?"

"Fuck if I have any clue. All I know is I'm alive and have tits now."

"Gan targeted her," I said, letting out a sad sigh. "She had it all worked out in advance, there ... wasn't anything we could do."

Tom put a hand on my shoulder. "It sucks, man, but at least she had one last ace up her sleeve: me."

Ed shook his head. "This is really fucking weird."

"Try living with him," I remarked.

"It's most exciting having the Freewill and the Icon under the same roof." Glen added, back in his corgi costume. "Bark!" Thank goodness nobody had challenged us bringing our *service dog* down into the station.

"I ... bet it is." Ed glanced sidelong at the little blob before turning back toward me. "I see things haven't been dull in my absence."

"That's a bit of an understatement."

As the trains to Manhattan were now on their evening schedule, it gave us time to relay the Cliff's Notes version of some of the shit that had gone down in his absence.

Ed nodded as I finished telling him about how Sally had trashed Falcon's warehouse. "Yeah, I heard some of it from my end. Dave brought me up to speed a bit when we were in Boston."

What? "Wait, what were you doing in Boston with Dave?"

"Mostly screaming and running for my life."

Tom clapped him on the back. "Same shit, different day."

"Starting to look that way again." He shook his head then turned serious. "He also told me that Kara flew in."

My eyes opened wide. "How the fuck did he know that?"

"Heard it from our gracious host apparently. I'm guessing Lucy Lunatic has been keeping tabs on you again."

I knew it! "So you're telling me she has Dave now, too?"

"Has is a strong word. The fucker's working for her."

"No shit?" Tom replied.

"Are you fucking for real?" I asked. "He told me he was down in Columbia closing up shop on that cursed hand cream of his."

Ed shrugged. "Why do you think she hired him in the first place?"

"To make more?"

"No, idiot! Because he figured out how to replicate your spit."

Holy crap. Was the psycho trying to clone me now? "Why would she need that?"

He pointed to himself. "Because now she wants to replicate someone else's spit."

"Oh ... oh!" I pulled out my phone again and dialed Dave's number. Unsurprisingly, it too went to voicemail. For fuck's sake! "I swear to God, Dave, I am going to jam my entire dice bag up your ass when I see you again!" I hung up and stuffed it back in my pocket.

"Feel better now?"

"Not really."

"Good. He deserves to get his ass kicked. So, about Kara..."

I spared a glance Tom and Glen's way, just as the train pulled in. "Yeah, about that... There's a bit more to the story."

I swear, life was so much easier back when I had a heartbeat. If someone asked, "What's up?" I could take care of it with a single, "Not much. You?"

That didn't cut it these days, especially with a friend who'd missed out on *not-so-minor* events such as werewolves trashing his stepdad's house.

"Werewolves?" Ed replied. "I thought they didn't..."

"Don't say it." I held up my hand. "We've already been down that road. Bottom line is they do, and both

Pop and Kara are fine. He's still down at his time share in Cape May, and she finally flew back home last week. I've been checking in with them every couple of days, just to be safe." Not to mention they'd kick my ass if I didn't.

But now that wasn't an issue anymore because Ed was back!

"Thanks for keeping them safe, man," he said, before adding, "So ... on a scale of one to ten, how pissed is she?"

"Oh, easily a twelve at first, but after she learned you were kidnapped it went down to maybe an eight." I let out a laugh. "Seriously, they're just worried about you."

"I guess I should face the music and call her once we're done at..."

"Wait," Tom interrupted. "You haven't heard the best part yet."

"There's more?"

"Fuck yeah. The werewolves weren't there for Pop. They were after *you*."

"*Me?* Why?"

"No fucking idea, man."

I nodded. "All we know is some guy named Hobart and his trailer trash witch both have hard-ons for you for some reason. They even called you the Progenitor."

"Shit! What the fuck is that about?"

"No clue. We haven't exactly gone back to ask."

Silence descended among us for several minutes as Ed slumped down in his seat – broken only by a little girl asking her mother if she could pet Glen, followed by her mom taking one look at him then grabbing her daughter's hand and walking to the next car.

Couldn't say I blamed her.

Ed finally raised his head and looked me in the eye. "Listen, man, I need you to do me a favor."

"Sure thing. Whatever you need."

"Good, because I want you to tell Kara that I'm still missing."

That certainly wasn't what I was expecting to hear. "Why?"

"I can't drag her back into this shit."

"She's already in it."

"I get that, but she's also over on the west coast. If she knows I'm free, one of two things is going to happen. Either she's going to fly out here again, or she's going to want me to come home."

"Yeah, that's generally how it works," Tom remarked.

"Which would be great if a bunch of monsters weren't after me."

I understood what he was getting at. Yeah, it was kind of shitty, and something she might very well never forgive him for, but there was a certain logic to be had in keeping her safe three-thousand miles away.

Even so, it didn't feel right. "She deserves to know."

"No shit, Sherlock. But it's safer for her this way ... at least until we know more."

"What about Pop?"

"I'll handle him. He'll understand."

I hated to lie to Kara, especially after I'd promised I wouldn't. At the same time, Ed was like a brother to me. If he was asking me to do this for him, how could I say no?

"Wait, what about your stuff?" Tom asked.

"My stuff?"

"Yeah, I managed to save some of your shit," he said proudly. "A mint condition Street Shark, the red Power Ranger, and a Rafael that might be missing an arm through no fault of my own."

"And the reason you thought I cared about that was...?"

"We all have our priorities, fucked up as they might be," I said, shaking my head. "But anyway, yeah, I can tell her what you want for now, at least until we figure shit out. Just ... don't take forever letting her know."

"Not planning on."

I nodded and let out a breath. "Okay. Well then, if

you need a place to crash while we sort our dirty laundry, your old bed's still waiting."

"I appreciate that, but...," He glanced down at Glen. "I thought it was already occupied."

"Nope," Glen replied, the corgi's face twitching unnaturally as he spoke. "I'm quite happy with my pail in the corner. Bark!"

"Yeah," I confirmed, "Glen doesn't take up much space and we have a fridge full of pig blood."

"I'll admit, it's a hell of a sales pitch." He grinned. "Okay, let's see how it goes."

Tom chuckled. "Works for me. I'll sleep better knowing you're not out there porking my baby sister."

"Says the guy inhabiting the body that Bill used to..."

"Can we maybe move on from the porking?" I interrupted, not needing that mental baggage on top of the growing pile already taking up space in my subconscious.

Tom grinned then elbowed Ed in the side. "Bill's just mad because Christy's finally growing wise to how limp his dick really is."

Before I could say anything to that, I remembered what I'd almost told her earlier this evening. It made me consider the kind of heartache Ed must've been feeling right then, knowing he was free, yet also realizing that freedom came with a price – making Kara a target.

My silence, however, only served to give Tom more ammunition. "Cat's got Bill's tongue, because that's all the pussy he's getting."

"I used to be a cat," Glen added.

"Trust me, I know," I replied, thankful for the distraction from my own feelings. "Just for the record, this costume is only marginally better."

"You mean there was a worse one?" Ed asked.

Tom merely shrugged. "Whatever works. It's just so he can go out during the day when we're..."

Wait ... during the day.

I ignored the rest of whatever Tom was saying as that

thought got stuck in my head. One of my biggest fears had been worrying that being a vampire again would drive a wedge between me and Christy. She seemed fine with it, don't get me wrong, but I couldn't help but think that some things would add up over time – such as the fact that I couldn't do stuff with her and Tina while the sun was shining.

But maybe that no longer needed to be a factor.

"Hold on," I said, focusing my gaze squarely on Ed. "This might sound weird, but once we get a couple hours of downtime, I'm gonna need you to bite me."

You don't know what that would do to us.

"Yeah, actually I do," I replied to my subconscious before realizing I'd said it out loud. "Um, sorry. What I meant is, I want the upgrade. I want to be able to walk in the sunlight again, sit next to Tom on the couch without igniting, all of that shit."

"Listen, Bill..."

"It doesn't have to be anywhere that's gonna freak you out. Hell, you can bite my fucking hand if you want to."

"The question being which one does Bill jack off with?"

I glared at Tom for a moment before choosing to ignore his stupid ass.

"I can't," Ed replied.

What?! "He was joking about that jerking off part." *Mostly.*

He waved me off, though. "I'm not worried about that. Well, I am a bit. But I still can't."

"Can't or won't?"

"Can't," he emphasized.

"Why the fuck not?"

"Because Gan gave me a parting gift before letting me go." Ed smiled at us, not an expression I was used to seeing on his face. Creepy as it was, though, it was his teeth that caught my attention.

The fuck?

Tom blinked a few times then shrugged. "Dude, grills went out like a decade ago."

What he was mistaking for bling, however, was apparently far more invasive. All the teeth on Ed's upper jaw, including his canines, appeared to be encased in metal.

"What the hell?"

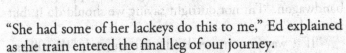

"She had some of her lackeys do this to me," Ed explained as the train entered the final leg of our journey.

Tom looked confused. "Why? Does she have a fetish for Jared Leto Joker cosplay?"

"Pretty sure she doesn't know what the fuck that is." He shook his head. "Gan got what she wanted from me. I thought that meant I was a goner, but fortunately she's still obsessed with not making Bill here angry."

"She's not really doing a great job with that," I remarked.

"Trust me, I know. But I can't complain either since the alternative is being dead. Anyway, I got the impression she wants to corner the market on making more vamps like me." He pointed at his fangs. "Not entirely sure what this crap is, I was kind of too busy screaming to get all the details, but I think it's silver topped with titanium."

I narrowed my eyes. *That little...* Silver wasn't particularly kind for vampires. Mixing it with our blood tended to cause explosive results. That, and it also retarded our ability to heal. It was why the First Coven's enforcers used to favor silver stakes. It got the job done with an extra helping of fuck you. That said, I remembered it being far less effective against neo-vamps.

That probably accounted for why Ed's face hadn't exploded. If so...

"Fuck that noise," Tom said. "I bet we could bash that shit right off with a hammer."

"What?"

"Hell yeah," he continued. "We smash it to bits then let the rest grow back. Right, Bill?"

He ... kind of had a point there, fucked up as it was. "I suppose..."

"I want to watch!" Glen bubbled excitedly.

Ed glanced sidelong at them both for a moment. "Yeah, well, count me out."

"Hold on," I said, not believing I was hopping on this bandwagon. "I'm not outright saying we should do it, but it could..."

"If it was just my teeth," he interrupted, "I'd still say no, because I'm not an idiot. But I'd maybe consider it as an option. It's not, though. Don't think for one second Gan didn't think of that, too. As a matter of fact, she handed me this right before letting me out of the car."

He reached into his back pocket and pulled out a piece of paper.

It was a copy of an x-ray, apparently of Ed's skull. I clearly saw the greyish bones of his lower jaw. The area encompassing his teeth, however, was much lighter, obviously highlighting the metal attached to it. What was far less heartening was how far she'd taken things. That lighter area wasn't just around his teeth, but his entire upper jaw and a good chunk of the skull around it.

In short, Tom's idea might still work, but in order to test it we'd have to smash most of my friend's head in the process.

7

BOOK OF REVELATIONS

"**D**ude, you're like Wolverine," Tom said, looking over the x-ray. "Except not in any good way."

Sadly, he was right. Gan had gone above and beyond on this one. How? Well, I had to assume, surgically speaking, one could get extra creative when operating on a patient that was hard to kill. As for why, I didn't even need to ask. The pieces of that puzzle were all there in front of us.

The old vampire race was almost like a plague, the sort of thing that could easily spread out of control without measures in place to contain it.

But this new breed was different. For reasons none of us understood, Ed was the only viable spreader. He was basically patient zero. Meaning, without him, the new strain couldn't propagate. Or at least that had formerly been the case.

But now I had a feeling that was no longer true. From the sound of things, Gan wasn't beholden to the First Coven's old rule against experimenting on the vampire genome. She'd brought in Dave, the fucker, to do the same voodoo he'd once done with my venom. It was no surprise that he, greedy fuck that he was, had a price when it came to screwing over the world, much less his friends.

I could certainly pick em, couldn't I?

Let's face facts. Gan wanted to be the sole source of these neo-vamps. She'd effectively elected herself CEO of an undead eugenics program. The good was that it would certainly contain things, as she was pretty selective about who she employed. The bad was there'd be little doubt that every new vamp she made would be loyal to her and her alone.

It was pretty fucking nefarious when you thought about it, even more so once she eventually figured out how Dave's methods worked and realized she no longer needed his disagreeable ass on her payroll – or alive for that matter. And he'd deserve it, too, the dumb fuck.

As for Ed, I doubted whatever she'd done to him was permanent. But it was likely designed to last long enough to keep us from recruiting our own army against her, which is almost certainly what a competent leader would do – meaning none of us.

Fuck that. All I wanted was to be able to go outside without bursting into flames, so I could take Tina to Coney Island or go walking in Central Park on a nice day.

Sure, I could crawl to Gan and beg for her help, but that would almost certainly come with the price of agreeing to be her personal sperm donor.

I swear, it was like a fucked up wish one might make to their dungeon master – like asking for your friend back but failing to specify what condition you wanted them back in.

Yeah, today was getting better by the moment.

Fortunately, I had better things to stew on. Ed was safe. That was the important thing. We could worry about his inability to walk through a metal detector at some other point. Sally was now the top priority, thanks to Gan's *pep talk*.

She'd claimed I was the one who had to do the deed, but that could've been nothing more than bullshit to throw me off her scent. We needed to get to Sally's place now and put both her and the coven on high alert.

After that, we could figure out the rest.

"Oh, tell her about Gan's Instagram," Tom prodded me.

"No."

"Already aware of it," Sally remarked, pouring drinks for us.

"Wait, you are? Don't tell me you're one of her followers."

"Please. Give me some credit here. Still, you have to admit, she really is something, isn't she?"

All things considered, Sally had taken the news rather well. A part of me had been worried that she'd blow again. I'd even advised the others to wait downstairs until I could bring her up to speed. They'd declined, being some combination of brave and too stupid to live. Or maybe they'd simply been as worried about her as I was.

"That's ... putting it mildly," Ed replied. "You look good by the way."

He wasn't wrong. The unnatural green of her hair had continued to bleed through the black dye she'd covered it up with, giving her a smoking hot Madame Hydra vibe. She'd also rethought her wardrobe to match her new outlook on life, wearing a short silk robe over an even shorter nightgown that left enough leg on display to distract even from Gan's craziness.

"I feel good," Sally said, her demeanor calm. "Not about what she told you guys, mind you. Just in general. I won't lie. I don't miss the old aches and pains."

She passed around the glasses, seemingly unperturbed to find she was now at the top of Gan's hit list. "To old friends returned. And to drinking better stuff than you would be if I wasn't here."

We raised our glasses, none of us contradicting her as I full well knew what was in our fridge back home.

After I'd taken a generous sip, I asked, "So, what do we do about it?"

"For starters, we worry about it tomorrow." When all eyes opened wide at her response, she added, "I'm serious. Ed's back. That's what we've been working toward. We shouldn't let her take that away from us because I guarantee that's what she wants."

"In addition to Bill," Tom replied.

They both had a point, sadly. However, I couldn't help but feel Sally was taking this rather well compared to past slights against her.

"Are you sure you're...?"

"Before you ask," she said, almost as if sensing my thoughts, "I'm perfectly fine."

"Yeah, but..."

"I'm serious. I went to see Matt the other day. He suggested some calming exercises I should try." She glanced down at the armored bracelet around her wrist, courtesy of Matthias Falcon. *Grr!* The paranoid son of a bitch wouldn't even let her take it off at home, although with her now a marked woman maybe that wasn't a bad thing.

After Sally's first lethal episode with her newfound powers, resulting in Stewart being utterly pulped, Christy had suggested bringing Falcon into the fold. His response to the whole thing had been to fit Sally with a magical arrest bracelet, one which instantly teleported her back home if she left the confines of the city for too long. So much for bringing in outside *help*.

"Calming exercises?" Ed replied.

She nodded. "Trust me, I'm as surprised as anyone that they worked. But so far so good. Anything to keep me from blowing up my own building, I suppose. After all, I paid cash for this place. Anyway, I've been doing his Magi yoga and it seems to be helping me find my Zen whenever I hear bad news."

"Yeah, well, this is pretty bad," I opined.

She grinned at me, remaining far calmer than she had any reason to. "Not the first time someone's put a hit out on me."

"Why am I not surprised to hear that?"

"Because you know me so well."

It was almost weird seeing her like this. In years past – hell, in weeks past – her response would've been to grab the nearest gun and declare open season on every asshole who'd ticked her off. But maybe Falcon was on to something, having her sit in the lotus position and chant some Oms.

Most of us had gotten a taste of what Sally was capable of, as well as what could set it off – stress and high levels of ambient magic being two such triggers. The magic part was a relatively easy fix, even if it meant she couldn't babysit Tina for now. The stress bit was trickier since Sally mostly existed in a constant state of low level annoyance.

Now that we'd heard what Gan had to say on the matter, though, I was forced to consider whether everything we'd seen so far was merely the tip of some proverbial iceberg. If so, then maybe this new chillaxed Sally was a good thing as she settled into this strange new phase of her life.

Speaking of which...

I raised my glass again. "To Sally Carlsbad and all the good she did after the Strange Days. May she rest in peace."

"Or as a piece," Tom added with a grin.

Oh crap.

I turned Sally's way, as her fuse toward him tended to be about a millimeter long on most days. To my surprise, though, she simply smiled and took a sip of her drink.

Damn, maybe I should ask Falcon about those exercises myself.

"So, have you decided who you're going to be now?" Ed asked.

She shrugged. "Still working on it. I thought I'd be Sally Carlsbad the rest of my life. Now, well, the future is wide open."

"Hopefully," I said. "Wait. Didn't you say you had a bunch of IDs with Jeff's last name on them?"

"Jeff?" Ed replied. "You mean Night Razor?"

"The one and the same," Sally said. "Yeah, but that was a joke for a different day and a different me. Think I'll pass on Sally Pemberton for now."

"Oh, I have a suggestion," Tom chimed in, drawing our attention. "You used to be Sally Sunset. Maybe this new you should be Sally *Sunrise*."

Ed snickered while I fully expected her to tell him to take his opinions and shove them up his ass sideways.

Instead, she inclined her head. "You know, I don't entirely hate that. It kind of tells the world that this is a whole new beginning."

It does? "Um, you do realize that makes you sound even *more* like a pornstar than Sunset, right?"

She shrugged. "That's everyone else's problem to deal with. Yeah. I think I kind of like it."

"Me, too," Glen replied.

Sally reached down and patted his head. "Good doggie."

He responded by vibrating his hindquarters in a gross mockery of a tail wag. "Bark!"

Okay, this was starting to get weird, unless she was just fucking with us. If so, I'm sure she'd reveal it any second now.

Yep.

Any ... second.

All right, then perhaps it was time to get back to something I could wrap my head around. "So, about Gan..."

She let out a sigh, like I was the wet blanket at this party. "What about her?"

"She wants you dead. For fuck's sake, she even wants me to do it. Said it's my destiny."

"Like we haven't heard that one before."

Tom nodded. "Yeah. If Bill said he was gonna take a shit, she'd be all, *fate has destined you to take the most glorious shit in all of history, Beloved*."

He probably wasn't wrong.

"Did she say anything else?" Sally prompted, sounding somewhat less than panicked.

"Mostly about her and Bill playing hide the sausage."

"I meant aside from that."

"Oh yeah. She handed him a Bible, too."

"A Bible?"

"Maybe she wants Bill to find Jesus," Ed offered.

"Doubt it," Sally replied. "That ship sank five years ago."

I raised an eyebrow. "What?"

"Never mind. It isn't important. What else?"

"Oh, I know," Glen bubbled. "Didn't she threaten to kill the Progenitor if you refused to murder Madam Sally?"

I shook my head. "That's what I thought at first, but then why bother letting him go?"

"Maybe he's got a bomb implanted in his skull along with all that metal," Tom replied.

"Thanks." Ed got up and helped himself to another drink. "Because I really need that in my head in addition to all the other nightmares."

I waved them off. "No. She specifically said it wasn't him."

Sally held up a hand. "What exactly did she say?"

"I don't know. She just implied that the people in my life could suffer the consequences. Typical Gan stuff."

"That's it?"

I shrugged. "She wasn't specific. I mean, Tom and

Glen were there, too, but she barely gave them the time of day."

"At least not compared to jamming her tongue down your throat," Tom said with a smirk. "Tell her about that part."

"I'm trying real hard to forget it."

"Not me. I can't wait for Christy to kick your ass when she finds out."

Wait, Christy... "Oh no!"

"What is it?" Ed asked.

Instead of answering, I turned and grabbed Tom by the shoulders ... for a moment anyway before his aura sparked to life.

"Dude, the fuck?"

I backed away, cradling my burnt palms. "You, you idiot. Remember what you said?"

"What?"

"About Christy losing her shit."

"Yeah, so?"

"You said it right in front of Gan, moron." I looked him in the eye. "She *knows* about us!"

8

FISHING EXPEDITION

God, how stupid can I be?

Back when I'd had a thing for Sheila, Gan hadn't been shy about letting us know she considered it a temporary inconvenience at best. As far at the murderous little nutcase was concerned, she and I were fated to be together, which meant all other romantic rivals automatically earned a spot on her shit list.

The only thing that had stayed her hand had been the modicum of respect she'd held for Sheila's role as the Shining One. But Christy was another matter entirely. Those two had started on the wrong foot and had never bothered to mend that fence.

Even before magic returned, Christy and I had agreed it was probably best if we kept things on the downlow while in the presence of the miniature Mongolian warlord, knowing her penchant for murderous violence.

I should've realized Tom's mistake the moment the words left his mouth, but I was too distracted by Gan acting like a lovesick lamprey. The problem was, where I was borderline ADD in my ability to focus, Gan was a freaking laser beam. She was Sherlock fucking Holmes wearing SpongeBob earrings when it came to noticing these things.

Sure, Tom hadn't outright said it, but his comment hadn't been remotely subtle either. That was the sort of math a second grader could put together, much less a three-hundred-year-old sociopath.

I realized now, there was no one else Gan could've been talking about in her barely concealed threat. She knew how strongly I felt about my friends. I'd reinforced that idea on her more than once. But she'd also seen the stupid lengths I'd gone to while pining for Sheila's affection — throwing myself into all sorts of unnecessary danger.

I had a feeling this was her own demented version of the Kobayashi Maru — forcing me to choose between Sally, one of my dearest friends, and Christy, the woman I lov ... was extraordinarily fond of. Either way, she won.

Needless to say, I was in a near panic as was Tom once he realized the implications of what he'd inadvertently done.

I quickly pulled out my phone and dialed Christy's number again, once more getting her voicemail. Fuck! Either Gan had already struck or that marketing meeting was running long. Both were equally possible. Gan was ruthless, but I'd dealt with marketers my entire career. Most of them didn't know when to shut the fuck up.

"We need to get to her place." I said.

"I can call us an Uber," Glen offered.

As ridiculous as that sounded, it was likely our best bet.

No, that wasn't true. The tunnels would be far faster, but I didn't mean waiting for a train. Vampire speed and stamina could more than make up the difference.

You know what's down there.

I silently told the tagalong inside my head to eat shit. I knew damn well what was down there. Hell, I'd purposely avoided the underground for the last week because of it. But this was a different matter entirely.

"What about Matt?" Sally asked, by far the calmest voice in the room.

"What about him?" I snapped, my temper fraying as every second lost was another second Gan could be...

"First off, calm down," she replied. "Christy can take care of herself."

"But..."

"Secondly, the pier isn't that far away. You can be there in a few minutes. Just explain what's going on and I'm sure he'll be happy to zap you over to her place."

"What if he's not home?"

"If he's not," she continued, her Zenlike repose starting to get on my nerves, "then you take the tunnels. If worse comes to worst, you can always borrow some of Ed's blood for a speed boost."

"That's..."

"Actually a damned good idea," Ed interrupted.

"Will it work?"

He shrugged. "I don't see why not."

I could think of one or two reasons why. Years back, for a short period of time anyway, his blood had been explosively toxic to vamps. But that had been a result of him being in some strange halfway point between human and becoming the world's first neo-vamp. With the transformation long since complete, hopefully that was no longer the case, even if now was probably not the time for a test run.

Sally next turned her attention toward Tom and Glen. "You two should probably call for that car now, since there's no way either of you are keeping up with two vamps."

"I dunno. Teleporting sounds faster."

"Yes, and if you were anyone other than the Icon, I'd agree, but we both know it won't work on you."

Tom paused for a couple of seconds, either thinking it over or waiting for her to call him a dumbass, but then he nodded toward Glen – who opened his mouth and disgorged a cell phone.

Goddamn we were such a weird fucking crew.

"What about you?" Ed asked her.

"Me?" Sally replied, still way too calm for my personal comfort. "I'm going to stay here, top off my drink, and continue trying to call her."

And just like that, Sally – whether Carlsbad, Sunrise, or Sunset – had taken our chaos and turned it into an orderly plan.

"Okay, so what are you all waiting for?" she added. "Get moving."

"I don't pretend to know what happened while I was vacationing at Club Psycho," Ed said, breaking the silence as we raced west toward the dilapidated pier that Falcon currently called home, "but did Sally seem a bit more ... sedate than usual? I mean, did she wake up like that or something?"

It was a welcome distraction from the horrors playing out in my head, most of them involving Christy being slowly skinned alive.

"Not even remotely. The only thing I can guess is she doesn't want a repeat of Stewart."

"Who?"

"One of the new Village vamps. He asked Sally to play a board game and ended up splattered against the wall."

"Harsh."

"It was an accident – a really gross one."

"Okay, so maybe relaxed Sally is a good thing."

Maybe...

It was late enough for most of the foot traffic to have cleared out, so we were able to move quickly, albeit not at top speed – much as I wanted to.

Thankfully, Falcon's place wasn't far. Sally had even

offered to call ahead. That would be our litmus test. If we got there and the wards were disabled, we'd head on in. If we set off even a single trap at the periphery of his property, then we'd take the hint and not waste any more time.

Of course, that was making a lot of assumptions. The last time I'd been there, the place had been thoroughly trashed. Though others from my circle had checked in on him since, I hadn't. Because, well, why would I?

We'd reached a comfortable détente when last I'd seen him – both of us fighting for our lives alongside each other, as well as me learning he wasn't actually trying to bone Christy as I'd feared. Go figure, uber-rich athletic mages with British accents tended to cause my inferiority complex to flare up.

Not helping my lack of self-esteem was the fact that his family was the envy of the Magi world – the guardians of an impenetrable mystical library with tomes dating back to the dawn of time.

Or *formerly* impenetrable anyway, since I'd managed to hack into it – not the most difficult thing as his minions were apparently too busy focusing on horrific death curses to worry about minor things like proper encryption.

Computer geeks: 1, Wizards: 0.

If he ever found out, I was probably as good as dead. For now, though, I was far more concerned with preventing a similar fate from befalling Christy.

We made it to the pier in short order, reaching the chain link fence that warned trespassers away from the dock beyond and the dilapidated buildings contained within.

Unsurprisingly, all looked sedate, although that would've been the case even had all hell been breaking loose inside, thanks to a glamour around the property which projected an aura of banal normalcy.

I swear, awesome as vampire powers could be, mages got all the cool toys.

"Be careful," I warned as I pushed the gate open.

A moment later, the air shimmered around us as we stepped through the glamour to reveal the reality within.

So far so good. All appeared quiet. Now to just hope...

"What's with the light show?" Ed asked.

I was tempted to ask whether he needed to get his eyes checked. The pier looked the way it always did – shitty and decrepit. The only lights to be seen were a few street lamps illuminating the lot, as well as... a fountain show? *What the?*

Just past Falcon's warehouse, looking only marginally less crummy then when last I'd seen it, multihued light was visible just beneath the surface of the water. They gleamed in one place, went out, then another spot would momentarily light up.

The hell?

This continued for several seconds until finally one of the flare-ups brought with it a heavy spray of water that shot up from the Hudson to about twenty feet past the dock.

"Huh," Ed remarked. "The Bellagio does it better."

I couldn't disagree. If this mystical waterfront display was Falcon's doing then he needed to keep working on it.

There came another flash of light, this one brighter than the rest, causing a wide swath of water to blaze an eerie electric blue. Then a massive spray, at least sixty feet wide by about the same amount high, shot up into the sky.

Hold on ... blue...

In that same instant, a purplish force dome appeared around the warehouse, much as it had during our battle there.

"I stand corrected," Ed remarked, a split second before something far less cheerful began to rise from the murky river. "Wait. What the fuck is that?"

For a moment, all I saw was a long dark shape obscured by the wall of water that had exploded from the Hudson. But then, parts of it lit up that same electric blue, enough for us to see it was some kind of monstrous appendage – a tentacle or maybe a tail.

It was hard to tell, other than the fact that it was both larger than anything that should've been in these waters as well as pants-shittingly terrifying.

No. Why now of all times?!

There was no doubt in my mind, though. Whatever the fuck I'd seen here two weeks ago was back, and this time it seemed a hell of a lot angrier.

9

CRUSH DEPTH

"Holy shit!"

Talk about an understatement.

I had no idea what we were looking at, other than there seemed to be some kind of ornate glyphs carved into the beast's scaly flesh, each of them ten feet high if an inch and blazing with blue light, as if they were filled with ionized plasma.

The ... *appendage*, for lack of a better term, continued to emerge from the roiling waters, rising up far higher than Falcon's warehouse. It turned slightly and I caught sight of some sort of serrated fin running the length of one side, dripping with what appeared to be a dark ichor that...

"Run, you bloody fool!"

"You don't have to fucking tell me twice, cabrón!"

Difficult as it was, I turned my attention away from the monstrosity rising from the nonexistent depths in this part of the Hudson and toward the sound of the voices.

Sure enough, Falcon came bolting from the door of the warehouse, headed our way, and hot on his heel was ... Char?

What the fuck is she doing here?

She was a blind vampire vigilante with badass fighting

skills, a hatred of skinheads, and – far as I was aware – a chip on her shoulder when it came to the police or those working for them, of which Falcon was one.

Mind you, that was probably a question best saved for a time when the Beast from 20,000 Fathoms wasn't about to shit stomp us all.

Almost as if reading my mind, the gargantuan tail thing slammed down atop the warehouse like the fist of an angry god. For a moment, the purple force dome held, but then it shattered like so much candy glass – giving way to the sound of splintering wood and shearing metal as the roof caved in.

Falcon looked back over his shoulder and cried out, "Get your bloody asses down ... *now!*"

Call me crazy, but I'd been mauled enough times during my short tenure as a vampire to know that when a wizard told you to hit the dirt, you hit the fucking dirt no questions asked.

Ed, no idiot, followed suit, just as the warehouse exploded in a fury of sparking lights, thunderous sound, and green flame.

Holy fuck nuggets! I sure as hell hoped the glamour stayed up this time, because otherwise this was gonna be about ten times harder to explain away than that film from the other week.

All of that could wait, though, as debris rained down around us, coupled with what appeared to be heavy droplets of some kind of thick black sludge.

What the fuck? Had Falcon been storing vats of black tar heroin in there or something?

I quickly stopped worrying about that as a steel girder slammed into the ground barely ten feet away, sending chunks of asphalt flying. *Shit!*

Bad as it was for us all, Char seemed to be experiencing double the fun. She was lying next to Falcon about fifteen yards away with her hands pressed to her ears. I still wasn't sure what was up with her or how she was even blind, being that vampire healing was awesome and all. But the sounds of destruction were bad enough for me, so I could only imagine how terrible it was for someone who relied on their ears.

A splitting headache, however, was loads better than being dead. She could deal.

Beyond where they lay, the thing which had just finished smashing Falcon's nest to kindling apparently took umbrage at all the fireworks still going off. It pulled back from the wreckage, making the damage Sally had caused there two weeks earlier look like a minor scuffle in comparison. Then it rose into the air again, like one of the titans of Greek myth, before finally slamming down into the Hudson – hard enough to send a small tsunami cascading over the docks and into the lot beyond.

Several minutes passed as we all waited to see if we were fated to be the first casualties in a *Cloverfield*-sized rampage.

"Is it gone?" Ed finally asked, raising his head.

"I fucking hope so." I pushed myself to my knees. Aside from the still churning waters of the Hudson, the only sounds to be heard were the lick of flames rising from the destroyed warehouse.

"Stay here." I got to my feet and headed toward where Falcon was helping Char up. Both of them, amazingly enough, appeared to be in one piece.

Falcon looked up, saw me approaching, and raised one hand wearily in greeting. "Freewill."

"Yeah, hi. So, um, quick question. What the fuck was...?"

I was interrupted by a sound like that of waves breaking at the beach. *What now?* There came another massive splash, sending spray flying everywhere, then something was launched up out of the Hudson, rocketing high into the sky.

My mouth dropped open as I watched the dark shape

catapult upward until it was silhouetted against the night sky, looking like some kind of long spindly mass.

Then it began to grow larger, making me realize it wasn't as spindly as I'd thought.

It's not getting larger, my subconscious screamed. *It's falling, right ... toward...*

"Oh shit."

Us.

"Get out of the way, Freewill!"

In the second or two before impact, my mind inexplicably raced back to me laughing in the theater at that scene from *Prometheus* where the characters were running from the collapsing ship – chuckling that the idiots could have simply picked any other direction and easily survived. In that moment I finally understood. When faced with the reality of being crushed like a grape, rational choices – like getting out of the fucking way – were few and far between.

It was small comfort as the massive thing crashed down upon me, erasing all thought other than I really should've heeded Glen's advice and just called for a car instead.

"You need to work on your reflexes, Freewill. After all, you're dodging for two again."

I sat up with a start at the voice and looked around, finding myself ... back in my apartment? *The fuck?*

Across from me, planted on the loveseat, sat ... me. Except it wasn't. The soulless black eyes told me everything I needed to know. So much for my wishful thinking. The thing in my head was Dr. Death after all, my evil alternate self – the beast that lurked inside of me, waiting for a chance to...

Oh crap! "You can't take over. Not now! I need to get to..."

He held up a hand. "Wasn't planning on. And if you

73

remember, I already told you I can't. It doesn't work that way anymore."

"Huh?" What the hell? Was he trying to trick me into letting my guard down, thinking I was stupid enough to fall for it?

"I think naïve is the more fitting term, don't you?" He let out a sigh. "We really do need to sit down and have a good long chat about this at some point."

I was almost afraid to ask, but I did anyway. "What's stopping you?"

"The same thing that keeps me from answering at your beck and call. It takes a tremendous amount of effort on my part to push through when you're conscious. I'm afraid I'm still recovering from the trauma of our joining."

I guess that made sense. The first time I'd gotten vamped, it had taken a good six months for him to rear his ugly head – almost causing me to hulk out in the middle of freaking SoHo.

But if he was too weak now to make a play for control then perhaps that was something I could use to my advantage.

"I already told you. I'm not trying to take over," he replied, seemingly plucking my thoughts from thin air.

Grr! "If you're not then convince me. Right here. You wanted to talk, well, let's talk."

He shook his head, though. "Alas, our time is up. Your healing is kicking in and there are people out there counting on us."

"But..."

"I'm afraid it's time for you to go back."

Ugh. In the blink of an eye my apartment was gone, replaced by darkness and pain. Everything hurt, and I do mean everything. A massive weight pressed down upon me, pinning me to the ground and leaving several of my favorite bones pulverized.

To make matters worse, there was an awful fishy flavor in my mouth, as if I'd just gone down on a chick who douched with expired sardine cans.

But hey, at least I couldn't breathe, busy as I was being crushed, because I'm sure this thing smelled equally as bad. Small victories and all.

Before I could pass out again, though, I caught the faint sound of voices, hard to make out from beneath whatever I was under.

A few moments later, the rubbery weight pressing down on me began to heat up – going from cold and slimy to hot and slimy in short order.

Oh great. It was a choice between being crushed and turned into a salmon soufflé. Lucky me.

However, just before the heat became scalding enough to crisp me up real good, some of the weight lifted off – enough for me to take a breath ... and realize I was right about how awful this thing smelled. Cooking it apparently didn't help much.

"Help me get this thing off him!"

Ed?

"Ugh, this is one heavy puta."

"No shit. Come on. Just a little more..."

Whatever was lying atop me was rolled off, but not before dumping a scalding pile of steaming innards on my face. *Eww!* Yeah, I really should've taken a car.

I reached up, with the arm that wasn't broken anyway, and wiped the gunk out of my eyes to find the blurry forms of Ed, Char, and Falcon staring down at me, as well as the bloodied remains of something massive off to either side of where I lay.

"Hold on," Ed said, reaching down. I thought it was to help me up, but apparently not as he plucked something from the ground next to my head. It was my glasses, amazingly intact aside from being a little bent. "You dropped these."

If only I could invest in a titanium skeleton to go along with my frames.

I weakly took them from him as I tried to get a sense of things. From what I could tell, it looked like they'd cut a chunk from the middle of whatever had fallen atop me.

"You okay?" Ed asked.

"I'll ... live ... unfortunately."

"You got luckier than you had any reason to be, Freewill," Falcon said. "Fate truly smiles upon you."

"Yeah ... lucky," I gasped, not wanting to think about fate as my insides started knitting back together.

"It's true. You fortunately landed in a pot hole when Kipsy here hit you. Otherwise you'd have certainly been crushed."

"Pretty sure ... I was."

"I meant the kind you don't get up from again."

"Point ... taken."

He pulled out his vape pen and took a long suck from it, before gesturing to the gory remains on either side of me. "Speaking of which, you might wish to dig in. I doubt it'll taste all that pleasant, but I believe its blood is compatible with your kind."

I looked at him as if he'd grown three heads. "What ... the fuck is this thing?"

"One big son of a bitch," Char said. "I'll tell you that much."

It was gonna take a while for me to heal, not to mention a decent amount of energy. Falcon was probably right about what I needed to do. But I preferred it not be while lying broken in a ditch. "Help ... me up, okay."

The two vamps helped me to my feet while Falcon continued to puff on his douche pipe. Ed mostly supported my weight as I turned to face what had landed on me.

"Sounds like you got stuff shifting around inside you," Char remarked.

"Nothing ... important, I'm sure..." The words died on my lips as I took in the remains of the creature lying before us, splayed out on the shattered asphalt like a nightmare fishing trophy.

It was at least fifty feet long, or would've been if it was still in one piece. Snakelike, but with two sets of webbed claws, it was black in color, covered in thick scales, and had a frill of sorts along its back. Worst of all was the head, like a massive python's but with fangs at least a foot long. All in all, it kinda looked like the classic depiction of sea serpents you'd find in old drawings and paintings.

Whatever the case, even minus the chunks that had been carved out of it, this thing had to weigh tons. No wonder it had flattened me like a pancake. Falcon was right, I'd gotten seriously lucky.

"What the hell is it?"

A naga, the voice in my head replied. *I told you about them once, remember?*

"The locals used to call it Kipsy," Falcon replied. "The great serpent of the Hudson. In actuality a river naga. In fact it's *the* naga for these parts, or was anyway. It's been the guardian of this river since back before your war for independence."

I glanced at him. "You knew about this thing?"

"Of course. I've found it best to be in the know regarding the locals, in case the need for parlay ever arises."

I turned toward the still burning remains of his warehouse. "I'm guessing this particular parlay didn't go well."

"Oh, this poor blighter didn't cause any of this mess."

"It didn't?"

Ed shook his head. "Look at it. This thing's big, but nothing like what we saw."

"Precisely. Also, notice if you will the bite marks around its neck. No, I'd say something else has moved in, taken over, and tossed this poor sap out along with the trash."

"What?" I asked. "I mean, why?" Ugh, healing was taking a lot out of me, causing my head to get all foggy – meaning I probably had no choice but to opt for some seafood. Yuck!

Falcon put a hand on my shoulder. "Save your strength, mate. I think I get your meaning." He too glanced back at the warehouse. "After the attack two weeks ago, I decided to lay some trap wards in the water, just in case the apkallu decided to pay me another visit."

"The ap-what the fuck?" Char asked.

"Those fish-eyed buggers we fought earlier."

Wait, earlier?

"Oh. Didn't realize they had an even stupider name."

"Be that as it may," he continued, "it seems my bait caught something a bit larger than anticipated." He turned and locked eyes with me. "Remember how I said I saw a shadow in the water after the fight here?"

"It ... was a lot more than a shadow. Believe me."

"Not doubting that, at least not anymore."

"So what was that thing?" Ed asked.

Falcon shook his head. "Big. That's all I know for now. I'm going to need to access the Archives, put my people to work on some research."

"Maybe ... have them watch *Jurassic World* while they're at it," I wheezed.

"Dinosaurs in the Hudson, Freebill?" Char replied.

"Maybe." I glanced her way. "So what brings you back here, aside from the all-you-can-eat seafood buffet? And what did he mean by earlier?"

She shrugged. "What, you my babysitter now?"

"I kinda like this one," Ed remarked.

"Figured you would. Ed, Char. Char, Ed," I said by way of introduction, not that I could pretend to know her all that well. I was still trying to figure her out, but for now it was enough to know she seemed to be on our side.

"I was helping Charisma here out with a personal matter," Falcon explained. "Perhaps we should leave it at that."

I nodded. It was probably none of my business anyway. Besides, being steamrolled by a giant eel was more than enough for me to handle at the moment. I was only here because...

Shit! Christy! I'd allowed myself to get distracted by Moby Prick's appearance.

No doubt about it. There was something nasty in the Hudson. But right then I couldn't afford to spare another second its way, not when Christy's life could be on the line.

"Did ... you get ... Sally's call?"

He raised an eyebrow, causing his stupid overinflated mustache to twitch. "Sally, no? We'd actually just gotten back when my wards out there began to trip like mad. Why? Is something wrong?"

"I ... she ... Gan..."

Ed put a hand on my shoulder. "Here's an idea. Let me handle the recap while you grab some sushi. I think it'll go a lot smoother that way."

10

DEAD WITCH WALKING

For the record, river naga didn't taste nearly as bad as some of the shit I've had the displeasure of sinking my fangs into. A little briny maybe, with a fishy aftertaste, but Falcon was right about it being good enough to fill up the tank again.

Not to mention, it beat accidentally running into any of Christy's neighbors in the hall and mistaking them for dessert.

Speaking of which, Ed brought Falcon up to speed while I noshed on river monster blood.

As I drank, I tried not to think of whether we'd have made it there by now had we simply opted for the tunnels. Instead, I kept reminding myself there was an equal chance we'd have gotten eaten by something nasty along the way.

Falcon, for his part, listened while sucking on his vape pen like this was a hipster kombucha bar. But whatever. So long as he helped us, I didn't really care what he sucked on.

Either way, we both finished at pretty much the same time. I turned to face them, now covered head to toe in bloody naga chunks.

"How do you feel?" Ed asked.

"Like what was left of Alex Kintner after the shark got through with him. How about you guys? We good here?"

"I fear I'm far from good, Freewill," Falcon said, glancing back toward the ruined warehouse. "The evening's events have left me a bit scattered. I can get us to Christine's place, but I may not be of much use if anything is afoot."

"Fair enough." I turned to Char. "You in? Care to meet more of the gang?"

"Much as I appreciate how it's never boring when you're around, Freebill, I gotta sit this one out. Personal stuff. You understand?"

I nodded. "Okay. Do what you gotta. Oh, but maybe try avoiding the waterfront for now."

"No shit, pendejo." She turned and started walking away. "Good luck fighting the good fight."

With Gan involved, I'd take whatever luck I could get.

Falcon in the meantime finally put his vape pen away and got down to business. "Everyone join hands and then I need you two to visualize her flat."

"Can do."

We did as asked, then I closed my eyes and pictured the inside of Christy's apartment, trying desperately not to imagine it coated in her blood.

Teleporting tended to be an unpleasant experience for me. It was like being pulled apart piece by piece, thrown in a dark closet, then reassembled again, usually with my stomach feeling like it had been shoved in backwards.

But, even knowing that, this was a brand new experience.

All of that other stuff happened, mind you, but then it was as if I slammed face first into a metaphysical brick wall. All at once, the nothingness around me started to spin, a pretty impressive feat for the void to pull off, and then, just as I was certain I'd astrally upchuck, reality came screaming back into place ... and I do mean screaming.

We reappeared midair in what seemed to be a dark alleyway. That was all I had time to notice before plummeting face first to the garbage strewn pavement fifteen feet below.

That itself wouldn't have been so bad had someone not landed atop me.

"Ow!" Not cool, especially since my ribs had just started to heal.

"The fuck was that?" Ed cried from a few feet away.

"Bloody hell, Freewill," Falcon snapped, climbing off me. "You were supposed to visualize a place outside her wards."

I shot him a look as I slowly pushed myself up. "How the fuck was I supposed to know that?"

"Christine is an experienced witch and a mentor," he explained, taking a tone as if schooling a child. "Of course she's going to have protective wards."

"Yeah," Ed replied, dusting himself off. "Duh."

"I think I liked it better when we didn't know where you were." I turned away from them and got my bearings. *There!* Far as I could tell we were right across the street from Christy's building.

Unpleasant landing aside, we'd made it. Now to hope we weren't too late. "Come on. Follow me."

Both foot and street traffic were thankfully light, doubly good considering I looked like the prom scene from *Carrie*.

There was no time to waste on pleasantries like waiting to be buzzed in. I grabbed the knob of the security door and twisted, putting my back into it until I heard it give way under the pressure. "Let's go."

I took off toward the stairs at a run, panic starting to settle in again now that I was so close. Gan wasn't one to make idle threats, especially against people she couldn't stand. Worse, she'd had all the time in the world to get here while we were busy in Manhattan.

Visions of horrific torture settled into my subconscious as I raced upstairs, all concept of caution pushed to the side in favor of speed. I'd never forgive myself if I was even a second too late. And God forbid Gan had dared lay a finger on Tina. There would be no safe place for her in this world or any other.

I heard Ed coming up behind me, doing his best to match my pace, but I neither paid him any mind nor heeded Falcon's warning from far below, telling me to be careful.

None of that mattered, not compared to saving the life of the woman I...

There! Her apartment. The door was shut and there didn't appear to be any signs of a struggle in the hall, but that meant nothing.

Please be okay!

I ran to her door and put my shoulder into it, snapping the lock and sending it flying open.

"Christy! Are you...?"

The door immediately flew back the way it had come, with equal or greater force, hitting me in the face like a Mack truck and sending me flying into the opposite wall with a crunch.

Oh yeah. Forgot about that one.

Falcon was right. Christy *had* warded her apartment against intrusion – something I would've remembered had I stopped to think for a moment.

But at least now there was time to slow down and reflect on things as I slumped to the floor in a daze.

"Uncle Bill got booped by the door."

"This isn't funny. Go back inside please."

"But..."

"Do as you're told, young lady."

"Go on, kiddo. I'll be there in a minute to play with you."

"Okay, Uncle Eddie. I'm so glad you're back."

"Glad to be back."

"Just for the record, I'm happy to see you, too. It's just this is..."

"A bit distracting? Yeah, I get it. Look! I think he's coming to."

I shook my head to clear the cobwebs, noting that Christy had cast a hastily constructed glamour in the hallway. Or at least I assumed that was the case as the air shimmered around us while her neighbors peeked their heads out, no doubt to see what the ruckus was.

"Kind of late to be getting furniture delivered," one old geezer complained.

"Sorry," Christy replied to him. "They were supposed to bring it earlier."

"Well, keep it down. Some of us need our sleep."

"You got it, Mr. Henderson. I'll try to be more mindful."

She kept up the cheerful demeanor as her neighbors quickly lost interest in what to them must have seemed like no more than a mundane disturbance. Then, when the last of them finally closed their door, she turned to me, eying the blood encrusted on my clothes. "Are you okay?"

I gave her a thumbs up. "Peachy. Don't ... mind this. Had a run in with a fish."

"Uh huh. So mind telling me what's going on?"

Before I could answer, Falcon finally made his appearance. Slow poke limey. She turned his way and nodded. "Guess that explains why my sending wards flared up a few minutes ago."

"My apologies," he replied. "But I was told it was an emergency."

Christy's tone suddenly grew serious. "Oh? What happened?"

"Not to us," I explained, extracting myself from the imprint I'd left in the plaster. Hopefully she had some magic that could fix it. "Well, okay, it was mostly to us. It's been a bit of a night. But the important thing is you're okay."

"Why wouldn't I be?"

I gestured toward her apartment. "Maybe we should go inside and talk."

She nodded. "Okay. But just so you know, you owe me a new door, mister."

I couldn't help but chuckle. "Actually, I think I owe you two."

With everything seemingly normal for now, aside from me barging in like a maniac, I figured it wouldn't hurt to take a breather long enough for Christy to dote on our recently returned friend, which she was quick to.

She wrapped her arms around him in a big hug. "Hey you!"

"Hey yourself," Ed replied, returning the gesture.

"Did you see what was on TV, Uncle Bill?" Tina asked me as I gave them a moment. She was standing there all wide-eyed in her pj's, obviously doing everything she could to forestall bedtime now that things had gotten interesting.

"Your Uncle Bill hasn't had time for TV tonight, Cat," I said.

She wrinkled her nose. "You smell funny."

"It's nothing twelve or thirteen showers won't fix."

Christy in the meantime stepped back and punched Ed in the arm. "Jerk. It figures. We work our tails off to find you and you come waltzing back in."

He let out a laugh. "What can I say? I'm inconvenient like that."

"Does this mean we don't need that spell anymore, Mommy?"

Oh crap.

Leave it to a child to almost spill the beans about the incantation we kinda stole from Falcon's precious archives. Oh well, at least it hadn't been Tom this time.

"Um, we'll see, baby girl. Why don't you go get ready for bed? The grownups need to talk."

I made it a point to quickly change the subject as she headed to her room, lest we end up with some uncomfortable questions. "So ... I take it you didn't get my messages."

Christy flashed me a grateful look then replied, "Sorry. I put my phone down to charge, and then the Zoom call ran long. I was just turning off the news to go grab it when you ... knocked." She turned toward Falcon, a pleasant smile on her face. "Speaking of which, I didn't expect to see you so soon after our last call, Matthias. You look well."

"That's a damn sight better than I feel." He chuckled politely, turning on the charm. "But likewise. I'm glad to find you in good health."

She raised an eyebrow. "So I've heard. Am I maybe safe in assuming you've all had a more exciting evening than me?"

"That's a fucking understatement," I muttered.

Tina's voice immediately answered. "Ooh, you said..."

"Yeah yeah, I know. Quarter in the swear jar."

"It's a dollar now," she called back.

"Why?"

"Daddy told me about this thing called inflation."

"Son of a..."

Why was I not surprised?

I brought Christy up to speed on the last few hours, while making it a point to leave out a good chunk of what Gan had told us about Sally – which Ed thankfully didn't contradict.

Falcon was an ally, but he already had his concerns about her – being the one to insist on her magic tracking bracelet. The last thing we wanted was to convince him she was the threat he already feared she might be. Instead we spun it more as Gan merely being pissed that Sally had ruined her big moment – which, in all fairness, didn't sound all that far from the truth.

Tom and Glen finally showed up just as we were finishing, a stalled truck in the Midtown Tunnel having led to their delay.

I swear, had Christy's life actually been in danger we would have been the tits on this rescue party bull. Hell, on the scale of eighties sword and sorcery movies, we were currently *Deathstalker* when we should've been *Conan the Barbarian*.

We needed to do better.

For now, though, it was enough knowing she was safe.

Too bad she was quick to throw a bucket of water on even that.

"So, let me see if I have this straight," she said, once we were done. "You left Sally, who Gan definitely threatened, to get to me, who she *might* have threatened."

"Well, when you put it that way," Ed remarked.

"There's no might about it," I interjected. "Tom spilled the beans. She knows about us, and you know damn well that Gan doesn't like sharing her toys."

"Fuck you, dude," he shot back. "Don't pin this on me."

"You know your dad is cursing, too," I called out, hearing crickets from Tina's room. *Figures.*

"Fortunately there's an easy fix to this," he said.

"Hoping Gan gets hit by a bus?"

"Yes, but that's not what I'm talking about." He

glanced Christy's way. "It's simple. You just need to dump his loser ass."

I opened my mouth to respond, before abruptly closing it again. He actually had a point. Of all our options, it was the road I most wanted to avoid, but it was quite possibly the path of least resistance if we wanted to...

"That makes sense," Christy said after a moment or two.

"Wait, it does?" Had my heart still been beating, I'm sure it would've leapt into my throat.

"Damned straight," Tom replied triumphantly.

"Yes, it's a win-win for her. Either way she gets what she wants." She threw an apologetic glance my way. "And let's face facts, we both knew this day would come, probably sooner rather than later."

She took hold of my blood-stained hands in hers and looked me in the eye.

God, she was beautiful.

It was as if time itself stopped as I tried to savor the moment, knowing it was all about to crash down, leaving me in flaming ruins.

Welcome to Dumpsville, Bill. Population...

"So I say let it come."

Wait, what?

"We've danced around that arrogant little bitch for far too long." Christy's voice turned hard as steel. "So if she really wants to come for me, then she's welcome to try."

11

DESTROY ALL MONSTERS

or several moments I couldn't do anything except sit there in stunned silence.

"So ... you're not breaking up with me?"

"That has yet to be determined," Tom was quick to reply.

Christy, however, let out a laugh, although whether it was at me or Tom's dumbass remark I didn't know.

As rational thought took hold again, I realized I shouldn't have been surprised at her reaction. Her and Gan's dislike of one another was a two way street. And it's not like Christy was left holding the short end of the stick. She was a seasoned battle witch, having survived a show-down with the freaking White Mother – basically the messiah of all mages.

If she had one weakness, it was Tina. But I'd also seen how that *weakness* manifested itself. We're talking less frightened tears and more a Liam Neeson "I will find and kill your ass" attitude.

And that assumed Tina was even vulnerable, some-thing highly questionable as she possessed enough eldritch energy to qualify as a weapon of mass destruction.

"Are you sure?" I asked. "Gan's..."

"Responsible for this world and the things trying to

claw their way back into it. I don't care about her motivation, and I don't care how many Magi lives she may have saved in the process." She tossed a look Falcon's way, but he didn't say anything, probably wise of him. "She doesn't get a pass, and she sure as hell doesn't deserve forgiveness. She paved this road to Hell with selfish intentions. And for that, I'm okay with burying her once and for all. Anyone disagree?"

Nobody said a word, except for Glen. "Can I watch?"

"It's not a spectator sport," I told him.

"Who knows?" Christy countered. "It might be."

"What?"

"Don't think for a second she's not going to want you there when she finally strikes."

Oh fuck, she was probably right. Gan was so far off her rocker that she probably thought slaying someone's girlfriend in front of them was the perfect aphrodisiac.

Silence descended in the room for several long seconds as Christy's words of defiance sank in. Of course, it might've just been the rest of us being too afraid to argue with her.

Finally, Falcon stood up. "If I may be so bold..."

"I swear, Matthias, if you're going to lecture me on our people's neutrality..."

"Nothing of the sort, luv. Far be it from me to talk anyone out of a good old fashioned blood feud. I was merely going to point out, that if you're planning on taking a stand, you may want to rethink some of your wards."

"You mean the same wards that pimp-slapped us in the face?" Ed asked.

"Hardly." He turned back toward Christy. "It's just that I couldn't help but notice the slight drain I felt upon stepping in here. This whole flat practically reeks with binding magic, does it not?"

"You're right," she said. "I guess I'll have to find a way to adjust those a bit."

"Adjust what, Mommy?" Tina asked reappearing again, apparently not nearly as asleep as we'd thought.

Christy knelt in front of her. "Never you mind, dear. Go back to bed. No school tomorrow."

"Yay! Am I sick?"

"No, but we need to work on some new spells and it can't wait."

"New spells?" Falcon asked.

"Defensive magic," Christy explained.

"But she's only a child."

"Remember when you first examined Sally, and I mentioned her radiating ambient magic?"

"Vaguely. To be honest, I thought you were just having a laugh at my expense."

She grinned at him. "Show the nice man, sweetie."

Oh, this is gonna be interesting.

"Really?" Tina asked, her eyes lighting up as if she'd just learned Christmas was coming early this year.

"It's okay. Just a little bit, though."

A moment later it was as if the tyke went Super Saiyan 2.

Prismatic energy began to crackle up and down her body, causing my hair to stand on end. It continued to grow in intensity until it was hard to look at her. Halfway across the living room, Tom's faith aura crackled to life – although, judging from the look on his face, it was an uncontrolled reaction to what was going on.

At the same time, sigils and glyphs appeared on every surface – lighting up with a ghostly glow as if someone had turned on a light switch.

Holy shit, and those were designed to *dampen* her power. A part of me was curious to know what would happen if they were ever turned off, while the rest – the sane part – was utterly terrified of the concept.

"That's enough, dear."

"Okay, Mommy."

Just like that, she became a normal little girl again.

Christy had obviously been teaching her control and, from the look of things, it was paying off in spades. Thank goodness, because the last thing anyone in New York needed was a human hydrogen bomb prone to temper tantrums.

Falcon, for his part, looked utterly gobsmacked.

"Your mustache is funny," Tina said with a giggle.

"All right," Christy replied, "fun time's over. We have a lot of work tomorrow. Say goodnight then get in bed, and this time stay in it."

"I'll come tuck you in," Tom offered.

"Me, too," Glen said, still in his creepy-ass corgi suit.

That seemed to please Tina to no end.

Christy nodded gratefully to them as the little tyke ran around the room hugging us all in turn.

"Don't forget about the swear jar, Uncle Bill," she said when it was my turn, the gravitas heavy in her voice.

"As if you'd let me forget. Now go on, Cat. Get your butt to bed before a vampire bites it."

She giggled and then ran off with Tom and Glen in tow.

"That ... that," Falcon sputtered before taking a breath. "These wards, they aren't..."

"No. They're not, but they'll do for now."

"Who ... how? I don't understand how she could be like..."

"She's my little girl. That's all *anyone* needs to know." Christy fixed him with a stare. "I really hope I'm making myself crystal clear about this."

Falcon excused himself shortly thereafter, still looking shellshocked at having witnessed Tina's power. Hopefully he remembered to be discrete about it – for his sake.

Christy offered him the use of the sending circle in her bedroom, designed to punch through her wards, but he declined, claiming he could use a bit of air after the night he'd had.

Oh yeah, in all the ruckus we hadn't even touched upon that *minor* detail yet. It spoke to what a crazy night it had been that we'd so casually forgotten about gargantuan sea monsters in the Hudson.

Regardless, I didn't want to leave Falcon high and dry. He'd done us a solid after all.

As I showed him to the door, I made it a point to ask, "You gonna be okay?"

He actually chuckled. "I'll admit, I might need a nip or two to get to sleep after seeing that display. I swear, I've seen grand mentors who'd be hard pressed to generate that kind of power. And she did it all without blinking."

I kept to myself that she was almost certainly holding back. "I meant, do you need a place to crash, seeing that your warehouse is ... well, you know. It's not much, but I've got a couch if you want it."

He clapped me on the shoulder, looking pleased. "I appreciate that, Freewill. I honestly and truly do. Says a lot about a man to offer his flat to a bloke. But don't worry about me. One of the perks of being a consultant to this fine city is they'll gladly comp me a hotel room." He turned, then stopped and grinned over his shoulder. "And if not, my family has a standing suite at the Lotte I can always *crash* at."

Goddamn, sometimes I truly hated the rich.

I watched him walk down the hall before turning and wedging the door shut behind me.

Once I was back in, Christy put a hand on the wall, closed her eyes, and mumbled a few words. "There. I don't think Matthias would scry us, but just in case."

Smart girl.

"So, mind telling me the real story now? And this time, I want every last detail."

Between us all we did a pretty good job of regurgitating the full details of Gan's visit, including, much to my dismay, our game of tongue hockey.

Thankfully, Christy was understanding, probably helped by my fake dry heaves as Tom gleefully told her about it.

That didn't mean she was happy about our ordeal. She was even less so when Ed and I filled her in on why it had taken so long for us to teleport over from Falcon's place.

"Destroyed?"

"Yep, completely."

"We're talking something straight out of an old Godzilla movie," Ed added, "except a lot more realistic looking."

"And glowing bright blue, like those fish things we fought," I continued. "Because what's a giant monster without the accompanying radioactive fallout?"

"I missed all that?" Tom replied, sounding put out. "Fuck!"

"Trust me, I will happily trade places with you next time. You, too, Glen."

"I appreciate it, Freewill."

"I think the bigger question is what the hell do we do about it?"

I glanced Ed's way, wondering if perhaps Gan had kept him sealed in an airtight container? "Do? Nothing. Whatever that thing is, it's way out of our league. Call the Navy if you want, but otherwise it's not our problem."

"That might not be entirely true," Christy said, her face grim.

"I'm gonna pretend you didn't say that."

"Remember earlier?" she replied, ignoring me. "I said I was watching the news before you arrived."

"Yeah, so? What, did Betty White finally die or something?"

The others looked at me aghast, as if I'd just eaten a busload of orphans in front of them. Jeez, everyone was so touchy these days. Christy, however, merely grabbed the remote and turned on the TV – flipping channels until she found a newscast that was replaying what had been on earlier in the evening.

"Air traffic controllers still have no explanation for the radar anomaly that appeared on their scope in the minutes leading up to flight 1105's crash. Online conspiracy theorists, however, were quick to offer up their own ideas, proposing theories ranging from UFOs to Russian MiGs to outright claiming photos of the wreckage prove this was the work of a living creature. Interestingly enough, some eyewitnesses from the ground reported seeing..."

"Okay," I said. "A plane went down. And?"

I trailed off as the report switched to an aerial shot of the crash, the still smoldering remains of a mid-sized passenger jet lying in a field somewhere. The top of the fuselage was mostly intact, making the damage stand out that much more. Just behind where the cockpit should have been, three massive triangular gouges ran across the roof of the cabin. The section around them was partially crushed, almost as if something had reached down from above and...

No way. That couldn't be right.

"So who had Rodan on their bingo card?" Tom asked.

"You're kidding right? I mean, there's gotta be an explanation. Explosive decompression maybe?"

Except the report picked that moment to zoom in, showing the jagged metal from the punctures clearly pointing inward.

Don't be so quick to dismiss this. It fits what she told us.

"Not now, asshole."

"Not now what?" Ed asked.

"Sorry. Dr. Death's acting up in my subconscious again."

"As if we didn't have enough to worry about."

Look first, he continued, ignoring the shit out of me, *to the sea...*

"Shit!" I shook my head, hating that I had a sentient being in my subconscious that enjoyed reminding me about things I'd sooner forget. "There's ... something else Gan said."

"What?" Christy asked, leaning forward.

"She handed me a Bible and... Yeah, it's not what I was expecting either. Anyway, she said something about looking to the sea first, then to the sky. I think it was supposed to be some kind of warning."

"About what?" Ed replied.

"Fuck if I know. This is Gan we're talking about. She's the mayor of Crazy Town. But there was something else about the Bible. She said it contained prophetic knowledge or some shit like that."

"Oh, yeah," Tom said. "And then I told her..."

"About some dude banging his brother's wife. Yeah, I remember."

Ed turned toward him and sighed. "You need to lay off the hentai, man."

"She's not wrong," Christy replied, a worried look on her face.

"About hentai?"

"No. The Bible. It's well-documented among Magi historians that several mystics were involved in its writing. Some texts even refer to them as seers. If one reads it less as parable and more as history, many of the events documented within line up with actual occurrences – both in mundane history texts and those that have been hidden from the general populace."

I glanced at the less magically adept in the room, which was pretty much the rest of us. "Do I want to ask?"

She shrugged. "The great flood for instance."

"Let me guess," Ed replied. "It was a bit different than some old guy collecting two of every animal."

"Somewhat. Thousands of years ago a gathering of

Magi elders attempted to raise the level of the Mediterranean to destroy an invading force. Their gambit succeeded, but one of the enemy generals, a vampire, was able to escape on his warship."

I raised an eyebrow. "So you're saying Noah was a vampire?"

"How else do you think he lived to be nine-hundred and fifty?"

"Point taken." *Ask a stupid question...*

"Always cracked me up that dude had a son named Ham," Tom remarked.

Ed glanced sidelong at him, but thankfully decided not to go down that rabbit hole. "Okay, so where does that leave us? All we know for certain is there's a sea monster in the Hudson and Gan still wants Bill as her personal cabana boy."

I glared at him. "Next time you get kidnapped, remind me not to look for you."

"I need to do some research on my end," Christy replied, "see if I can connect the dots. Might take a while, though. I won't lie. My Bible studies are a bit rusty."

I nodded. "Same. In fact, I'm pretty sure everyone in this room qualifies as hell-bound heathens."

Glenn cocked his corgi head, "My people don't believe in Hell, unless you count the great pile of simmering refuse that waits for us at the end of..."

"Wait a second," I interrupted, facing Christy. "You said you heard back from Kelly, right? Well, that's it then. Vincent's our ace in the hole. Guy's a former Templar. He probably recites Bible verses in his sleep."

"Good idea," she replied. "I'll shoot them a text, then see what I can find out on my own."

"Maybe check to see what Witchipedia has to say about it."

Ed turned my way. "What's that?"

"The Falcon Archives," I explained. "Our buddy Matt just so happens to be the guardian of the Magi equivalent of the New York Public Library, which yours truly may have sorta hacked into."

"Seriously?"

"If I'm lying I'm dying ... again."

"Way to go!" He held up a hand and we high-fived.

"This isn't a laughing matter," Christy snapped. "I already told you how wrong that was."

"And ... yet you still used it to find that tracking spell." It was probably petty of me to point out, but we were kind of past the finger pointing on this one.

She sighed. "I know, and like I said, I'm not mad at you."

"But it's okay if you are," Tom said, throwing me under the bus.

She fortunately opted to ignore him. "I'm more concerned about myself."

I inclined my head. "What for?"

"Because I *like* having access to it, that's why. Every night before I go to bed, I find myself combing through the archives, picking some branch of arcane lore and seeing where it leads me."

"So? Nothing wrong with a little light reading."

"There's nothing *light* about it. There's a reason so many of the Archive's tomes are considered forbidden. Just the other day, for instance, I came across a chapter from Gryzhinya's Manuscript of Dark Dreams."

"Manuscript of... That the new D&D supplement?"

"It's a long lost book of prophecies, a good deal of which are nonsensical ramblings that could be interpreted any of a thousand ways."

"That doesn't sound so bad," Glen said.

"It could be in the wrong hands. My people are at a delicate point in our history. Many are still picking up the pieces from their shattered lives, looking for direction. Others are still drunk on their returned power. I know it hasn't even been two months yet, but a part of me wonders if our culture – a society that's survived thousands of years – will ever recover. The very last thing we need right now are false prophets using the old texts for personal gain."

"Okay, so crazy prophecies are a bad thing," I replied, throwing a glance Tom's way. "No argument from me on that one."

"It's not just that. I've come across incantations and rituals that haven't been performed for millennia. I don't even know what half of them do, yet it's testing the limits of my willpower to keep from trying them all out."

I looked around the room. Tom, Ed, and I were all gamers, to some degree or another, the kind who would sacrifice our own guilds for a minor artifact. I had a feeling her entreaties fell on deaf ears. Still... "So, then don't. Simple as that."

"Except it's not. Forbidden fruit once tasted," she replied, looking me in the eye. "But what makes it even harder is everything that's happening. Gan's ultimatum, Sally's powers, and now the threat of giant creatures – whether in the river or sky."

When she put it that way...

"The sad truth is," she continued, "as forbidden as some of this knowledge may be, we might have to consider it if we want to survive whatever's coming."

12

SLEEPING AROUND

Christy's worries aside, I had full faith that she wasn't going to go all Dark Phoenix on us. As the saying went, worrying that you were losing your mind was usually a sure sign that you weren't. It was the unrepentant nutballs like Gan you had to watch out for, even more so when they had a shit ton of followers.

We talked a bit more, filling in any other blanks we might've missed, then Christy took some time to examine what had been done to Ed's skull.

Sadly, it looked like her apartment door was going to be the far easier fix.

"Can't you just, I dunno, zap it out of there?" I asked.

She shook her head. "The silver makes it tricky. Not only is it toxic to the undead, but its highly resistant to transmutation. That's why we use it in summoning circles. It has a high degree of eldritch conductivity as well as resistance."

"So what you're saying is, if you zap it out, most of his head might come with it?"

"I'm willing to take the risk," Tom said, only to get slapped upside the head – Ed being far less vulnerable to his flare-ups.

"Let me think about it for a bit," Christy offered. "Maybe there's something I can do."

That kind of brought us to an impasse. Not to mention, it was getting late. "So what now?"

"I guess we'll see what tomorrow brings," she replied. "You said it yourself, Gan told you there's still time left. Much as I'd love to ram some killing magic down her throat, I see no reason why she'd lie about that."

I nodded. "Yeah, not really her style. Okay, then I guess we'll head back to..."

"Hold on," Ed interrupted. "I know I just got back, but let's think this through. Even if little Jenny Genocide wasn't lying about that part, she still wants Sally dead and she's planning to use you as leverage to get Bill to do the deed."

"We don't know that for certain," she replied.

"No, but I'd put good money on it. Anyway, my point is, at least two of us are in danger. So, we're what – just returning to our respective corners to sleep on it? Is it me, or is that somewhat less than smart?"

Leave it to Ed to be the voice of paranoid reason. Guess the rest of us were either too overwhelmed or tired to realize it. "What do you have in mind?"

"Strength in numbers. Remember last time when things started going to shit? We moved the girls into the apartment right below us. That way if anything happened we could at least deal with it together."

"Oh yeah," Tom said. "That was right before you got kidnapped by that Calibra chick."

"Thanks for the reminder because I so do love reliving my personal failures."

"But you do it so well," I replied. "I get what you're saying, though. The problem is it's easier said than done. Last time, we had the advantage of the building being mostly empty, but right now I'm full up. No vacancies."

"So kick someone out," Tom offered.

"In the middle of the night? Yeah, I bet a lawyer would love to hear about that one. No thanks."

"What about Sally's place?" Ed asked. "She's got more than enough room."

Christy shook her head. "I can't risk taking Tina there. If she sets off Sally's powers again..."

I held up a hand. "Point taken. Blowing up SoHo, not particularly subtle."

"I got it." Tom hooked a thumb toward the door on the far side of the living room. "You still have the place next door. So why don't I just move in?"

Much as his idea made sense, I couldn't help the small worm of jealousy that knotted in my gut. Fortunately, he was overlooking one minor detail. "Not a good idea."

"Says you."

"Yeah, says me. Don't forget, you're the Icon. And what do Icons do?"

"Kill dumb fucks like you?"

"Yes, I suppose. But what else? They fuck with magic. So if Gan comes knocking, the last thing Christy needs is you tripping over your own two feet messing up her spells."

"I don't trip over my own..."

"Bill has a point," she said. "Your powers are more likely to affect me than her."

"There's also the fact that you wussed out earlier," I added.

"I was merely being cautious."

"The fact remains. *I* should be the one to take the apartment next door."

Tom let out a laugh. "Not even if I found the world's smallest chastity belt for your micro-penis."

"All right, enough," Ed interrupted. "I don't know what kind of dick measuring contest you two have going on, but it has nothing to do with me. So *I'll* take the apartment. It'll give me a place to crash while I figure out ... well, stuff."

Tom and I glared at each other, both of us no doubt thinking up plenty of reasons why that was a dumb idea. Too bad it actually wasn't.

Damn it! I mean, it's not like I would've used it as an excuse to pop by Christy's bedroom and ... well, I wouldn't have used it much anyway. *Grr!* "Fine," I conceded. "That works."

"I agree," she said. "Besides, I need to stay here anyway. I meant what I said about Tina earlier. Much as I don't want her in this, she needs to be properly trained. And right now, this place is as well warded for that as anywhere ... at least during the day."

I raised an eyebrow. "What do you mean?"

"I'm not too worried about anyone trying anything when we're all awake and alert, but nighttime is a different animal. Much as it breaks my heart, if I'm a target I'd prefer she not be here after dark."

"So where's she going then?" Tom asked.

I rolled my eyes. For fuck's sake, he really was too stupid to have produced such a wonderful kid as Tina. "I think she means with us, dumbass."

Christy nodded. "Bill's right. I know you'll keep her safe, and I don't doubt for a second she'll be tickled pink to spend more time with her father." She then nodded toward Glen. "Or with her favorite babysitter."

"It will be my pleasure to watch over her, Madam Witch. Maybe she'll do me the honor of giving me another bath or two."

Uh, yeah. "Okay, so that's settled then."

Christy faced me next. "Almost. Sally needs someone, too."

"Agreed," Ed replied. "Besides, she likes you a lot more than Tom."

That was an understatement. They were also right. I'd been so focused on Christy being Gan's potential target, I'd sort of neglected that Sally was her ultimate goal.

It was selfish of me. Yet, at the same time, it was hard

to ever think of Sally as vulnerable. She was, though, especially now with us having only the barest clue as to her powers. Also, let's be realistic here, if she truly was the harbinger of something horrifically dark and evil, well, it might not be the worst idea to keep an eye on her.

It would also give me an excuse to hang with the coven more, something I was trying – and mostly failing – to be better at.

Much as I preferred sleeping in my own bed, the proposed accommodations made perfect sense, at least until we had better intelligence to work with – and I don't mean Tom's.

With no objections on the table, Ed stood up. "Okay, so let's head back to Bill's, grab what we need, then we'll split up to our temporary digs." He turned my way. "Please tell me you didn't throw out any of my luggage."

"Tempting, but I held onto it."

"Awesome."

"I wanted to sleep in your suitcase," Glen replied, "but the Freewill wouldn't let me."

The proposed living arrangements might've made sense, but that still didn't mean they weren't weird as fuck.

"One caveat," Christy said. "Tina can stay here for tonight. Trust me, you do not want her waking up cranky."

Considering the tyke's power, I couldn't help but think there was some wisdom to be had there.

"Sounds like a plan. Let me just tell Sally to..." I pulled my phone from my pocket, only to find it was now a broken pile of metal and glass, courtesy of my earlier flattening. *Not again!* "Okay, so maybe someone else can text her instead."

The trek back to my place wasn't a long one.

Or it normally wouldn't have been, but we had what you might call a bad influence among us.

"Don't wait up," Tom called back as we left Christy's. "This might take a while."

"Why'd you tell her that?" I asked as we headed downstairs.

"Dude, are you dense or something? The Edster is back."

"Yeah, I noticed."

"And you're okay with letting this night pass without a celebratory beer between bros?"

Huh. He actually had a point there. We'd had a few drinks at Sally's earlier, but this was *us* we were talking about – the original amigos. I mean, yeah, Tom was technically an *amiga* these days, but that didn't matter.

There were, however, a few snags to his plan.

I gestured toward Glen. "He needs a leash and..." One sniff of the air told me all I needed to know, *ugh*. "I could use a shower."

Tom was not to be deterred, though. He held out an arm to Ed. "Care to escort a lady to an all-night liquor store while Bill scrapes squid shit off himself?"

"If you can find me a lady to escort, sure, but otherwise that sounds like a fine idea."

About forty five minutes later found us all back at my apartment. I smelled a lot better after a quick shower, and the mood was far lighter with beers in hand.

Hell, even Glen joined us, enveloping one inside his body, bottle and all.

"I do so enjoy a Corona," he bubbled, a few of his eyeballs blinking lazily.

"Matches your color, too," I added.

Ed grabbed the clothes he'd left at my place back when he'd first flown in at the start of this mess, enough to tide him over for a few days. I packed a bag as well, tossing in a few extra changes knowing how disgusting vampire life could be.

It was decided to let Tina bunk in Ed's old room while temporarily relocating Glen's pail to my bedroom, on the condition that he not store his meat suit there.

That done, we settled in to polish off the six packs they'd picked up. I mean, it seemed rude not to.

Besides, this was Ed. If we couldn't spare at least a few minutes of good cheer together, then were we really any better than the monsters we fought?

Okay, rhetorical question, since none of us were repulsive spider rats or troglodyte pixies, but still. I liked to think what truly separated us from the animals was our ability to sit around a fire, or TV, and get shitfaced together.

Because wasn't that what life was all about?

We killed the next two hours, but then it was finally time to get a move on.

I called a car from the landline, then we bid Tom and Glen a fond adieu as we headed out.

"Don't fuck with the plan," Tom called after us. "I'm gonna call Christy to make sure."

I flipped him off over my shoulder as Ed let out a chuckle.

"I don't know if I'm ever gonna get used to him being in that body," he said to me as we headed downstairs.

"You should've seen him when he got his period."

Ed grimaced. "Ugh. Remind me to thank Gan for not letting me go sooner."

"I'm sure you'll get the chance. She's a bad penny that keeps turning..."

I paused as I spied a figure in the vestibule, but then relaxed as I recognized him.

"Oh hey, Mr. Ryder ... I mean, Bill," Mike said in greeting as we opened the inner door. He gave Ed a quick nod in turn. "Sir."

"Hey, Mike," I replied, surprised to find him there. Most of my tenants were blue collar types, meaning they favored the early to bed, early to rise lifestyle – which was ideal for those of us who tended to slip out during the wee hours. "Late night?"

He nodded, inclining his head toward the street. "Couldn't sleep. Got me a touch of insomnia. Figured I'd do some people watching to set my mind at ease."

Ed chuckled. "Good luck. At this time of night, the only people to watch are the ones puking on their own shoes."

"Oh, this is my friend Ed," I said as way of introduction. "Ed, this is Mike H..." I trailed off, biting my tongue before I could say Hunt. "He's new here."

"Pleasure," Mike replied with another nod.

"Good luck living with this clown as a landlord." Ed remarked jovially, adding after a moment, "Hey, do I know you from somewhere?"

"Me? Nah. I think I just have one of those faces."

And one of those names.

Mike quickly turned his attention back toward the street. I followed his gaze to see a late model Kia Sedona pulling in up front.

"I think that's us."

Ed let out a sigh. "Looks like we're riding in style tonight."

Next to him, Mike appeared to tense up for a moment, something easily missed unless you had vamp senses. "Everything okay, man?"

A moment passed, then he nodded. "Yeah. Just not used to the city yet is all."

"All right, well, have a good one."

"You, too, sir. Take care."

"I can't believe he called you sir," Ed said as we tossed our bags into the minivan and climbed in.

"Be nice. City life was brand new for us too once."

"Fair enough."

We settled into the backseat. Our driver was a young guy, probably borrowing his mom's soccer van to earn a few bucks on the side. He glanced at us in the rearview – the yellow glow from the street lamps lighting up his face – then pulled away from the curb, seemingly content with listening to the radio.

That was fine. Couldn't say I was a big fan of the talkers anyway.

Ed turned to face me. "So how are things with you and Christy? Was meaning to ask earlier, but figured I'd wait until a certain someone was out of earshot."

"Good call. Not always easy when your best bud is also your worst cockblocker."

"What does she think of all of this?"

"Oh, she's happy as can be he's back. And it's awesome that Tina can get to know her dad now ... even if most of what he's teaching her is stuff Christy immediately has to unteach."

He chuckled. "Let me guess, he's not exactly the role model for restraint?"

I nodded, suppressing a shudder at the fact that he was going to be hosting a series of unsupervised sleepovers with his insanely powerful daughter. "That's why liability insurance was invented."

"So getting back to you three. Is he...?"

"Still in love with her? Oh yeah. No doubt there. Although, it's Tom's idea of love, which, well, we're not exactly talking *Princess Bride* here."

"No kidding. Pretty sure the only fairy tale he relates to is Jack Be Nimble, and only because most of it rhymes with dick."

I couldn't help but laugh. He wasn't wrong. "Christy is ... I dunno. She still cares for him, but..."

"Five years is a long time?"

"Exactly. Still makes things awkward, though."

"I bet. And how do *you* feel about her?"

"Me? Well, you know. I ... um..." I felt a sudden stab

of annoyance that Ed was the one who'd be spending time with her and not me. It was ... unpleasant. "She's Christy. She's awesome."

He let out a laugh.

"I say something funny?"

"Nope. It's just that I know you. And you usually only sputter like an idiot when ... well, actually there's lots of reasons you sputter like an idiot. But when a woman's involved it usually means you're head over heels." I narrowed my eyes but kept my mouth shut. "Have you said anything to her yet?"

Something isn't right.

I told Dr. Death to stuff it. No shit. There were *lots* of things that weren't right. "Of course not. I mean, it hasn't even been that long." That was true, even if the last several weeks had felt like years.

"Yeah, but you've known her for a long time, and things like that tend to count a lot in situations like these."

"I know."

He was right. Christy had gone from being an enemy, to an ally, to one of my closest friends, to ... so much more.

That last part had kinda snuck up on me, mostly because it felt so natural. She'd been a part of our inner circle ever since that clusterfuck in the Woods of Mourning, and she'd never had reason to leave – not even when things went back to normal. Tom was gone, Sally was focused on trying to make amends for her years as a vampire, and Ed had drifted away as he and Kara worked to start a life together. Hell, even Sheila and I had settled into an awkward friendship for most of it. But Christy had been there the entire time.

I just hadn't realized it until recently. I don't think either of us had.

So, of course, it would figure that shit would turn crazy now that I finally understood just how deep my...

The scent here is all wrong.

Oh for Christ's sake. Couldn't the asshole let me inner monologue in peace? I took a sniff of the air. *Of course it smells wrong, shithead! Who the hell knows what kind of dirty asses have sat in this same spot in the last day alone?*

That's not what I mean.

"Hey, buddy," Ed said to the driver, "I think you missed our turn."

I looked out the window, noting the same thing. Easy mistake to make in the rat maze that was Brooklyn. "Yeah, he's right."

The driver glanced back at us in the rearview mirror, the yellowish glow of the streetlights once again illuminating his...

Hold on. I glanced out the window again, noting we weren't currently passing any streetlights.

Uh oh. "Um, hey, fella, did you hear my friend? We're going the wrong..."

That scent. I think ... it's magic, my subconscious cried out.

Oh crap. The front seat suddenly lit up with blinding light, leaving stars in my eyes. "What the fuck?!"

However, if that bothered our driver at all, he didn't show it.

When it cleared, he was no longer alone. A red-haired woman sat in the passenger seat, her body aglow as she tapped a finger to the driver's head before turning to face us. "Howdy, boys."

"Who are...?"

"Myra," I snapped, leaning forward and taking a swing at her hick face.

She was ready for that, as a purplish wall of force immediately sprang up between us, leaving me with nothing more to show for it than a bruised fist.

"Let me guess," Ed remarked. "You two know each other."

"That we do, handsome. As for you...," she said with a

twang, turning my way. "I *told* you not to fuck with us, Freewill. Now you gonna find out."

In the next instant, the back of the van crackled to life with blue energy, causing every muscle in my body to seize up.

It was like sitting on a giant stun gun with bucket seats.

Myra let out a cackle as she turned the voltage up, making me twitch in places I didn't know I was capable of twitching.

Consciousness began to fade as a smell akin to fried bacon permeated my nostrils.

That settles it, I considered as I passed out, *no fucking way am I tipping the driver now.*

13

THE WOLVES OF WALL STREET

*Y*ou really need to start paying better attention, *Freewill.*

Oh, for god's sake, Dr. Death, can you maybe lay off the fucking I told you so's?

That's another thing, the voice in my head continued. *I'd thought we'd made a breakthrough, but you're back to calling me that when you know it to not be true.*

Well then who...?

"Wakey wakey eggs and bakey, you bloodsucking fucks!"

I was roused from comfortable unconsciousness, partly by the voice beckoning me, but also by the warm wetness that followed, dousing my face and neck.

I cracked my eyes open and then immediately wished I hadn't. Some shit-kicking asshole in overalls and a baseball cap was taking a leak on me.

"It's true what they say," he said with a grin. "Better to be pissed off than pissed on."

Goddamn it. This was what I truly hated most about being a vampire, the fact that it could be gross as fuck.

He shifted the stream toward Ed who was lying next to me – proving that pee-drenched misery loved company.

Then the asshole stepped in and kicked him once for good measure.

"Okay, okay, I'm awake," my friend snapped. "Enough already!"

"Y-you all right?" I asked, spitting out a mouthful of fresh piss.

"That depends. Are golden showers all right in your book?"

You could always count on Ed to look at the bright side. Speaking of looking, we appeared to be in an underground lot or maybe a parking garage, judging by all the cars.

Not the most subtle of locations, but when you had a trailer trash witch on your side you could probably afford to skimp on stealth.

Myra was standing next to Piss Boy, looking pleased as punch with herself. I'd first had the displeasure of meeting her a couple of weeks back at Ed's stepdad's place. She was a hillbilly witch who, for some reason as yet unknown to us, seemed to have put her lot in with a clown named Hobart and his hayseed buddies.

In addition to them, I spied three others close by — two men and a woman, all of them busy getting undressed as if we were the guests of honor to a good ole boy gang bang.

I knew better, though.

I tried to sit up, but found my hands bound behind me as well as my legs tied together at the ankles. Flex cuffs from the feel of it. Hell, probably nothing more than cheap-ass wire ties considering the company.

"H-how?" I asked, trying to ignore the unsavory flavor still on my tongue. Damn, I really needed to start carrying a bottle of mouthwash with me.

"Easy as my grandma's apple pie," Myra replied, pointing a finger at me while making sure to not actually touch my piss-soaked self. "See, some dummy went and left his car at Jacob's house, complete with registration in the glove box."

Oh yeah. Should've guessed. Was *still* waiting for my insurance to take care of that.

"You left your car there?" Ed asked.

"Not on purpose. We were kind of in a hurry."

"Wouldn't have mattered none," Piss Boy said, slipping his overalls off. I had a bad feeling I knew where this was going. "We got your scent, Freewill. Might have taken us a bit longer, but we'd have found you eventually."

Suddenly Gan didn't seem so bad in comparison. At least I'd never woken up to find her marking her territory via my face – not that I really put it past her. As for this joker, I didn't recall seeing him at Pop's, but that didn't mean anything. The only two I really got a good look at there before the shit hit the fan were Myra and her beer-bellied fuck nugget friend Hobart.

Cooter here was rail thin by comparison, with straw colored hair and about as many teeth as IQ points.

"And lookie here," he continued, sliding off a pair of underwear that might've been white once upon a time. "Our patience paid off."

"Okay, fine," I replied, opting for a different route. "You got me. But leave my friend here out of it."

"No can do, Freewill. Not when providence has provided."

"He's not a part of..."

He grabbed hold of my hair to look me in the eye. "You think we're stupid or something?" *Well, actually...* "Yours ain't the only info we got from Jacob's place." He pulled a photo from his overalls, one clearly depicting Ed and his sister. *Fuck!* "Can I get a halleluiah, friends? The Progenitor is ours, meaning we can end this nightmare before it begins."

"Pretty sure you're too late for the nightmares, pal," Ed groused.

"Oh, not yours, string bean. I'm talking ours. The only

thing you got left to do is meet your maker and hope he's kinder than us."

Oh crap! "Hold on there, Jeb."

He rounded on me, his eyes furious. "How the fuck do you know my name, vampire?"

Huh. What were the odds? "Um, lucky guess."

Jeb turned to Myra. "He pulling some sort of Freewill mind trick on us?"

Oh for Christ's sake.

"How the hell am I supposed to know?" she replied. "You see fangs sprouting from my cooch?"

"You're the one with the magic know how."

She let out an indignant huff. "Talk to Hobart. He's the one who decided to burn my old coven alive, along with all their books and stuff ... even though I told him not to."

"Speaking of which," I said, trying to buy more time before the biting started, "where is old Hobart? What, was there a NAMBLA convention he needed to be at?"

Jeb turned his head and spat. "Someone's got to stay behind to mind the pack, remind them of the lies our lives were before the Strange Days. Remind them what the Top Coven did to us for all those years."

"It's the First Coven," I corrected. "And what exactly did they do, make you wear glittery collars at the Westminster Dog Show?"

"Way to win them over, Bill," Ed muttered.

"Don't look at me. You're the one who keeps getting kidnapped. Nobody asked you to bring me along for the ride."

Jeb planted a solid kick to my face, no doubt growing tired of listening to me mouth off. Thankfully, there wasn't much behind it other than normal human strength.

"I retract the collar remark," I said, trying to sound conciliatory. "But seriously, what did they do to you and why do you think Ed here has anything to do with it?"

"What didn't they do?" he cried, turning to his friends. "Am I right?"

Replies of, "Hell, yeah!" echoed through the garage.

Oh yeah, because that was useful.

"Centuries of hate," he said, after taking a moment to scratch his ass. *Eww.* "Maybe more. Who can say how long it went on for? They kept us cowed, hid our true nature from us. They made us think they were our saviors, that we should be grateful for them. But now we know better."

"Any of this make sense?" Ed whispered, low enough that I was probably the only one who heard him.

I gave my head a quick shake, no more clued in now than I had been a few weeks ago when Christy had dug up some moldy old text talking about the wolves of men and the kingdom of Ib.

"Same way that we know who you are," Myra said, glaring at Ed. "The one man, the one *thing,* that can start it all up again."

"We ain't gonna let that happen, are we? The vampires won't rise up and we will never again be their slaves."

"Just one small problem with that," Ed replied. "I can't start shit. Take a look for yourself." He opened his mouth wide, showing his metal coated teeth.

"The fuck?" Myra asked, leaning in. "Why you gone and done that?"

"I didn't, genius!"

"Well, I'll be dipped in shit," Jeb replied with a chortle. "Looks like someone gelded the Progenitor."

His buddies, now all naked as jaybirds save for Myra, all had a good laugh at that, which I couldn't really blame them for.

Ed turned his head to glare at me. "Not a fucking word."

"Wouldn't dream of it."

"There's still a threat out there, though," Ed continued, raising his voice again. "I can't make new vampires anymore, not that I even want to, but there's someone else who can. Someone who's working to replicate this ... um ... curse. Believe me, she's the one you want, because I guarantee she's working to bring back all that bad stuff and more."

"And who might that be?" Myra asked, sounding unconvinced.

"Her name is Gansetseg."

"Ganwhatseg?"

"It's Mongolian," I explained. "Trust us, she's the real deal. If you're afraid of ... whatever it is you're afraid of, then she's the one to keep tabs on."

"You heard him," Jeb cried. "Once we're finished with these two, we got some mongoloid bitch to look for."

What?! "That's not what I said..." *Oh fuck it.* I turned Ed's way. "You ready to get medieval on some motherfuckers?"

"No, but when has that ever mattered?"

Gotta love a positive attitude.

These chucklefucks had known where to find us, so it wasn't hard to make the leap that they'd been staking out my place.

Although how they knew when to strike had me baffled.

That was a worry for another time, though. Things didn't look great for us, but I liked our chances better than when we'd been waylaid at Pop's. There, they'd brought a whole pack with them, meaning we had no choice but to beat feet. Here, it was five on two. Not great odds, but maybe workable.

More importantly, I knew something they didn't. We weren't nearly as trapped as they thought.

Anyone in the know understood that vampires had several advantages over normal humans. For starters, if you were going to cuff them, you needed to make sure you didn't cheap out.

With a quick tug of my arms I snapped the ties binding my hands, then set to work on my legs.

I doubted these degenerates expected to hold us for long but, judging by the look on Jeb's face, he'd been expecting more time than we gave him.

"Myra!" he cried. "Do it now!"

Sadly for us, Myra was more on the ball. She raised a purple force dome around herself and was already working to conjure another spell, one that I was certain would create a fake full moon – a weird as fuck concept in the confines of a parking garage.

I scrambled to my feet with Ed a step behind me, still working his ankle cuffs. "You waiting for an invitation?"

"Sorry. I'm not as used to this crap as you are."

"Excuses, excu ... oh fuck!"

Myra *had* been prepping another spell all right, just not the one I'd anticipated. Rather than throw out a glamour, she instead let loose with a blast of angry green energy.

I dove at Ed, knocking him out of the way just as the hellfire slammed into the asphalt where we'd been standing, blowing it to pieces.

Then, as we were busy untangling ourselves from each other, she cast the spell I'd been expecting.

I needed to remember that. Myra might've talked like it had taken her five tries to pass the third grade, but she was apparently more than capable of thinking a few steps ahead.

The moon spell was different this time. Before, she'd shot a magical flare high up into the sky to create it. This was more a full blown illusion. The ceiling of the parking garage suddenly disappeared, replaced with an image of a night sky complete with – you guessed it – a full moon high above.

Christy had theorized there was more to it than that,

which made sense. Otherwise these dipshits would wolf out the second a nighttime scene came on the TV. But right then I didn't care much as my ears caught the sound of rippling flesh and crackling bones.

No doubt about it. Shit was about to get real hairy for us.

FREEWOLF

14

FREEWOLF

"Should we run?"

While I hated being elected de facto leader, I had at least one advantage over Ed – I'd seen this crap before. Last time, it had caught me by surprise, resulting in me standing there gawking as the creatures transformed.

This time I knew better. Waiting around while these fuckers added several hundred pounds of muscle to their frames was a chump game – one I didn't care to play again.

"I have no idea where we are," I quickly replied, "and I'd be willing to bet they're faster anyway. So, instead of hide and seek, let's play *tag* instead."

"If you say so," he replied dubiously.

"And don't hold back because they won't. Trust me on this." Much as I hated to advocate for wholesale murder, I'd just barely walked away from our last tango. Whatever their issue with Ed was, it didn't involve hugging and singalongs.

I launched myself toward the nearest wolfman, some beefy guy with muttonchops – as if he were unaware the seventies were over. He was in mid transformation, his body still reforming, meaning he wasn't in any shape to put up a defense.

So, rather than give him time to finish – standard operating procedure in most horror movies – I leapt on him, burying my teeth in his rapidly expanding neck.

Most people were familiar with wet dog smell. I had to assume, however, far fewer were familiar with its taste. *Lucky me* to now count myself among that exclusive club.

Needless to say, as far as tasty treats went, their blood ranked only slightly higher than Jeb's piss.

Regardless, I wasn't above tearing out an asshole's throat if it meant evening the odds a bit. Also, being that I'd just gotten zapped, a little drink to whet my whistle didn't sound so bad either – and since these guys were partly human, I was hoping their blood would be good for at least that much ... *ugh!*

What the fuck?

The werewolf's blood hit my stomach like a lit roman candle – not entirely dissimilar to the sensation of drinking vampire blood, yet different all the same. It was, in a word, weird as fuck.

Not to brag, but I'd tasted the blood of a decent number of creatures, both normal and otherwise. From a nutrition standpoint, human blood was by far the most satisfying, but I could make do with livestock like cows or pigs.

On the freakier side of things, Sasquatch blood might as well have been bottled shit for all the good it did me. I'd also recently learned that proto-leprechauns seemingly had the equivalent of magic mushrooms flowing through their veins.

Vampire blood was unique, though. Not only was I the only person who could drink it, but it somehow temporarily allowed me to *borrow* the donor's power, willingly or not – giving me a boost.

Nothing else had ever affected me in the same way. Nor had I expected it to.

As I stepped away from the partially transformed werewolf, though, shoving him to the side like yesterday's trash, I began to feel ... strange.

The first thing I noticed were my fangs. They refused to retract. Next, the smells of the garage, already crystal clear, grew even stronger – practically inundating me with the odor of every car, person, or piece of trash that had been there recently. Oh, and piss, too. Let's not forget about that.

There came the sounds of ripping and tearing as I backed away holding my head. When I looked down again, I was both surprised and horrified to see my toes popping out from the ends of my sneakers, the nails on them blackened and thick.

Oh no. This can't be happening.

Continuing from there, my pants were now ripped in several places and the top button had popped, my belt being the only thing still holding them in place – and it looked to be barely hanging on as it was.

Then there were my hands, the backs of which were now covered in a fine coat of brown hair – as if I'd been reverse masturbating.

"Holy shit, Bill! Are you all right?"

I turned to find that Ed had worked over the female of the pack with his claws – sporting guy that he was – likewise catching her while she was vulnerable. "I ... I don't know." Go figure but it was hard to talk, as if my jaw was deformed.

"Is it him?" Ed asked. "Dr. Death, I mean."

If it was, it was like nothing he'd ever done to me before. Hell, I hadn't even been in mortal danger, unless one counted wanting to die thanks to being piss-soaked.

I turned toward the nearest car window so as to catch a glimpse of my reflection.

It wasn't as freaky as I'd feared, but it was far from normal. From the look of things, I'd put on a few inches in height. My face had taken on what seemed to be an almost Neanderthal-like appearance. My jawline was heavier and thicker, as were my fangs, while my hair had grown out a couple of inches. My eyes were still black, but I could've sworn I saw some red in the irises.

This was no normal Dr. Death takeover.

No. It was like I'd taken on some of the physical traits of the asshole I'd bitten, albeit thankfully short of a full transformation. Either way it was unreal – as if his blood had affected me in ways not dissimilar to vamp blood, but with added physical side effects.

I flexed my hands, noting I certainly felt stronger. However, this bizarre change had left me feeling seriously awkward and not just emotionally. It was like I suddenly didn't quite know how to move my own body, as if the controls had changed and I hadn't been given the instruction manual.

"H-how?"

The beast inside my subconscious was quick to answer this time, but sadly in no way that even remotely helped.

I wish I knew.

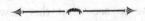

There was barely time to breathe, much less have any hope of figuring out why werewolf blood had the reaction in me it did. We'd taken down two of these assholes, leaving them lying unmoving in pools of their own blood, but that still left two more – both now fully transformed.

That evened the odds numerically, outside of Myra anyway, but it still wasn't great as they possessed most of the advantages here.

Most wasn't all, though.

The two monster wolves snarled. One of them – Jeb I think – remained standing on two legs, towering over us both, even with my newfound growth spurt. The other squatted on all fours and ... apparently decided now would be the perfect time to take a steaming shit on the asphalt.

Guess I should watch where I step.

"They're t-tough," I said, slurring the words as my tongue felt way too long for my mouth, "but dumb. Not much s-smarter than dogs."

"Yeah, kinda got that impression."

"Is that what you think?" Myra cried, still safely behind her force field. "Got a new trick to show you."

I had to open my mouth.

Myra let loose with two bolts of yellowish energy – mind magic if my knowledge of color coding held – both of which struck the werewolves in question.

On the upside, that seemed to drain her batteries, as she slumped down inside her magic shell looking winded. The bad was that the werewolves blinked a few times, then their expressions changed – going from rabid dog to cunning in the space of seconds.

The second wolf finished taking its crap then stood up tall while Jeb stopped snarling and instead cracked his knuckles.

That wasn't good. Guess you *could* teach an old dog new tricks.

Oh well, time to see what this new body of mine could do.

I tried to race forward to meet Jeb head on, but instead ended up lurching toward him like some sort of Frankenstein's monster. The unexpected power boost was nice, but I could've done without being stuck in some weird middle state, like in that one episode of the old *Incredible Hulk* TV series, except grosser looking.

Jeb took a swing, catching me in the shoulder. It didn't hurt as much as it should have, but when I tried to return the favor I may as well have been moving in slow motion.

The awkwardness of this partial transformation had effectively negated my speed, leaving me marginally stronger but a hell of a lot slower.

Sadly, against creatures like these, now enhanced even further by Myra, speed made all the difference.

Jeb spun, catching me with a clawed backhand that flayed open my cheek. I saw the attack coming, even tried to block it, but I simply couldn't move fast enough.

Let's face facts. People and dogs were physically pretty different. The fact that these werewolves had found a halfway point that worked for them was probably a minor miracle unto itself. I had a feeling I was shit out of luck with this half-assed form I'd unwittingly adopted.

The only plus in my favor was being a bit tougher, meaning I made a really good punching bag for this inbred fucker.

Jeb started to get into it, peppering me with blows and sporting a raging red rocket as he began to drive me back.

God, I hope I don't have one of those.

Out of the corner of my eye I saw Ed wasn't faring much better, mostly getting the ugly slapped out of him. Neither of us were fighters, but at least I'd been put through the wringer enough times to have picked up a few survival skills along the way. Though he'd technically been a vamp for the last five years, his powers had been dormant for most of it, meaning he had, at best, a few weeks' experience doing this shit – and most of that had been as Gan's personal suck puppet.

Back on my end, Jeb continued toying with me. Though it was hard to tell with his rottweiler-like face, I was fairly certain he was grinning as he slowly cut me down to size.

Hell, I couldn't even get in a spite kick to his balls, being that I was still trying to figure out which way my legs wanted to bend.

The ramifications of this are ... disturbing, my subconscious said.

I cocked my head, sending back a big ole, *No shit, Sherlock!*

You don't understand what this could mean...

Our internal dialogue couldn't have come at a worse time as Jeb pulled back and delivered a double fisted axe handle blow, catching me squarely on the jaw.

Ouch!

Between his size and strength, it was more than enough to plow through my defenses and send me flying.

I slammed down onto the hood of a car, a Beemer by the look of it, pretty much instantly trashing its resale value.

The crackling of bone caught my dazed ears as I lay there – *you broke me, you bought me* – only to be drowned out a moment later as the car's alarm started to blare.

The horn was disturbingly loud to my ears, but apparently it was even worse for Jeb and his buddy, both of whom threw back their heads and howled. *Heh.* Guess there were some things even a magical intelligence boost couldn't fix.

On my end, that crackling noise continued. Along with it came the feel of my skin crawling, as if I'd landed atop an anthill instead.

As I pushed myself off the hood of the car, though, I realized I was moving a lot more easily.

About fucking time!

The blessing of being a Freewill was the ability to subsume the power of other vamps. The downside was it didn't last long. It was a case of use it or lose it, meaning it had fucked me over more than once in the middle of a fight.

However, some fuckings were more pleasant than others. I swear, I never thought I'd be so happy to see a boost finally end. My clothes were a mess, but I was back to being me again.

Equally as good, Ed was cognizant enough to take

advantage of the car alarm to deliver an uppercut to his werewolf's crotch.

It's howl quickly turned into a whine as my friend backpedaled to where I was still shaking off the effects of that last hit.

"You about done fucking around?" he gasped, bruises coloring his face.

"No. I figured I'd tire them out by letting them kick our asses some more."

"I'd tell you to eat shit, but here, eat this instead." He shoved his hand into my face. "Come on! We don't have all fucking day."

Dazed as I was, it took me a moment to realize he wasn't just being weird. *Ah, I get it. Time to trade a bad boost for a good one.*

Before I could get distracted worrying about stupid things, like whether this was the hand he'd cockpunched his wolf with, I bit down and hoped for the best.

Thankfully, Neo-vamps, much like the original model, were a part of this nutritious breakfast. The only difference was their blood tingled for some reason, like downing a bag of Pop Rocks while chugging soda. One of these days, I really needed to figure out why. For now, though, I simply enjoyed the sensation of not exploding.

"Ow, not so hard, asshole!"

Pussy. I didn't take a lot since he needed to finish this battle, too, but I took enough. Ed's blood hit my stomach like an M-80 and I instantly felt his power added to my own.

Oh yeah. This was more like it, even if I couldn't let the moment pass without some trash talk. "Yuck. I don't know where you've been."

"How about we focus more on where we're going?"

"Sounds good to me," I said with a grin. "What say we take these fuckers on a tour of Hurtsville?"

15

DOGPILE

I didn't fool myself into thinking there was any great strategy or battle acumen on our part. The truth was we'd gotten lucky. Jeb had allowed us to get the drop on two of his number, while Myra had exhausted herself with one too many parlor tricks.

Still, I wasn't one to look a gift wolf in the mouth.

The boost from Ed was marginal at best, nothing compared to sucking on an ancient vampire – unfortunate wording aside – but it was enough to make a difference. My strength, speed, and healing were already formidable, enough to keep me from being instantly creamed. But with his added to it, the tide started to turn.

Ed focused on keeping his wolf busy, doing his best to stay alive while I took the fight to Jeb.

"Get that son of a bitch," Myra cried, reduced to little more than a cheerleader inside her shield.

I quickly began to understand why she hadn't dropped it though.

Ducking Jeb's first blow, I slashed at his midsection, drawing four rivulets of blood. Then, when he spun, hoping to catch me like he did earlier, I kicked out instead, driving my foot into the side of his knee.

That staggered him enough for me to clock him upside

the head. It felt like punching cinderblock, but I took some pride in seeing a few of his teeth crack.

I was prepared to press my advantage when Jeb let loose with a primal snarl. In the space of an instant, the intelligence fled from his face, leaving feral red eyes staring back. In the next moment, he leapt at me snarling and biting.

I couldn't exactly claim this to be a good thing, being he was still a dangerous monster. However, gone was any sense of strategy on his part and in its place was left little more than a wild animal.

One on one, these things were dangerous, no argument about it. But add intelligence and they became downright deadly. Their leader Hobart had given me a firsthand lesson in that, nearly taking me apart singlehandedly. Then there'd been that other wolf, the one who'd appeared from out of nowhere and helped us to escape.

Still no idea what was up with that one, but now wasn't the time to worry about it.

With Ed keeping Jeb's littermate busy, I had to focus on the task in front of me. Jeb gave one more guttural snarl, then he put his head down and charged forward recklessly.

With my body back under my control, though, I was able to sidestep him neatly. *Yes!*

The werewolf pounced upon the spot where I'd been standing a moment earlier, leaving his flank open. So of course, I, sporting fellow that I am, stepped in, grabbed him by the scruff of his neck, and slammed him face first into the side of a nearby Dodge Ram. It was a good truck – nice and solid, just how I was hoping it would be.

Then, just to drive the point home, I repeated it several more times, leaving both the truck's side panels and Jeb's face little more than crushed messes.

I dropped his unmoving form to the ground then turned to help Ed.

His werewolf, though still possessing whatever intelligence Myra had gifted him, took one look at the downed Jeb then backed away, piss running down his legs. *Eww.* What was with these things?

He threw Myra an apologetic glance, then dropped to all fours and took off running.

"You're a fucking coward, Larry!" Myra shouted after him. "Don't think I ain't gonna tell your wife."

I held up my hand until Ed, exhausted though he appeared, threw me a high five.

"You okay?" I asked.

"I'll live."

I turned toward where Myra still waited behind her purple force dome. "Got enough left in you to spank a mouthy witch?"

"Oh yeah."

"You wouldn't dare," she snapped.

"Normally you'd be right," Ed replied. "But my chivalry kind of goes out the window when you sic a fucking dog pack on me."

"Damn straight," I said, continuing with the tough guy routine. "Although, I'll offer you this. Your chances of walking out of here with your teeth intact will be a lot higher if you stop fucking around and tell us what's going on."

"I ain't telling you shit lickers anything."

Her voice was defiant, but I saw the doubt in her eyes. "What say we make this canary sing?"

Before we could make another move, though, the empty space directly to our left lit up with blinding white light.

Goddamn it. What now?

Ed and I adopted defensive stances, which, to be fair, didn't look all that impressive. But then the light faded away, revealing who it had been containing.

"Christy?"

Talk about a sight for sore eyes.

In the space of a few seconds, she surveyed the scene, her eyes opening wide as she beheld Jeb's unconscious body.

"Who the fuck are you?" Myra snapped.

Christy turned toward her, eyes narrowed. "Nobody you want to mess with."

She gestured and the inside of Myra's force dome lit up with blue electricity, dropping the hayseed Circe like a bad habit.

That's my girl!

With Myra down for the count, her spells dissipated. First went the force dome, next was the strange glamour – erasing the moonlit sky above us and leaving nothing but ceiling.

"So much for getting answers," Ed remarked. "Not that I'm complaining about the assist."

Christy shrugged. "She forgot to ground the floor beneath her. Amateur mistake." Then she turned to us, eying me in particular. "Are you okay?"

I gestured down at myself. "Long ... and weird story, but yeah, we're fine. We... Wait. How are you even here?"

She cocked her head and grinned. "Tom called to make sure you were on your way to Sally's. When he told me how long ago you'd left, I decided to scry you both." At my raised eyebrow, she added, "At this point, I consider it best practice to keep a few strands of everyone's hair handy."

Ed chuckled. "In another life that would be creepy as all hell. Considering the circumstances, however, I'm all for it."

I nodded. "Saved by the spell." And my roommate's petty jealousy, of course. "Seriously, though, I could kiss you right now."

She smiled in return. "What's stopping you?"

Ooh, now there was an invitation I wouldn't have

minded taking advantage of. Sadly, the mood was quickly shattered as there once again came the disturbing *schlup* of shifting flesh, just barely audible over the dying whine of the car alarm.

Talk about the opposite of make out music.

Before our eyes, Jeb began to shrink, turning back into a human, his body rearranging itself from werewolf to bare-assed dickhead.

But that wasn't all.

"Um, guys, you might want to check this out," Ed said, pointing elsewhere.

Our celebratory smooch sidelined, Christy and I both turned to follow his gaze toward the werewolf whose throat I'd torn out. This one, too, was busy returning to his human form, leading me to wonder whether he was as deceased as I'd thought.

A moment later that fear was confirmed as the wound on his neck knitted itself back together and he took a breath.

"The fuck?"

"It's not me is it?" Ed asked. "This guy was dead a minute ago, right?"

"Pretty sure that was the case."

He sure as shit wasn't now. Neither was the woman for that matter. All of them began to stir, groaning as if waking up from a bender.

Between all the blood, the damage we'd caused, and the fact that most of the people on the ground were naked, this was quite the scene – once again leaving us with questions we had no answers to.

But maybe we could still fix that. "C'mon. Let's grab Jeb. Maybe he can..."

Unfortunately, our window of opportunity picked that moment to slam shut. Whether because of the car alarm still weakly blaring or just dumb luck, headlights appeared as another vehicle rounded the corner to this section of the garage.

"Time's up," Christy said, grabbing hold of both me and Ed. "We need to go."

"Not yet. We can still..."

My words fell silent as reality heeded her call and we winked out of existence.

The only upside to the adrenaline rush of getting my ass kicked was that it slightly muted my gag reflex upon reappearing in Christy's summoning circle.

The door to her bedroom was open and for a moment I had to blink twice, as I could've sworn I saw her out in the living room as well. When I looked again, though, the only Christy was the one standing between us.

"Wait, was that...?"

"Yes."

Ah! That made sense then. It was the same spell she'd used a few weeks back at Sally's apartment, allowing her to effectively be in two places at once. As she sat on the bed wiping her brow, I also remembered how taxing it could be.

"Are you all right?"

She nodded. "Sorry about the quick exit, but I didn't want to risk leaving Tina by herself longer than I had to."

"Or bring a werewolf back here with us, I presume?"

"That, too."

"Is she still awake?"

"Thankfully not. That definitely makes it easier, not having to carry on two conversations at once."

"I bet. And no worries about the rest. We'll get them next time."

"I'm missing something here, aren't I?" Ed asked as we headed to the more spacious living room.

"Magic stuff."

"We can talk about that later," Christy said. "First things first."

I grinned. "Oh yeah. That kiss you were..."

"I was joking earlier." She held up a hand while wrinkling her nose. "No offense, but you two kinda smell like the bottom of a toilet bowl."

Thankfully, between Christy's apartment and the one next door, she had two working showers. While Ed and I were cleaning up, she took care of the rest. I didn't ask any questions as to what voodoo she may have performed, but there was a pile of brand new clothes waiting for us once we were finished, tags still attached.

Holy shoplifting spell, Batman.

Oh well. It's not like we hadn't committed worse crimes against humanity.

"Okay, so what happened?" she finally asked once we were dressed.

For the fourth or fifth time that night I made with the exposition, explaining how Ed and I had been shanghaied by Myra the moonshine witch and then filling her in on the weirdness I'd experienced.

"So you not only got stronger but physically changed, too?"

"Yeah," Ed replied. "It was pretty freaky to watch."

I chuckled mirthlessly. "Far freakier to live through."

"Hah. I'm half surprised you didn't bend over and lick your own balls."

"Tom would have."

"No doubt."

"Be that as it may," Christy said, no doubt trying to steer us back on track. "It's potentially another piece to this puzzle, maybe an important one."

"How so?"

"I don't know yet." She shook her head. "You're sure this has never happened before, right, with another species I mean?"

"Nope. The hairy knuckles were definitely new. As for the rest, before today I thought it was a vamp only thing."

"I see. It almost suggests ... a kinship of some kind."

"You mean we're related to dogs?" Ed asked.

Christy shrugged. "It means I have no idea, other than adding it to the pile of research already on my plate."

I raised an eyebrow. "We talking about the Archives here?"

She let out a sigh and nodded. "I won't lie. It's still bothering me. I meant what I said earlier, about how dangerous it could be, even more so since there aren't any checks and balances in place."

"Then stop using it. We'll figure something else out."

"I can't."

"Can't?"

"We need answers. That, and..."

"You like having a finger in the cookie jar?"

She narrowed her eyes but didn't disagree.

"Okay, fine. Then just be careful."

"I'm trying to. It's just ... you don't understand how unprecedented this is. Archive librarians have to pass a rigorous gauntlet of tests, and even then are only allowed to catalog the specific subsections assigned to them. It's exceedingly rare for even noted scholars to be granted unfettered access. There are always restrictions in place, safeguards."

"What about for Falcon?" I replied.

"That's different. The Falcons have been keepers of the Archive since the beginning. Members of his bloodline are purposely raised to respect the vast knowledge contained within. They know not to dig further than is needed, and to respect that which is not meant for mortal eyes. And in cases where access to forbidden knowledge is warranted, well, there's one final safeguard in place. It's well known that members of his family are..."

She trailed off, shaking her head.

"Are what?" Ed asked.

"It's not important. I'm just saying I'm worried that I might..."

"I'm not," I interrupted, looking her in the eye. "I know you, Christy. Of all of us, you have the best head on your shoulders."

Ed nodded. "In some cases by far. Hell, you're pretty much the last person I worry about going mad with power."

"I ... appreciate that," she said, placing her hand atop mine. "From both of you." After a moment or so, she brightened up. "This is probably for the best anyway. Matthias already has his hands full, so I doubt he has time to spare helping us."

I considered what happened at his place earlier. "You ain't whistling Dixie."

"We have more pressing concerns, though," she continued, the mood turning serious again.

"Are we back to Gan?"

She shrugged. "Partly. I mean, she's still the reason most of this is happening. But specifically I was talking about our new living arrangements."

Ed blew out a breath, turning to me. "The werewolves. They know where you live."

I nodded. "Which means no sleepovers for Tina."

"It means no sleepovers for any of you," Christy said, "At least not for right now. We can't defend against one threat if we're watching our backs for another."

Shit! She was right. "And since they have no way of knowing where we zapped off to, that's the place they'll keep their eyes on."

"Exactly."

There was also no way of faking them out since, between them, they now knew all our faces. That meant we had no choice but to abandon the apartment for now and hope they didn't sniff us out otherwise, at least until we solved our number one problem – Gan.

It all added up to one thing: we were one step closer to being stuck between a rock and a hard place.

UNSAFETY DANCE

16

UNSAFETY DANCE

I put on the TV as Christy went to brew some coffee.
It was late and even those of us with inhuman consti-
tutions were starting to feel it.

Alas, there was no comfort to be had in mindless info-
tainment. As for the news, the top story had switched at
some point to the increased risk of terror attacks. An
unidentified aircraft had apparently violated New York
City's airspace in the last few hours. From the sound of
things, fighter jets were close to being scrambled when the
contact simply disappeared from the scope.

I quickly turned it off, remembering the crash from
earlier. It was yet another rabbit hole demanding attention, although one that would hopefully be taken care of
by more qualified personnel – such as the U.S. Air Force.

A part of me was tempted to ask Christy if there was
any part of the research I could maybe take over for her.
That would certainly ease the burden of temptation. It was
probably a useless endeavor, though. Figuring out the
Archive's web interface had been a piece of cake. The rest
... not so much. I was about as useful at interpreting
ancient Sumerian tablets as I was at giving Gan the hint.

I swear, those fucking werewolves couldn't have picked
a worse time to rear their ugly mugs again. Pretty soon I'd

need eyes in the back of my head to keep watch for whatever threat decided to strike next.

No matter which way you looked at it, we were at the disadvantage, having to play the waiting game while the assholes around us...

Rather than wait for our foes, why not take the battle to them instead?

Hold on. Was my internal hell-beast suggesting we actually ... go to war?

The thing was, he might've had a point. Ever since everything started back up again, we'd mostly been reacting – putting out fires as they sprung up.

Hell, the last time we'd taken the initiative had been when we'd zapped down to The Source to free a kidnapped Sally from a vamp named Komak and his witch girlfriend Liz.

It hadn't worked out quite the way we'd hoped, but it had beat sitting around with our thumbs up our asses.

As far as tangible threats went, the werewolves kind of felt like the low hanging fruit – something we could potentially handle. The problem was we didn't know dick about them or what they wanted, outside of Ed. And, well, we'd just gotten him back. Seemed kind of dickish to just hand him over and hope they went away.

I was still convinced the thing in the Hudson wasn't our problem, but that might've been because it scared the absolute shit out of me. Also, once again, we knew next to nothing about it other than it was big and terrifying.

That left only one option on the table, a certain someone Christy herself had already expressed interest in ending with extreme prejudice.

As she returned with steaming mugs of coffee, I decided to gently test those waters. "So, what if, rather than waiting for her to show up, we took the fight to Gan instead?"

Probably a good thing I didn't wait for anyone to start drinking.

"What?!" Ed sputtered.

"I'm just talking hypothetically here, but think about it. We're kinda stuck either splitting the party and waiting to see who gets picked off first, or gathering everyone in one place and hoping Sally doesn't explode. But what if we figured out a way to go on the offensive instead? Hunt down the little nutball and make her tell us everything she knows."

The look on Ed's face suggested that he would've sooner licked werewolf taint than purposely seek out his former captor. "You do realize how much easier said than done that is, right?"

Christy, however, seemed a bit less perturbed by the idea. "Gan has called the shots for every single dealing we've had with her, and I have absolutely no doubt she's anticipated almost every defensive move we've considered."

I nodded. "You just know she'll be waiting for an opening we didn't expect, like one of us getting up to use the bathroom."

"Or stopping for gas," Ed remarked, a trace of bitterness in his voice.

I reached over and patted his shoulder. "Nobody blames you, man. Being captured is your thing."

"Eat an asshole."

"Already got my recommended daily allowance of bodily fluids, thanks."

"Which makes me glad I didn't take you up on that kiss earlier," Christy remarked.

I chuckled. "Fair enough. But back to the matter at hand..."

"Yeah, about that," Ed replied. "I'm not sure this is as straightforward as you're making it out to be."

"Of course not. This is Gan."

"Exactly. All I know is the mansion she kept me holed up in was a veritable..."

"Hold on." I held up a hand. "You've been at a fucking mansion this entire time?"

"Yeah, mostly. Except for that trip up to..."

"We're talking a dungeon down in the basement, right?"

"No. It was a suite on the second floor."

"That you were kept chained up in?"

"Not really. I had the run of the estate, but..."

"There was an estate, too? And what did this estate have, pray tell?"

"Um, a couple of swimming pools, a tennis court, and..."

I blinked a few times. "Tennis court?! Why the fuck were we looking for you again?" I turned to face Christy. "New idea. How about we surrender to her instead? My backswing needs a bit of work."

"You're missing the point, numbnuts," Ed replied. "It was still a prison."

"A really *nice* prison."

"And I was a prisoner."

"With access to an Olympic-size swimming pool."

"Pretty sure it was bigger than that."

I narrowed my eyes. "Of course it was."

"But it still sucked balls. She kept forcing me to bite her people against my..."

"A vampire snacking on people, in between tennis lessons and soaking in the hot tub. The horror."

He glared at me. "Then I was forced to sit through Dave milking my fangs."

I remained unimpressed. "Been there, done that. It's not exactly thumbscrews."

"Listen, asshole..." He slapped a hand onto the coffee table, making a loud bang, then cringed as he turned toward Tina's room. "Sorry."

"It's okay," Christy said with a wave of her hand. "I assumed things might be noisy when we got back, so I activated the sound dampening wards on her bedroom door ahead of time."

Huh. Too bad they never seemed to work whenever I said a curse word.

"Good thinking," Ed replied. "Anyway, back to what I was saying..." He pointed at me before I could open my mouth. "I will remind you, I know where you keep your cloud backups, including your *special* directories."

I made a zipping my lips motion, making a mental note to change my password.

"Special directories?" Christy asked.

"Just ... old projects from back when we worked together." I shot him a look, not appreciating the shit-eating grin I got back.

"Now that that's settled, what I was trying to say is there's a reason I didn't escape, and believe me I tried. We're talking practically every single day here. Gan has that place wired top to bottom, and that's not even counting the security team. It's led by this guy named Paladin..."

"Paladin?"

He nodded. "Trust me, I said the same thing. He's some ex special forces guy who wouldn't know a twenty sider if you slapped one upside his head, but he knows his shit. Worse than that, he was one of the first people Gan had me bite."

"So her security chief is a vampire, too. Not exactly unexpected."

"As are most of his team," he continued. "And believe me they are paranoid as fuck, mostly because I got the impression Gan executes anyone who isn't."

"Huh. Wonder if she posts that to her Instagram page as well." Okay, jokes aside, this was getting less good by the moment, but it still wasn't insurmountable. So long as she didn't have any...

"Oh, one other thing. Pretty sure she has some Magi on her payroll, too."

Shit! That's exactly what I didn't want to hear. Down at The Source, Gan had swayed a buttload of mages to her side, but I'd been hoping they were nothing more than temporary allies – desperate bed fellows there to bring magic back and nothing more.

"That's not surprising to hear," Christy said after a moment.

I turned to her, eyebrow raised.

"Never discount the value of a paycheck during uncertain times." She let out a sigh. "I've been reaching out to some of my old friends, those who'll still talk to me, and it's not good. Even in our former strongholds – Salem, Amherst, places where the most established covens in the country are rooted – it sounds like only a handful have gotten their act together."

"What about Boston?" Ed asked.

"Boston?"

"Yeah, I ran into some Magi up there. Sounds like they're working on cutting some kind of power sharing deal with the crew Gan's trying to install."

"Oh, yeah. I almost forgot about your little furlough."

He glared at me. "Don't start with that shit again."

"Hmm," Christy replied. "I wasn't aware of that."

"Yeah, they're apparently being backed by some big corporate syndicate ... Grove Industries I think. Anyway, the reason we were up there was that Gan had a bug up her ass about exploring what was left of that old carwash."

The carwash? "I thought that place got turned into a crater."

The Boston Prefecture was a marvel of over-engineering, my subconscious replied. *The lower levels were spread over a vast area and hardened against attack.*

Huh. Good to know, except for the part where it really wasn't.

"Why?" Christy asked.

"Because she was looking for something she wanted." He held up a hand. "The good news is, she didn't get it."

"What was she searching for?"

He looked away for a moment, as if debating what to say.

"I don't know for certain, but we ran into something pretty nasty down there. Something called ... a Nameless One."

My God, he actually did it, Dr. Death said.

"Did what?" I asked, before once again realizing I was talking aloud. "Sorry. I meant, what was it?"

"Remember that moderator from the Woods of Mourning?"

I nodded. "Been trying to forget it."

"Yeah, well, it was like that, only angrier."

Christy for her part didn't say anything, but the look of worry on her face told me this was yet another item to add to our growing shit list. Wonderful.

"The point I'm trying to make," Ed continued, "is that Gan came out emptyhanded, and she was pissed about it."

I couldn't believe I was going to suggest this but, "So are you saying we should search it ourselves before she decides to try again?"

I would highly recommend against that.

"Not really. Things are all weird as shit down there. Oh, and there's some kind of magical barrier around it, too. Tough stuff. We barely got through as it was. One of the dryads who came along had to make a deal with some freaky Earth spirit just to get us past it."

"Wait, dryads?" I replied. "You mean like ents?"

He shook his head. "That's what I thought, too. But they're more like people with plant powers."

"Plant powers?"

"It's not as lame as it sounds. There was this one chick who was basically a walking joint, and not the cheap kind either."

"For real?" Feeling the glare of Christy's raised eyebrow, I quickly added, "Not that I care about such things anymore."

"Okay, enough." She held up a hand. "The fact that Gan didn't get what she was after is a good thing, but I'm not sure it really helps us. I'll make a few calls and see what I can find out about this Grove Industries, but it sounds like this is low priority for the time being."

"Fair enough," I said, forcing my thoughts away from the awesomeness of sentient ganja. "Okay, so is there anything *tangible* in our favor here then?"

Ed took a sip of his coffee, seeming to consider this. "Maybe. The security team were actually pretty cordial, when they weren't busy fucking up my every escape attempt. Anyway, they were dragging me back one night when I overheard a few of them laughing about how I set off just about every alarm imaginable..."

"You're like an anti-ninja."

He flipped me off before continuing. "So I kind of casually wondered out loud why no cops had shown up."

"Let me guess," Christy interrupted. "They weren't notified."

"Bingo. She's completely off the grid."

"What happens in GanBerg stays in GanBerg," I mused.

Christy nodded. "Possibly useful. But it also means that however hard we might hit her, she's free to hit us back harder."

"And I don't doubt she can." Ed chuckled but there was little humor behind it. "Anyway, there you have it. Two vampires, a witch, an Icon, and a blob of snot against an impenetrable fortress. Place your bets."

I blew out a sigh. "And Tom's powers aren't nearly as useful against neo-vamps. Not exactly a lot of checks in our plus column."

Christy turned to me and smiled. "Don't underestimate us or yourself, *Freewill.*"

"Amazing how little that title seems to mean these days."

"Not to some of us." She put a hand on my knee, instantly making me wish Ed was anywhere but here at the moment.

"I'd tell you to get a room, but that would make Bill way too happy."

Christy laughed but she didn't correct him. Oh, God. I'd had way too weird of a day to be this horny. Sadly, rather than suggest Ed go and make an extended run for ... anything, she steered us back on track. "Anyway, what I meant is that's not all we have in our favor."

Um, okay. I mean, I guess we had Kelly, too – once she was done showing her husband all the other positions besides missionary. Other than that, though, I was drawing a blank. I doubted I could convince Char to cross the street much less help us kill someone she didn't know. As for Falcon, well, I wasn't sure I wanted to discuss a bunch of premeditated crimes with someone on the NYPD's payroll, even with the old vampire treaties back in place.

Seeing the clueless look on my face, Christy explained, her voice growing cold, "If Gan wants Sally dead, that must mean she's afraid of her. Which means she might be the perfect weapon for us to use."

17

NUCLEAR OPTION

I sat there for several seconds waiting for a punchline which didn't seem to be coming. On the upside, all thoughts of boning had fled ... mostly. "You're kidding, right?"

"Not in the slightest."

Christy's voice had taken on the same cadence she'd once used to explain how she would kill anyone and anything who threatened her unborn child. She could be a person of limitless caring when it came to friends and family, but I was well aware she wouldn't hesitate to scorch the Earth and then salt it afterward if shit got real.

Oh boy. All at once I was wishing I'd kept my mouth shut on this *hypothetical* scenario.

"Sally does sort of dislike her, I'll give you that," Ed remarked.

That was an understatement. Hell, she'd put a bullet in Gan's head down at The Source. Too bad it hadn't been of higher caliber. Would've saved us a lot of trouble.

There was just one small problem. "Let's back up here. We don't know the extent of Sally's power or how to control it. All we know is that bad things happen when she goes off."

"Then that gives us impetus to figure it out," Christy replied.

"Also, let's be honest here," Ed added. "If bad things are gonna happen, Gan's a good candidate for them to happen to."

"True. But let's not forget that whole Great Beast incident down at the docks."

"You mean earlier when…"

"Different Great Beast thing," I corrected. "While you were still busy sampling the catering at Club Gan."

He looked confused, probably because he hadn't been there, but Christy knew what I was talking about. And I couldn't help but think it was a wee bit more pertinent now considering what had happened to Falcon's pier.

She shook her head, though. "For all we know, that might've been nothing more than a reaction to being assaulted by the apkallu, or the fact they're not part of the natural order."

"Or it could have been something much worse."

"Perhaps, but the bottom line is we simply don't know. Hell, we don't even know if we can help Sally, or if eventually we'll be forced to…" She trailed off before she could finish, even though I knew where she was going with it – a direction not entirely dissimilar to Gan's. I swear, some days it was hard to deny the logic of *The Dark Knight*. You either died a hero or lived long enough to become the bad guy.

"Yeah, but…"

"*But*," she continued, "we'll never get the opportunity to figure it out so long as Gan is out there threatening us." There came a crackle of power from behind her eyes, one that said I was venturing into dangerous territory if I persisted. "And I will not risk that little girl in there becoming collateral damage because we decided to play it safe rather than end this when we had the chance."

Oh yeah, I'd definitely opened Pandora's Box by

suggesting we go on the offensive, and I had a nasty feeling there'd be no closing it now.

The wee hours of the morning saw me heading out once again. Neither of my friends wanted me to go alone, but I was fairly certain we'd given Myra and her hairy dicked friends enough of a bloody nose for one day. That, and Christy was clearly exhausted. I didn't want her expending any more energy than she had to, not knowing when she might need it for real.

Besides, I wanted some time to get my head on straight.

Mind you, I wasn't insane enough to take needless risks. Fuck that noise. I at least waited for the start of rush hour, meaning it was still dark enough for me to make the trek, while also offering the safety of numbers.

My first stop was an all-night convenience store, where I picked up an overpriced burner phone along with a prepaid data plan. I quickly shot out some texts, letting my friends know how they could reach me. Then I hopped onto the subway, just another schmuck headed into Manhattan for the work day.

Despite the fact that we'd been periodically checking in with her via text, getting back generic *all's well* responses, Sally had been left alone long enough. As the train raced underground, I wondered if maybe that had been part of Gan's plan all along – distracting us by threatening Christy so that we'd focus our efforts elsewhere.

If that were the case, though, why bother showing up to my apartment at all? She could've simply popped by Sally's at any point and put a bullet in her head without the rest of us being any wiser.

That told me she likely hadn't been lying about believing I was the only one capable of getting close enough to do the deed. It also told me she was worried.

Hell, if not for the batshit aspects of it all, Christy's plan was solid – take the one person Gan was afraid of and use her to our advantage.

And Ed was right. I doubted Sally would mind much.

The thing was, we were still figuring out what had happened to her in that rocky cocoon. We simply didn't know how deep it went. I couldn't help but remember back to the fight at the pier. Something had changed in her when she'd flared up, enough to cause all the bad guys there to give her a wide berth. The implications hadn't exactly been promising.

We still didn't know who or what was behind the attack in the first place, or how they'd managed to ensnare a disparate group of degenerate monsters to do so. Once Sally had declared herself the herald of the so-called Great Beast, though, well, much as I hated to admit it, that kinda put her on the suspect list.

And I think my friends, her included, understood that, too. After all, why else would there have been an unspoken agreement to keep that little tidbit from Falcon?

Goddamn it all!

Making it worse, if that was even possible, had been the Sword of Damocles Gan had hung over my head back before magic returned – proclaiming that fate wasn't done with me yet, that *great* things awaited.

I swear, some days I wished I could convince my friends to find a deserted island for us to hide on while this shit played out. Let destiny pick some other dickhead to shove into the great toilet of the universe and get a metaphysical swirlie.

Hell, it almost made me long for the days when my biggest concern was keeping Jeff, AKA Night Razor, from kicking my ass. Yeah, that had seemed a big deal at the time, but a good chunk of it had been mostly normal crap – beer, bullshit, and me hanging with my buddies. Those were the days when it seemed the world was happy to keep spinning without the need to shove dire prophecies up my ass.

I took a deep breath, immediately regretting it since the subway car was pretty packed. *Uck*. Regardless, I still had some hope. For instance, the giant radioactive dinosaur in the Hudson could very well be someone else's problem. If so, then I didn't need to give a shit.

That still left a lot on my plate, though. Worse, Gan had made it personal. So, big or small, there was no way I could ignore it.

I just hoped Christy was right about Sally and we weren't making an even bigger mistake dragging her into this.

I ran into Jessica and Leslie on the way up, having just beat the sunrise to Sally's place. They were hanging out in the hall – no bodies, blood orgies, or any of that. It was nothing more than some girl talk. I swear, it was so mundane as to be almost glorious.

"Ladies," I said greeting them.

"Coven *leader*," Leslie replied with a grin, probably waiting to see if I'd correct her. Screw it. Maybe Craig was right and master was a shitty term for the position. Just because there was some logic to the coven system didn't mean I had to adhere to every stupid-ass rule the First Coven had made.

"Hey, do me a favor and pass the word. I need you guys to keep an eye out for anyone who doesn't belong. Raise the alarm if you notice anything dodgy."

Jessica inclined her head. "What do you mean by doesn't belong?"

So much for letting them enjoy their normalcy. I gave them a brief rundown on Gan and how she likely had this place under observation. And then I doubled down that they were not to do anything about it other than let Sally and me know.

I didn't consider any of the new Village Coven vamps to be alpha dogs, but it seemed safe to reinforce that. I already had Char running around playing undead Daredevil. I didn't need one of these guys deciding their powers made them a half-assed Batman – especially where Gan was concerned. There was little doubt she could easily play the Joker to their Jason Todd.

"I swear," Leslie replied, "who'd have ever guessed being a vampire would be this stressful?"

"You don't know the half of it." I was about to head past when I remembered to add, "Oh, and stay away from the docks. There's some weird shit going on."

That got their attention. When you were undead and someone told you that something was weirder than that, it was an instant warning sign.

"Okay, you two be good," I finally told them. "I need to head up and see Sally."

"Oh, I think she might be asleep," Jessica said. "Craig went up to ask her about something earlier and she told him she was turning in."

I waited a beat, but thankfully there was no follow up regarding him being blown into a million bloody chunks. Talk about a relief.

Nevertheless it was kinda odd. Far as I was aware, Sally had been unable to sleep ever since waking up in her new green-haired hottie form – a side effect of whatever had happened to her.

Maybe this was a positive sign then. Perhaps it meant that whatever had been done to her was starting to normalize in some way. Who knows? Maybe that whole herald of the Great Beast thing was a limited time offer, one that expired if you didn't immediately sign away your soul in blood.

I sincerely doubted that was the case, but it would be

nice. And fuck it, a bit of hope wasn't exactly a bad thing after the last twenty-four hours.

I headed up to her floor, thankful she'd had an interaction with the coven that hadn't ended with her calling in some shady cleaners to take care of the mess. It was a small victory, but a good one since she was kind of their den mother in my absence.

Reaching the door to her fifth floor apartment, I was about to knock but then remembered what Jessica had said. The last thing I wanted to do was wake Sally up if she was actually sleeping. I obviously didn't want to set her off in a way where I'd end up like Stewart. And even if not, well, who really wanted to deal with a cranky Sally?

Fortunately, I had a spare key, as I was the one who'd gotten her door fixed back when she'd been busy playing statue.

I let myself in, trying to make as little sound as possible. It was only once I'd locked things up again, though, that I noticed the bathroom door was open and a cloud of steam was wafting out.

It was the space of a moment to realize I'd quite possibly paved a road to Hell with my good intentions.

In the next instant I picked up the sound of soft footsteps, the kind people tended to make when barefoot.

Fuck! Then, before I could turn and correct the horrific mistake I'd just made, Sally came strolling out wearing nothing but her magical arrest bracelet and a towel around her hair.

She turned my way, her eyes opening wide as they met mine.

Oh shit!

This was it. I was so dead they were going to need to squeegee me off the wall twice.

18

THE NAKED TRUTH

O nce upon a time this would've been a dream come true. Hell, I might have even tried to snap a picture for posterity's sake, despite it being a near certain death sentence.

But I'd also been younger, single, and far stupider back then.

These days I was older, a bit wiser, and had a girlfriend I was super fond of. There was also the slightly worrisome part about Sally being infinitely more dangerous.

On the upside, at least I didn't have to worry about waiting to see if the world was gonna end or not.

I braced myself, hoping the impending explosion was at least quick.

"Hey, Bill," she said casually, as I stood there waiting to die. "When did you get here?"

"I ... uh..." *Don't stare at her tits. Do not stare at them, Bill!* "I ... let myself in. J-Jessica said you were ... um ... taking a nap."

Oh God! They were as perky as I'd imagined.

"I was." She placed a hand on her hip, somehow making it both better and worse. "It was nice. First bit of sleep I've been able to get since, well, you know. But then I woke up and figured I'd grab a shower."

"I can ... see that." Inside my pants, little Dr. Death let out a silent roar of triumph as I realized the carpet didn't match the drapes ... because there was no carpet! *Oh, dear lord.* "Listen, I'm sorry. I didn't realize you..."

"Oh this?" She gestured at herself as if finally realizing she was playing centerfold to my sudden twelve-year-old grasp of reality. "It's nothing you haven't seen before."

My jaw dropped open. "What?"

"You remember, right?" she replied, sounding disturbingly nonchalant. "That time in the woods, right after you fought Turd? We had a celebratory roll in the hay."

"T-that was Dr. Death, if you recall."

She let out a chuckle, as if this whole thing was hilarious. In some ways that made the blast I was still expecting far worse. "I know, but I figured you were still in there somewhere watching." She cocked an eyebrow at me.

Oh no. Here it comes.

"Are you actually blushing?"

What?! "Me? No. Of course not."

"Oh my gosh, you are!" *Gosh?* "Seriously, Bill, you're an adult and this is just a naked body. Hell, you've seen Christy's, haven't you? Or at least I really hope you have."

Not nearly as often as I preferred, but that was beside the point. The fact that she was just standing there, neither tearing me a new asshole nor fetching her gun, was seriously messing with my head.

What the fuck kind of bizarro universe had I stepped into and why hadn't it happened years ago when it would've been the best fucking thing ever?

Not that it wasn't awesome now. Because believe me, it was.

Some people looked good in clothing, but then when you saw what was going on beneath you were all like, "What happened?" Not Sally. She was like Margot Robbie from that scene in *The Wolf of Wall Street*, except with different colored hair. And, damn, if that wasn't the hottest fucking thing in all of creation I didn't know what was.

She finally let out a sigh, as if she found all of this somehow quaint. "All right. Hold on for a minute, Mr. Puritan. I'll go put something on."

Then she turned and walked into her bedroom, giving me a view of her perfect ass to drive home how utterly insane my life had suddenly become.

With supreme effort, I forced myself to look away, waging a silent battle of wills with my dick as I silently explained to it that something strange was going on and now was not the time for a Loch Ness Monster sighting.

Why the hell had I even come here? It was like my mind had gone blank. All that existed was my name and Sally's naked body. I mean, shit, what else did one need in this world?

She truly is as lovely as ever.

What the...? "Keep it in your pants, asshole!"

"Excuse me?" she called back.

I forced myself to turn around, finding her now clad in tight yoga pants and a t-shirt. It was still distracting as all hell, but was at least enough to dial my pants down from DEFCON 1 ... slightly.

"Nothing," I replied, trying to force rational thoughts back into my brain now that blood flow had been partially restored. "I came over to sleep with you ... I mean stay with you."

"Come again," she replied, her voice still disturbingly calm.

Talk about a poor choice of words. "Okay, let me back up. I meant our plan. I was going to stay here with you and the coven for a while."

"Oh yeah." She nodded. "Christy called earlier and told me. Huh. Took you long enough to get here."

"We kinda got sidetracked."

That's it. Talk about getting my ass kicked. That always kills the mood. I explained how Ed and I had been waylaid by werewolves, leading to a brawl in a parking garage before Christy could bamf us out of there.

However, where I expected snide comments as to my lack of fighting prowess, she instead simply listened and nodded.

Now that the crisis of her nakedness had passed – albeit it would live on forever in my memories – it was beginning to hit home how *not right* all of this was.

Hell, barely a week ago, she'd nearly blown my head off as I was running for my life, only to tell me to suck it up. Now here she was, acting like she'd just showered in Xanax. It was kinda creepy.

Hmm. Come to think of it, she'd been similarly laid back when we'd popped by yesterday to check on her.

Regardless, chillaxed or not, Sally's mind was still sharp as a tack. "So the werewolves found out where you live? I'm guessing this means plans have changed again."

"Pretty much."

She stepped into the kitchen and poured herself some orange juice, as if we were discussing nothing more than the weather. "How'd they know you were going to be in that car?"

"No idea, but they have that witch. Maybe she was snooping on us."

"Maybe." She took a sip before setting the glass down. "Or maybe they've got someone keeping an eye on you guys. An inside man, if you will."

"I doubt that's the..."

Wait a second. Hadn't we run into my newest tenant on the way out? Yeah, Mike had been there, waiting at the front door for some reason. Huh. Like that wasn't suspicious at all. Not only that, but the fucker had only moved in a few days ago. "Son of a bitch!"

"It was Tom, wasn't it?" Sally replied with a smirk. "Let me guess. They pretended to be telemarketers and he told them everything they needed to..."

I waved her off. "No. Not Tom. At least not this time."

Although, she had a point. I probably needed to talk to him about that. "But I think I know who."

She shrugged as if unperturbed by any of this. "Well, then you might want to have a word with them at some point."

A word? "I might try being a bit more persuasive than that."

"Never hurts to try talking first. Carrot before stick."

Oh yeah, something was off here. I knew Sally. She typically wasn't above the concept of torture. Hell, she'd once bitten a Templar, compelled him to tell us what he knew, then blown his head off once we had what we were looking for. I could practically hear her voice in my mind telling me I should slowly snip Mike's balls off one at a time until he squealed like a pig.

I held up a hand. "Okay, let's forget about that for the moment. The more important part is what we discussed afterward, back at Christy's."

She grinned at me, but it wasn't a normal Sally grin. There was too much of a ... cutesy quality to it. "Aww. Did you finally tell her how you feel?"

"What the fuck are you talking about?"

"Come on, Bill, it's written all over your face. You have it bad for her. Trust me. I can read you like a Harlequin Romance."

"Wait. You actually read those things?"

A confused look passed over her face for a moment. "Actually, I don't. But you know what I mean."

I did, but that wasn't what I wanted to discuss right then, especially with the image of her naked flesh seared into my mind's eye. Goddamn. I could understand why people turned to therapy. "No. That's not what we talked about." *Okay, here it comes.* If this didn't get her fired up, nothing would. "We discussed taking the fight to Gan."

"Oh? How so?"

"Still working that out, but violently would be my guess. Rather than sit around waiting, we go after her.

And, if we just so happen to take her out in the process, then *boom* – half our problems are solved right there."

"I suppose so."

"What do you mean you suppose so?"

"Well, for starters, what if she's right about me?"

"She's not!"

"But she could be."

"She isn't. And even if she was, that doesn't give her a free pass to threaten your life or Christy's."

"No, but I'm not sure why we should let that bother us. They're just words after all."

"Words can kill, especially where Gan is concerned."

"Fair enough," Sally replied, still as calm as a lake on a sunny day. "All right. Well, if you feel you have to, good luck!"

"I wasn't finished. Christy ... I mean *we* kinda want you to be a part of it."

"What for?"

Grr! This was getting tedious. "To help us blast the shit out of her obviously."

She inclined her head. "That sounds kind of unnecessarily brutal."

"You do realize we're talking about the same person who dubbed you a whore the moment you met, right?"

"Of course I do," she replied with an eye-roll, but even that somehow felt sedate. "I'm not going to lie and say we'll ever be besties. It's just, I don't know. I mean, once upon a time I wouldn't have minded putting a bullet in her, but now..."

"You already did."

"Oh yeah." She smiled as if remembering a pleasant memory. "But that was a different me."

"Yeah, you were still a blonde."

She ran her fingers through her hair. "Oh, I dunno. This new look is starting to grow on me."

"Me, too." *Gah!* No fair distracting me by changing the subject back to her looks. *Focus, Bill.*

Almost in response to my self-castigation, my subconscious added, *Yes, please focus, Freewill.*

"Oh butt out."

Sally raised an eyebrow. "Talking to yourself again?"

"Can't be helped."

"That's so weird. For thirty years I had one of those things inside my head, yet I can't recall ever having a single conversation with it ... minus a few weird dreams maybe. I wonder if it's a Freewill thing."

The bonding is slightly different for everyone, or so I am led to believe.

I mentally shot back, *Who gives a flying fuck?* Goddamn, and he claimed *I* was the one who needed to focus.

"Regardless," I said, trying to force us back to the subject at hand, "this is probably the closest thing we have to a plan of action right now. It's either this, or we sit around and hope for the best which, oddly enough, never seems to work out. Oh, and before you give me that 'you were a different person back then' bullshit, I'll remind you that less than two weeks ago you threatened to blow a guy's head off, and that was *before* you knew he was a werewolf."

"Amazing the difference a couple of days can make, isn't it?" She lifted her arms and stretched, her t-shirt raising up over her tight stomach.

Goddamn. Somehow she managed to ooze sex appeal even acting like she'd switched to an all OxyContin diet.

"I was angry, scared," she continued. "And I couldn't even seem to turn off my brain long enough to sleep. But now, I just feel so relaxed. I swear, I wish I'd met Matthias years ago. If he'd only shown me those breathing exercises back then, well, imagine how different my life might've been."

Wait ... Falcon!

Was he responsible for this? But why and, more importantly, how?

I'd never been much into exercise crazes, or exercise itself for that matter, but my mother had been. Growing up, there'd been Sweatin' to the Oldies and Jazzercise tapes interspersed throughout our entertainment center. Over the years she'd tried Tae Bo, yoga, Kegel exercises, and more. I think Dad might've gotten some enjoyment out of that last one, but not a single workout had ever succeeded in making Mom any less high strung.

Hell, the only time I'd seen her in a state similar to Sally's was when she found the pot brownies I'd brought home from college that one time, thinking I'd taken an elective in home ec.

Hold on. I sincerely doubted even Magi exercises could chill someone out this much, but what if there was something else in the mix, something of a chemical nature?

"Hey, mind if I ask you a question?"

"Go right ahead. I'm an open book."

Oh yeah, she was definitely out of her gourd. I mean, hell, it had taken two years of us surviving all sorts of crazy shit together before I'd even learned her real name. "Listen carefully. Did Falcon give you anything to go along with those exercises?"

"Like what?"

"Oh, I don't know. Anything really. You know ... vitamin supplements, energy drinks, maybe a pack of hypodermics."

She let out a laugh. "No."

"You're sure?"

"Positive. Last time I saw him we talked for a bit, he readjusted the settings on my bracelet, then he told me about those relaxation techniques. That's it. Oh, wait, there is one more thing."

I leaned forward. "What?"

"He asked if I'd seen any more of those leprechauns."

"That's all?"

"Yes, that's all, Bill. I'd tell you if there was more. Trust me, the only thing I'm high on right now is..."

"I swear, I'm throwing myself out the window if you say life."

She shrugged but didn't seem overly concerned. That was the whole problem. She didn't seem concerned about *anything*. It was like she was...

Hold on a second. I glanced at the bracelet still on her wrist, where two small LEDs were currently lit up green. "Exactly what kind of adjustments did he make?"

"I don't know. The magical kind, I guess."

"No shit. So you mean you weren't paying attention?"

"Not really. He took it off me then went into the other room to work on it while I waited."

"He did, did he? And that didn't ... annoy you?"

She appeared to consider this. "Come to think of it, it kinda did at the time, but I got over it. Rome wasn't built in a day after all."

It wasn't proof positive, but it was all I had to work with. "Put some shoes on."

"Why?"

"We're going out."

"The sun's up."

"I know but this can't wait."

She shook her head. "I can't just leave."

"What do you mean you can't?" Had that fucker done something else to her, maybe warded the place so she was stuck here? If so, he and I were going to have a chat that involved my foot up his ass.

"It's Craig," she replied. "He came up to see me a few hours ago, right when I was getting ready to turn in. Anyway, I promised to play Scrabble with him and the others after I got up and I'd hate to break a promise."

Oh yeah. This was far worse than I could have ever imagined.

19

SIDETRACKED

T he first thing I did was try to rip the bracelet off Sally's arm. That was a mistake as I soon found my body enveloped in a bolt of blue defensive magic, knocking me to the floor to twitch like a bug.

"Are you okay?" she asked my prone form. "Need me to make you some tea?"

"N-nothing a new set of skin won't fix."

I should've guessed as much. Falcon seemed to have a hard-on for his wards. In a typical D&D campaign, you'd run across the occasional magical trap on things like treasure chests and secret doors. In real life, though, mages apparently put them on every fucking thing they owned. Maybe it was a good thing Dave wasn't here to see this. Might give the asshole ideas.

Okay, Plan A was a bust. So, once I was able to stand again, I considered our next course of action. And no, it wasn't Scrabble, despite Sally's protests to the contrary.

The pier wasn't far, but it had gotten shit stomped the night before, because why the fuck would anything be easy? It was possible Falcon would be there anyway, using his magic to set up shop again. If not, there might be something in the wreckage we could use to get the bracelet off.

Mind you, digging through debris in broad daylight wasn't exactly my idea of a party.

Okay, maybe we could save that one for Plan C. For now...

Wait. Hadn't Falcon said something about his family, his *rich* fucking family I might add, having a place somewhere in the city? I took a few moments to wrack my brain. It had been some hoity toity joint, definitely more upscale than a Courtyard by Marriott. But what?

I believe he mentioned the Lotte, my subconscious offered.

Huh. Glad one of us had been paying attention.

I knew of it, but had never been there. Regardless, looking down at myself, I had a feeling I was barely dressed well enough to make it through the lobby.

Unless I wasn't alone.

I turned Sally's way. "I need you to get changed."

"Changed? Why?"

"We're going uptown and you need to look the part. Go find your slinkiest dress and do your makeup." I glanced down at her current attire. "Think less Peg Bundy and more high priced hooker."

Not too long ago a remark like that would've gotten me decked. For a moment, no more, she threw me some side-eye, making me think an ass kicking was incoming. Hell, I'd have almost welcomed it.

But then she simply shook her head. "Okay, if you say so, although I'm not sure why." She got up without further protest and went to do as I'd asked. It spoke volumes to how fucked in the head she was.

"Oh, and grab your gun while you're in there. We might need it."

＊＊＊

No, I wasn't planning on shooting Falcon – not unless he tried to play dumb.

It was more for protection.

The vamps downstairs had some high SPF sunscreen I could borrow, a must have for any vampire coven, but I didn't fool myself into thinking it'd be enough to survive the trek uptown without burning to a crisp.

Summer was over and fall was on its way, but it was still unseasonably warm out, probably enough to dissolve any covering if I risked an extended stay above ground.

I briefly considered phoning Christy and asking for a magical lift, but then thought better of it. Let her get some rest. I could handle this ... probably.

Goddamn, I really needed to get my ass another car at some point, and change insurance companies while I was at it. This was bullshit.

Unfortunately, that left me only one option – the reason I'd asked Sally to grab her weapon. We were going to have to risk the sewers. It was the only way to...

Holy shit!

She stepped out of her bedroom wearing a slinky off the shoulder minidress that was one hundred percent the old her, minus the changes to her hair and eyes. At least on that last front, she was wearing contacts that gave the impression of her having pupils. Mind you, I was pretty sure her eyes were the last thing anyone was going to look at.

Sadly, there was no way she was going to be able to traipse through the sewers of Manhattan and not ruin that look.

"Are you sure this is appropriate?" she asked. "Feels kind of gaudy."

Wow. She was going downhill fast. No doubt about it.

At least she'd brought her favorite gun along as requested, a massive five shooter – because the bullets were too big to fit six.

"Quick change of plans. I need you to grab a raincoat or maybe a jacket, too."

"Why? Where are we going?"

"To the Lotte?"

"Why do I need a raincoat for the Lotte?"

"It's not for the hotel, it's for the sewer. That's how we're going to get..."

She cocked her head. "And is there a reason we can't just take a fucking cab?"

I stopped and blinked a few times, her words sinking in. She ... kind of had a point there. We weren't going to some magical warehouse or den of evil. Our destination was one of the premiere luxury hotels in the city. Why do it the hard...?

Wait a second ... fucking cab? "What did you say?"

She raised an eyebrow, for a moment looking like her normal self. "A cab, idiot. You know what those are, right?"

"Yeah." Okay, this was getting weirder by the second. "How are you feeling, by the way?"

"Like I'm the only one in the room with working brain cells, as usual." She put a hand to her head. "Hold on a second. I think I need some Motrin. I can feel a stupidity induced headache coming on."

What the hell? It was like watching some sort of Jekyll and Hyde transformation.

Her search for aspirin wasn't to be, though. As I stood there trying to figure out what was going on, Sally's body lit up with a soft bluish light, causing us both to stop in our tracks.

I quickly glanced down at the bracelet on her wrist, having seen this before ... just as it let out a single beep.

Shit!

In the next instant, the light around her intensified to a blinding brilliance.

I leapt toward her hoping to catch a ride but was a second too late, landing on nothing but the floor where she'd stood a moment earlier.

For some reason, the bracelet had teleported her away, despite us not venturing outside the city this time. And lucky me, she'd still been holding her gun when she vanished.

The hell? Was the damned thing reading her thoughts now? Okay, maybe that wasn't too farfetched considering who had given it to her.

That wasn't all, though. In the moment before she'd disappeared, I'd noticed something else about her bracelet. Of those two green lights I'd seen earlier, one had changed to red.

The only questions now were what did it mean and where the hell had it sent her?

Christy made the most sense to call next, and under any other circumstance that's exactly what I'd have done. But I wanted her safe behind her wards. Hell, I needed her to be safe, at least until she could rest up. Besides, with both Ed and Tina there – and by that I meant Tina – someone would've needed a small army to breach her defenses.

And that was apparently what I was reduced to, counting on a five-year-old mega-witch to make all the difference. I kind of felt like a shit for it. At the same time, I'd seen what Tina could do when someone threatened her loved ones. No fucking way would I want to be in that line of fire.

Yeah, Christy would probably bitch me out later for keeping her out of the loop, but it's not like I hadn't been bitched out before. Hell, it was practically an everyday occurrence.

That said, I wasn't a complete moron. With Sally gone who knows where, that raised the stakes considerably. What was going to be an angry confrontation with Falcon had now escalated to a potentially violent one. That meant calling for backup.

Fortunately, I had more than one option there, and

was persistent enough to let it ring until he finally answered.

"Hey, Tom. It's me."

"Ugh. The fuck time is it?"

"Time to wake up. I kinda need a favor."

"You really should remember to take the trash out *before* sunrise, asshole."

"Not that! I need you to head into Manhattan and get to Falcon's pier."

"Wait." he replied, sounding like he was finally awake. "Are we talking about the same pier you said was all *War of the Gargantuas* last night?"

"Yeah, but I'm sure it'll be fine today..."

"And you're heading there, too?"

"Not yet. I have to check the Lotte first to see if Sally's there."

"Back the fuck up, dickshake. You want me to go to that shithole while you shack up with Sally in a luxury hotel?"

"I'm not going there to get a room, numbnuts. She zapped out of here. I think Falcon did it, but I'm not sure where he sent her." I let out a grunt of frustration. Last time this had happened, she'd gone back to her apartment. But being she was nowhere to be seen, it seemed a safe bet he'd updated the settings at some point.

"Okay, then why don't you check the pier and I'll go to the five star resort instead?"

"Because the sun's up."

"Not really winning me over here."

"Listen, it's an emergency. She's acting all weird."

"When is she not?"

"Weirder than usual."

"Okay, so have you tried calling her?"

"Of course," I snapped. It had been the first thing I'd done. "She took a page out of your playbook and left her phone on the charger."

"Jesus fucking Christ! Fine, but how about this? I'll meet you at the Lotte..."

"But..."

"If she's not there then we'll both go to the pier together. Because if I'm gonna get stomped by a kaiju, you're coming with me, dude."

Grr! He had a point, though. "Deal. Just get your ass moving. Oh, and dress decently. I mean for a woman. We'll be lucky to make it past the lobby as it is."

"Gotcha. Let me go wake Glen up and then we'll head out."

"Wait! No. Don't bring..."

I was too late, though. He'd already hung up and I didn't want to waste further time calling him back to argue.

Son of a... Oh well, fuck it. Corgis were all the rage with rich fuckheads. Sure, Glen's was kind of obviously dead, but maybe it would work out okay.

Oh who was I kidding? This was gonna be a clusterfuck.

Fortunately, those were second nature to me and my friends.

Less fortunate was that time was now of the essence, and I could traverse the sewers a hell of a lot faster than any cab could crawl across Midtown during rush hour.

Fuck! I turned toward Sally's bedroom, certain she owned more than one gun. The problem was I didn't know where.

She had a safe in there, true, but I had a feeling it would take me far longer to break into it than I was comfortable wasting. I was strong but not *that* strong. So, of course, that left me right where fate usually did – shit out of luck.

Guess it was another trip through the sewers without even a can of roach spray to my name.

I paused halfway to the door, an idea forming.

Maybe I didn't need much more than myself.

I raced downstairs to where the coven was likely settling in for the day. I hated to rouse them, but this was kind of an emergency.

I knocked on the door, giving it a good hard pound, sure to catch the attention of vampire ears. A minute or two later, Jessica opened it wearing a pair of striped pajamas.

Remembering that I was talking to a different breed of vampire now, one that I preferred to encourage, I said, "Hope I didn't wake you up."

She shook her head. "Nope. Was just reading a bit before turning in. I downloaded this awesome superhero book by Drew H..."

"Yeah, that's nice. Listen, I need you to gather the others real quick. I have a bit of a favor to ask of you guys."

Or perhaps I should've said *a bite* of a favor...

20

HAUTE SEWER COUTURE

O
h yeah! This was more like it.

I sidestepped the glob of acid spit, then grabbed the fucker by one of its many legs and tossed it against the wall, watching it splatter with a satisfying *crunch*.

A part of me felt bad using the coven like this, but they hadn't seemed to mind – outside of being slightly weirded out.

I'd asked them each to volunteer a bit of blood, cutting their palms over a borrowed coffee mug.

Some years back, I'd learned my little blood boosting trick had a handy dandy bonus feature. I could drink the blood of one vamp and gain their power – something that could be daunting with older vampires, since most of them hadn't liked me much. Or, by taking blood from multiple vamps, I could get a cumulative boost.

That meant my coven's combined blood amped me up to a level I wouldn't see for a couple hundred years yet. Better still, it was Sally who'd originally come up with the idea, making it fitting I use it to save her.

I just needed to remind myself this was something best saved for *special* occasions. It would be way too easy to fall into the trap of using them as my personal batteries, something an asshole like Night Razor wouldn't have hesitated to do had he been a Freewill. I needed to be better than that.

For now, though, I simply enjoyed carving a path of destruction through the monstrosities inhabiting the tunnels beneath Manhattan.

It also didn't hurt that there seemed to be less of them around. Maybe it was the time of day, or maybe they'd found some other corner of the city to haunt. Either way, I didn't question my luck. I just punched the shit out of whatever was in front of me then moved on to the next until the way was clear.

That done, I sped uptown, popping from the sewers over to the subway lines – as they were both less disgusting as well as useful for location context. After all, the last thing I wanted to do was get lost and end up in the Bronx by mistake.

I finally headed to the surface at an M-line station a few blocks from the Lotte. Perfect timing as my power boost was starting to wear off.

One quick stop at a nearby McDonald's bathroom – so I could wash off the mutant bug guts and slather myself with more sunscreen – and I was ready to head to my five star luxury destination.

Oh who was I kidding?

Looking and smelling as I did, it would probably take a small miracle to make it past the reception desk without the cops being called.

◆———◆◞◟◆———◆

"Can I help you ... sir?"

The only thing saving me from being tossed out was the fact that not all rich assholes dressed the part. Sure, there were plenty of three piece power suits to be seen, as well as ladies dressed in the latest fashions concocted by whatever overpriced chimpanzees were en vogue these days. Thankfully, enough weirdos were present, too, so as to make it feasible that I might've actually belonged there.

"I'm here looking for Matt ... Matthias, I mean, Falcon. Can you check to see if he's in? Tell him Bill ... Bill Freewill is here to see him."

Almost as if on cue, the familiar voice of my roommate picked that moment to sound off from back near the entrance. "Hey, Bill! We made it!"

"Bill Freewill and guest," I amended.

"Bark!"

Oh God. "Make that guests plural."

Thank goodness this place was pet friendly.

I made the mistake of looking back and immediately regretted it. Pet friendly they might be, but freak friendly was a whole other issue.

Glen looked like he was about to burst from the dead corgi, its bloated corpse missing an ear as well as fur from several places. And don't even get me started on the two mismatched eyeballs nearly popping out of its skull as he waddled by Tom's side.

Sadly, my other friend wasn't much better. He'd once worn a suit every day, back when he worked in the financial district. But that had been as a guy. As a woman, his sense of style was ... let's be kind and say still *evolving*. Worse was the fact that he'd apparently taken my request a step further and had attempted to wear makeup, resulting in an eyeshadow and lipstick combo that would've looked more at home in a seventies porno.

Fuck me.

I really should've saved some of that blood cocktail. If so, I could've simply compelled the staff to let us in without causing the scene that would surely...

"Mr. Falcon is in," the concierge said. "You can go right up."

"Um, thanks," I replied, biting my tongue to keep from adding, "really?"

He gave me the room number as well as which

elevator to take. Then I waved my friends over before he could change his mind.

"Ooh, I bet all the rooms have gold plated pails," Glen remarked as the elevator doors closed.

"I'm sure they've gotten stranger requests."

"So, are we here to kill that wizard?"

"We'll see how it goes."

"Because I'm ready this time." The corgi meat suit opened its mouth wide, disgorging a tentacle of slime holding a GoPro.

Dear God, is this my life now? "Where the fuck did you get that?"

"I bought it for him," Tom said. "Figured it was waterproof, so that should mean its Glenproof, too."

"I was thinking of starting a YouTube channel."

I glanced down at the little blob, watching him swallow the camera again. "Let's not and say we did."

"Oh, I came prepared as well." Tom patted the art bag hanging over his shoulder, lowering his voice to a conspiratorial whisper. "My sword's inside."

"Really? And here I thought you were gonna paint me a copy of Whistler's Mother."

The elevator stopped only once before our floor, for some older couple looking to get on. However, they took one look at us and opted to wait for the next car.

Couldn't say I blamed them.

At last we reached Falcon's floor, the doors opening to reveal the type of place I'd probably have to mortgage my whole life just to afford a weekend vacation at. Much as I loved my parents, there was something to be said for being born into obscene wealth.

Falcon's room was at the end of the hall, complete with a Do Not Disturb sign – which I proceeded to ignore by giving a polite knock. I figured he'd at least earned the right to explain himself before we kicked down the door and hung him out the window by his ankles.

"It's unlocked," came Falcon's smarmy voice from inside.

I opened the door, but Glen pushed past me.

"Please allow me to intimidate him on your behalf, Freewill. Bark bark bark!" Glen waddled into the posh room, but then the little slime gremlin skidded to a halt just inside the entranceway. "Holy shit!"

Huh. That was unusual language for him. Guess it was easy to be impressed when you slept in a slop pail. I mean, the place was nice, but it wasn't that... Just then, however, I noticed the air around his rump shimmering, as if he'd partially stepped through something.

Ah ha. Magic no doubt.

As I followed him into the suite, reality changed around me, going from really nice to utterly mind-blowing. Gone was the hotel room, and in its place was a magnificent underground grotto, complete with a shimmering pool of crystal clear water. Falcon, wearing swim trunks and holding a tropical drink, waved to me from the raft upon which he lounged.

Holy shit indeed.

"It's a recreation of this charming cave system down in Jamaica," he explained. "I figured I could do with a relaxing soak after the evening I had."

"Everything cool, guys?" Tom asked from behind us. I turned to see him still standing at the doorway, a stark contrast to the glorious cavern around us – like we were in a freaking holodeck.

Except, how could you float on an illusion?

"It's quite all right," Falcon said. "The Icon's presence shouldn't disrupt anything. This is more a pocket dimension than glamour. So long as she doesn't flare up, all should be well." He turned Tom's way. "Just be sure to close the door behind you, luv. Wouldn't want housekeeping barging in by mistake and losing the plot, now would we?"

"It's *he*," Tom corrected, looking nonplussed, at least

until he stepped inside. "Fucking A! Remind me why I live in that shithole with you again, Bill?"

I didn't really have a good answer to that. Fortunately, we weren't there to discuss real estate, or how much it apparently sucked to not be a wizard.

I remembered Christy telling us about pocket dimensions, kind of like what that time dilation spell of hers created. But I also recalled it wearing her out quickly. Yet Falcon was floating along like he didn't have a care in the world.

How fucking powerful was this guy? More importantly, how arrogant was I to assume I could just waltz in here and intimidate him?

"So, fuckstache," Tom said, throwing any sense of caution right out the window, "where's Sally?"

"Pardon?" Falcon replied, looking at us over a pair of sunglasses. "What about her? Oh, by the way, please feel free to join me. I'd be happy to have the concierge send a few swimsuits up."

"Why not just conjure them?"

He let out a laugh. "Because that would be, as you Americans say, a vulgar display of power."

Of course it would.

I put a hand on Tom's shoulder, hopefully to clue him in that it might be best to dial down the attitude. Glen, on the other hand, decided to live in the moment – puking himself out of the corgi and slithering down into the water, where he floated on the surface like a giant slick of dog vomit. *Eww.*

"Come on in, the water's fine."

"Maybe later," I replied, trying to focus on the task at hand. "So back to what Tom was saying. Where's Sally?"

"Pleasantries really are lost upon you lot aren't they?" He replied with a sigh. "Anyway, I assume she's back at her flat. Why do you ask?"

I narrowed my eyes at him. "Because she bamfed out of there about an hour ago."

"Bamfed? You'll excuse me for not being familiar with that vernacular."

"Teleported. We were standing there in her living room when all of a sudden her bracelet beeped and *poof*, she disappeared."

He sat up, looking surprised. "It did? And in her living room, you say? What in bloody hell did you do to set it off?"

"Don't ask me. It's your stupid charm bracelet."

"Bill, check this out. Mango daiquiris!"

I turned to find that Falcon apparently had a fully stocked wet bar in here, too, and that Tom had, unsurprisingly, wandered over to it like a moth to a flame.

Forget being rich. Next life I was coming back as a rich wizard.

"Just ignore him," I said. So much for bringing backup. "Anyway, I didn't do anything. The stupid thing beeped, one of the lights turned red, and then she was gone."

Falcon popped off his raft and began wading to shore, giving me a much unneeded reminder that the guy was absolutely chiseled, too. "A red light? Which one, right or left?"

"Mine or hers?"

He grabbed a towel from a nearby beach chair, along with his vape pen. "Hers of course, you git."

Oh, it was so tempting to walk over there and rip that stupid mustache off his face, but first things first. "Left, I think."

He took a suck from his pen. "Hmm. That's not good."

"No shit. First she was acting like she was stoned outta her gourd, then she fucking vanished in front of me. So I want to know where to."

He shook his head, looking none too pleased. "The warehouse, I'm afraid."

I spared Tom a dirty look as he topped off his drink. "See? I told you to go there first."

"How the fuck was I supposed to know?" he shot back. "Ooh, brain freeze!"

"And you," I continued, rounding on Falcon. "Why the hell did you send her there of all places?"

Falcon pursed his lips. "In case you've forgotten, chum, my humble waterfront abode was reduced to matchsticks last night. You'll forgive me if I haven't had time to sweep it all up yet." He took a deep breath. "Unfortunately, that's where it was designed to take her in case the built in reservoir malfunctioned ... or unexpectedly ran dry."

"Wait. What reservoir?"

He shook his head. "You have to understand, I'm dealing with several unknowns here. There was no way I could have anticipated she'd metabolize all of it so quickly."

I narrowed my eyes at him, even as over his shoulder Glen continued to float along blissfully, as if having the time of his life. "Let's back up for a second here. What exactly was she metabolizing?"

Falcon let out a sigh, then grabbed a t-shirt and slipped it on. "It's an alchemical extract, non-addictive but not dissimilar to Fentanyl in its effect. It creates a moderate euphoric high."

"I'm all for recreational drugs, don't get me wrong, but why exactly was Sally taking that shit?"

"She wasn't. I modified her bracelet to deliver it transdermally."

"So you've been what, shooting her up like she was some kind of methhead?!"

"Not at all," he replied. "The system was designed to monitor her vitals. If heightened levels of anxiety were detected, it was supposed to give her enough to mellow her out, keep her calm."

"Well, I hate to break it to you, but something ain't

working right. She's been walking around, acting like she had a front row seat at Woodstock. She's..."

Except maybe it had worked after all, just too well. I'd been thinking about this same thing earlier, noting that Sally mostly existed in a constant state of low-level annoyance. And what had the last twenty-four hours brought? Gan's threats, me walking in on her naked, oh and let's not forget about Craig inviting her to play Scrabble. All were things that could easily set her off, especially these days.

If so, that probably meant Falcon's bracelet had been working overtime to pump happy drugs into her, at least until the well had run dry.

Shit!

"You don't know Sally like I do," I explained. "She tends to be irked about something at any given time. Hell, I'm pretty sure she's at her happiest when she has something to bitch about."

"Oh. I could see how that might be a complication."

"Ya think?" I let out a frustrated breath, then, in need of some mellowing myself, I stomped over to where Tom stood and ripped the glass out of his hand.

"Hey, asshole, that's mine."

"Some of us need it more." I chugged down the contents. *Huh.* He was right. It was tasty. Maybe I could ask Falcon for the recipe, assuming I didn't end up kicking his stupid teeth in.

For now, I simply glared at him. "So why exactly did you feel the need to drug her in the first place?"

"For her own protection, mate, as well as those around her. Simple as that." I opened my mouth, but he wasn't finished. "You saw what she did to my little home away from home, and we both know how that vampire bloke fared against her."

"But..."

"Not to mention, I managed to get my hands on a high resolution copy of that video making the rounds." When I raised an eyebrow, he smirked. "Perks of working with the boys in blue, chum. Anyway, do you know what I saw? The apkallu. They swarmed her and she utterly annihilated them."

I waited for him to say more, to tell me he'd heard what she'd said about the coming of the Great Beast. However, I guess the audio hadn't captured that part, which was damned lucky for us.

Still, Falcon had already been wary that Sally might be *dangerous*. In fact, he'd already threatened drastic action. The fact that he'd drugged her against her will told me he was more worried than we suspected. At the same time, it was worth noting that he hadn't tried implementing any final solutions yet, which probably meant he wasn't to the point of, "if it bleeds we can kill it."

Maybe there was still a chance to dial this back.

Mind you, that was contingent on Sally appearing at the dock and not immediately being swallowed by the whale-sized monster in the Hudson.

It likewise assumed that thing wasn't the Great Beast she'd been talking about, something I didn't care to speculate on. If so, then we'd likely gone from bad to apocalyptic by sending her down there to have a face-to-face chat with it.

Goddamn, I needed a bottle of aspirin for the stress headache I could feel building. Either that, or maybe Falcon could hook me up with my own magic drug delivery system. Can't say I'd have turned down some euphoric happiness right then.

Instead, the phone began to ring. I looked around the tropical cave for the source of the muted chiming. Guess that was one downside of Falcon turning the place into his personal sex grotto.

He was one step ahead of me, though, picking up a conch shell that was sitting on the bar next to where Tom was once again filling a cup.

"Hello?" he answered cheerfully. My ears immediately

caught the voice of the front desk concierge from the other end.

"Come on in, guys. We can play Marco Polo," Glen called out, distracting me from my eavesdropping.

"Yes, send her right up. Thank you." Falcon hung up the conch. "Alas, we'll have to put the kibosh on this holiday. That was the front desk. Sally is downstairs."

"She is?" I replied, letting out a sigh of relief I didn't know I was holding. Guess her unexpected sojourn to the docks had been less interesting than I'd feared.

"Yes. Although that means I'll need to release all the incantations in this room post haste. Can't have her..."

I waved him off. "Just do what you need to."

He paused to take a suck on his vape pen, because spell casting apparently required a pineapple flavored nicotine hit, then he closed his eyes and gestured with his hands.

Mere seconds later, the grotto faded from existence around us. My feet touched down on carpet instead of stone as the cave turned back into a hotel room. Glen, who'd been paddling around about twenty feet away, suddenly plopped down onto the floor maybe a yard from me. Tom likewise appeared a lot closer than he had a moment earlier, his drink cup disappearing from his grasp.

"Son of a bitch."

"Sorry," Falcon replied. "A necessary evil where our dear Ms. Carlsbad is concerned."

"Sunrise," I corrected. "Or something like that."

"Pardon?"

"Her former identity met with an untimely death."

Falcon shrugged as if making note of it, then he stepped to the corner of the room and picked up a strange object I hadn't noticed before. It was about a foot tall and milky white, like a shard of quartz crystal, except it was glowing brightly from within.

He repeated the action, hastily retrieving similar items from the remaining corners of the room.

"Orbs of Amun-Ra," he explained. "Had the folks back at the academy send me a fresh batch this morning."

"How convenient." Yeah, I definitely needed filthy rich parents in my next life.

He'd mentioned these things once before, back at the pier when angry leprechauns had been trying to eat our faces. They apparently functioned as a sort of arcane battery pack, allowing the user to work complex magic without exhausting themselves.

Normal magic – if such a term even applied – didn't set Sally off. Otherwise I'd have been dead meat once she'd zapped out of her apartment. An overabundance, however, was a whole other ball of wax. Judging by how quickly Falcon worked, as well as the fact that we'd just been hanging out in a fucking pocket dimension, I had to guess these orb thingies fit the bill.

Almost as if echoing my thoughts, he pulled a reinforced looking suitcase out from under his bed and quickly stuffed them inside.

"The case is lined with both silver and brighdril," he said. "It's a rare extradimensional metal found only in the kingdom of the fae..."

"I didn't ask."

"Oh, well then..." He snapped the case shut. "I suppose all that really matters is that it'll ground any ambient magic from escaping."

Ah. That was good. I had a feeling the Lotte's owners would be less than thrilled if we managed to blow the top five floors off by accident.

Falcon stuffed the case back under the bed, not a moment too soon as there came a knock from outside.

"I'll get it." I stepped to the door and pulled it open.

Sure enough, Sally stood there looking hot as the sun in her minidress, the trip to the docks having barely mussed her hair.

She raised an eyebrow upon seeing me. "Hey, Bill."

"Hey. I'm glad you're oka..."

"That's nice. Is Matt in?"

"Yep."

"Good. Is he still alive?"

"Well, yeah. Why wouldn't he be?"

She elbowed past without letting me finish, pulling her hand cannon from her bag as she strode toward Falcon.

"You have three seconds to give me a good reason why I shouldn't blow your fucking head off."

So much for us dialing it back a notch.

21

LIKE SHOOTING FALCONS IN A BARREL

At least two of Falcon's remaining seconds passed as I tried to wrap my brain around the difference an hour or so could make to a person's demeanor.

The silence was finally broken by Glen. "Might I say, Madam Sally, that you are looking exceptionally radiant today."

"Thank you," she replied, keeping her eyes focused on Falcon.

As the little blob bubbled happily at her response, I quickly stepped to her side. "Maybe this is one of those times we could use our words instead."

She shifted her aim and I suddenly found myself looking down the barrel of the oversized revolver. "Speaking of words, I'd better never *ever* hear a single one from you about anything you may or may not have seen at my apartment today."

"Heh. You know me. Poor short term memory and all."

"Oh? What did you see?" Tom asked cluelessly.

"Nothing but you shutting the fuck up."

"Good call," Sally replied, turning the weapon toward Falcon again. "Now where were we?"

He appeared to consider his options. Sadly for him, he

was in a bad spot for a Magi, filthy rich or not. Any spells he might try could set Sally off – assuming they even worked with Tom in close quarters.

Though his face remained unreadable, I could only guess he was regretting not calling security when he had the chance.

Finally, though, proving he was a cool cucumber, Falcon raised his hands and replied, "Please allow me to offer my sincerest apologies for any miscalculation on my part."

"Miscalculation? I just spent the last day feeling like little Miss Muffet snorting her cocaine tuffet. Tell me, do I strike you as someone who grew up wanting to be a Disney princess?"

"That's actually not Disn..."

She shut Tom up with a glare. "Don't make me throw your dumb ass out the window, because I might enjoy it."

"Ooh. Can Icons fly?" Glen asked excitedly, his GoPro making an appearance.

"Yeah," I replied, "but only in one direction."

To her credit, I'd seen Sally kill people for less. The fact that she hadn't ventilated our wizard friend the moment she walked in told me she was open to hearing him out. But I also knew her patience was far from limitless.

"Tell her what you told us." Noting her finger was still on the trigger, I added, "And you might want to skip the boring parts."

To be fair, Falcon did have the best of intentions. But, like most Magi I'd met, he'd gone about it in the most arrogant condescending way possible.

In short, he'd treated Sally like a child, doing something for her own good without bothering to consult her first. Then, due to not having good enough intel on her condition, he'd fucked it up. Instead of mellowing her out whenever she was about to redline, he'd ended up drugging her like a lab rat – failing to take into account that when she came down off her high she'd be seriously pissed off.

The fact that she'd managed to hold it together so far without turning us all into paint splatters was a near miracle unto itself.

When he was finished, she held the gun on him a moment longer before finally lowering the barrel. "Next time ask before slipping something into my drink. It's only polite."

"You might have said no and..."

"The funny thing is, you're wrong," she interrupted. "And no, I'm not bullshitting. I've been doing nothing but self-medicating since realizing what I could do. Hell, I've probably put all of Johnnie Walker's kids through college this past week alone." She narrowed her eyes before continuing. "Had you been straight with me, I'd have heard you out and we could've done this the right way. Do you think I want to hurt anyone? Well, anyone who doesn't deserve it anyway."

I zipped my lips for that one.

"We can try again," Falcon offered. "I can use the telemetry data from the bracelet to adjust..."

"The only thing you're going to do is take this thing off me once and for all. We're done."

Falcon sat on the edge of his bed, no doubt realizing we were past the shooting part of our program. "I'm afraid I can't do that. What I said to you back then still stands. You have to understand, I'm here at the bequest of the NYPD to assess threats to this city."

"And you're saying Sally's a threat?" Tom asked. "Because..."

"I'm saying nothing of the sort. All I know is that there haven't been any recent incidents with her powers. That's a good thing, but I would still be remiss in my duties if I let her go about her business unmonitored."

I shook my head. "Dude, there's a dead sea serpent rotting on the docks that was killed by a bigger meaner sea serpent. Offhand, I'd say we have bigger fish to fry right now."

"You think I missed that, Freewill?" he shot back, losing his cool for a moment. "This isn't a zero sum game. You do realize that, right? I can't simply drop one case file because another lands in my lap. It simply does not work that way. If that were the case, I'd be happily ignoring the fact that the a'chiad dé danann, the apkallu, and now the tekutokatl are all running wild in..."

"The tech-what?" Tom asked.

"An ancient race of monstrous insectoids that once plagued the Aztecs. I've uncovered evidence suggesting they may have appeared in this city's underground."

I raised my hand. "I can probably vouch for that being a bit more than a possibility."

He glanced at me sidelong and let out a sigh. "Either way, every single one of these occurrences requires my attention. So to ask me to turn a blind eye to this particular issue, when a solution is within our grasp, is simply unacceptable." He turned his focus once again toward Sally. "I appreciate the help you and your friends have provided, but I must insist that we continue with the measures we have in place."

"Really?" she replied, her tone making me think she was reconsidering filling him full of lead. "And what if I were to ... try and remove it myself?"

She placed the gun down and reached for the bracelet with her free hand.

"I must warn you," Falcon said. "There are counter-measures in place against that."

He wasn't kidding. I'd gotten a good taste of it earlier when the damned thing had left me twitching on the floor.

"You don't say." She threw him an eyeroll. "I'm more

interested, however, in what those countermeasures might do."

"Sally...," I warned.

She ignored me, though. "Let me guess. It'll zap me with magic before I can rip it off."

Falcon nodded. "To put it mildly, yes. I will warn you, it's not lethal but it is painful."

"Of that I have no doubt, but I'm far more curious as to whether it'll be stressful enough to cause a reaction. Oh, and before you ask, I'm already pretty fucking stressed."

Oh shit.

She grabbed hold of the bracelet and began to tug on it as Falcon's eyes opened wide.

Couldn't say I really blamed him. Hell, right at that moment I was considering my chances of surviving a fall out the window in broad daylight.

Sally continued clawing at the bracelet as blue sparks began to dance across her fingers.

Even Tom seemed to get the hint, backing up as if that would do anything.

Of us all, only Glen seemed blissfully unaware that we were standing at ground zero – adjusting his camera and pointing it Sally's way. "This is so exciting."

Yeah, exciting was one word for it as she gritted her teeth but refused to let go.

What the fuck was she thinking?

Was she really so pissed off that she'd risk the lives of so many people? Or had the Great Beast taken control again, overriding her sensibilities in favor of whatever chaos it sought to cause?

Either way, I couldn't stand by and let her do this – at least partly because she was about to murder the shit out of me, too.

I clenched my fist, preparing to deck her upside the head – hopefully with enough force to knock her out. Sally no longer had her vampiric strength, but she'd proven surprisingly resilient nonetheless during our battle two weeks prior.

Whatever the case, I was only going to get one shot at ...

"Bloody hell!" Falcon cried. "Enough already! Stop!"

Sally merely raised an eyebrow, as if telling him the ball was still in his court.

In return, he mumbled a couple of incomprehensible syllables. A moment later, there came a *click* as the lock on the bracelet disengaged.

Sally slipped it off and tossed it onto the bed. Then she smoothed her dress a bit, grabbed her gun, and stuffed it back into her bag. "Thank you. Was that so hard?"

"You do realize I won't be able to protect you if you walk out that door without it, right?" he replied.

"And I hope you realize I never asked for your protection to begin with. Next time treat me like a person, not property. I'd tell you to ask the last guy who made that mistake, but you'd need a Ouija board to reach him."

A few minutes later found us back in the hallway, beating a hasty retreat to the elevator – including Glen who was back in his zombie corgi suit.

Despite Falcon's warning, I wasn't too worried. For starters, the treaty between the vampires and New York City was back in place. As for my friends, well, I doubted he was prepared to rat them out. Though the separation between the normal and the supernatural seemed to be on thinner ice than ever these days, I doubted he wanted to be the one responsible for shattering that illusion once and for all.

The world had already gotten a taste of that back during the Strange Days. There were still unpleasant holdovers from that time – religions that had sprouted around the idea, particularly up in Boston where nearly half the population had been turned into magical trees thanks to the Feet.

I'd joked with my coven about revealing the truth, but I didn't honestly think there was much chance of me getting away with it had I been serious. The truth was, I wouldn't have been half surprised if some interested party or another decided I needed a silver bullet to the brainpan had I moved ahead with it.

Fiction liked to show us worlds where magic and the mundane lived side by side in harmony, and it might even be possible, but it would take a long time to get there. Before that happened, though, it would be Hell on Earth – with the population warring over whether to worship, dissect, or exterminate anything they decided wasn't natural. That wasn't even counting what the other side might do to make it even worse.

No. Falcon wasn't the worry there, at least for now.

That didn't mean it was all sunshine and unicorns, though.

"The fuck were you thinking?" I asked once the elevator doors shut on us. "You could have blown half the fucking building to hell."

"I bet that would have been marvelous to behold," Glen opined.

"With you in it?"

His mismatched eyes blinked a few times. "Okay, perhaps marvelous isn't quite the word I wanted."

Sally glanced at all of us in turn before rolling her eyes. "Goddamn, I am seriously overdressed for this bunch. But to answer your question, Bill, do I strike you as a fucking moron?"

"Well..."

"It's a yes-no question by the way."

"Then no."

"You'll notice his slight hesitation," Tom remarked.

"Did I ask you?" She elbowed him in the side, causing

Glen and me to both flinch lest he flare up. "Sorry about that."

"Um, no problem," I replied. "Just maybe don't do that in close quarters."

"My bad. I sometimes forget some of us are pussies. Speaking of which, I have to say I'm impressed."

"That Bill's a pussy?"

"No," she replied, facing me. "Out of the corner of my eye I saw your fist clench. You were going to try and stop me, weren't you?"

I shrugged. "You noticed that?"

"I wasn't born yesterday. I know what it looks like when someone is about to deck me. But it was the right move. You did good. Would have probably backfired horribly had I really been pushing things, but it was the right sentiment."

"Hold on." I raised an eyebrow. "What do you mean really pushing it?"

"Exactly that. The batteries behind that stun spell were almost dead," she explained. "Between you setting it off then the bracelet teleporting me, there wasn't much juice left."

"How do you know that?"

"Because I tried removing it again after I reappeared at the docks. Figured it was a safe enough place to try. Couldn't budge the damned thing for shit, but all I got in return were a few sparks, barely enough to feel it. I realized that might be the ace up my sleeve in case Matt Falcon wanted to play chicken."

Tom let out a chuckle. "So you bluffed his pants off? Fuck yeah! High five."

She, of course, left him hanging. "If I wanted a guy's pants off, I wouldn't need to bluff."

I opted to ignore that part, since I preferred not having my balls ripped off and fed to me. "He's going to figure it out, you know."

She nodded. "Probably sooner rather than later. But

that's his problem now. Regardless, we should probably find somewhere else to be." She paused for a moment before adding, "I don't know about the rest of you fuckheads, but acting all pleasant works up an appetite. Who wants lunch? I'm buying."

"I wouldn't mind letting a burrito dissolve in my vacuoles," Glen replied. "Bark!"

Sally glanced down at him then sighed. "On second thought, maybe we should grab takeout instead."

PART II

PART II

22

TIME FOR A BREATHER

I t's amazing how quickly a break in the action could stretch out.

Mercifully, things settled down to a dull roar following our little run in with Falcon, allowing us to actually do some of the stuff we'd previously just talked about. Our focus shifted toward defense at least until such time as we felt ready to do otherwise.

With my place compromised, Ed took the spare apartment next to Christy's, while Glen agreed to be Tina's personal puppy for the time being. Meanwhile, Tom and I relocated to Sally's building – where I had plenty of time to ponder how much I hated social media after seeing Gan's Instagram post proclaiming, "just snuggling with my bae," and the number of likes it had garnered.

Anyway, the living situation wasn't ideal, but it was the best we could come up with after much bickering. As a group we had the quagmire of some of us either affecting, setting off, or negating another's power – not to mention at least one of us who was determined to remain a cockblocker.

I swear, you didn't see the Avengers ever having to deal with this shit.

Unfortunately, it also gave us the opportunity to waffle on things we should have done.

On my end, I put off confronting Mike about whether he was indeed a werewolf spy, as I sorta had no real proof. Lacking anything solid to accuse him of, I'd do nothing more than end up looking like a nutcase.

Far worse, however, on the sin of sloth scale was Ed. He seemed to have no shortage of excuses when it came to calling Kara and telling her he was free. In all fairness, his argument that it was too dangerous for her to fly back to New York was pretty convincing, especially since reports of strange sightings in the sky continued to trickle in.

Still, there was little doubt he was purposely procrastinating. Ah love, such a many splendored thing.

On the upside, at least I wasn't the only one not getting any quality time with my significant other.

To be fair, though, Christy was probably the busiest among us. She took some PTO from work so she could focus on research and training Tina – splitting her hours between her place and Sally's so we could also continue brainstorming how to take the fight to Gan.

All that said, it still left plenty of free time – for some of us anyway. I mean, yeah, I monitored the internet for more Hudson monster sightings, but the reality is a good chunk of my nights ended up being mundane shit – picking up groceries, surfing porn, and babysitting Tina.

Mind you, not necessarily at the same time.

Four days later found us out and about, breaking up our routine to do some patrolling, since there were still plenty of freaky-ass things haunting our fair city.

"Batter up!" I punted the deformed little gremlin trying to gnaw on my shoe, sending it flying in Tom's direction.

He swung his sword at the proto-leprechaun, the blade igniting with white fire ... and promptly missed.

"Strike."

"Fuck you, dude. That was a shitty pitch." He turned and stabbed the weapon – now adorned with action figures wire-tied to the pommel – through the body of the downed leprechaun.

Faith magic wasn't quite as good as potatoes when it came to keeping the little fuckers down, but his powers seemed to retard their insane healing somewhat, making sure they stayed put long enough for us to drop a spud or two.

Speaking of which, I tossed him one from the grocery bag at my side, which he then spiked into the face of the creature he'd just impaled. The skin immediately began to sizzle as the spud melted its flesh, leaving behind a potato-sized hole where its head had been. Crazy shit, I tell ya.

Though we'd come up with an adequate, if utterly ridiculous, defense against these things, I was still worried. Barely a month ago our focus had been hunting vampires, trying to keep in check what Dave had unwittingly unleashed.

Nowadays, though, it seemed we were running into fewer vamps – feral, asshole, or otherwise' – and more creepy fuckers like these. A part of me wondered if there was some cause and effect going on there, especially since the ugly little troglodytes didn't seem overly picky about what they ate.

Either way, we seemed to be on our own again. I hadn't seen Char since the pier, and it had been radio silence from Falcon following our confrontation at the Lotte. Even Christy's attempts to reach him had netted nothing but silence. Oh well, it was a small price to pay compared to having Sally back to normal.

"Come on," Tom said, dragging me from my thoughts. "Let's find the rest of these assholes. Pretty sure I saw at least three more scurrying away from that dead dude we found earlier."

"I think we're too late. Look." I pointed toward the far end of the park, catching sight of the rest of our *party* – namely Tina and her mother.

I wasn't overly pleased they were out here with us, but I couldn't really say anything about it either. After all, it had been Christy's suggestion to have our patrol double as a training exercise. Yay for multitasking.

Above the two witches, three tiny figures could be seen floating in midair about fifteen feet off the ground, their brutish bodies silhouetted by a nearby street lamp as well as the purplish magic around them.

"Very good," Christy said, her voice carrying to my ears. "Hold them there just like that."

Tom and I headed their way, ostensibly in case they needed help, but mostly because I was curious to see what would happen next.

As we got closer, I caught a better view of the struggling leprechauns – their jaws working overtime as they attempted to *devour* the magic holding them. I was more concerned, though, for Tina, standing there with one hand raised as her mother instructed.

"Now do as we practiced," Christy told her.

One of the proto-leprechauns bit into the force construct holding it, gnawing at the spell as if it were a physical thing. That was the horror of these fucking abominations. They healed scary fast and could somehow consume magic itself – normal magic anyway.

Tina, however, was on a whole other level. It was truly something to behold.

"That tickles," she said with a giggle.

"Focus."

"Sorry, Mommy."

Tina lifted her other hand and it began to glow with prismatic color as she began reciting words in a language I couldn't hope to comprehend.

Water began to pour into the floating force bubble from seemingly out of nowhere. Smart. It was the leprechauns' sole known weakness, aside from potatoes that is. Yeah, you couldn't make this shit up.

The liquid cascaded into the magical prison, slowly at first, like it was the world's freakiest fish bowl. Then the trickle abruptly became a tidal wave, filling the force construct within seconds.

Whoa! Drowned in midair. Talk about a bad way to go.

Tina apparently wasn't finished, though. The leprechauns began to convulse as they flailed about, their eyes bulging from their heads. There came a crackling sound like that of bones snapping and then their bodies simply collapsed in on themselves, as if they were under tremendous pressure.

Holy shit!

Did I say a bad way to go? Make that utterly terrifying, even for these creepy pieces of shit.

Christy let out a sigh. "That was too much."

"I just added a little extra."

A little? She'd crushed them like they were at the bottom of the goddamned Marianas Trench.

"I understand, sweetie, but you need to control it better, otherwise you're going to tire yourself out."

That was debatable. I'd seen plenty of Magi in action, more than I really cared to. Most were double-barreled shotguns. Dangerous as all hell at the start of a fight, but limited in ammo.

I didn't claim to know dick about magic, but what my goddaughter had just done seemed the sort of thing that would've driven most witches to their knees. Yet she stood there looking like she could've done it all day.

"That's my girl!" Tom cried, drawing a big grin from her. "Here to kick ass and chew all the bubble gum."

"Ooh, can I have some gum, Daddy?"

"Sorry. As the saying goes, you're all out."

Her face dropped. "Oh poo."

"All right," Christy said. "That's enough. Let's get rid of this mess before anyone sees us. Bill?"

"Potatoes standing by."

"Let me do it, Uncle Bill." Tina wrinkled her brow and there came a flash of light from within the drowning pool. When it winked out, the mangled leprechauns, along with all the water, were gone.

"Where did you send them?" Christy asked, her tone far less freaked out than I felt.

"Back to where the water came from."

"That's good, but next time ask permission first. We need to make sure we do this properly."

"Okay, Mommy."

To say this was all a bit ... weird was an understatement.

At first, Christy had been exploring ways to bind her daughter's magic. But that was like tying up an elephant with dollar store twine. She'd then turned her focus toward teaching Tina restraint. Now, however, after everything that had happened, we'd somehow ended up here.

She was still hammering Tina with lessons about control and the proper use of her powers, but she'd coupled it with training in the art of battle magic. And now we'd apparently graduated to field work.

Unsurprisingly, Tom had been all for it, but I still had my doubts. I mean, we'd gone from '*don't use your powers*' to '*drown these fuckers with magic*' in less than a week.

I didn't like to criticize what I didn't understand, but that seemed a bit of a leap.

I couldn't help but feel things were progressing a bit quickly. It had been less than a month since we'd first seen these leprechaun things and nearly been overwhelmed by them. And now we were using them as a child's training exercise.

It felt kind of reckless, and this coming from a guy

who'd once been the reigning Everclear pong champion of his dormitory.

"Can I go swing?"

And just like that, we switched from battle magic to having a five year old with us that, despite the late hour, wanted to do five year old things.

Technically the playground was closed, but that didn't matter to any of us. I mean, yeah, on the surface we were a single mom with a young daughter, a programmer, and a guy leeching off the bank account of the woman whose body he inhabited. But the reality was, we were part of the things that went bump in the night.

If there was anyone who could break the rules and use a fucking swing set after hours, it was us.

Christy shook her head, probably about to tell Tina that it was bedtime, but I stepped in first. "Why don't you ask your dad to push you?"

Tom pursed his lips at me. "This better not be so you two can sneak off for a quickie behind the slide."

"What's a quickie, Daddy?"

A red crackle of energy flashed in Christy's eyes, but thankfully it wasn't directed at me.

"Here's an idea." I put an arm around her, albeit more to steer her away from the situation than anything intimate. "Why don't we let Tom answer that while we take a little stroll?"

"You'd best be staying where I can see you," he called after us while Tina extolled him to help her onto the swing.

"Not too high," Christy said over her shoulder.

Talk about crazy. Less than ten minutes ago we were murdering leprechauns via a magical flood, and now we were worried about playground safety.

God, what a strange world we lived in.

Aside from us, the park was empty. Partly because it was closed, but also because the proto-leprechauns had eaten everyone else in the vicinity. On the upside, it was a nice night – if one ignored the lingering stench of death in the air.

"That was really something," I said, trying to ease into the conversation with small talk. I swear, some days I envied Gan's ability to cut through the bullshit and get right to the point.

Christy nodded. "She's a magical savant in every sense of the word. I'm still coming to terms myself with the fact that she's able to manipulate energy as easily as most people breathe."

"She's that good, eh?"

"Maybe better. The truth is I have no idea whether this is the peak of her power or if it's going to grow with her."

"How does it normally work with you guys?"

"Not like this. Our powers usually awaken during puberty. Gradually for some, abruptly for others."

"What was it like for you?"

"Let's just say my parents weren't too understanding when the family car suddenly burst aflame in the driveway."

"Ah, one of those."

She nodded. "It was especially difficult since neither of them had the gift. But that's how it works sometimes."

"Gotcha. You're one of those mudbloods they talk about in the movies."

She let out a laugh. "Such a ... not great term, but also not really an issue for the most part. The Magi typically don't judge based on one's parents..."

"That's good."

"Unless those parents are filthy rich or descended from renowned lineage."

"Normal or otherwise, it always comes down to the Benjamins."

"True." She turned to face me. "But you didn't ask me here to talk about the conceits of Magi society, did you?"

"Fascinating as I find those conceits, you're right. I ... I'm worried."

"About what?"

"Everything. It just seems like it's all moving so fast, and now this."

"Life tends to do that when you can do the things we can."

"I get it, but remember you're talking to someone who once took five years just to ask a girl out. I'm not what you'd really call a dynamic type of guy. Hell, if I hadn't run into Sally on that subway car way back when, I'd probably ... well, still be living where I am, but I'd be worrying more about weekend bar hops than werewolves."

I glanced back, hearing Tina's cries of, "Higher, Daddy!"

"But I also know we can't keep letting things pile up and do nothing but hope for the best. We have to start fixing some of our problems before we get buried beneath them."

She nodded. "I agree."

"And Gan's definitely one of those problems."

"No argument here."

"The thing is... Not to question your parenting skills, but..."

She stopped and turned toward me. "Of course I'm not planning on bringing her with us."

"You're not?"

She cocked her head. "*That's* what you're worried about?"

All at once I felt kind of stupid as I stared into her eyes, finding myself rapidly becoming lost in them. "Sorry. It's just that ... well, you know I love you ... *guys*. And um..."

"I know." *You do?!* "She's your goddaughter. You've

been with her since she was born. Heck, you probably know her as well as I do."

Oh. I quickly tried to recover from my tailspin. "Yeah ... minus the magic stuff anyway."

She nodded as if that was a given. "I understand your concern, though."

Behind us, Tina continued to yell, "Higher!"

"The thing is," she continued, "I can't keep my head buried in the sand anymore. Since the moment she was born, I wanted nothing more than for Tina to have a normal childhood. Then magic came back and I realized what she was capable of. My first instinct was to fight it, to force normalcy on her. But I'm beginning to see that was wrong. This is who she is. The more I push back, the more she's going to pull away from me."

Now it was my turn to chuckle. "She's five. So long as she has toys, cartoons, and the occasional ice cream cone, I'm pretty sure she's not eying the front door."

Christy shook her head. "This might just be me projecting. I don't talk about my parents much in case you hadn't noticed."

"I have."

"Harry was more of a father to me than my real dad, and ... I just don't want that for her."

My left eye twitched at the mention of Harry Decker's name, but I kept my opinion on the matter to myself as we started walking again.

"That means keeping myself from going down that path before I even get started. I love my daughter more than anything in this world and I never want her to think I don't accept her for what she is." She let out a sigh. "If that means training her in our ways a bit earlier than planned, so be it."

"But this..."

"Harry always said experience was the best teacher." She inclined her head my way. "Did I ever tell you how, during our first week together, he sealed me in a cave with an angry water pixie?"

"Think you might have skipped that one."

"It was ... a learning experience all right." She smiled as if it were somehow a pleasant memory. Witches, go figure. "But it's more than just that." All at once her tone turned deadly serious. "Tina needs to be prepared."

"For?"

"*Everything*. The rules have changed. This world. Ever since magic returned, it's felt familiar yet not – as if we woke up in some kind of dark mirror."

"Maybe I should ask Dr. Death to grow a goatee."

Fortunately, she opted to ignore my stupidity. "Power attracts power, Bill. Don't ever doubt that. And Tina has it. Sooner or later they'll come, whether it's to worship, recruit, or try to destroy her. And I want her ready." She turned my way. "I'm sure you'll find this entertaining, but I sincerely debated going after Matthias the other night and blanking his memory of what he'd seen her do."

I considered some of the magic he'd been responsible for, like that insane hotel grotto. "Would that have even worked?"

"Who can say? But the fact that I actually considered it is the point."

"What stopped you?"

"I realized that no matter what I do, the Magi are going to find out about her. She's a secret that can't be kept. So instead, I'm using it – Gansetseg, Matthias, all of it – as impetus to get off my butt and do what I should've started doing weeks ago."

I grinned, trying to lighten the mood. "Then I guess it's not a bad thing that Tom's the new Icon. Will save him a lot of hurt if he ever tries sending her to bed without supper."

"There's more, though. I need to face facts about what's coming."

There was so much on the *what's coming* scale that I wasn't sure what she was talking about.

She turned to me, taking both my hands in hers. "The truth is we're planning to do something that's both foolish and dangerous. It's necessary, don't get me wrong, but it doesn't change the fact that if we take the fight to Gan, there's a good chance not all of us will come back."

"There's always a chance of that..."

"I know," she said, her voice becoming hard as steel. "But *I* need to take it seriously. And, more importantly, if anything were to happen, goddess forbid, then I want whoever or whatever comes for my daughter to know, without a shadow of a doubt, that I prepared her for them."

23

BUMPING UGLIES

Tom and I waited for Christy and Tina to teleport back home. Then, once they were gone, we turned to make our way back to Sally's place and the apartment we shared there.

"I'd call that a good night," he said as we got on the subway back to Manhattan.

"The world should thank us for making it a few leprechauns lighter."

"Yep, that too. But I was mostly talking about making sure you went to bed with blue balls."

I glanced at him and sighed. It was time to do the old song and dance. "There's way too much crap going on to worry about romance."

"Dude, how long have we known each other?"

"In that body or the other one?"

He flipped me off. "You know you can't bullshit me, right?"

"And yet I seem to do it several times each and every day."

"I meant for real shit. The stuff that counts."

"Like?"

He let out a derisive huff. "You're talking to the motherfucker who lived with you all throughout the Sheila years.

I saw that wistful dry-dicked expression you'd get every single time you thought about her. It was like living with a horny forlorn puppy." He shook his head. "Oh, just for the record, I know this is her body and all, but if I ever see that look on your ugly mug when you're facing my direction, know that I will stab you in the dick with my sword."

"The point?" I asked, glancing around and noting the subway car wasn't nearly as empty as I'd prefer for this conversation.

"The point is, you've been getting that same look whenever you talk to Christy, especially as of late." He paused for a moment. "Except it's different now. Less desperate, more mature I suppose. What can I say? You're getting old, fucker."

"Living with you ages a person."

"It's the ... how do I say it ... it's the same look my dad used to give my mom, usually after nights where I'd be awake listening to their bed creak. Damn, they really should've oiled that thing."

"I think they were too busy oiling..."

He held up a hand. "Anyway, what I'm saying is, I know what I see. I don't particularly like it, and I think it's doomed to failure because Christy likes her men like me – hung and with a bionic tongue."

"Hung?"

"I'll admit, I'm going through some issues with that part at the moment. But I'm not talking about me. This is about you and the bullshit that you're somehow only allowed to think pure thoughts when shit gets real. We both know how that worked out for you last time."

He was right. In trying not to distract myself, I'd done nothing but. "I can't believe I'm asking this, but what do you suggest?"

"And I likewise can't believe I'm telling you this, but you're my bro. Always have been, always will be. Talk to her. Tell her how you feel. If she dumps your ass, deal with it and move on – knowing you will always be second to me. But if she doesn't, then figure out where you stand with each other ... while still knowing you'll always be second to me."

"That's ... almost good advice."

"I have my moments."

"And you're okay with this?"

"Not really, but it is what it is. Sometimes you snooze you lose, especially if it's for five years. But at least I can always take comfort in knowing I was the first to plow those fields."

I couldn't help but smile. Beneath all that assholery, Tom was a good friend, the best I could hope for.

Well, maybe not the absolute best, but he was a good guy nevertheless.

I considered what we'd discussed for the rest of the trip back to SoHo. Maybe, he was right. I was older now. The things that used to terrify me, well, they still did. Let's not go crazy here. But they terrified me a bit less than they used to, and no longer to the point where my jaw would seize up and refuse to speak.

Talking about this with Christy wasn't going to be easy. Hell, I'd probably need a bit of liquid courage ahead of time, not to mention hoping Dr. Death didn't interrupt with some stupid bit of distraction when I least needed it. But it probably had to be done.

And Tom was right. Even if she did give me the old "it's not you, it's me," speech, I could do any wallowing in my spare time.

If it worked out, though... Well, it would be dangerous and uncertain, no doubt about that. But maybe it could be wonderful, too.

That was what I tried to hold on to as we got in,

offered the coven our greetings, then headed upstairs to turn in.

I was so used to being stuck between miserable and worried, that I barely took the time to consider how good something might be if I just let it happen. I really needed to stop with the pessimism at some point.

I mean, I knew it was possible for it to work between witches and vampires. There was Liz and Komak for instance ... at least before Gan killed his ass and Christy threatened to murder Liz if she ever laid eyes on her again.

Okay, maybe a bad example, but still...

Christy and I came from two different worlds, true, but not nearly so different as, say, a witch and a Templar hooking up. Kelly and Vincent seemed to make it work. Besides, who was to say Ed might not eventually get his bite back? If so, our lives might even have a shot at something approaching normalcy, allowing us to do things like take Tina to the park during the day, when it wasn't overrun by evil Irish gremlins.

Yeah, a bit of a positive outlook might not be a horrible thing, I considered as I closed my bedroom door, turned off the lights, and prepared to crash.

So, of course, there I was thinking happy thoughts when a flash of light appeared from directly behind me. It took me a second or two to realize it wasn't just Tom barging in to offer one last nugget of wisdom.

By the time I tried to react, a pair of arms had grabbed hold of me from behind. I found myself dematerializing, my atoms coming undone as the room around me disappeared, leaving only the void.

So much for having a positive outlook.

Reality reasserted itself less than an instant later, leaving me momentarily disoriented as Magi teleportation always did.

Someone was still holding onto me, though, reminding me of the last time I'd gotten a surprise like this. Gan was no mage, but that didn't mean she couldn't conscript one to fulfill her sick kinks.

Not today, you little SpongeBob-wearing...

I spun, fist raised, a second before realizing the room I'd reappeared in was a familiar one, as were the blue eyes staring up at me.

"Christy? What the hell are you...?"

She silenced my question by pressing her lips to mine, her tongue finding its way into my pleasantly surprised mouth.

After far too few seconds of that, she pulled back and smiled.

"I realized after you left that I've been so focused on our problems, that I've been neglecting the good things in my life."

"Good things?"

She pressed herself up against me. "Or at least one of them anyway."

Oh ... oh! "And what did you have in mind, pray tell?"

Christy grinned wickedly as she shoved me down onto her bed.

"I'm a witch. So why don't you sit back and let me show you a bit of magic."

Oh God, I so missed sex. Almost too much, at least before I was able to slow things down a bit and find my pace. After that, well, let's just say having vampiric stamina never hurts. Oddly enough, neither did a bit of magic. That stun spell of hers, turned way down and applied in just the right places, was actually pretty awesome. Never thought I'd ever be happy to get zapped, but there you have it.

I stayed with Christy until the sun rose, enough time for us to try for round three. *Oh yeah, TKO, baby!*

Sadly, as much as I would've liked to have stuck around and spent a lazy naked day in bed – watching TV, then getting all sweaty, then rinsing and repeating – there was too much to be done. Tina would be up soon, not to mention both Ed and Glen were in close quarters. That, and eventually Tom would wake up and realize I'd ding-dong ditched for a romp with a witch.

Despite his words from earlier, I didn't doubt for a second he'd have two barrels of bullshit ready to fire at me if he guessed that I'd zapped out of Dodge to go cuckoo on Christy's Cocoa Puffs.

So, it was with no small amount of regret that we got dressed so she could teleport me back to Sally's, hopefully with no one being the wiser.

As we prepared for our bamf of shame, I grabbed hold of her and kissed her one more time. Then, as seemed to be my modus operandi, I brought up a topic that was almost certain to ruin the mood.

"Tom and I had a chance to talk last night."

"Oh? About what?"

"You. And, while I don't think he's quite ready to give us his blessing yet, I think he's starting to come around to us ... slowly."

"That's actually not surprising to hear," she replied.

"It isn't?"

"No, silly. Tom may have a ... unique way of expressing it, but he only wants what's best for us. That includes you, too. He may give you a lot of crap, but he really does care about your happiness."

"I know, and I'm glad he does, even if I'm not always convinced happiness is in the cards for me."

She put her arms around me. "I know this life isn't what any of us expected, and I likewise understand that things are uncertain right now. But I don't doubt we'll find our place in it all, even if that means figuring out how to make our own happiness."

If that wasn't a cue to tell her how I felt, I didn't know what was.

"I know of one thing that makes me happy. Y..."

"Pancakes!"

Huh? "Um, yeah, I suppose. That's not really what I..."

"No," she said, pulling away. "I totally forgot. I promised Tina I'd make blueberry pancakes for breakfast today, as a reward for all the hard work she's put in."

"Drown evil leprechauns, get pancakes. Seems a fair trade."

She chuckled. "The things that motivate children. Nevertheless, we should probably get a move on. Wouldn't want Her Highness to think I welched on a deal."

So much for our talk. Oh well. Far be it from me to deny Cat a stack of well-deserved murder pancakes. Besides, it's not like there wouldn't be another chance. Who knows? Maybe I could convince Christy to make last night's magical kidnapping caper a regular thing. If so, we could time our heart to heart talk with a little crotch to crotch action.

That would certainly put a spring back into my step.

A part of me was tempted to stick around. Christy's pancakes were nothing to sneeze at. I doubted she had the type of *syrup* I preferred, though. Besides, it was probably best to zap back on an empty stomach, lest I end up yakking all over Sally's floor.

"You ready?" she asked, taking hold of my hands.

I actually wasn't, but the world didn't stop spinning for my whims alone. "Let's do this."

"I think we already did."

I let out a laugh. "Seriously, last night was..."

"If you say magical I'm going to kick you."

"How about awesome?"

"That works."

She directed us to the metal circle in her bedroom

floor. A moment later, a blinding flash of light erupted around us and I once more found myself blasted into billions of tiny molecules across space and time.

Goddamn, I so hated traveling this way.

Mind you, I liked it a lot less when it involved once again slamming into a wall of pure metaphysical force. Good thing I had no body at the moment, as I'd have almost certainly broken it into pieces.

Less good was a moment later when reality reformed around me at the speed of thought.

Much like the week prior, I found myself crashing face first to the ground below.

This time, however, when I rolled over and looked up, I saw the sun smiling down on me like the asshole that it was.

A second later, my exposed skin burst into flames, erasing the good start to my morning, and ensuring I almost certainly had a long day ahead of me – assuming I survived the next few minutes.

24

BUILDING BLOCKS

I t's amazing how difficult it is to consider your options when your skin is busy melting off.

I had no idea where I was or what was happening, save that I'd somehow landed outside in full view of the giant ball of angry fire in the sky.

Had Christy somehow zigged when she should have zagged. Or had the sex maybe been less good than I'd hoped?

Goddamn, talk about the harshest Dear John letter in the history of dumpings.

Fortunately, I was far too busy immolating to let that thought wallow.

To your left, the voice in my head screamed.

I think we're beyond stop, drop, and roll here.

No, you fool! There's shade to your...

Before I could do much of anything, except turn extra crispy, a half dome of purplish energy winked into existence above me, turning opaque a moment later.

With the fuel to this fire blocked, I rolled over and began to beat the flames out. Then, turning in the direction Dr. Death had mentioned, I saw he was right. There was both shade there next to a building as well as a filthy mud puddle.

Fuck it. Beggars couldn't be choosers.

I threw myself into it, dousing the last of the flames and making me glad I hadn't taken the time to shower yet.

"Are ... you okay?"

I pushed myself up, noting my hands and arms were a charbroiled mess. As I opened my mouth to answer, feeling the less than wonderful sensation of my lips cracking, I realized the rest of my upper body probably wasn't in much better shape.

Oh boy. This was gonna be seriously unpleasant once my nerve endings got the message to start working again.

Glancing down, I caught a glimpse of my reflection in the water, the image slightly distorted due to my glasses having warped from the heat. *Good thing I sprang for reinforced frames.* No doubt about it. I currently looked like Wade Wilson's uglier cousin. A few more seconds and I'd have been toast.

"I... I'll live," I said, turning toward where I'd heard Christy's voice.

She was sitting on the pavement, a goose egg rising on her forehead from where she'd probably hit the ground, but otherwise she appeared in much better shape than me.

"W-what happened?"

"Wards," she said, giving voice to what I already suspected. "But how?"

I took a look around, realizing we were in the small parking lot of Sally's building. We'd reached our intended destination all right, but something had gone horribly wrong in transit.

That's when I got my first clue as to what had caused our wrong turn. A glyph, a good seven feet high, had been burned into the exposed masonry of the building. It glowed with unearthly silverish light. Turning my head, I spied two more in either direction. Though I couldn't see past the corner from my vantage point, it wouldn't have surprised me to learn they ringed the building.

"I'm ... going to ... guess those aren't yours," I said, my words slurred thanks to my ruined lips.

"No, they aren't," she replied wide-eyed.

Subtle these things were not, pretty much a glowing neon sign that screamed, "Hey, New York, come check out this shit!"

Yet, I noticed as I turned once again, this time toward the sidewalk, people continued walking past as if nothing were amiss. City commuters tended to have a bit of tunnel vision, but this was ridiculous.

Unfortunately, I also knew better.

I'd seen something like this once before, back during Village Coven's heyday – or more precisely at the exact same time that heyday came to an explosive end. It wouldn't have surprised me in the least to stroll a few yards in any direction, only to turn back and see nothing but stark normalcy. It had to be a glamour, an illusion designed to make people see something other than what was actually going on. A pretty big one, too.

There was no need for me to point any of this out. If I noticed it, then it was painfully obvious to Christy. Besides, I was distracted by my healing kicking in enough for my nerves to fire to life like a nest of angry hornets – ensuring that any further insight I had would almost certainly come out in the form of a horrific scream.

I bit my tongue to keep that to myself as my mind turned to less savory topics, like who had done this.

As far as I was aware, there was only one other mage who was based in the city, knew where Sally lived, and had the mojo to do this. And apparently he was in sore need of having his feathers plucked.

First, though, I needed to get inside, both for my own sake and to make sure my friends were okay.

"Cuh-come on." I clambered to my feet and lurched for the door, tears streaming from my eyes.

"Wait, Bill! Don't."

"You'd do well to listen, Freewill," another voice

replied – female with a British accent. Something about the cadence was off, though. There was an echoey quality to it, as if the user were amplifying their voice from afar. "It would be *unwise* to get any closer."

I glanced back, seeing no-one else.

Fortunately, Christy was more on the ball than me. "Up there!"

I turned my head skyward. It was hard to see thanks to the glare of the morning sun, and I wasn't about to step from cover to get a better look, but I spied a figure on the rooftop next door, one wearing a flowing white robe of Magi design if I wasn't mistaken.

That itself was bad enough but, whoever they were, they weren't alone.

My vantage point was limited and I was in no position to improve upon it, at least not without turning myself into ashtray remnants, but I saw enough to know we were likely dealing with a full coven here.

That was surprising, especially since Christy had insisted a good chunk of the Magi world was still far too busy trying to turn lead into cocaine to bother with chaos like this.

The voice that had warned me off, though, hadn't sounded like a magical meth addict. No. It had been dripping less with drunken disorderliness and far more with condescending arrogance.

Guess some things were finally starting to get back to normal after all.

Movement from out near the street caught my eye and I turned to see Matthias Falcon step into view. *Son of a bitch.*

The air shimmered for a moment as he stepped through the boundary of whatever glamour separated us from the usual insanity of Manhattan. He looked me in the eye then averted his gaze – although whether from shame or the fact that I was a walking horror show, I couldn't tell. Probably the latter. When dealing with wizards, it was always safer to assume hubris was at play.

I expected whatever came out of his mouth next to confirm that, anticipating something conceited like, "You brought this upon yourself, Freewill."

So instead I was surprised when he simply said, "I'm sorry. I tried to stop this, but it's out of my hands now."

What the?

Thankfully, Christy was there to pick up my slack, allowing me to focus on regrowing my skin.

"What is this, Matthias?"

In response, there came a flash of light to Falcon's immediate left. When it cleared, it revealed an older woman in her sixties or seventies wearing a white mage robe. Emblazoned on the front was a golden emblem in the shape of a bird.

"L-let me guess," I slurred, unable to help myself. "May the odds be ever in our favor."

The woman threw me a sour look, no doubt judging me beneath her contempt. "This, my dear, is what happens when a situation is not properly contained." She inclined her head at Falcon. "Matthias."

"Aunt Marjorie," he replied with a nod, refusing to meet her gaze.

Huh. Another member of the esteemed Falcon family. I should've guessed based on the conceited haughtiness alone.

"I don't believe we've met," Christy said, her tone measured. "I am Mentor..."

"*Former* Mentor," Marjorie corrected. "I seem to recall you being accused of treason, Ms. Fenton, by one Julius Robertson, late Grand Mentor of the Great Plains. May the White Mother have mercy upon his essence. As I do believe the charge was never formally dismissed, Magi law dictates you no longer have any official standing among our people ... other than perhaps that of traitor."

Ooh, look at Dame Judi Dench here throwing some shade.

"You have no right to judge me," Christy shot back, "not when you invoke the same White Mother who betrayed our people and led them to ruin."

Oh boy. Here we were stuck outside with no idea what was happening to our friends, but apparently still with time enough to clap back at each other.

"Do not take the wretched status of our *colonial* brethren to be indicative of us all, child. The fact that you yourself are not lying passed out in some brothel alongside your sisters speaks well for you, but it does not exonerate your misdeeds."

"Marjorie," Falcon hissed.

"Oh you're quite right, nephew, I've forgotten my manners. You may address me as Grand Mentor Falcon, high priestess of the order of Kala the White, and executor of the board of trustees for the Falcon estate."

"That's a bit of a mouthful," I replied, my tongue finally feeling unburnt enough to talk. "How about we call you Large Marge instead?"

"Ah yes, the Freewill. I dare say, your kind has not been missed these past five years."

"The feeling's mutual." I turned my attention toward Falcon. "So what's the deal? I thought you were in charge of the Falcon Academy, the Falcon Archives, the Falcon Cave, the Falcon Toilet, and whatever else your name's stamped on."

"Foolish creature," Marjorie replied. "My nephew here has inherited the patriarchy of our family name, yes, as well as the duties it entails. However, the board exists to ensure our vast holdings are managed appropriately ... and to act when we feel more *prudent* judgement is necessitated."

Prudent judgement. That meant Matty here had done

fucked up somehow. Judging by the fact that Sally's apartment building was currently in magical lockdown, I had a feeling that could be traced back to us.

Because that's how this shit always seemed to work.

"You see, Freewill," Marge continued, "despite my nephew's naïve insistence on being a so-called *man of the people* in dealing with the quirks magic's restoration has brought with it, the board of trustees has chosen to take a somewhat different stance. We have been monitoring this situation from afar and have found it somewhat disturbing."

"Join the club." I looked down, glad to see the skin on my arms was finally mending. Too bad that brought with it a rumble from my stomach. Guess I should've stuck around for those pancakes after all.

"Between the reemergence of species previously thought lost to time and other occurrences that our experts are still attempting to classify, we thought it best to step in and take a more active hand in matters."

I glanced toward Sally's building and the burning sigils still glowing upon it. "Active hand, you say?"

She stepped forward. "Yes. You see, my nephew has been providing us with status reports. Coupled with data we have been gathering independently, it paints a rather unpleasant picture. To be perfectly frank, Matthias's recent *failing* to mitigate this situation necessitated us to act in his stead."

"This *situation* has a name you know."

"Be that as it may, the threat *it* represents warrants isolated containment ... at least until such time as we can determine the best way to dispose of it."

25

URBAN RENEWAL

"**Y**ou can't do that."

As far as comebacks went, mine was lame. Sue me. I'd just spent the last several minutes waiting for my skin to decrispify, and now my stomach was demanding payment for services rendered.

It didn't exactly leave me in an overly clever mood.

"Bill's right," Christy said. "Your coven has no authority to come here and unilaterally decide someone is a threat. There are..."

"Protocols in place?" Marjorie interrupted. "Whose family do you think wrote those protocols? Certainly not yours. Besides, as you yourself said, the current state of our people leaves much to be desired. Until such time as that changes, I will not hesitate to be the firm hand this world requires."

"That's nice," I replied, "but I'm pretty sure nobody's asking you for a reach around. Besides, if you're so concerned about this shit, where were you when the world was being cornholed to make thirteen new baby Sources?"

"I don't answer to your kind."

"You do when you fuck with my friends."

"It's not that simple, Freewill," Falcon stated.

"Seems that way to me. You drugged Sally and got

caught, so you decided to run back home and cry that we took your ball."

Marjorie let out a huff. "Quite the opposite actually. My nephew was adamant on handling things his way. Recent events, however, have caused us to reconsider."

"Like?" I asked, feigning ignorance.

"You may not be aware, Freewill, but my family are the custodians of a vast library dating back to before your people first sullied this Earth."

"You don't say," I muttered, noticing Christy's warning look. "I mean, yeah, I've heard of it."

"And are you similarly aware that we have had teams scouring it for weeks now, trying to piece together the ramifications of the Source's return? Or that we have recently learned of a being seemingly born of this incident, one possessing abilities that mock the fundamental building blocks of magic?"

I guess I could see how that might unnerve the Magi a bit.

"What else have you learned?" Christy replied, her tone telling me she wasn't just asking about Sally.

"Only that Matthias's operation here has accomplished nothing save to make it worse."

"That's not bloody true and you know it," he shot back, apparently finding his balls sometime in the last thirty seconds. "Not every problem can be solved by analyzing it to death from afar."

"And yet here we are regardless, cleaning up your mess."

I shook my head. "You know, rather than swoop in like a flock of magical assholes, you could've tried talking to us first."

"Exactly what I would expect your kind to say. For too long the Magi have sat back and done nothing but talk. All the while, our people declined as the world's problems grew. And yes, I count your First Coven among those problems. Because of their ineptitude and our people's unwillingness to act, you were born, giving rise to the very Icon who nearly ended us all. You'll forgive me if I am hesitant to repeat that mistake now that we've been given a second chance."

Oh, fuck this noise. I pulled out my cell, only to find the cheap burner phone had been fused shut during my morning flash fry. *Goddamn it!* That was two in one week. I turned toward Christy. "Can I borrow yours?"

"I wouldn't waste my time." Marjorie said. "That barrier isn't like others. It's a lost technique, only recently rediscovered in the Archive. Strong enough to hold back an army or withstand the fires of creation itself."

"Uh huh. Should I go out on a limb and assume it blocks cell service, too?"

She grinned like I was an idiot, but didn't contradict me.

"Okay, so where do we go from here?"

"We? There is no..."

"Perhaps we can sit down and talk this over like adults," Falcon said, glancing his aunt's way. "*All* of us. Maybe then we can come to an arrangement that..."

"That what, Matthias?" she asked derisively. "We hold the advantage here. What reason do we have to negotiate with a single disgraced witch and this *low* creature?"

"Because this is their city."

"Something else perhaps in need of change," Marjorie opined. "If the covens here aren't up to the task, then perhaps it's time to seed them with Magi who still possess a sense of duty that goes beyond their selfish needs."

Okay, I was beginning to get the sense that Marge here had never gotten over a little thing called the Revolutionary War. Either way, this witch had a chip on her shoulder the size of Big Ben.

Made me wonder if all Magi from the old country had such massive sticks up their asses.

Unfortunately, it was starting to look like talking wasn't going to resolve this mess. Too bad for these assholes that Magi blood was a part of this balanced breakfast.

Christy was apparently of the same mindset, minus the blood drinking part. There came a flash of power from my periphery as her body began to glow red.

"Enough of this," she said. "You have no authority in this place save what you claim. You say I'm a disgraced Mentor, but I say your words are meaningless here."

"Really girl?" Marjorie replied. "And do you presume to fight us, your betters, as well as the acolytes I've brought with me?"

That was a good point. I had a feeling we were surrounded and, far as I could tell, they held the high ground. There was also the fact that I was a wee bit limited in my options by the sun still rising in the sky.

Why the hell did these assholes have to pick a sunny day to start shit?

Despite the odds being against us, Christy smiled – telling me she either had an ace up her sleeve or the sex last night was so bad that death was preferable. Man, Tom would never let me live that down.

Wait ... Tom! He was still inside. That gave me an idea.

Christy, in the meantime, was already forging ahead. "You have us outnumbered, true, but I'm guessing that construct requires a lot of concentration to hold." She took a moment to look at it. "Concentration that they can't afford to drop by fighting us."

While this was going on, I scoured the parking lot, or at least the shady portion, for some stones. Fortunately, there were several asphalt pebbles within easy reach.

I looked up, not even remotely sure where anyone's bedroom window was from this angle. But at least I knew what floor Tom was on. If I could get his attention...

Fuck it. As Christy continued to mouth off against the Falcons, a wizard dual no doubt imminent, I chucked a handful of the pebbles up toward the fourth floor –

hoping there was a good reason Marjorie had warned me from approaching the building earlier.

Sure enough, as the rocks closed in, the barrier around the building sparked, causing each of them to blow apart explosively as if I'd tossed a bunch of firecrackers instead.

Tom could be a lazy fuck when he wanted to be, but surely that was enough to catch even his attention.

"Really?" Marjorie cried. "Rocks? Is that truly the best the legendary Freewill has to offer?"

"Yep," I replied, throwing Christy a wink. "Because I know something you don't. Sally's not the only one trapped in there. You also managed to catch the one person your magic won't do dick against – the Icon."

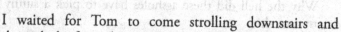

I waited for Tom to come strolling downstairs and through the front door, negating the force field.

Yep, any minute now...

Shit like this always worked in the movies.

Regardless, it definitely caught Marjorie's attention.

"Matthias," she calmly said, as if my revelation hadn't ruffled her feathers one bit, "As head of the board of trustees, I hereby order you, on pain of binding, to protect me from this fallen Mentor."

What?

She then glanced my way. "As for you, Freewill, I am well versed on your shared history with the Icon."

"You are?"

"And you are correct. This barrier cannot hold her. But perhaps the threat of losing you will. The question now being, does your former lover still have enough feelings left for you to stay her hand?"

I raised my index finger. "Yeah, I'm thinking your intel may be a bit out of date." Guess Falcon's status reports hadn't included *everything*, not that I could blame him. His interactions with Tom had probably been just enough to convince him the Icon had a screw loose, but perhaps not enough to figure out what had really happened.

"Well then, I suppose we shall see." Marjorie began to glow, her body lighting up an angry green, telling me she meant business.

Christy, in turn, dialed up the energy already crackling off her, no doubt meant to be an intimidation display before the fireworks started. Somehow, flashing my fangs felt a bit inadequate compared to them both.

Falcon stepped in front of her, though, raising a purple force wall between Christy and his aunt. "I-I'm sorry, Christine. I have no choice in this matter."

"I am too, Matthias," she said, the asphalt beneath her feet starting to steam.

Oh boy.

Once again my stomach rumbled, reminding me how good it would feel to sink my fangs into that old witch's throat – something that would almost certainly drive even more of a rift between us and Falcon. But oh well. These things tended to happen when dealing with assholes.

I just needed to focus on not letting the hunger distract me too badly. Marjorie had me between a rock and a hard place, leaving me perhaps ten feet of shade to operate in – not a lot of room to avoid a fireball. There wasn't even any cover for me to hide behind – the one dumpster in sight sitting across the parking lot in the sunlight as if mocking me.

I considered my options. If I made a run for it, I might be able to round the corner. There, the shadows were long, allowing me a lot more freedom to dodge, but making it required not getting shot in the back first.

I somehow doubted Mary Poppins there would be that sporting. Hell, she was probably imagining herself on horseback and me as some little Freewill fox to be hunted, jolly good show and all.

Christy, thankfully, was no idiot. She wasn't so focused on blasting Marjorie that she'd forgotten about me.

She nodded my way then began to shift her position – using her own magic to afford me the cover the surroundings lacked.

I backed up, trying to gauge the best moment to run for it, but then stopped as my ears suddenly picked up the sound of footsteps. They were distant and muffled, which meant they were coming from inside.

Yes!

Maybe we could tip the odds here. Tom wasn't the most useful person to have in a fight, but lately he seemed to be getting his shit together a bit. I still didn't trust him with his sword, but at least he'd gained a modicum of control over his powers. It was probably too much to hope that he'd finally figured out how to use that crazy-ass Kamehameha wave he'd blasted the werewolves at Pop's place with, but so long as he could play the tank and soak up some magic, it would work in our favor.

I turned as the footsteps neared the door. Now to hope I hadn't accidently woken any of the coven instead. If so, I'd need to warn them off fast before they got fried. Still, none of them should've had any reason to come to the door during daylight hours. They all hopefully knew better than that.

There came the click of the inner door opening to the vestibule and then the outer door was pulled open revealing, not Tom, but Sally. And, of course, she was armed with her hand cannon because that's exactly what we needed to make this situation less tense.

Shit!

"Stay back!" I cried. "Don't move. There's a barrier..."

"Do I look like a fucking idiot, Bill?" she replied, raising an eyebrow.

Okay, guess she'd noticed the exploding rocks. That said, she had to be within a foot or two of the unseen barrier. Knowing how her body tended to react to too much magic, I found my ass cheeks clenching preemptively.

However, she merely continued to stand there looking annoyed.

I glanced back toward where the mages continued their Mexican standoff.

"Did you think we would come unprepared?" Marjorie explained haughtily. "That incantation is entirely self-contained. No ambient magic runoff."

That was good ... sorta.

"My apologies," Falcon called out, sounding oddly sincere. "I didn't want it to come to this."

"You know what the best apology would be?" Sally replied. "Dropping this bullshit and getting off my property."

"Unacceptable!" Marjorie powered down enough to converse but not enough to leave out the possibility of vaporizing me at a moment's notice. "You had your chance but chose to ignore it. You had to know there would be consequences."

"Last I checked, I don't answer to... Wait, who the fuck are you anyway?"

"Oh, this is Falcon's aunt Marjorie," I replied conversationally. "She's Grand Mentor of a bunch of shit I didn't bother to remember."

Needless to say, that didn't win me any points in Professor McGonagall's book, judging by the sour expression she threw my way. On the other hand, she was old, English, and wealthy as fuck. That might just have been how she normally looked at peons like me.

"That's nice." Sally leaned against the door frame, checking her weapon. "Doesn't change the fact that I didn't order any magical Grubhub. So kindly leave and take your horse shit with you."

"You are in no position to give orders here, girl."

Huh. Guess Marge didn't realize Sally had a few more years under her belt than her looks implied. Or maybe she just didn't give a shit.

"Let me explain using small words. This is private

property and New York is a stand your ground state, so I think that gives me some wiggle room when it comes to warning your ass."

"Actually, it's not," Falcon said. "If you check the statutes..."

"There's the letter of the law and then there's the spirit, Matt. This is Manhattan. Trust me when I say we don't like to be fucked with."

"Enough of this." Marjorie turned toward the rooftops, where the rest of the Falcon flock waited, and gave a nod.

A moment later, the sigils around Sally's building began to glow even brighter, at least those not immediately around the entranceway. A few seconds passed and there came the sound of masonry cracking. I looked up to see sections of the building's stone façade starting to crumble.

The fuck?

"What are you doing?" Christy cried. "There are people inside!"

"Consider this a final warning," Marjorie said, her voice cold as ice. "This particular incantation was designed for siege warfare against city states. It can contain whole armies and, if necessary, compress them to pulp, crushing them and all they hold dear."

"You're bluffing," Sally replied, sounding unperturbed.

"I can assure you, I am not."

"Christy's right," I called out. "There are others in there. Our friends..."

"Do you think I care a single iota about the Icon," the witch replied, "or for any others who might associate with your kind?"

"Aunt Marjorie..."

"This is for the good of the world, Matthias. Now please be silent."

"He's right," Falcon continued, dropping his force shield. "At least let the others out. Then we can resume negotiations."

Marjorie shot him a look that would've melted steel. "Is that what you think we're doing here, negotiating? I've read your reports, had our acolytes do the research, and I've seen the news, too. Something is attempting to enter our world, something so old I fear that even the ancient texts barely hint at it."

He shook his head. "Something is *always* trying to enter this world and you bloody well know it. Why, right now up in Boston the gates of Hades are about to..."

"Foolish boy. We're not talking about anything of the sort."

Huh. Didn't realize the gates of Hell were so passe these days.

"The Olympians, the Æsir, the Kami, all the known pantheons," she continued, "they adhere to rules. They can be reasoned with, bargained with. We are dealing with something primal, something savage. It only has a toehold for now, but it wants more." She pointed Sally's way. "And that thing inside there is the one that shall open the gate."

"Don't even think about making a keymaster joke, Bill."

I smirked at her. "Wouldn't dream of it."

"Liar." Sally turned her attention back toward Marjorie. "You're right about one thing. This *isn't* a negotiation. Leave."

"Or what? You have no leverage here."

"Oh no?" I half-expected Sally to make a show with her weapon, for all the good it would do, but instead she raised her free hand toward the entranceway.

What the fuck?

"Far be it from me to tell anyone how to play chicken," I said, "but Tom is still..."

"The meathead is built for shit like this. He'll be fine, probably. As for the coven, well, there are always more vamps to recruit."

No!

In that moment, I couldn't help but think her strange

green eyes reflected the cold inhumanity Falcon's aunt was accusing her of.

"You can't be serious," I whispered.

"Never negotiate with those who think they're better than you, Bill," she replied, her voice flat, devoid of emotion. "If you give them an inch, they will never stop taking. Trust me, I know that better than most."

"Go right ahead," Marjorie said, oozing confidence. "Prove to everyone here you deserve to be put down like a rabid dog. I think we both know you don't have the..."

"You don't know shit about me, lady," Sally interrupted, her eyes never leaving mine. "But you're about to find out."

I opened my mouth to scream for her to stop, but was a moment too late.

There came a spark of power where her hand touched the barrier – then, a split second later, it was as if everything good and pure about this world simply ended in one massive explosion.

26

ALL RETREAT, NO SURRENDER

I knew the drill, having already lived through it more times than I ever cared to.

My legs were already in motion in the same instant Sally's hand sparked against the barrier. I couldn't see what happened to her, the flash of power inside far too bright, but it couldn't have been good.

All I knew for certain was that if she did survive the initial flare up, whatever came next would be even worse.

Using every bit of speed at my disposal, I turned and leapt for where Christy stood. Angry red energy continued to surround her, not to mention she was standing in the sunlight. Talk about two kicks to the balls for the price of one. And there I was lining up for both, as if telling the universe, "Thank you, sir. May I have another?"

I hit her hard enough to crack a normal person's ribs. Fortunately, for her anyway, the magic around her body served to mute my blow, mostly by directing a good chunk of the force back into me.

My flesh began to sear from both ends – the spell like a blanket of living flame, the sunlight above unforgiving in its fury. It figured. And my hair had just started to grow back, too.

More important was that I managed to knock her

down, landing atop her just as there came a whoosh of power from behind us, back where Sally had just given Marjorie the most lethal middle finger in history.

I felt the kinetic energy rush over me, a tornado force of unearthly power strong enough to turn me into puree – had I been stupid enough to still be standing. Crazy how in that moment Christy's death magic was the lesser of two evils.

Far worse than the pulse of Sally's power, however, were the sounds of destruction that followed. Concrete crumbling, windows shattering, and support struts exploding into dust.

"Get us out of here!" I screamed, forcing my burning mouth to work even as the sunlight was blotted out above by a plume of dust and debris.

I prayed I hadn't hit her hard enough to stun her or worse. If so, I had no idea what would happen. My body was badly injured, *again*. Even with my vampire healing, I doubted I could survive being buried in that much rubble. As for Christy, her magic was formidable, but her body was as fragile as any human's. If my survival was iffy, hers was...

I tried not to think about it as the noise grew ever louder around us, becoming nearly deafening, until it suddenly stopped – cutting off in an instant and leaving me in a hell of infinite nothingness.

Okay. If this was Hell, at least it had decent flooring.

The emptiness of the void retreated as a wave of nausea rolled through my guts, telling me Christy had done it. She'd managed to teleport us away before we could be crushed like bugs.

My eyes refused to focus properly, my glasses seemingly both melted and fused to my face, but I could see enough to recognize that we'd reappeared exactly where we'd left, inside her bedroom's sending circle.

There wasn't time to celebrate, though, as the queasiness passed, leaving behind a pit of raw hunger. I'd been horrifically injured twice in a short period, my body working overtime to repair all the damage I'd sustained. For a vampire, it came with a heavy price.

For a moment, I found myself fixated on Christy, still lying beneath me. Her eyes were closed and she appeared to have taken a pretty good hit, no thanks to me. If I had to guess, she probably had at least a mild concussion. But I was less concerned with her head in that moment as I was with her throat – the rush of blood through her arteries practically a song to my ears.

And it was a tune I wanted to sing along with, as I drank deep of her and...

No!

I reached up and slapped myself, the feeling far less than pleasant considering my freshly charred skin. *Ow!* But at least it cleared my head for the moment.

Christy moaned beneath me, her eyelids fluttering. We were both a mess, covered in dust and grime, although she still somehow managed to make it look good. Less good was me leaving her on the hard floor. I lifted her up as gently as I could, almost stumbling as my own head was swimming from the energy I'd expended.

Man, I really needed to properly hydrate next time I went hunting leprechauns, followed by hot sex then getting blown to hell twice in a row.

Finally I managed to get the job done, laying her on her comforter as I leaned over to make sure she was...

The bedroom door burst open, revealing Tina. "It's pancake time!"

I was about to tell her that her mommy and Uncle Bill were having a bit of a morning, but then I saw the smile on her face fall, replaced first by horror then by outrage.

Oh yeah. My fangs were out and there I was – shirt in

tatters and with my face and torso burnt beyond recognition. In short, I looked like a nightmare given form.

Fuck me.

"You leave my mommy alone!"

A prismatic aura of energy flared up around Tina, utterly vaporizing the door frame wherever it touched.

Oh boy. I could feel the raw power radiating from her. Had my eyebrows not already been burnt off they would have surely started smoldering.

I had a feeling that if I didn't head this off at the pass and fast, I'd be dealing with another disaster similar to what had just happened at Sally's.

Oh God, Sally...

No! As much as I needed to know what had happened to her back there, if she'd somehow managed to... I wouldn't be able to do dick if I ended up dead.

"C-Cat, it's me!" I cried, forcing my mouth to work as best it could. "It's Uncle Bill!"

"Uncle Bill?" she asked, her eyes aglow with furious power. I felt like Krillin standing there like a deer in the headlights while Vegeta prepared to go all Super Saiyan Blue on my ass.

"Y-yes, it's me! Your Mommy and I went out, but ... we ran into some trouble." *Talk about an understatement.* "She brought us back home but hurt her head. I was just putting her on the bed to..."

All around us the walls lit up as sigils and wards activated, no doubt attuned to Tina's power. I watched as the energy around her began to collapse, going from a thousand watts down to maybe three hundred – which was still two-hundred and eighty more than she needed to finish me.

She's a child.

I raised a brow at my subconscious's less than stellar advice. *No shit.*

Use that to your advantage.

Use that to my...? How? Did he want me to take

advantage of my superior reach and deck her or something?

Wait a second. What was the one thing that got children everywhere to snap to attention? Parent voice!

"Cat, I need you to stop that right now. Your mommy is going to be okay, but I need you to go get her ... a glass of water and a couple aspirin." She hesitated, energy still crackling around her as the wards continued to pulse. Time to go for broke. "*Now*, young lady!"

"Okay, Uncle Bill."

With that, her power winked off like a light switch. She turned and headed toward the kitchen, leaving a large chunk of wall missing in her wake.

I let out a heavy sigh as I collapsed in relief. "Goddamn, what a morning."

"Ooh, you said a bad word!"

Son of a bitch.

Much as I hated to leave Christy right at that moment, I didn't have much choice in the matter. I pulled myself up and stepped from the bedroom, headed toward the apartment next door.

Glen was already in the living room, sans his dog costume. Nevertheless, as several of his eyeballs turned my way, he cried, "Halt, stranger! Bark, bark, bark!"

"Not now, Glen."

"Oh, so sorry, Freewill. Didn't recognize you. Did I miss anything exciting?"

"You could say that."

I opened the door leading into the other apartment and immediately turned toward the kitchen. *Please don't be empty.*

I'd helped Ed stock up when he'd moved in, via our new living arrangements. Thankfully, he hadn't been a glutton about it, there still being several pints of pig blood waiting in the fridge.

Pity I couldn't say the same of myself as I tore the lid from one and guzzled it down like there was no tomorrow.

Oh god that's good! Everything about vampires was attuned to making blood as awesome as possible. Gross as that might be for normal folk, our tastebuds transformed it into the best meal imaginable – like Thanksgiving dinner in viscous liquid form. Needless to say, it hit the spot.

So did the pint after that, my body demanding more even as I felt my healing begin to accelerate.

"What the fuck happened to you?"

Apparently it wasn't fast enough, though.

I turned to find Ed standing in the bedroom doorway wearing shorts and a t-shirt – there being little need for him to be nocturnal since sunlight didn't bother him.

"I've ... had a bit of a morning," I said between slurps.

"I can see that."

"Do me a favor and go check on Christy. I think she's okay. Just make sure. I would, but..."

Thankfully, there was no need for me to finish that sentence, crispy as I looked. "You got it. Just save some for me."

"No promises," I replied, downing another mouthful before reaching for the next pint.

27

PICKING UP THE PIECES

I tried to focus on anything other than what happened as I finished making sure I was safe to be around again.

That done, I went into the bathroom to wash up, noting my burns were starting to sort themselves out. Heck, I even had lips again. My glasses were completely shot, meaning it was like looking at the world through cotton candy, but I could take care of that soon enough.

For now, I went into Ed's room and helped myself to a t-shirt before heading back over.

Christy was sitting on the couch, still covered in dust but awake – her black hair now a chalky white – while Ed was in the kitchen making coffee.

She turned my way then glanced down at herself and smiled weakly. "You look like you've seen a ghost."

"Probably closer than I ever want to come to it."

A moment later, Tina came skipping out of the bathroom with a wet washcloth for her mother.

"Thanks, baby girl."

"You're welcome." Cat turned my way and nodded approvingly. "You look less scary now, Uncle Bill."

"Thanks. I feel less scary."

Glen slithered over to where I stood. "I want to hear what happened."

"Later. Let's turn on the news first."

Christy nodded solemnly as I took a seat next to her, both of us no doubt avoiding the six hundred pound gorilla in the room, at least until we could learn how bad it really was.

It didn't take long.

The news cut to an aerial shot of SoHo, but most of what was on the screen was heavily obscured by dust. What we could make out, though, didn't look promising.

"Holy shit!"

"Ooh, Uncle Bill..."

"It's okay, sweetie. Uncle Bill gets this one for free," Christy said as we turned our attention to the news report.

"It's difficult to make out from here, but a section of the street appears to have caved in, resulting in at least one collapsed building – which I'm told was the former home of late philanthropist Sally Carlsbad. A handful of nearby properties likewise sustained damage in what authorities are claiming was a tragic accident. Though it's clear that several people were injured, the city has yet to release a statement on the number of casualties. Now over to Kelly Ortez who's on the ground with an eyewitness."

The shot switched to an overly cheerful reporter. She was apparently a few blocks from the scene of the destruction – a plume of dust visible in the background.

It was who was standing next to her, though, that caught my attention as I squinted at the screen.

Son of a...

"I'm here with Matthias Falcon, special consultant to the NYPD. Mr. Falcon, what can you tell us about this terrible tragedy?"

Falcon was covered in dust, his mustache looking like an albino ferret had climbed onto his face and died there. Otherwise, he looked as fit as ever.

"It's Mentor Falcon if you please, Kelly." *Smarmy*

motherfucker! "Rescue efforts are still underway, however, we believe the adjacent buildings were mostly empty at the time of the incident."

Mostly empty. Obviously not counting anyone who might've been turned to dust or worse.

"Tell me, should New Yorkers be concerned that this may have been a terror attack?"

"Obviously an investigation is forthcoming and our hearts go out to those who were injured in this regrettable episode, but I assure you there's no cause for alarm."

"How can you say that with such certainty considering what happened?"

"We've been in contact with numerous agencies, and at the moment believe a seismic event is to blame."

"A seismic...?"

"That's all I can say on the matter, I'm afraid. I'm told an official statement will be issued shortly. Right now the only thing left to do is thank the heavens it wasn't worse."

"No thanks to you!" I yelled, as if the prick could hear me.

"Look," Christy said, pointing at the TV.

Sure enough, a snooty older woman could be seen in the background, looking pissed off as if someone had dared interrupt her tea time. Fucking Marge.

It would figure that she'd survived, too. Bad pennies always seemed to turn up.

Unfortunately, that was all the insight to be gleaned. Neither a casualty list nor estimate of those injured had been released yet. I had little doubt Falcon had his hand in that, too.

Ed stepped from the kitchen carrying a tray of mugs. "Goddamn, you weren't kidding. What the hell happened?"

"Honey, why don't you go make yourself a bowl of cereal and take it into your room?"

"I thought I wasn't allowed to eat in there."

"Just for this morning. We'll do pancakes tomorrow. Okay?"

"Okay, Mommy!"

I glanced Tina's way as she ran to grab breakfast, noting she didn't say shit to Ed about the swear jar. Figured.

It was only once she was safely in her room, and I'd taken a few sips of the heavenly ambrosia, did the conversation take a turn for the darker.

"Do you think they...?"

"I don't know," I snapped at Ed. "It all happened so fast."

"Tom's power might have shielded him," Christy said, her tone telling me she was grasping at whatever straws she could.

She wasn't wrong. Sheila's aura had once protected her from something similar up in Boston. However, that had merely been a collapsed section of roadway. We were talking an entire building here. Even if Tom hadn't been crushed outright, he could easily be trapped with his air running out even as we... *No!* I pushed that thought away. "We need to go back."

"No offense," Ed replied, "but neither of you look like you're in any shape to go anywhere. Not to mention, that place is going to be crawling with cops."

I nodded bitterly. "Including the asshole responsible."

"Wait. You mean that Falcon guy did this?"

"Pretty much, at least indirectly."

"Holy shit."

"I just don't understand the sudden escalation," Christy said.

"Well, Sally did kind of lose her shit over that bracelet incident."

She shook her head. "I understand that, but it doesn't seem enough to warrant going to war over, not when he could have come to us and discussed it. We could have easily found a workable solution that didn't involve ... this."

She kind of had a point. Falcon had previously struck me as cool under pressure, but maybe he simply had a better poker face than some of us.

And then there was Sally. What she'd done... It had been beyond anything I would've ever expected from her. She knew there were others in the building. Knew that Tom was...

I shook my head to chase that thought away. This wasn't her fault. She didn't start this. No. It fell entirely on the Falcon family's lap.

Sadly, now wasn't the time to worry about them.

They would get theirs, no doubt about it, but first we needed to focus on our friends. I let out a deep sigh, trying to hold onto some hope, but even I was finding it hard to believe anyone could have walked away from...

Christy stood up, wiping her eyes. "I'll try scrying the area, assuming they haven't warded it off yet."

"And if they have?"

"Then I'll break out that blood magic spell again and punch through it."

"Yeah. That sounds like a... Wait, what do you mean *again*?"

Before she could answer the phone began to ring.

It was probably either telemarketers or more bad news, nothing any of us needed at that moment.

"I'll get it." Ed stepped over to where the receiver lay. "Huh. That's odd."

"What is?" I asked, not really paying attention.

"Caller ID says it's coming from the apartment."

"You mean this one?"

"No. Our ... I mean your place." He picked up the phone. "Hello?"

My place?

"Holy shit!" he cried. "How the fuck did...? I mean, are you all right? Yeah, okay, I guess that is kind of obvious. No, you don't have to be a prick about it... Okay. We'll be over in a few."

What the?

Ed put the phone down. "Huh. Asshole hung up on me."

"Who...?"

"Tom," he replied wide-eyed. "He's not only alive, but he brought company with him."

Ed didn't have any more details to share, but it was more than enough for us to cast off our misery and put our game faces back on. Tom was apparently back at our place, and he'd brought the coven with him. I had no idea how or why, but I couldn't say I really cared either so long as they were okay.

Christy wanted to zap right over, but I ixnayed that. She was still shaky on her feet and, well, teleporting hadn't exactly been kind to us as of late.

Fortunately, that wasn't the only option available. I might've still been carless, but she wasn't. That said, a two door coupe was a smart choice for the city, but it kind of sucked when a whole group needed to go somewhere.

That meant some hard choices had to be made.

In the end, despite everything we'd already been through, she and I were the ones who ended up heading out. It was her car, so her rules. And, well, Ed was still at the top of the werewolf hit list – just in case something dodgy was afoot.

Thankfully, downing all that blood had gone a long way toward putting me on the mend. One stolen hoodie from Ed's closet later and I was ready to once again brave the outdoors.

It was a short drive to my place, but that didn't mean it wasn't tense. Hell, I'm surprised we didn't run anyone over on the way. It was probably a good thing Christy chose to drive because, even had I been able to see where I was going, I'd have probably snapped the steering wheel off in my anxiety.

Finally, we pulled onto my block, lucking out and finding an open spot close to my place. Not only that, but the sky had clouded up a bit since our earlier foray, making it a bit less risky for me.

Once parked, we raced up the stairs and opened the door ... only to find Mike standing there in the fucking vestibule.

For fuck's sake, did the guy live there or something? Oh yeah, this wasn't suspicious at all. All at once, I was regretting my decision to not confront him earlier in the week.

I tensed up, preparing to extend my talons when Christy put a hand on my shoulder, reminding me that this wasn't why we were there.

"Hey, Mr. Ryder," he said cheerfully enough, having no clue how close he was to having his day permanently ruined. "Haven't seen you around in a few..."

"Enough," I interrupted. "Just ... go back to your apartment, okay?"

"Huh, what?"

"I've gotten complaints from the other tenants. They don't like you always hanging out here like some kind of weirdo."

It was weak sauce as far as confrontations went, not to mention a lie, but at least I'd said *something*. Besides, I could always beat a confession out of him later when Christy wasn't around.

I pushed past and headed for the stairs, not caring if he had anything to say.

Around the second floor landing, I turned back toward Christy. "Just for the record, if there are any were-wolves waiting upstairs, I'm killing that guy on the way out."

"No argument here."

That alone told me tons about her current mood. She was the most wonderful person on the planet, but mess with her loved ones and she'd turn into a fucking honey badger, with no fucks to give as to whose ass needed kicking.

We slowed down as we finally reached the top floor. Christy started to glow in preparation – not as brightly as she had earlier, but it was more than enough to singe some mutt if need be.

However, my ears picked up the sound of conversation from inside. Better yet, they were all familiar voices – including one I'd known since childhood, even if the pitch was a bit more feminine than back then.

Trusting my senses, I pushed the door open and stepped in ... only to find I should've heeded caution instead.

Myra stood there, hate in her eyes and a fireball at the ready, unleashing it my way before I could even scream.

Just fucking with you.

Life's no fun if you can't occasionally be an unreliable narrator within your own mind.

"About fucking time," Tom *greeted* as I stepped inside, a sight for the sorest of eyes.

He was a bit on the grimy side and he certainly didn't smell wonderful, but none of that mattered. I grabbed hold of him anyway. "Holy crap! We thought you were dead. We thought you all were."

"Yeah yeah, pry your sexually harassing mitts off," he said with a grin. "No free feels, asshole."

I stepped back and looked around, noting the entire coven was present as well: Jessica, Craig, Leslie and the rest – all of them dirty but otherwise hale and hearty, for vampires anyway.

Christy powered down and joined us, closing the door

behind her. Oddly enough, when she stepped in to give Tom a big hug he didn't say a word against it.

Dickhead. But at least he was a living dickhead.

"How?" she asked. "The entire building came down."

"Yeah," Jessica said. "So we heard on the news."

"Crazy shit, eh?" Tom replied.

I raised an eyebrow. "Wait. What do you mean heard on the news?"

Craig let out a laugh. "You don't think we were actually in there when it happened, do you?"

"You weren't?"

"No fucking way, man," Tom said. "We were long gone by that point."

"Wait. How did you know it would...?"

"Sally, of course. It was all her idea. I mean, what did you think we were doing while all those wizards were outside dicking around?" He narrowed his eyes at me. "Speaking of which, where the hell were you this morning?"

28

HALF-ASSED HERO WORSHIP

om explained that Sally had apparently been more than aware of what had been going on outside. In fact, it almost sounded like she knew they were coming. She'd roused him and the coven, then had ordered a building-wide search for me when it became obvious I wasn't where I was supposed to be.

Oops.

Unable to find me, she'd then directed everyone down to the subbasement sewer entrance. Despite the barrier already being up by then, Tom was able to fizzle it out enough to get both himself and the coven through with no more than some minor singeing.

"From there we simply ran," Leslie said, "while trying not to get killed along the way."

Tom shook his head and let out a laugh. "Falcon wasn't shitting us about the big ass bugs down there."

"I could've told you that."

"Thankfully they didn't seem to like her light," Jessica said, before quickly amending, "Sorry, his light."

"Yeah," Craig added. "Every time we ran into them, he stepped forward and drove them back with his sword so the rest of us could get past. It was ... badass." He nodded toward Tom. "Seriously, you really saved our bacon down there."

Christy and I both turned his way. I wasn't sure her thoughts on the matter but I, for one, was somewhere between dumbfounded and amazed. "You actually did all that?"

"Fuck yeah," he replied proudly. "This Icon isn't just another pretty face. Like he said, I'm a badass with a..."

"You could've stopped at ass," I interrupted with a grin. "Seriously, man. I'm proud of you."

"We both are," Christy said.

Wow. Talk about things I never expected to say. Things really were getting weird if Tom was successfully playing the hero. Hell, he'd saved my coven, which was more than I could say for myself. Instead, I'd been out...

"Oh yeah," he added, almost as if reading my guilty conscience. "Where were you, by the way? Sally was pissed. She kept muttering about how she was gonna shoot your ass if we found you jerking off in a closet somewhere."

I glanced Christy's way but, interestingly enough, she'd found something on the wall to stare at. Guess it was up to me to serve this bullshit sandwich. "Um, coffee. I couldn't sleep, so I went out to grab some coffee."

"Despite the sun coming up?"

"It was *really* good coffee."

Out of the corner of my eye, I saw Christy smirk. She no doubt enjoyed watching me squirm.

Tom blinked a few times, making me think there was no way he was gonna buy my obvious lie, but then he shrugged. "Next time you could at least grab me something, too, asshole."

Before his three watt bulb of a brain charged up enough to wonder how that had led me back to Christy's place, I changed the subject back to more sobering matters. "So then what happened to Sally?"

At least now I understood why she'd been so coldly

calculating against Marge. She knew the building was empty. But if so, why end it like that? We could've stalled on her behalf, maybe returned with reinforcements to fight our way in. What could have been going through her mind to do what she'd done?

Maybe she simply had enough, my subconscious said, *and this was her way of doing it on her own terms.*

Was that possible? Could she have just been ... tired of it all, tired of the games, the manipulation, being treated like a pawn? But if so, why hadn't she said anything? When last we'd talked, she'd sounded like, well, Sally.

Leslie, however, spoke up before those dark thoughts could consume me. "I don't know, but she didn't sound like someone who was preparing to sacrifice herself. Maybe ... something went wrong after we left?"

"Or went right," Christy said, her eyes narrowed.

I turned toward her. "What do you mean?"

"Think about it. There was no reason for her to have done that. She could've kept talking, bargained, or done a million things differently."

"I don't know. It's possible this was some sort of final fuck you."

"Yes, but why? Bad as that situation seemed, we've been in worse. Her back wasn't so up against the wall that there weren't options."

That was a good point. She could've simply left with Tom and the others when they escaped, but had purposefully chosen to stay behind. Why?

I mean, it was always possible that she considered dropping a building on herself to be a better fate than dying with Tom in the sewers. At the very least, that was in character as something she might say.

But not as something she'd do. Sally was a survivor. She'd been one long before we met. She'd even gone so far as to kill off her public persona so as to not be hindered by it in her newly rejuvenated form. Why bother going through the trouble if she was simply planning on checking out like this?

Besides, there was one other thing I was forgetting. The Sally of old always had a plan up her sleeve. Why should now be any different?

I locked eyes with Christy. "What do you think?"

"I think," she said, "that we're missing a piece of this puzzle. But it's not one we're going to solve by standing here talking about it."

I took a few minutes to change clothes and grab my spare pair of glasses. Oh, it was so nice to have the world back in focus again.

Christy in the meantime gave the coven the lowdown on white trash werewolves, wood alcohol sipping witches, and the guy downstairs who seemed to like hanging out in the hallway a bit too much.

I handed over my spare set of keys to Leslie, along with a warning not to fuck with the Wi-Fi settings, then we headed out again, this time with Tom in tow.

The apartment wasn't the safest place in the world these days, but beggars couldn't be choosers. At least it was a roof over the coven's head with a fridge that still had some blood in it. That last one was particularly important since I really didn't want to come back to find all my leases rendered null and void due to the other tenants' untimely deaths.

As for the rest of us, we had things to do, specifically figuring out whether Sally had somehow cheated death. I desperately hoped so because I'd already mourned her once. I didn't care to do it again. For now, though, I held onto that, telling myself that she wasn't one to go quietly into the night.

Mind you, blowing up her own building was pretty

much the opposite of quiet, but you get where I'm going with this.

The drive back to Christy's was mostly done in silence, at least by two of us. Tom sat in the backseat expounding on his awesome heroics, until you'd have sworn he'd singlehandedly delivered the One Ring to Mordor. Still, it's not like I could begrudge him a bit of pride.

That said, he was still kinda ripe thanks to his trek through the sewers, so I cracked open a window which also served to drown his boasting out a bit.

"Daddy!" Tina cried upon our arrival, running from the bathroom where she'd apparently been giving Glen a bath, or his meat suit anyway. "Mommy was afraid a building got dropped on you. I'm so glad it didn't."

Ah, leave it to a child to be direct.

"Mommy didn't say that," Christy scolded. "And you shouldn't eavesdrop."

"I wasn't," she replied innocently. "You were thinking it earlier and I heard you."

Wait, what?

"What did I tell you about using mind magic, young lady?"

Tina lowered her head. "Not without permission."

And apparently this was a normal conversation now.

"Oh yeah," Tom proclaimed, ruining any chance of discipline. "Who's an ass kicker like her dad?"

He bent down to pick her up, causing her to wrinkle her nose. "Eww, you smell funny."

I, in turn, pulled out my wallet and handed a few bills to her. "Of course he does. That's because your daddy is full of shit."

Totally worth it.

Unfortunately, we had few leads to work on from there. Sally wasn't answering her cell, scrying didn't turn up anything, and there was no way we could get back to her place to search for clues – at least not during daylight hours.

So, with at least half of us exhausted from both a late night and far too exciting a morning, we decided to settle down until evening came.

Ed offered to entertain Tina while the rest of us showered – alone sadly – and then retired to grab some much needed shuteye.

Tom and I took the apartment next door, with me getting the couch.

Oh well. I'd passed out on far worse. So long as I didn't wake up with dicks drawn on my face, I could look forward to finding out what had happened to my friend.

"Bark, bark, bark!"

I wasn't sure how long I was asleep, but when I next opened my eyes the room was dark, telling me the sun was finally down.

I roused myself to see what was setting the little weirdo off, stepping into Christy's apartment only to realize someone was knocking at the front door. Glen, once again in his dog suit, repeated his cry, to which I replied, "You could've just asked who's there, you know."

"Yes, but I'm still in disguise."

"Uh huh, real convincing as usual. Where are the others?"

"Madam Witch and the Progenitor are tucking Tina in. They asked me to see who it was."

"So instead you're standing here barking?"

"I'm a good watchdog. Also, I can't reach the peephole."

The knocking continued, causing Tom to cry out, "Someone answer the fucking door already!"

"Oh for fuck's sake," I muttered, fortunately not loudly enough for my goddaughter to overhear.

I tried not to get my hopes up that it was Sally. Besides, she knew better than to come here while Tina was present – wards or not. The last time had been warning enough for us all.

Still, seeing her alive would've made it worth it.

However, as I pulled open the door, I realized our visitor was the exact opposite of the good news I'd been hoping for.

My eyes instantly darkened as I unsheathed my claws.

"Falcon."

Much as I wanted to knock out his teeth, that wasn't really my style.

There was also the fact that it was fangs and claws against a guy who'd created an artificial reality within the confines of his hotel room. I mean, yeah, in the comics Wolverine always acted the part of the tough guy, but against, say, Dr. Strange ... well, I knew where I'd put my money.

Falcon for his part looked somewhat worse for the wear, a few bruises covering his face, no doubt from our earlier block party. "Are you going to let me stand out here all night or are you going to invite me in, Freewill?"

So much for intimidating the guy. God, I really hated smug, self-esteem filled assholes.

I gestured for him to come in. Besides, Christy probably wanted first dibs on the prick anyway.

As I closed the door, Glen opened the dead corgi's mouth wide and puked himself out.

At the sight of him Falcon bent over and began to make retching sounds.

Heh. Of all the shit that had happened, *this* was what caused him to lose it? *Newb.*

However, just as I was starting to feel superior, Glen perked up. "Why thank you, Mister Falcon! I wasn't aware humans could perform my people's customary greeting, at least without regurgitating their internal organs."

What?!

"Just takes a bit of practice, mate."

Grr. Showoff!

Thankfully, I was spared further indignation as the rest of our group joined us in the living room, Christy first and foremost.

"You have a lot of nerve coming here."

"Yeah," Tom replied. "You tell him, babe."

Falcon held up his hands, no doubt hoping to diffuse the situation. "You have every right to be cross with me. I fully admit it. But what happened earlier was a necessary..."

I narrowed my eyes. "I swear, if you're gonna try telling us that Sally's death was necessary for the good of the world, I'm going to..."

"If you'll allow me to finish, I was going to say it was a necessary ruse."

"What?" the rest of the group cried in unison.

"I assure you, your friend is alive and well. I'm here to take you to her, unless, that is, you'd prefer to do whatever you were about to threaten me with instead."

29

HARSH REALITY

D ecisions, decisions.

Okay fine, that wasn't a hard one to make. Still, I didn't trust this asshole, not after this morning.

"Where are you holding her?"

Falcon let out a sigh, pausing for a moment to take a suck from his vape pen.

"You do know those things make you look like a douche, right?" Tom said.

"That only matters if one cares for the opinions of others."

"Touché."

"Back to your question, Freewill, I'm not keeping her anywhere. If anything, she's less a prisoner than I am."

"Explain," Christy ordered.

"Yeah," Glen said. "Bark!"

"I will," Falcon replied, "but not here."

"Why?"

"Isn't it obvious? This place is under observation." He held up a hand as Christy made to speak. "And no, the wards you have in place will not stop them. You may be surprised to learn this, but there's an ancient blood scrying ritual known to very few that has the power to punch through common wards."

I glanced sidelong Christy's way, but she was much cooler under fire than me, barely blinking at his mention of it. "If that's the case, then they already know you're here."

"Not necessarily." He reached into his shirt and pulled out some weird-ass necklace, a bunch of feathers tied together with what looked like chicken bones and dried foreskins. *Eww.* "This is a hat'oshk fetish. It comes from a little known tribe of ghost warriors that live deep in the jungles of Barundi. A primitive people but extraordinarily paranoid when it comes to keeping to themselves."

I made a hurry along gesture. "Yeah, fascinating I'm sure. So if you're invisible with that thing, then we're good, right?"

"Not quite." He let go of the necklace, shaking his fingers as if it were hot. "The fetish is powerful, but short lived and extremely volatile. So, if you don't mind, I'd prefer we go somewhere where we can speak freely before it burns me alive."

A few minutes later found the five of us squeezed into Falcon's vehicle, an unmarked patrol car no doubt on loan from the NYPD.

Christy had offered the use of her sending circle, which would have worked for all but one of us. Before Tom could throw a snit, though, Falcon informed us that his aunt's people would likely be watching for any sending magic. As such, we needed to do this the old fashioned way.

Glen offered to stay behind and babysit. Christy didn't like leaving her child while hostile eyeballs were potentially keeping watch, but Falcon assured her Tina was in no danger. Mind you, his assurances didn't keep her from activating every protection ward at her disposal as we left. If anyone so much as looked at the building the wrong way, she'd be alerted.

And, worst case, Glen had his phone floating inside him somewhere.

Falcon tossed the now red hot fetish out the window as we pulled away from the curb, insisting we keep it to small talk until we could get where we were going, just to be safe.

Guess that tribe in Africa weren't the only paranoid ones.

Speaking of which, I couldn't say I was comfortable riding in the back of a cop car with Tom in between Ed and I, but I took some solace in knowing Christy could vaporize Falcon from the passenger seat if he tried anything stupid, like aiming for too many potholes.

Rush hour was over and it was late enough that we made good time heading toward Manhattan, not hurt by the fact that our gracious host was able to turn on his flashers whenever some doofus tried pulling in front of us. It was good to be the fuzz.

I became concerned once I saw us approaching Sally's block, most of the street cordoned off. However, then we passed it by, heading west ... toward the docks.

"You're kidding, right?"

"Alas, it made the most sense," Falcon replied to me. "It's uninhabited and still a bloody mess."

"But?"

"But, the security glamours are still functional and I placed those fetishes at the four corners of the property. Fortunately, the asphalt is already in poor enough shape, so I'm not too worried about any new holes being scorched into them."

I was less concerned about that and more about Sally being alone there, especially with what was swimming around in the Hudson.

Apparently my worry was easy to read, though. "Don't worry, Freewill. I won't claim to know her as well as any of you lot, but I've seen enough to know she's no fool."

No, Sally wasn't, but I still wasn't convinced we weren't idiots to trust this self-absorbed magical dandy, no matter what he claimed.

At least if this was a trap, he was in close enough quarters for one of us to gank his ass first. Small victories and all.

Amusingly enough, as we closed in on the pier, the scene before us was one of banal normalcy – the glamour showing nothing but what the outside world was meant to see. Needless to say, we all knew better. This place had seen more shit recently than Pompeii after Vesuvius erupted.

Falcon waved his hand and the chain link fence that served as *security* opened up, allowing us to pass. A moment later, we drove through the glamour, revealing how things really were. Thankfully, that didn't include a *Pacific Rim* sized fish monster waiting for us, but the damage it had left behind was still evident – including the rotting remains of the dead naga.

"My goddess," Christy whispered, seeing the carnage.

"Fairly sure she has nothing to do with this shit," Tom replied.

I, however, was far more interested in the lone figure I spied waiting for us – sitting on a crate just outside the wreckage, casually polishing an oversized handgun as if all this were the most normal thing in the world to her.

Sadly, these days that might've actually been true.

I noted Sally's hair was back to its full brilliant green, the dye job she'd gotten from Alfonzo having finally given up the ghost. Nevertheless, she was a sight for sore eyes.

Needless to say, we barely waited for the car to come to a halt before hopping out and double-timing it across the pier to where she waited.

"Hey, guys," she lazily called out as we neared her, a disturbingly pleasant smile on her lips as she placed the weapon down next to her, "I don't know about the rest of you, but I hope your day's been more interesting than mine."

I stopped dead in my tracks. *Motherfucker!* Falcon had somehow managed to drug her again.

However, a moment later the easygoing grin turned into a smirk. "Oh, lighten up, Bill. I was just fucking with you."

I glared at her. "I thought you were dead."

"We all did," Ed added.

"Like that's the first time you've ever been wrong where I'm concerned."

The impasse broken, we all stepped in for a group hug, even if a part of me was tempted to deck her instead. If there were any punches to be thrown, though, they were best saved for a certain little birdie who was finally catching up to us.

"How did you...?" Christy started.

Sally held up a hand before turning to Falcon. "Are we good to talk?"

He shrugged. "As good as we're going to get I'm afraid."

"It is what it is. And it's not like I can hide forever. That insurance claim isn't going to file itself, y'know." She turned Tom's way. "I see you made it out okay."

"The coven, too," I replied. "He saved them all."

"Huh. Will miracles never cease? Guess they're right. A blind squirrel does occasionally catch an acorn. Glad I didn't bet against you for once."

"He told us what you did," Christy said. "Thank you."

Sally waved her off. "You think I'm just gonna let a building fall on him after all the shit we went through getting his stupid ass back?"

Tom grinned. "You're like my guardian Lorna Dane."

"Uh huh, I'll pretend that means something. Anyway, since you're all probably wondering, the truth is all of this is because of him." She hooked a thumb Falcon's way.

"The good and the bad I'm afraid," he replied, stepping forward.

I raised an eyebrow. If we were about to hear how he changed his mind at the last second, digging her out because he realized the error of his ways, it would probably keep him alive – but might not stop us from tearing his fucking mustache off and pissing on it.

"Explain," Christy said.

"Matt showed up at my place around three a.m. asking to be buzzed in."

"And you let him up?" I asked.

"Yep, after double checking that my gun was loaded, of course."

"Which I can't fault you for," Falcon replied in a conciliatory tone. "I will admit, I was a bit ... put out after our confrontation at my hotel room. But, after thinking about it, I realized, good intentions aside, my actions were uncalled for. I should have treated you like an adult, not as a..."

"Ticking time bomb?"

"More or less."

How ... heartwarming. Coming soon to the Hallmark Channel: the story of a rich wizard who rethinks a life spent drugging women against their will and learns to love again.

"So anyway," Sally said, "I let him in, then almost shot him anyway once I saw he was carrying that stupid ass bracelet."

The rest of us turned his way as he held up his hands. "It's not like that, I can assure you."

"He's right," she continued. "He was actually there to warn me. Told me his relatives were in town and what their plan was. I'll admit, I was a bit skeptical at first."

Falcon nodded, still in apology mode. "And rightfully so."

"But hey, what can I say? Something about a British accent makes shit sound so much more sincere. So we sat down and made a plan of our own."

As she explained it, the entire standoff was staged. Falcon left to go rendezvous with his aunt, having given her some bullshit about working a case. In the meantime, Sally waited for them to raise their barrier spell, knowing if she acted too early it would tip them off that she was in the know.

We knew what came next – rousing Tom and the coven so they could escape through the subbasement exit. Falcon's aunt wasn't after them, so it would've simply seemed a desperation move on their part had they been detected.

That's about when Sally came to the front door and gave them that dog and pony show.

"I suspected the barrier would cause her powers to react, having already seen the effect an overload of magic has on her," Falcon explained. "In all fairness, though, I didn't expect her to level the entire building in the process."

Sally rolled her eyes. "Trust me, I wasn't trying to. All my stuff was there."

"And this is why people masturbate," Tom said. "You keep that shit pent up too long and it gets all over everything."

She narrowed her eyes. "Why exactly did I save your ass again?"

"Forget about that," I said. "I'm more interested in how you walked away without a scratch after dropping said building on yourself."

"That's where the bracelet came in. You probably didn't notice in all the confusion, but I was wearing it around my ankle. Matt recalibrated the teleporter…"

"Sending spell," he corrected.

"Whatever the fuck. Do you want to tell this story? Anyway, he fixed it to go off at the first sign of explosive kinetic discharge, which zapped me here before the whole place could come down on top of my head."

Holy shit. That was actually pretty clever of him. Much as a part of me still didn't want to trust Falcon after the last week, I forced myself to eat crow. "Thank you."

"My pleasure, Freewill."

I turned back toward Sally before things could get too sappy. "Why didn't you tell any of us? We were losing our minds thinking you were..."

"Which is exactly your problem," she interrupted. "You should leave the thinking to those who are better at it. But to answer your question, I tried. I came looking for you after Matt left, but *someone* wasn't there."

Oh.

"Bill went out for coffee," Tom replied.

"Really?" Sally asked, raising an eyebrow. "Because I checked the security feed and it showed you coming in with the meathead, but not leaving again."

"That was my fault," Christy said sheepishly. "I wanted ... coffee, too, so I popped in and got Bill."

"Seriously?" Tom cried. "You could have woken me up if you guys were going out. I drink that shit too, you know."

"You looked kinda tired," I replied.

"Fuck that. You just wanted a coffee date without me."

Sally, no idiot, smirked. "I'm guessing there wasn't enough nondairy *creamer* for three."

Ed snickered in response, the asshole.

"Um yeah, something like that." Was it hot out there or was it me? "But anyway, why didn't you tell Tom then?"

She shrugged as if that wasn't even a consideration. "Because he's an even worse liar than you are."

Goddamn, talk about picking the absolute worst night to disappear for a booty call.

"The important thing is you're okay," Christy said, no

doubt trying to steer us away from that minefield. She stepped forward and put a hand on Falcon's shoulder. "I'm sorry, Matthias. I was wrong to judge you."

"Not entirely," he replied. "Alas, my aunt's right, I am somewhat caught beneath her boot heel, or at least I need to pretend to be, but enough of my ruse. At this point it's more important to focus on why it was even necessary to begin with. I'll admit to being caught off guard by her arrival, and with barely an hour's warning at that. It's unlike her."

"How so?"

"I don't say this for a laugh, Christine, but Marjorie absolutely loathes the states and this city in particular. The fact that all of this was in part due to outside influence is equally worrying."

"Hold on," I said. "Outside influence?"

"Yes," he explained. "You have to understand the history of my family to know why this is unusual. The Falcon clan have always been rather insular. Even with regards to the circle of Grand Mentors, we tend to keep our own counsel on matters of importance."

"My own counsel will I keep," Tom and I said almost simultaneously in Yoda-speak.

"And now I wish I'd let the building fall on me," Sally muttered.

Falcon glanced between the three of us for a moment, before Christy bade him to go on. "Anyway, between my family, the academy's instructors, and the Archive itself, it's rare for us to accept outside advice before choosing to act." He paused for a moment, letting out a long sigh. "However, it's positively unprecedented for us to take said advice from those within the vampire nation."

"Wait, vampires talked to your aunt?" I asked, all thoughts of *Star Wars* fleeing in an instant.

"Not vampires," he replied. "Just the one, I'm afraid. But I fear she was enough."

I didn't need for him to finish to feel my eyes blacken in anger. There wasn't anyone else he could be talking about.

"Gan."

30

WHEN TWO TRIBES GO TO WAR

"Let's back up for a second here, Hoss. Why did Gan reach out to your aunt?"

Considering what had happened, I had a feeling I knew the answer but wanted to hear it anyway.

"I'm not entirely certain," Falcon replied. "Whatever the case, it seems to have stirred up quite the hornet nest among the Board of Trustees regarding Sally here. Far more than my last report certainly did."

"What exactly was in that report, if I may be so bold to ask?" Ed replied.

"Not a great deal I'm afraid. Most of it was dedicated to the creature that attacked this pier, and my subsequent inability to identify it." He glanced Sally's way. "No offense, but you only received a passing mention, a note that your case was progressing following a slight setback."

"Drugging me was a slight setback?"

"No, but your finding out about it was."

He really needed to learn more about Sally's nuances. Just because she hadn't shot him yet didn't mean the option wasn't still on the table.

"Regardless, before today the Board, and my aunt in particular, had seemed mostly disinterested in my coming here, thinking I was off sowing my oats or some such nonsense. As if I'd actually leave Gerald behind for no other reason than to get a bit of adventure out of my system."

"Gerald?" Tom asked.

"My husband of course."

"Your hus ... oh!" He turned my way and smirked. "You are such a fucking dumbass, dude."

"Takes one to know one."

"At some point in the last few days, however, this Gansetseg somehow managed to make direct contact with Marjorie. How, I'm uncertain. The Falcon family has had few dealings with the First Coven over the centuries, much less recently. None of that lot should have been able to reach any of the trustees, not without going through several layers of security first." Almost as an afterthought, he added, "Which I would've heard about."

I was finally convinced he hadn't been lying to us about working with Gan to reopen The Source. Anyone who'd ever met her would almost certainly not be surprised to learn she'd figured out a way to game the system in her favor.

"What did they talk about?" Christy asked, looking none too pleased.

Sally let out a mirthless laugh. "I'm gonna go out on a limb here and assume it was me."

"You're not incorrect," Falcon replied, "albeit I'm not privy to the specifics. All I know is that Marjorie contacted me in the middle of the night, letting me know she'd be arriving post haste. When I asked the reason why, she accused me of downplaying the severity of one of my cases, stating that my methods of *containment* were woefully inadequate. There was only one case that came to mind."

"So, rather than set out tea and crumpets, you headed over to Sally's?" Ed opined.

"Precisely. I know my aunt's predilection for ceremony,

so I properly assumed there was more than enough time to do so without being missed."

"I guess my question is why?" When Sally raised an eyebrow, I clarified, "No offense, but why help her? I mean, a few weeks back you were clamping that bracelet on her wrist and warning her not to take it off."

"I'll admit, my initial reaction was based on knowing her history as a vampire." Before I could say something to that, he added, "Following our first meeting, Freewill, I, of course, did my due diligence with regards to your known associates. One of the perks of the job."

"Are we talking wizard or cop here?"

"Yes," he replied. "Regardless, it's a stance I've since come to rethink. That you all came to my aid when my humble pier was besieged, despite having no reason to, went a long way toward changing that opinion." He turned to face her. "There's also the fact that, despite having good reason to, you didn't shoot me at the Lotte. Needless to say, I now believe that, whatever may have befallen you, it was through no fault or desire of your own."

Sally shrugged. Considering she'd gotten this power after shooting Gan in the face, I had a feeling there was maybe a wee bit of desire involved. But perhaps it was best to keep that little factoid to ourselves.

Christy had been mostly quiet for the last part of his tale. When she finally spoke again, though, it wasn't what I was expecting. "Am I correct in assuming this pier is warded against sending?"

Falcon inclined his head. "Most of my protective glyphs have been buggered to hell and back, but yes. I placed a few sending wards around the periphery this morning."

"A wise precaution."

"Hopefully. Anyway, so I was thinking our next step should be to..."

"No," she interrupted. "*Your* next step is to return to

your aunt. Find out whatever you can and throw her off our scent for as long as possible. We'll take care of the rest."

We will?

"Not that easy, I'm afraid. My aunt's crew got dinged up a bit, but nothing that'll hamper their efforts. It won't take them long to get past the NYPD's security measures and determine the building was empty at the time of its collapse. Once that happens..."

"We'll be ready, now that we know they're coming."

I glanced toward the rest of our group, not sure where Christy was going with this as her face was currently unreadable. If my friends had any insight, though, they weren't sharing. Or at least two of them weren't.

"It's time, isn't it?" Sally replied.

Both Falcon and I turned toward her. "Time for...?"

"You've done enough here, Matthias," Christy interrupted again. "I'm grateful. I truly am, but I have to insist you don't put yourself at further risk on our behalf."

He actually chuckled at that. "Risk is all part of the..."

"I'm serious. Please."

I wasn't sure what she was getting at. I mean, yeah, it was good to have an inside man keeping an eye on the old hag before she went all aggro on us again. All the same, I wasn't sure where that left us, as we were rapidly running out of safe havens to retreat and regroup.

Christy and Falcon locked eyes in a silent battle of wills ... for a few moments anyway.

"Very well. If you insist," he said at last.

"I do, not to mention you look like you could use the rest."

"I won't lie and pretend I couldn't do with a cuppa."

She nodded. "Come on, I'll walk you out."

Falcon inclined his head our way before following her. "I'd tell you to help yourself to whatever's in the ice chest, but you'd have to find it first under all of this mess."

Talk about giving me the opposite of a warm fuzzy. I

turned toward the Hudson. The surface was calm for the moment, but that didn't mean much. Twice now that thing had appeared out of nowhere, in water that wasn't nearly deep enough to hide something of its size.

How the hell could something do that?

Fuck it. So long as it didn't show up in the next few minutes, let it be someone else's problem. Right then, we had a coven of asshole mages to deal with – precisely the kind of dickheads that had made me firmly against reopening The Source to begin with.

Goddamn, when did we become such trouble magnets? All I wanted was to wake up next to a smoking hot witch and hang out with my friends, preferably not at the same time. Was that so much to ask for?

"We're gonna have to kill them, you know that right?" Sally said after a few minutes, breaking the silence that had descended – albeit not in any positive way. "All of them."

If I'd had any doubts that Falcon's magical happy juice had worn off, that silenced them for good.

Crap. Five years of not killing anyone or having anyone try to kill us. Now here we were, barely two months into this new world of magic and casually talking about bumping off an old lady in the most violent way possible.

And the worst part was, I couldn't even disagree. *People* tended to be able to talk out their differences, in small groups anyway. It didn't always work, but there was at least a chance.

But we weren't people, at least not anymore, not fully. Violence and the supernatural went hand in hand. Where vampires and Magi were concerned, though, you could add a healthy dollop of arrogance to the mix. And Marjorie was obviously old school when it came to this shit. Much as I hated to admit it, our best bet for convincing her to back off was probably snapping her spine. I said as much.

"Oh yeah," Ed groused. "There's no way Kara's not dumping my ass."

"You do realize you gotta call her first for that to happen, right?"

"You mean you haven't yet?" Sally replied, as if that were the most interesting thing going on. "That's the kind of pussy shit I'd expect from Bill, not you."

I glanced at her sidelong. "Don't drag me into this crap."

"Dude," Tom said, ignoring me, "I know my sister's type. She digs bad boys. You break that old bag's neck and she won't be able to rip her panties off fast enough."

"Remind me to never take romantic advice from you."

"Hey, you're the one who started banging her after I died. I'm just trying to help your sad ass out since you're still ignoring her."

"I'm not ignoring her," he said. "I ... just don't want to bring her into this while we're being hunted by all this crazy shit."

"When are we not?" Sally asked. "I mean, seriously, you act like all this is new."

I heard Falcon's car start, distracting me from my friends' increasingly inane small talk. Glancing that way, I saw the shimmer of air as he passed through the glamour and accelerated away from us.

Christy watched him go but then, instead of heading back in our direction, she started walking toward the street. I was about to call out, wondering where she was going, when she stopped and turned back – a soft yellow glow suffusing her body.

What the?

Sally was right, she said, her voice echoing in my mind instead of my ears. Just what I needed, even more voices in my head.

"Right?" I asked, unsure whether this was a one way street or not. "About...?"

There's no choice. We have to end this. The longer we

wait, the worse it's going to get.

Huh? "Wait. What are we...?"

She'll fill you in on the way.

Looking back, I saw that the rest of our group had apparently gotten the broadcast too – except for Tom who continued yammering on, magic being an absolute null to him.

"Fill us in on what?" I called out.

I need to take care of some stuff first, she continued. *Find a car and meet me up in Salisbury Mills. Ed knows where to go. Park about half a mile away. I'll find you.*

"The fuck?"

The broadcast abruptly ended. Christy turned and continued walking, passing through the glamour and out onto the street beyond. For a moment, I considered going after her. With my speed, it wouldn't be a...

Before I could take a single step, though, her body lit up like a magnesium flare and then she was gone.

"Is it me or did that Falcon guy specifically say *not* to do that?" Tom asked, finally noticing what was happening.

"It's called being an independent woman," Sally replied before turning toward the rest of us. "All right then. Since I'm guessing none of us have any other plans tonight, what say we get to stealing a car?"

"Wait," he said. "Why are we stealing a car?"

"Because Christy asked us to, duh."

"She did?"

"Yeah," Ed replied, looking none too pleased. "I guess this was finally the straw that broke the camel's back."

"What camel?"

I turned Ed's way, having a sinking feeling I knew the answer to my next question. "What's in Salisbury Mills?"

"The estate where I was held prisoner," he replied after a long moment. "I guess we're finally doing it. We're going after Gan."

Somehow I knew he was going to say that, although I couldn't lie and pretend it made me feel any better.

31

THE ROAD TO RUIN

"**W**-who, what are you?"

"Isn't it obvious?" the glowing figure in the road replied. "I'm ... *the blessed one,* an angel sent from the Lord himself. Fear me, foolish mortal!"

"Y-you are?"

"*Now,*" Sally whispered to me, her strange green eyes aglow as we hid in the shadows next to a dumpster, "before the idiot fucks it up."

"Now what?" I asked.

"The driver's distracted. Punch his fucking lights out."

"Why me?"

"Because you're the one with vampire strength, and you need the practice."

"Why do I need to practice punching innocent people in the face?"

"Fine. Then you can practice covering your balls instead, because if that guy gets away with our car I'm cutting yours off."

Most of what were parked in the neighborhood closest to the pier were late model cars, probably a testament to the fact that a good chunk of the old buildings there had been converted into high priced apartments. Sadly, that gave us a much better shot of setting off an alarm than hotwiring anything. So that left us the next best thing – a good old fashioned carjacking.

Ed was working as our spotter, keeping an eye out for breaks in the traffic so we could hopefully strike without being seen. Tom was running point as our distraction, stepping into the street and lighting up like a beacon. His aura was bright enough to dazzle a driver and, on the off chance they didn't stop, it would protect him from being run over – in theory anyway. As for the shit he was saying, well, maybe we should've written a script first.

That left Sally and I to do the dirty work, which mostly meant me.

"When you put it that way," I muttered before racing out into the street.

"Jesus knows you've been masturbating," Tom continued, blazing like a burning road flare. "He wants you to stop wanking your crank."

"My wha... oof!"

I was there in the next instant, slamming my fist through the open driver's side window and dropping the guy like a bad habit.

"Good shot, Bill!" Tom cried, dousing his aura.

"Could you maybe not say my name in the middle of a crime?" I snapped at him.

"Oh yeah, sorry. Good shot ... um, Pedro."

Dumbass! I turned back toward the fellow I'd clocked, my mind going blank, likely due to it being some time since I'd casually committed felonies out in the open like this. "Um ... what should I do with him?"

"How the fuck should I know? You're the one who hit him."

"Well ... think of something!"

"Wait! I've got it. Stuff him in the trunk. That always works."

"Yeah. Good idea." I opened the door, unhooked his seatbelt, then quickly located the trunk release. Thankfully, vampire strength made tossing this guy over my shoulder no more difficult than carrying a bag of groceries.

I stepped to the rear of the car as Ed broke cover and hopped into the driver's seat, mostly because he knew where we were going.

"What the hell are you doing?" Sally asked just as I slammed the lid shut on the sedan's roomy cargo space.

"Putting him in the trunk."

"Why the fuck would you do that?"

"Because Tom told me to."

"You two idiots deserve each other, you know that right?"

"Okay, so what was I supposed to do with him?"

"Anything but that!"

"Should I take him out?"

"No. Just leave him and get in the car. We've wasted enough time as it is."

"Wow, you're snippy when you're not on drugs."

"Do I need to remind you that I brought my gun?"

"That's not much of a plan."

"It's not supposed to be," Sally replied. "The more moving parts, the better chance of someone fucking it up, meaning you or the meathead."

"Okay, so let me see if I have this straight," I said. "We're just doing some reconnaissance first. If things look quiet, we make our move. But otherwise..."

"Exactly," she interrupted. "Just play it cool once we're there and we'll figure the rest out as we go."

From the driver's seat, Ed threw a look our way via the rearview mirror.

Sally locked eyes on him. "Got a comment from the peanut gallery?"

"No. I'm just ... making sure this is the way we want to do this."

"Want is debatable, but I think it's our best shot."

"Okay," he replied. "If you say so."

Guess he was in agreement with me. Still, that didn't mean we had to be stupid about it. "Head to Brooklyn first," I told him.

"Why? Christy said..."

"I know what she said, but if we're potentially going all Alamo on Gan's ass, we should at least grab a few things first."

"Like what?" Tom asked from the shotgun seat.

"Like your sword for instance, dipshit. You know, that thing you forgot to bring when we left for Christy's."

"Get off my ass, dude. It's been a stressful day."

"Try having a building dropped on you," Sally grumbled.

"Oh, you should grab your old Templar armor while you're at it," I said, ignoring her.

"Why?"

"Because it's fucking armor, that's why. You think I wouldn't be grabbing a Kevlar vest if I had one?"

"No way. That shit is lame."

"I dunno. Sheila always looked good in it," Ed remarked. Then, after a beat, he added, "What? She did."

He wasn't wrong.

"And that's precisely why I'm not wearing it," Tom replied. "You two fucks can jack off to some other cosplay fantasy. Not to mention, it pinches in the vag."

"I take back everything," Sally said. "Do what Gan asked and put me out of my misery."

"Oh come on," I told her. "You missed this and you know it."

"Maybe, but at least back then I could always look forward to the Feet smashing my skull in if it got to be too much."

"Don't worry," Ed replied. "I've seen where we're headed. There's all sorts of fun ways for us to die up there."

"There you go, threatening me with a good time again."

Our stop in Brooklyn made and the banter played out, we headed toward upstate NY, the discussion in the car giving way to silence.

Well, almost anyway.

Thud, thud.

"Let me out! Please! I didn't see anything, I swear. Just..."

Sally turned and glared at me as I smiled sheepishly back.

Heh. In all the excitement, guess we'd forgotten to dump that guy back when we'd stopped.

"Knock it the fuck off," Sally cried, elbowing the seat behind her.

"I have money!"

"And I have a gun, which I will use to shoot you through this fucking seat if you don't shut up. Am I clear?"

Silence resumed, for a moment anyway.

"Okay," I remarked, "so maybe bringing him wasn't the best idea."

"Ya think?"

"Sorry, I don't react well under pressure."

"No shit," Tom said, "Hey, remember when we first moved into the apartment and kept getting all those stupid magazines every month, like Crochet World and Fishing Digest."

"Oh yeah," Ed replied. "All because Bill couldn't say no to some telemarketer."

"It was only for a year and then I cancelled," I told Sally.

She let out a sigh. "How the fuck are you still alive again?"

"Just lucky to have good friends, I suppose."

"Better than all the enemies we seem to make," Ed groused.

"Tell me about it." Tom turned around to face me. "I don't know what it is about witches, man, but they don't seem to like you much."

I glared at him. "I can think of one who does."

"I'm sure she'll eventually come around to the idea of *alternate* lifestyles. And when she does..."

"Yeah, about that," Sally said. "Not whatever your dumbass point was, I meant Falcon's aunt."

"What about her?"

"Does anyone else think something stinks about all of this?"

I shrugged. "Well, she was kind of old. Had that mothball smell hanging around her."

"Not that, idiot. Gan. Remember what Falcon said, that he was surprised she was able to get through to his aunt?"

"What about it?"

"People like that, old money I mean, you don't exactly find their direct number in the phone book. Hell, anyone trying to cold call me at the Pandora Foundation had to get through at least three layers of receptionists first, and that assumed I was in the mood to pick up."

I considered this. Gan was the type who specialized in being in the know, and I sincerely doubted even the Falcon family's wealth compared to the vast resources she'd inherited from the First Coven. If Gan truly wanted to reach out and touch someone, I didn't doubt she could.

But that led to a whole other problem. Marjorie was an old school witch. That much was painfully obvious.

There was none of that new age "let's all be friends" vibe about her that we'd gotten from others. Liz and her vampire dildo Komak, for example, had given us a whole hippy-dippy spiel about the old ways being dead – all while holding us at gunpoint, mind you. Nevertheless, they'd obviously found common ground, working together in ways that vamps and witches usually didn't.

Marge, however, didn't strike me as the progressive type. That meant she was likely full of herself up to her highbred eyeballs.

The thing was, it also probably meant she considered vampires to be lower than trampled dog shit.

"Kind of funny how Gan was able to convince her to act, isn't it?" Sally asked, giving voice to my thoughts.

Ed scoffed. "Hell, remember those witches up in Canada? We were just barely able to convince them not to kill us ... and that was supposed to be a peace conference."

I nodded. "Exactly. Or when Harry Decker blew up the Loft, along with everyone in it. Afterward, James couldn't even get the fucker to so much as apologize."

Don't remind me, the voice in my head replied as Sally pretty much said the same thing.

Um, yeah. Whatever. "Anyway, you all get the point. In the past, witches like Marge would've sooner swallowed cyanide than ask a vamp for the time of day."

Ed glanced at me in the rearview mirror. "And yet one phone call and she was willing to travel three thousand miles to cause a terrorist scare in an American city known for being paranoid about those things."

"I take back what I said," Tom remarked. "Witches *definitely* don't like you."

"That," I replied, "or they're already in Gan's back pocket."

I remembered back to that day, just before The Source was reopened. All had seemed to be going well, but then Tom and I had stumbled onto a hidden cache of supplies and communications equipment. We'd suspected Komak was behind it, but that had been nothing more than a red herring.

Gan had pulled a fast one at the last second. Once she gave the word, at least a quarter of the Magi there had abruptly donned black robes and set forth to do her bidding.

Plenty had died during the ensuing scuffle, but many more had escaped – no doubt to ditch their fetish wear and pretend everything was hunky dory now that magic was back. The thing was, Christy suspected that had merely been the tip of the iceberg – something I didn't doubt. There'd almost certainly been others involved. At the very least, there were those Magi present at the other sites – the hidden spots where they'd worked to set up thirteen new Sources, thirteen portals to beyond the veil, opening up the floodgates of magic in ways not seen in millennia.

Who knew how far it stretched, how many Magi she'd gotten to go along with her mad scheme? It wouldn't have even been difficult to do – the promise of getting their powers back more than enough to convince most. Even Christy had admitted it would've been a tough bounty to turn down.

That was the real problem. How many were, even now, still beholden to her? Hell, owing Gan even a single favor was a terrible price to pay, because she was someone who never forgot a debt.

That settled it as far as I was concerned. Falcon had assured us he'd known nothing of Gan's plot, and had since earned the benefit of the doubt. But who was to say his organization, his family even, hadn't been a part of it? And wouldn't this Board of Trustees be in prime position to stonewall any efforts on his part to dig deeper?

The more I thought about it, the more it made sense, and the more it made sense, the less I liked it.

32

STAND OFFISH

I had to hand it to Gan. Of all the things we'd prepared for following her sudden reappearance at my place, finding out she'd called in favors from one of the top Magi families in the world wasn't one of them.

Everyone has a price, I told myself as we crossed the town line into Salisbury Mills. *Even when they're already filthy rich.*

There was a rustic feel to the town proper, a real salt of the Earth vibe. At the same time, as we continued onward, I began to see signs of there being a whole other social class who called this place home.

Quaint homesteads gave way to farmhouses, and those gradually gave way to McMansions before continuing even further up the food chain.

No doubt about it. This was a county that was trying to figure out its identity – spacious and old timey on the one hand, but with plenty of the rich raising property values as they bought large tracts of land within which to erect their personal strongholds.

Ed stopped at an intersection, looked around for a bit, then eventually turned left.

"You do know where this place is, right?"

"Not really."

"But Christy said..."

He shook his head. "I know where it is in a general sense. I mean, it's not like the people there didn't talk. But as I told Christy, I mostly only saw it from *inside* the gates. So..."

"You have no fucking idea where we're going," Tom surmised.

"More or less. Not helped by you two stealing the one car in the city without a working GPS."

"Yeah, because GPS works so well when you don't know the address."

Sally made a sound of disgust. "I knew I should've kept some of Falcon's drugs handy."

I nodded. "Can't say I wouldn't accept a hit of happiness right about now."

"Give me a break," Ed groused from the driver seat. "It's not like I'd planned to ever find this place again, at least not until recently. Excuse me for not becoming Gan's Stockholm Syndrome gimp."

"If at first you don't succeed..."

"Yeah, about that. Don't let her capture me again, even if it means..."

"Seriously?" I asked wide-eyed.

"No, not seriously, dumbass. Just do a better fucking job of rescuing me next time."

"At least you acknowledge there probably will be a next time," Tom said with a smirk.

"Eat my unholy ass, *Blessed One*."

We drove around for far longer than we should've. There weren't that many estates capable of housing Gan's base of operations, but there were enough – all of them on tracts of land with ample space to hide the main house from the road. If we picked the wrong one, well, that was yet another felony to add to the evening's growing list of crimes.

I was almost beginning to reach the fuck it stage, figuring we could choose one at random, toss Tom over the fence, and then see if a tactical team descended on his ass. But, as we turned down one dark lonely stretch of road, I realized that might not be necessary after all.

"There!" Ed cried, pointing up ahead.

I followed his lead and spied a woman standing on the side of the road, along with a misshapen thing next to her that could've been a dog ... maybe.

"It's just some chick walking her mutt," Tom said.

Nice of a night as it was, I doubted that was the case.

Ed glanced at him for a moment, shook his head, then pulled over to the shoulder, the headlights illuminating Christy and Glen.

"What took you so long?" she asked as we got out of the car.

"We let Ed drive."

"Bite me," he said.

"Depending on how this goes, I may need to."

"Bark!"

I looked down at Glen. "You do realize you probably don't need to wear that where we're going, right?"

His two mismatched eyeballs blinked a few times. "How else am I going to catch our foes by surprise?"

"Um, fair point I suppose. I... Hey, who's watching Cat?"

"Her name's Cheetara, dude," Tom replied. "But yeah, what Bill said, but pretend I asked first."

A small part of me was disheartened that Christy had kept her word and left Tina behind, as the tyke likely possessed the power to rip through Gan's defenses like a fat man opening a Big Mac. However, the rest of me was relieved, mostly because I wasn't an inhuman monster – at least on the inside.

"Her Aunt Kelly will be taking good care of her until this is over."

Okay, that worked. I still wasn't sure what Kelly and Vincent had been up to on their little lover's retreat, aside from fucking, but there was no doubt in my mind they'd both protect Tina with their lives if necessary. Although, hopefully it didn't come down to that.

Sally hooked a thumb Ed's way. "So how'd you manage to find this place when a certain someone kept driving us around in circles?"

Christy shrugged. "Mind magic. I pulled the images from his memory last week."

Amazing how mundane that almost sounded coming from her mouth.

She flashed me a smile. "Fortunately, Matthias's aunt isn't the only one with access to forgotten scrying magic. I was able to use the spell to pinpoint where Ed's presence had recently left a heavy psychic imprint. From there, well, I've been trying to learn whatever I could in the time I've had."

Huh. And here I'd been mostly scouring YouTube for shitty sea serpent videos.

"Look at you going all *Mission Impossible*," Tom replied, pulling his gear from the back seat.

Speaking of gear, I noticed Christy was brandishing a backpack, one of Cat's judging by the Winx Club logo emblazoned on it.

She inclined her head Sally's way. "I have those supplies we talked about, if you're still willing to..."

"Oh definitely," Sally said. "Now more than ever."

"Wait," I replied. "What supplies are you...?"

"Please let me out! I can't breathe in here! I won't talk, I swear."

Oh yeah, I'd almost forgotten about Trunk Guy. He certainly had a healthy set of lungs for someone who claimed to not be able to breathe.

"What was that?" Christy asked, as Glen spun toward the car and let out a series of pathetic barks.

"Oh, that's just the guy the two dipshit brothers here kidnapped," Sally remarked. "You know, because stealing a car wasn't a big enough thrill."

Christy raised an eyebrow but I was ready for that. Before Tom could say anything, I pointed a finger at him. "Don't look at me. It was all his idea."

I hated for Christy to waste any power before a potential throw down, but I hated the idea of going to jail a lot more. Sometimes you gotta pick the lesser of evils.

Thankfully, she was up to the task. I figured she'd maybe zap the guy with mind magic, then let him wander off into the night to ... I dunno, probably get eaten by a bobcat or something.

Instead, she placed her hands on the trunk, causing it to light up brightly from within. A moment later, the man's surprised cries ceased.

Jesus H. Christ!

"Holy shit," Tom cried. "Did you just fry that fucker? Hardcore."

"I didn't fry anyone." She popped the trunk, revealing it to be empty. "I sent him back."

"Hold on. I thought Falcon said his aunt was keeping an eye out for that shit."

"So he did. That's why I sent him back ... to the Bronx. It'll give them a wild goose to chase." She threw Tom and I some side-eye. "As well as hopefully make the gentleman in question's story a lot less believable when he goes to the police."

Okay, point to her for thinking this through better than us.

"Should we wipe the car for prints just to be safe?" Ed asked, as Tom stepped away to put his chainmail on.

Christy was on that particular ball, too. Her body glowed yellow, right before the vehicle itself took on the same hue for a second or two. "Done."

"Um, should you be using your magic like that?" I asked. "I mean, it kind of feels like firing all of our bullets before the gunfight even starts."

She smiled. "It's okay. I've brought a couple of extra clips with me." *What?* "Besides, those spells take up less power than battle magic, not that it really matters."

"It doesn't?" Maybe she didn't expect tonight to amount to much, which I couldn't say would bother me. If things went south, though, it's not like we could fight Gan with nice words alone.

"Not at all," Glen said, quivering with barely concealed excitement inside his corgi costume.

I raised an eyebrow. "And why's that?"

"Because we'll be too busy marching up to the gates."

"What for?"

"So we can surrender, of course."

"Oh, it'll be so exciting."

I opened my mouth, fully intent on asking Glen when he'd lost his gelatinous mind, but Sally stepped in first.

"Okay, enough dicking around. It's probably safe to assume the hills have eyes and ears this close to Gan's place. Time to zip it for everything but small talk."

I was about to say something when Christy replied, "She's right. We need to go."

Hopefully Glen was just fucking around to lighten the mood a bit.

I mean, it's not like Gan would take us into custody, spill the beans on her nefarious plan, then allow us to make with some James Bond-esque escape after pushing her into a tank full of sharks – awesome as that sounded.

That was all well and good for the movies, but this was

reality. Gan didn't fuck around. She was just as likely to order everyone else's immediate execution before spending eternity trying to stuff her tongue into my various orifices.

I was all for taking one for the team if necessary, but that seemed a bit over the top even to me.

As Tom rejoined us, I realized nobody else appeared to be freaking out. Guess I was overreacting. I probably needed to have a word with the little blob about his sense of humor when it came to Gan, but oh well. It's not like a little levity could hurt at a time like this.

About as ready as we were going to get, we set off down the road in relative silence, with Christy taking the lead as she obviously had more of a clue where we were going.

As we walked, a reinforced wall became visible just past the trees to our left, running parallel to wherever we were headed.

"This is starting to look familiar," Ed remarked.

"Good," Christy said. "Because it's time for a distraction."

I turned her way. "What kind of...?"

Alas, it was a moot point as her body lit up bright blue. For a moment, nothing else happened, making me think her strategy involved little more than a light show. Then there came an electric sizzle from all around us, followed by sparks falling from every tree in sight.

"What did you do?"

Sally let out a whistle of appreciation. "Off the top of my head I'd say she shorted out their entire security system along this stretch."

Christy raised a finger to her nose. I fully expected her to tell us to make a break for the wall, but she instead kept ambling along as if this were nothing more than a pleasant moonlit stroll.

More and more I was starting to get a bad feeling about this. It wasn't helped by the fact that purposely walking into Gan occupied space made my balls want to shrivel up and die in my pants. That was okay, though. If things went badly, I'm sure the extra space in my jeans would rapidly be filled with shit.

Regardless, I couldn't help but feel I'd been left out of the loop on something. Why was Christy going off script on what was supposed to be a fact-finding mission, and why was Sally so fucking blasé about it? I kept waiting for one of them to change course and bolt over the wall.

At the same time, this was Gan's property, which meant there was no telling what awaited us inside – be it Mongolian Death Worms, crazed hordes of berserkers, landmines, or all the above.

Either way our window of opportunity was running out, as I spied a break in the trees up ahead – where the wall ended at both a heavy iron gate and a guardhouse before continuing on again past it off into the distance.

Whatever their play was, it needed to happen soon. The entrance ahead suddenly lit up like the middle of the day. Floodlights turned on and vehicles could be heard racing this way from the interior, not that there weren't plenty of folks already waiting for us. And yet Christy kept strolling right along, even as I slowed to a stop.

Something wasn't right here.

I grabbed Sally's arm. "Wait, are we actually surrendering?"

"We might be."

"Since when?"

She shrugged. "Since I may have left out a few details about our plan."

"What? Why?" I shook my head. "Fuck this noise. I'm calling it off."

Now it was Sally's turn to grab onto me instead. "Don't," she hissed. "It's too late anyway."

"Fuck that shit."

Her green eyes bored into mine. "If you've ever trusted me, Bill, trust me now when I say that trying to stop this, trying to stop Christy, would be a very bad idea."

I held her gaze for a long second. *Damn it all.* "Fine. But after this is over, we are having a seriously long talk."

"Deal. You can buy the drinks."

Christy, for her part, had fallen silent as several flashlight beams were pointed our way, despite my nose telling me a good chunk of the *people* up ahead were, in fact, neovamps.

Apparently Gan had modernized a bit since the early days, as I didn't notice any yak skins or horned helmets among the waiting minions. Nope, it was all crisp suits or tactical gear.

I continued to focus on Christy out of the corner of my eye, expecting her to do *something*, but she didn't appear in any hurry to do much more than enjoy the night air. If anything, she looked ridiculously calm.

Despite Sally's warning, it seemed unwise to let things continue as they were, especially with a good dozen of Gan's finest heading our way.

Fuck it!

I probably should've stayed the course and done as I'd been told, but that simply wasn't my forte. It was time to *improvise* ... by grabbing Ed and dragging him with me to the forefront, ahead of Christy.

"What say we go greet this welcome wagon, *Progenitor?*"

"What?!"

"Hey, at least you already know these guys. So ... I dunno ... say something to them."

Unfortunately, it was the space of a few seconds to realize I'd overestimated their mutual familiarity, because we suddenly found ourselves with several guns and tasers trained our way. Crap!

I see you are as sound a strategist as ever, the voice in my head opined.

Stuff it where the sun doesn't shine, asshole.

"The hell with this," Tom said from somewhere behind us.

A moment later, he strode up to our position.

"What the fuck are you doing?" I hissed, really hoping not to get shot.

"Making up for your bullshit by being awesome. Duh!"

I turned Christy's way to gauge her reaction, but she remained silent – seemingly content to let us take the lead here. Talk about poor timing for letting us grow into our roles.

"Oh, this is so exciting!" Glen opened his mouth wide, producing a tendril containing both an eyeball and his camera. It was so nice to see someone was enjoying this.

No doubt running with his own insane version of my failed improv idea, Tom stepped confidently in front of us before glancing over his shoulder. "You fuckers might want to back up a bit."

"Hands up!" one of the guards ordered. "Or we *will* open fire."

Don't let that hero thing from earlier go to your head, I mentally pleaded at him. *Now is not the time to ... oh, fuck me.*

Rather than do anything smart, Tom put his hand on his sword, still adorned with action figures. "I'd tell you cum stains to suck my dick, but how about sucking on this instead?"

He drew his blade in the same instant the guards opened fire, filling the night air with sound, fury, and blinding white light.

33

THE YELLOW ROSE OF SURRENDER

I 'll admit to silently kissing my ass goodbye. Vamps were tough, but enough lead could ruin our day just as thoroughly as anyone else's.

A moment later, though, I realized we were all still unharmed as Tom's aura continued to flare up, spreading out wide enough to provide the rest of us with cover.

Guess he really had been practicing.

Maybe a bit too much, as Ed and I quickly backpedaled, smoke already rising from my hands.

Fuck, that stings!

I had to hand it to Tom, though. A couple of weeks ago he could barely get his powers to turn on. Now he was wielding them, not quite at Sheila's level, but at least approaching the same ballpark.

Mind you, the plastic figurines tied to his sword and scabbard sort of ruined the whole badass warrior vibe, but whatever worked.

And it definitely did, as neither bullets nor taser darts penetrated his shield.

Cool as it was, however, I wasn't sure what it meant for the rest of us, especially since we were just standing there like morons while this played out.

"Christy?" I turned to face her, but she appeared oddly

tuned out toward everything that was going on. What? Were we boring her or something? Had she led us down this path then mentally checked out ahead of time due to apathy?

Doubtful, as that wasn't her style, but it's not like now was a particularly great time for insight.

"This is going to look so awesome in high definition," Glen cried, proving at least one of us was paying proper attention.

"Now you know, dick biscuits," Tom shouted as the barrage died down, his attackers no doubt realizing they weren't accomplishing shit. "And knowing is half the fucking battle."

Ugh! All at once I felt the urge to wade into the field of fire.

"Yeah, that's right," he continued. "I'm the Icon. That means anything you dish out, bounces off of me and sticks to you!"

I really needed to sit down with him at some point and explain the concept of witty banter.

Still, there was no denying...

That we were fucked, as three of the guards drew black-bladed knives instead. *Shit!* Had this been anyone else's fortress of solitude, I'd have laughed them off as merely painted that way for macho tactical bullshit reasons. But this was Gan's place, and she was fully aware of how best to fight an Icon – with blades that had been soaked in the blood of Baal, making them capable of penetrating Tom's shield.

I opened my mouth, prepared to shout a warning since my friend had just written a check with his mouth that these assholes were about to cash. However, before I could say anything, there came the roar of another engine closing in on our location.

A moment later, a vehicle came racing out of the now open gate – a side by side, the kind hunters and wilderness types favored. It skidded to a halt and a man leapt out. He had dark hair, dark eyes, a dark complexion, and a muscular build over a – say it with me now – dark suit.

"Stand down," he ordered, the authority in his voice evident. Then he stepped forward, seemingly not intimidated in the least. "Shining One, I presume."

"Um, do I know you, dude?" Tom asked, dialing back his lightshow.

"No. But I know you, or of you anyway." He stepped to the side, his gaze landing upon my other friend. "Didn't expect to see you back here so soon."

"Didn't expect to be back, Paladin," Ed replied with a sigh. "In fact, I was really hoping not to, but life's a prick like that."

So this was the guy he'd told us about, Gan's number one lackey. I was surprised. In the past, she'd surrounded herself with folks from her own neck of the woods who'd been raised to die at her whim. Yet somehow I had a feeling this guy's loyalties stopped short of committing seppuku whenever the wind blew in a direction that annoyed her. That didn't mean he wasn't dangerous, though.

Mind you, that never stopped me from throwing some shade. And since it looked like the organizer of this *plan* of ours had checked out, I guess it fell to me to at least put forth the illusion that we had some semblance of control here. "Personally, I always favored barbarians myself."

"A pleasure to finally make your acquaintance, Freewill," he said, an easy grin on his face.

"Should I assume my reputation proceeds me?"

"Not really. My employer has an entire hard drive full of data on you."

I wasn't surprised to hear it, yet was still infinitely creeped out nevertheless. Glad to see Gan could have that effect on me without even being present.

"Oh, and you may be surprised to learn this," he continued, "but the word paladin dates back much further than some board game. They were Emperor Constantine's elite bodyguards."

"Is that before or after *Justice League Dark*?"

"Huh?"

"And just for the record, I hope you multiclassed. Paladins in 5E just aren't what they used to be."

"Well, if this was a dork war, you'd certainly win," Sally said, finally speaking up and drawing Paladin's attention.

"Ma'am," he said with a nod to her. "If I'm not mistaken, you're Ms...."

"I'm Glen," the little corgi-wearing blob said, waddling forward. "Pleased to meet you."

It figured. This guy had the Icon, the Freewill, the Progenitor, a witch, and a green-haired Sally standing in front of him, but the thing that finally cracked his resolve a bit was Glen. Somehow that just made sense.

Mind you, it was only for a moment. The burly security chief stopped and raised a quizzical eyebrow the little blob's way before once again turning his attention toward Sally. "Ms. Carlsbad."

"She's dead," Sally replied. "So is Ms. Sunset. Still debating my other options."

"What happened to Sunrise?" I replied.

"Amazing how much less convincing that sounds when I'm not stoned."

Sobriety truly was wasted on her.

Finally, our *host* seemed to notice Christy, still standing there behind the rest of us as if she had all the time in the world. "Ah, you must be..."

"Surrendering," she interrupted, piping up as if finally noticing our predicament. "Along with the rest of my companions."

"Are you now?"

"Yes."

Paladin's feathers weren't so easily ruffled, though.

"Normally I'd send you all packing, no harm no foul. If we took every random gawker into custody, we'd never get anything else done. However, being that you just destroyed tens of thousands of dollars' worth of surveillance equipment, maybe I should turn you over to the police instead."

"Do you think the police are prepared for anyone like us?"

"No, I don't suppose they are."

"Good," Christy replied. "Then I repeat, we surrender ourselves to your custody. Please take us to your employer Gansetseg."

"I'll accept your surrender," he said with another nod, gesturing his people forward, "but I must regretfully inform you that my employer is not on the premises this evening."

"Wait," I said, "Gan's not here?" *Son of a...*

"I'm afraid not. She's offsite, attending to other matters. Now kindly surrender your weapons so I can figure out what to do with you – some of you anyway."

"Some of us?"

"Yes, the one's who'll eventually be allowed to leave. As for the rest, you should perhaps make yourselves comfortable as your stay here will be of a somewhat more permanent nature."

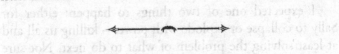

"This really isn't comfortable," I protested.

There was absolutely no doubt that Gan had prepared her crew for us. First they relieved us of our stuff – backpacks, Tom's sword, Sally's gun, et cetera – stowing them in the back of one of the vehicles.

They used normal handcuffs on Tom, while two guards flanked him with those black-bladed daggers. Extra heavy duty cuffs were the choice de jour for vampires such as Ed and me. For Christy, they unsurprisingly produced a set of sigil-etched manacles, the kind that dampened Magi powers.

Nobody seemed quite sure what to do with Glen. Paladin ordered him out of his disguise, but then, when one of his people tried to pick him up, he simply oozed out of their grasp like the ball of slime he was. Eventually, they had someone fetch a plastic storage tub to stick Glen in until they could come up with something better.

That left Sally.

She stood there looking bored as their guns remained trained on her. After a minute or so, she held up her hands. "Seriously? The one person here who actually likes handcuffs and you're not going to offer me a pair?"

"As if they would do any good, Ma'am," Paladin replied. "At least according to what I've been told. However, we do have a little something prepared for you."

"Oh? Breaking out the nipple clamps already?"

Paladin barely blinked at the suggestion, making me wonder if Gan had switched to hiring eunuchs. "Not exactly."

He gave a nod then, quick as a snake, a woman stepped in from behind Sally and jammed a syringe into her neck, quickly depressing the plunger.

Shit!

I expected one of two things to happen: either for Sally to collapse or explode with power – killing us all and at least solving the problem of what to do next. Not sure I'd have minded that latter option now that I knew we'd managed to storm the castle on the one night Gan was out playing cribbage – or whatever psychos did to relax when they weren't plotting world domination.

Neither happened, though. Instead, Sally's strange green eyes opened wide in surprise for a few moments, then her expression relaxed into a lazy grin. "That was ... mean."

"Sorry about that," Paladin replied, "but I bet you're

feeling a lot more relaxed now, as well as less likely to ... lash out."

"The only lashes I want, handsome," she slurred, sounding drunk off her ass, "are twenty across my bottom."

"I second that," Tom said, quickly adding, "hers, not mine."

Christy threw a glare at the clueless moron, but then turned her attention back toward Paladin. "What did you do to her?"

"Nothing you don't already know about. Our intelligence informs us that certain compounds have proven quite effective at managing the harbinger's mood."

Intelligence? That bitch Marjorie. It had to be. It was simply too convenient, especially knowing Falcon had been sending her regular status reports.

Wonderful. It was one thing to deal with mages who simply didn't like me for being a vampire. Now we had to also worry about who else Gan was keeping in her back pocket.

"Harbinger?" Christy asked as if discussing the weather.

"Of what will come to pass should steps toward *remediation* not be taken." Paladin took the syringe from his underling and held it up in front of me. "A little something one of our staff whipped up. I believe you know Dr. Cheng. He speaks of you quite often."

Grr! "As a guinea pig or former player he used to fuck over?"

Paladin threw back a grin. "A bit from both columns, actually. Can't lie and say I really listen to him much. He's..."

"An asshole?"

"I was going to say not really a people person, but whatever shoe fits best I suppose."

34

POOR ESTATE OF MIND

Christy's eyes abruptly rolled back into her head and she stumbled as we were led into the estate. Sadly, I was helpless to do much to help as my breath suddenly caught in my throat.

Be careful! This place is...

Dr. Death's voice, however, abruptly fell silent in my head, just as there came a single feeble *thud* from within my chest.

What the fuck?

To the credit of Paladin's staff, though, they were right there to catch her before she could tumble onto the cobblestones.

After a few moments, she shook her head then stood again under her own power. "I'm okay now, thanks."

"My apologies, Ms. Fenton," Paladin said. "I should have warned you. The perimeter of the grounds are heavily warded. I don't pretend to know exactly how it all works, but I've been told it's designed to ground powers such as ours via the unique properties of the bedrock below us."

It was a hell of a security fence. For a second there I could've sworn my heart let out a beat before falling quiet again. Glancing Ed's way and seeing the confused look on his face, I had to guess he'd noticed something, too.

Hell, even Glen seemed to have been affected. "My pseudopods are tingling," he bubbled, his voice muffled from within the storage container.

What was up with that? Had Gan built her home over a cursed Native American burial mound or something? Knowing her, I wouldn't have doubted it. Hell, if she thought it would've benefited her, she'd have probably dug up the corpses and shit in their...

All at once, the area around us lit up a sickly green.

Okay, that's new.

I turned back to find Sally's still giggling form being led over the imaginary line in the sand that had just knocked the rest of us for a loop.

No, it wasn't just around us. That strange glow – roughly ten feet wide – seemed to lead off into the distance, following the wall that encircled the estate.

It was as if the entire perimeter was reacting to her presence.

What the fuck was going on here?

Almost as if in response, the radios of the security staff all blared to life.

"Sir!" a guard called from the gatehouse, "we're getting reports of sensors being tripped."

"How many?" Paladin asked, sounding unconcerned as he unclipped his radio.

"All of them!"

He quickly nodded to the people minding Sally. They dragged her along until she caught up with the rest of us. At that point, the strange glow faded away as abruptly as it had appeared. What the hell kind of weird-ass security did Gan have here?

"Stand down," Paladin said into his radio. "Conduct a perimeter sweep and system diagnostic just to be safe, but it appears to have been a momentary overload, nothing more." I couldn't help but notice he glanced at Sally for that last part.

She merely laughed, though. "Woo! That was trippy. Can we do it again?"

"Maybe later," Paladin said with a shake of his head, signaling his team to carry on.

I had no idea what that had been, but one thing was painfully obvious – we were going to have a hell of a time getting out of here without being noticed.

The light show apparently over, our group was split among a trio of utility vehicles, giving me a clue as to how big this place truly was if they needed to drive wherever we were going.

Sally and I, apparently being the VIPs, rated riding along with Paladin. Pity she was way too stoned for me to pry any more information out of her about our so-called plan. So I turned to our gracious *host* instead.

Before I could say anything to him, though, I found myself distracted. Holy shit, Ed was right. They did have a tennis court. Maybe being prisoner wasn't going to be so bad after all.

No, that was the wrong attitude. This wasn't some half-assed vacation in paradise, especially since I had a feeling Gan would be the only bikini babe waiting poolside.

Forcing thoughts of how swank this place was from my head, and damn it really was, I again turned toward Paladin. "So, what's your deal?"

"My deal, Mr. Ryder? Not sure I understand what you mean."

"I think you do. You don't seem like most of the evil fuckheads we normally deal with. I mean, aside from the cuffs and drugs, you've almost been polite."

"S-says you," Sally slurred. "Free drugs are the height of polite society."

"Good and evil are irrelevant," he said, rather than give

me the usual goon response of smacking me with the butt of his rifle and telling me to shut it. "I'm simply doing my job. Had you and your friends insisted on hostilities, you would have found my response somewhat less *cordial*."

"Does that mean you'd spank me for being a bad girl?" Sally asked, her eyes wide.

"Something like that," he replied, the pillar of professionalism.

"Okay, so then when did doing your *job* entail becoming an undead minion? Or was that always part of the bonus package?"

I expected that to earn me a backhand, but again this guy seemed to take no personal umbrage at anything I said. So much for him being a paladin. Hell, the Templar would've called me a devil spawn and tried to ram a rosary up my ass by now.

"I have to admit, all of this is pretty new to me. I've seen some strange things in my life, things that have occasionally caused me to question what I know. But finding out all of it is real, well, it's been eye-opening. As for this..." His eyes momentarily flashed gold before returning to their normal color. "It was a choice that was offered us, nothing more."

"It was?"

"You have to understand, Miss Khan favors loyalty above all else, even competence. Albeit, I can assure you a lack of such is not indicative of long term employment here."

Miss Khan? I guess that sorta made sense. Unless Gan was going for a Cher vibe, she'd probably want a surname for her day-to-day dealings with the mortal world. Khan was both a nod to her heritage as well as arrogant as fuck, two things that suited her.

"So you took her up on it?"

"I saw little reason not to. In my field of work, superior strength, speed, and reflexes are all a plus."

"What about drinking blood?"

He shrugged. "Every job requires some level of compromise. This is no different."

"So, getting back to that loyalty part? Is it me, or does that sound contrived when there's a paycheck involved?"

There was no getting under this guy's skin, though. He let out a laugh. "I'm afraid you watch too much TV, Mr. Ryder. Call someone in my position whatever you'd like, security consultant, soldier of fortune, even mercenary. Those are just titles. The bottom line is loyalty goes hand in hand with this line of work. Your stereotypical merc makes for a good story, I'll give you that. But trust me, those who gain a reputation for selling out their employers don't last long."

Interesting to know, not that I had any shot in hell of outbidding Gan. That said, when it came to atrocities, history tended to be less than kind to those who fell back on the excuse of just doing their job.

Let's face facts. I didn't see any way that someone could be Gan's chief of security and not commit a dozen crimes against humanity before lunch.

Sure, Paladin didn't seem like a bad guy, but that hadn't stopped him from cuffing us or shooting Sally up with enough happy drugs to have her hanging halfway out the door singing *Let It Go* at the top of her lungs.

I swear, where was Glen and his GoPro when you needed them?

We were driven to the main house, and what a fucking setup it was. I swear, had Gan not been a terrifyingly obsessive psychopath, I could maybe see the appeal of being a kept man in a place like this. Hell, you could've probably stuffed my entire apartment building into one wing of her mansion and had room left over.

I won't lie. A part of me had been expecting to maybe find a bunch of tents set up in the middle of a forest, some kind of weird-ass attempt to emulate her late father Ögedei Khan. But there was no doubt Gan had embraced the modern world in ways that her dear old dad had refused to.

The architecture alone spoke to that. I mean, it wasn't some ultra-modern pile of building blocks, but it was a far cry from the thousand-year-old castle the vampire nation had once used as their headquarters. Now to only hope the basement wasn't full of crazy blind nutjobs huffing fumes and prognosticating dire futures.

With any luck I wouldn't get a chance to find out.

We parked in front, prompting me to ask, "What, no servant entrance?"

Paladin smirked. "Not for you, Freewill, and I think you know why."

I did, but greatly preferred willful ignorance over reality.

"Our standing orders are to make sure you're comfortable and treated well ... should you ever grace us with your presence. Albeit, I have to admit, I didn't expect you to waltz up to the gate like you did. Tell me, what exactly was your plan?"

I wish I knew. Before today, I'd sorta expected a bunch of stuff to happen, ending with us standing triumphantly over a pile of dust wearing Gan's nametag.

Yeah, there's probably a good reason my friends usually didn't leave the planning to me, but he didn't need to know that. Oh well, I was already far up shit creek without a paddle. Might as well make with some improv and hope for the best.

"I won't shit you, cleric wannabe. Your boss lady threatened my friends. We're here to crumble up her ultimatum and shove it down her throat."

"With just the six of you?"

I didn't say it was a good plan. "Wouldn't be the first time someone underestimated us."

"Oh, we haven't, I can assure you of that. We have extensive files on you all."

"Even Glen?"

"Most of you anyway."

I threw a sly grin his way, as if to imply he'd made a tactical error.

Paladin raised an eyebrow then turned and glanced over his shoulder at where Glen was being unloaded, looking like ten gallons of yellow snot sloshing around in a fish tank.

It was bullshit on my part, born of nothing more than wanting to have something, *anything* to make this disaster feel like less than total shit.

The problem now was capitalizing on it. There was little doubt in my mind that Christy had something up her sleeve, but that still didn't solve the issue of Gan not being here. Hopefully whatever she was waiting to do could still prove useful for breaking us out – allowing us to slink home with our tails between our legs to wait for whatever Gan had in store for us next, which would almost certainly be less embarrassing than this clusterfuck.

Yeah, my frustration was boiling over, not helped by Sally acting like a first grader at Disney World.

She climbed the wide stone stairs leading toward the main entrance, then turned and shouted, "I'm king of the world!"

"Queen," I corrected with a sigh.

She stuck out her tongue. "See if I let you touch my royal scepter."

"Goddamn," a familiar voice replied. "Do I know my drugs or what?"

I looked past where Sally continued to preen, to see the door now open and Dave, my goddamned ex dungeon master, standing there looking like a fucking snake oil salesman in an Armani suit.

Damn it all to hell.

35

TUMBLING ASSETS

"**H**ey, Bill." Dave said, stepping forward while the rest of my friends were still being unloaded behind me.

"Fancy meeting you here," I replied. "Last I heard, you were supposed to be ... oh yeah, in South America shutting down production on that fucking vampire spooge you created."

He shrugged. "Relax. I took care of that over the phone."

"That's not the point, asshole! You're supposed to be our friend."

"I still am ... whoa there. Watch it." He stepped out of the way as Sally began to spin around the veranda like this was the opening from *The Sound of Music.*

"Oh really? You have an interesting way of showing it."

"Fuck you, asshole," Ed snapped from below, adding his two cents.

Dave let out a sigh. "What can I say? Gan needed my particular expertise."

"There's a phrase I'm thinking of when nutcases show up at my door asking for help with their evil schemes. It's pronounced *no!*"

"I get it, man, but it's not that cut and dry."

"How so?"

"Here, let me show you something." He pulled a slip of paper from his pocket and held it up so I could see.

"What am I looking at?" I asked, noting all the zeros.

"My last pay stub."

"Holy shit!" I shook my head, trying not to let it distract me from his betrayal. "Wait, do you just carry that around with you?"

"Well, yeah. Wouldn't you?"

In all fairness, I might, but that wasn't the point. On the upside, at least he hadn't sold us out cheaply.

"Besides," he continued. "It all worked out."

Dave had never been the most ethical of my friends, but I'd never suspected just how far round the bend he'd apparently gone. "How do you figure that?"

"Dr. Cheng," Paladin warned, but I waved him off.

"Chill for a sec, dwarven battlerager. We're just having a friendly chat here."

Dave shook his head. "You do realize there's not a single game pun I haven't used on that guy already, right?"

I nodded. "I'd be disappointed if you hadn't. So anyway, what you were saying?"

"Ed," he replied. "You know I'm the only reason he's free, right?"

I glanced back at my friend, but he was facing the other way so he could flip Dave off with both middle fingers.

"Ignore him. He's just mad because I was in charge of milking his venom."

"Poor word choice aside," I replied. "I remember."

"Anyway, I was able to create a method similar to how I replicated yours, with maybe a couple advances thrown in thanks to a certain someone footing the bill."

I narrowed my eyes. "Please tell me you're not selling Ed-infused hand cream now."

He inclined his head as if filing that idea away for later. Goddamn, what a dick. "No. I'm out of the moisturizer business ... for now anyway. But I've made it so she doesn't need him anymore. And since he's your pal and all, that meant she let him go instead of ... well, you know." He mimed shoving a stake through his heart.

I guess he sorta had a point, in a twisted, greedy, completely amoral sort of way.

"In fact," he continued, "you could kind of say I succeeded where you failed."

"You mean in providing Gan with an unlimited supply of vampires with which to take over the fucking world?"

"I meant rescuing Ed. Jeez, man, don't be so fucking cynical."

I turned halfway and showed him my cuffed hands. "You'll excuse me for being a Debbie Downer."

He glanced at them then shrugged. "Oh yeah, speaking of which, why the fuck are you even here anyway? I mean, this is the last place I'd expect to see you of all people."

"Looking for your boss so I can kick her ass."

"Oh. Well, she's not here."

"So I've been told."

"You probably shouldn't have brought *her*." He hooked a thumb Sally's way, then lowered his voice as if telling me a secret. "Gan's trying to..."

"So I've also been told."

He looked back at her. "Nice hair, by the way. Glad to see you're not still a statue."

"Bet I could still make you stiff as one," she purred in response.

He turned toward me again, a grin on his face. "High grade opioids are a wonderful fucking thing, aren't they?"

"That'll be quite enough, Doctor." Paladin said at last. "I need to secure our *guests*, after which, well, I would prefer you not converse with them without Miss Khan's express approval."

I looked at him then back toward Dave. "Call me

cynical, but I don't think you're gonna get him to the table if you ever decide to start up the game again."

"Never say never. By the way, since it sounds like you might be here a while, I could always grab a module or two if you want. What do you say? I could let you resurrect Kelvin from the Hell of Infinite Spiked Dildos."

Before I could answer him, Christy stepped forward, pulling away from the guard minding her and racing past me to the top of the stairs, where Sally continued to twirl like the sugarplum fairy's stoner cousin.

It spoke volumes toward Paladin's confidence that he didn't immediately try to stop her.

"Sorry to be the bearer of bad news," she said, turning around to face us, "but we won't be staying as long as you may think."

"Oh, Ms. Fenton?" he replied. "And why is that?"

In response, Sally stopped her little ballerina act and grinned, seeming to sober up in the space of a second. "Because this is the part where we fuck your shit up."

This was their plan? And people told me I sucked at strategy.

Two of Paladin's men walked up the stairs toward my friends, their casual pace suggesting they didn't take the sudden defiance all too seriously – at least until there came a clang of metal from behind Christy, her manacles dropping to the concrete.

Before I could question when she'd learned to pick a lock, she pulled her arms out from behind her revealing the reason for her sudden escape. She had no fucking hands.

Holy shit!

Her arms simply ended at her wrists, like she'd never had hands to begin with. That apparently didn't hinder her much, though, as she held them out before her. An instant later, two things happened: the pair of guards dropped to the ground as blue electricity arced around them and the lock on my own cuffs popped open, freeing me.

I could hear Paladin's people scrambling, but was too fixated on the insanity going on up front. It was probably a good thing, too, as Christy looked me in the eye and mouthed a single word. "*Duck.*"

It was a small miracle I'd survived as long as I had. I knew that much. However, I'd at least *tried* to pick up a few things along the way – not the least of which was knowing that when one of my friends told me to duck, I made sure to hit the fucking deck.

Mind you, that was easier said than done when my brain was currently busy short circuiting. That said, I doubted anyone could blame me as I watched my girlfriend begin to *melt* before my very eyes.

Jesus motherfucker!

It was insane. One moment she was Christy. The next, it was like she was reenacting *Raiders of the Lost Ark's* most infamous scene. Her skin turned the color and consistency of wax and began to dissolve, along with the rest of her – the runoff turning to smoke before it could even hit the ground.

As her flesh continued to liquify, a glow became visible from within her torso. There was something inside her body. It took me a moment – the horror of it all rendering my synapses nearly useless – but, as she melted away, I saw it was a large milky white crystal of some sort ... a vaguely familiar looking one.

An orb of Amun-Ra, my subconscious whispered.

Of course! It was one of those crystal things Falcon had used to create his ultimate hotel getaway.

The very same kind he'd rushed to put away ... before Sally had shown up.

Uh oh.

"Everyone hit the dirt!" I cried, finally heeding Christy's advice and throwing myself to the ground. I still wasn't sure what the fuck had just happened, but Q&A would have to wait.

As the last of *Christy* dissolved, the crystal fell to the ground where it pulsed brightly.

"Oh no you don't," Sally said, grabbing Dave by his sports jacket before he could run. "Remember when I promised to make you stiff? Change of plans, jackass. How about I make you *into* a stiff instead?"

With that, a pulse of pure destructive energy exploded from her, annihilating Dave's body from the waist up as surely as if she'd shoved a stack of lit dynamite down his gullet.

Holy fucking shit!

The wave of power pinned me to the ground as what felt like an F5 tornado washed over me.

Something disgustingly wet hit my back as screams filled the air, quickly drowned out by the sounds of destruction as the entire front façade of Gan's mansion blew apart.

From behind, there came the heavy crunch of metal, telling me the UTVs we'd been driven here in were probably being swept away like Matchbox cars.

Being drenched in Dave's innards was bad enough. What came next, though, was a wee bit more painful, physically anyway. For the second time in as many weeks, I found myself at ground zero for a building demolition.

Wood, plaster, masonry, and more began to rain from the sky as the pressure wave finally subsided, giving me a chance to turn over just in time to see...

Oh fuck!

I rolled out of the way as a baby grand piano slammed into the ground where I'd been a moment earlier.

I knew Gan wanted us to make beautiful music

together for the rest of our days, but this was perhaps taking it too literally.

Note to self: next time just fucking stay in Brooklyn.

Just as I was about to raise my head to chance another look around, a hand grabbed me by the shirt and began to drag me back to my feet, causing me to cry out in a manner most unmanly.

"Are you taking a fucking time out or are you gonna help?"

It was Sally and she looked neither hurt nor particularly happy.

"Y-you killed Dave!" I cried. "You..."

She slapped me across the face. "Focus, Bill. You can whine about it later. Right now we need to move."

"But..."

"Listen to me and listen well. We both know you'd have come up with some excuse to let him off the hook, but the asshole deserved it."

She was right, at least on that first part. But what Dave had said about helping to free Ed... If he'd been telling the truth then she'd just flat out murdered...

The thing was, I knew deep down that wasn't his real motivation. If that had been the case he wouldn't have flashed his paycheck in my face. No. Dave served his own interests first and foremost. Still, what she'd...

Now is not the time for this! We are not among friends here.

Almost as if heeding my subconscious, Sally's hand rocked across my cheek a second time, sounding like a shotgun blast.

It wasn't a hard hit, but it didn't feel like Christmas either. Besides, my inner demon was right. We weren't among friends. If anything, I remembered Paladin's words about how he would've been a lot less friendly had we been a hostile invading force ... which was pretty much what we'd just become.

I still had no idea what had happened, especially with Christy, but...

That was obviously some sort of solid glamour. It wasn't her!

I nodded to myself. Yeah. She also had that spell that could split her consciousness between two places. This whole thing had that written all over it.

Mind you, last time she'd used it, it hadn't been for wholesale destruction. Not to mention, that still gave me no clue as to where she was or what was happening to her, but I had a feeling I'd wasted enough time on this pity party.

"Okay, enough. I'm ... good," I said, holding up my hands in case Sally tried slapping the shit out of me again.

I dared a quick glance back at the mansion. Most of the front façade had been blown to hell, making it look like a giant doll house someone had left open ... after taking a hammer to the insides.

In the middle of it all, I spied a large steel enclosure, visible now that the walls around it had been blasted away. For a second, I thought it might be some kind of vault, Gan going all Scrooge McDuck. But I quickly realized it was probably a safe room.

Mind you, it didn't look particularly safe at the moment, the door twisted and warped from the sheer force of Sally's power.

No matter which way you looked at it, the under-writers behind Gan's homeowner policy were gonna shit a brick with this one. Perhaps even more than that, I real-ized as the scent of blood caught my nose from that direc-tion. I felt bad for any butlers who'd decided to work late this evening.

That couldn't be helped, though. I needed to focus on my friends and...

Oh shit, our friends!

I quickly spun back toward the circular driveway in front of the house. An ornate fountain had once stood in the center of it, now nothing more than a pile of wet rubble. There was little doubt at least some of Paladin's people had been taken out by the blast – both human and vamp, judging by the trails of blood that led across the paver stones, a few of which ended in scorched piles of dust.

They weren't my concern, though, so much as... *There!*

I spied Ed or, more specifically, the glowing figure he was lying atop. From the look of things, he'd thrown himself at Tom to knock him out of the way of the blast. Good thing, too, as the new Icon wasn't always so quick to take the hint.

"Get off me, fucker!" Tom cried from beneath him. "I'm not into your ugly ass."

Ed finally rolled off him, looking pretty damned singed from having just eaten a face full of faith aura, but they were both alive and likewise freed of their bonds. Now where was...?

I caught sight of shards of shattered plastic, beyond which lay a yellowish smear that stretched across the driveway out onto the lawn.

"Oh, fuck! Glen!"

I should've been focused on following Sally, who'd broken off toward our left, but I had to check on him. I'd already lost one friend today, or former friend anyway. If there was any hope that he was...

I made it to where the smear of goop started, seeing an eyeball lying in the middle of it staring unblinkingly up at the sky.

Oh no!

But then it shifted, turning my way as bubbles began to form in the sludge around it.

"F... Free..."

"I'm here, man."

"Freewill..."

I blinked away tears, unsure how – *if* – I could help him. "It's okay. Y-you're gonna be just fine."

"D...did...?"

"Yes?"

"Did ... you ... find my camera? I'd ... hate ... to lose the footage I already shot."

Seriously?! "Wait. Are you injured or not?"

"I ... seem to be a bit scattered," he bubbled. "Might take me a while to pull myself together."

"Um ... okay, you work on that, while I..."

A gunshot sounded from nearby, causing me to instinctively flinch. It hadn't been aimed at me, though. I turned to find Sally behind the trigger. She'd taken a gun from one of the downed guards then subsequently fired it into the back of his head. A moment later, his body flared up like he'd been doused in rocket fuel. Guess that answered whether he'd been human or not.

It also told me that someone had definitely woken up on the wrong side of the bed this morning.

Unfortunately, another shot rang out, this one far less friendly, clipping me in the side.

Argh!

I spun to find Paladin rising. He looked beaten to hell, but that didn't mean anything. He'd heal within minutes, and he wasn't alone. As much of the security team that had been taken out, more had survived. Worse, I saw head-lights from back in the direction of the gatehouse – rein-forcements no doubt.

Shit!

We needed to rally if we were going to walk away from this mess. Too bad I didn't see any way to...

"Come on!" Sally cried, already on the move toward one of the wrecked vehicles.

The utility vehicles! Paladin had locked our stuff in the trunk of one of them. We hadn't exactly come loaded for bear, but there were a few items there that might tip the odds a bit.

I waved to the others before taking off. "This way!"

I glanced back to find them following – Ed in the lead,

being he was a lot faster than Tom, but that was okay. As more shots rang out, Tom's aura flared to life. It wasn't as bright as before, but was still more than enough to act as a bullet sponge for the rest of us.

Ed caught up to me quickly enough, mostly because I was kind of lurching along thanks to the bullet in my side.

"Quick thinking with Tom," I said.

"Not really. Sally's power fucks with his, doesn't it?"

It took a moment for his words to sink in. "Wait, you knew about that?"

"She might have mentioned it to me."

"Did you know what she was going to do to Dave?"

His wide-eyed stare was all the answer I needed. "Sorry, man. I – I think that part was more spur of the moment. Holy shit."

I guess it was good to see he was shaken by Dave's supremely messy demise, too. But again, there wasn't time to sort out our feelings as the air was rapidly filling with the sounds of gunfire.

"She mention anything *else* to you?"

"Maybe one or two things," he remarked as we ran. "Why? You want to stop for a recap?"

"Not really."

I'll admit, I was having a hard time wrapping my head around this. I wasn't used to being the aggressor in these sorts of things. Don't get me wrong. Gan deserved a bloody nose for everything she'd set in motion, but she wasn't even fucking here. The second we learned that we should've hightailed it out of this place and rethought our plan ... or at least that's what I'd have done.

Maybe that was the problem, though. I didn't really consider myself responsible for a lot of the shit that had gone down five years earlier. Yet, at the same time, I'd always wondered whether I could've prevented some of it – Tom's death in particular – had I been more proactive.

The problem was, I ... didn't want to be. That wasn't me. I wasn't some vampire warlord, intent on waging war against anyone who slighted me. I was a fucking programmer by trade, and I liked it.

But when had fate ever given a shit about what I liked?

Sadly, now was a really bad time for introspection. Hell, the only thing that was keeping Ed and I from being mowed down by a hail of bullets was our speed and the fact that Sally was providing cover fire while Tom acted as a human shield.

"Slow down, you bunch of cocks!"

Albeit, judging from his cries behind us, he wasn't all too happy to have the job.

It was time to see if we could do something about that.

Afterward, we were going to have a good long sit down about all of this, but for now we needed to survive long enough to figure out how to escape.

36

BULLET TIME

Ed and I reached Sally's position, taking cover behind the downed side by side as my healing compensated for the gunshot I'd received. The only good part about this bullshit was that Paladin's team didn't seem to be outfitted with silver bullets – something I'm sure Gan would remedy after tonight.

Even so, regular old bullets were more than enough. A hit in the right place and it would be all over, even for folks like Ed and me.

Speaking of which, I ducked down as a shot ricocheted off the side of the vehicle about a foot away from me.

"Not him!" Paladin cried out as he rallied his people. "The other one! Take out the other one."

A few moments later, they stopped peppering the vehicle we were using as cover.

I popped my head up for a look and immediately saw why.

Paladin's forces were now fully focused on Tom, who'd managed only about half the distance thanks to lacking super speed.

"Thanks for waiting, assholes!" Despite his words, there was an undercurrent of panic to his voice. Bullets continued to be absorbed by his faith aura, sparking wherever they hit, but with each passing moment his shield seemed to grow smaller around him – shrinking as if their weapons were striking his confidence instead of his power.

In a way, I realized they probably were. Tom's aura rendered him almost invulnerable, true. However, whereas he'd inherited Sheila's powers when he took over her body, he hadn't laid claim to the unearthly confidence that had been hers upon taking up the mantle of the Icon – the same confidence from which their power stemmed.

That was potentially a problem. Faith magic was all about belief. If he didn't *believe* he was bulletproof then soon enough he wouldn't be. It was like watching a completely different person from earlier. When we'd first arrived, he'd been all bravado, stepping in front of us and waving his sword like some sort of half-assed...

His sword!

Tom had recently started attaching action figures to it, like it was a new bedazzling craze. The thing was, those toys were his source of confidence, as crazy as it sounded. I knew my friend, perhaps better than anyone else. He didn't believe in much but he had rock solid faith, ungrounded though it might've been, that his ragtag collection of toys, action figures, and trading cards would one day pay off big, resulting in a massive financial windfall.

It had been that same warped faith that had once allowed him to empower an Optimus Prime figure so that it burnt the shit out of vampires. He'd managed to latch onto that same faith in his new body to keep those fires burning bright. Without it, though...

"Shit! Wrong one," Sally said, popping the trunk and finding nothing inside. She pointed toward another wreck lying a ways off. "Come on. It must be that one."

"Tom needs his sword."

"You don't say." She handed Ed the gun she'd purloined. "There's a fresh magazine in it. See if you can dissuade these assholes a bit."

"Why me?"

"Because you're their precious Progenitor, stupid. They're not going to shoot you."

"How the fuck can you be sure of that?" I asked.

"Because I just took out the guy who designed their undead assembly line. If they kill Ed and then whatever that asshole did breaks down, that's it. No more of these new kind of vamps ever."

"Neo-vamps," I mumbled, trying to internalize what she was saying. She was right. Even had Dave's betrayal not made him a target, what he'd done for Gan had. In killing him, she'd effectively made Ed untouchable ... in theory anyway."

"Like I really give a fuck," Sally said, dragging me from my poorly timed reverie. "Move it!"

I threw Ed an apologetic glance before turning and following her. Interestingly enough, nobody appeared to fire at us as we ran – although whether that was because of me or Sally, I didn't know.

"Okay, here's the plan," I said, trying to bring order from this fuckery of chaos. "We get our stuff, scoop Glen up, and make a run for it. Once we're outside the wall..."

"Get with the program, Bill," she snapped. "We're not leaving, not yet."

"Gan isn't here!"

"Do you honestly still think we didn't know that?" she replied as we reached the downed UTV. It was lying on its roof, looking far worse for the wear than the one Ed was still hiding behind.

"Enough of this shit! What aren't you telling...?"

"Push this thing over onto its side," she ordered, ignoring my protests.

"Me?"

"You're the only one here with vampire strength."

"I asked you a..."

"We don't have time for this crap. *Do it!*"

Grr! She had a point, sadly. Answers would need to

wait until after we'd retrieved our gear. I grabbed the side of the vehicle and gave it a shove. "Ugh!"

"Come on, put your back into it."

"F-fuck ... you...," I replied, struggling. The side by side wasn't large by truck standards, but it's not like I was Superman. Vamp strength was awesome, but we started off much closer to Captain America than the fucking Hulk.

C'mon!

Finally, there came the groan of metal as, little by little, the vehicle began to tilt.

Plant your legs and push with your knees.

Seriously? Was my alter ego Richard Simmons now? *You know, this would be a lot easier if you just did your thing*, I replied back at him.

I already told you, I can't.

Can't ... or won't?

The question, however, was ultimately moot. Spurred on by my frustration, and also planting my legs like he suggested, I managed to upend the vehicle, wrenching my back in the process.

Even then, my work wasn't done yet. The trunk was all beaten to hell, requiring the use of my claws to rip it open.

Bingo! This time it was thankfully the right one.

In my haste, however, I acted stupidly, grabbing Tom's sword and earning myself a fried hand in the process before quickly dropping it again. *Ow!*

"Ladies first," I said, stepping out of the way. "And you might want to hurry."

I turned to see that Tom had finally reached Ed's location, his aura just barely still alit. Fortunately, Sally's theory seemed to be sound. None of Paladin's people appeared all that eager to pump Ed full of lead. The bad was that several of them had switched out their guns for stun batons and combat knives, no doubt looking to take this fight up close and personal.

Sally retrieved Tom's sword then pulled her hand

cannon out, checking to make sure it was still loaded. "Ah, much better."

"My turn." I stepped in again. *Now where is...* Ah, there! I grabbed hold of the titanium travel mug and clipped it to my belt via the attached carabiner. The only thing missing was... "Hold on. Where's Christy's pack?"

"Forget about it. It wasn't real to begin with, or at least that one wasn't."

Of course not. It had probably turned to smoke along with the woman I'd thought to be my girlfriend as she... "Wait. You knew about that? What the fuck is going on and where is Chris...?"

"Enough," she stated flatly. "We're in the middle of a fucking fire fight here. Save the quid pro quo for later." She looked past me back toward our friends. "Or better yet, ask her yourself."

I turned to see Tom and Ed, out of bullets and almost out of luck, hiding behind the vehicle like deer in the headlights as a trio of security goons closed in.

As the first of them raised their baton, though, seeking to bring the fight to my friends, their bodies lit up in a sizzle of blue electricity.

Two of the guards immediately dropped to the ground, humans most likely. The third managed to remain on his feet, trying to fight his way through the stun spell. The flash of yellow from his eyes identified him as a...

A corpse apparently, as a beam of red hot power sliced through his chest, causing him to combust where he stood. Ouch!

I followed the spell back to its source and saw Christy, hopefully the real one this time, step from around the side of the ruined mansion.

A purple force dome appeared around her as she then turned her attention toward the bulk of Paladin's men, unleashing hellfire their way.

"Come on!" Sally cried, heading back toward where our friends waited.

She didn't have to tell me twice.

With Christy now drawing the lion's share of the assault, we were able to make it back to the other vehicle with little trouble.

"Merry Christmas, dipshit," Sally said, tossing Tom his sword.

His skills with the blade were at best kind of pathetic, as evidenced by how he almost dropped it. But there was no doubt of its effect as once again his aura blazed to life.

Any port in a storm, I suppose. "You guys good?"

"Better now," Ed replied, stepping clear of Tom's power and pulling a fresh magazine from one of the downed security mooks.

"I'm ready to kick the tires and light some mother-fuckers on fire," Tom said.

"Me, too!"

I turned to see Glen rolling our way like a pus-filled bowling ball, having apparently managed to pull his goopy self together.

Christy was likewise closing in on our location, her force dome deflecting all the firepower directed her way.

When at last she reached us, she asked Tom to drop his aura before quickly extending her spell to encompass us all, giving us a momentary breather. Heck, she even opened a small slit in the bottom so Glen could slither through. I didn't fool myself into thinking she could hold it forever. For now, though, she appeared to be in good enough shape for me to approach her.

"Are you actually you this time?"

"Of course," she replied, her face a bit smudged but otherwise a sight for sore eyes. "Who else would I be?"

Despite having mixed feelings in that moment, I immediately grabbed hold of her and held her tight, although not so hard that she dropped her spell.

"Hey!" Tom cried. "Keep it in your pants, asshole."

"Oh relax. What are we going to do, bone while they're shooting at us?"

Sally shrugged. "Wouldn't be a first for me."

Why did I not find that surprising?

"Fine." I stepped back, turning my attention to the dome around us. "I thought all those crazy wards were supposed to keep magic from working in here?"

Christy shook her head. "No. They're to prevent sending and to slow down any mystical creatures long enough for the security staff to deal with them ... in theory anyway."

"That assumes whoever they're dealing with aren't simply the diversion," Sally added.

"Exactly."

Okay, enough of this crap. "Listen, I know we don't have much time, but can someone please tell me what the fuck is going on?"

"Yeah," Tom agreed. "I don't know about Bill, but all this stuff with you melting and shit is giving me a headache."

Christy looked confused. "It's what was supposed to happen when..."

Sally raised a hand. "I ... may have held off on divulging certain details on the ride up."

"You didn't tell them?!"

Ed nodded sheepishly. "And I might've gone along with her, too."

"Why?" Christy and I asked simultaneously.

"Simple," Sally said, her expression defiant. "In order for this to work, we needed it to look convincing. That was the only way we were going to get them to drop their guard." She turned to face me. "No offense, but the more I thought about it, the more I remembered you two have the shittiest poker faces on the planet."

Ed nodded, looking guilty. "She's right. You two are cut from the same cloth, in that you're both terrible liars and, well, I knew the kind of pros we'd be dealing with here. Vamps or not, they can smell bullshit a mile away."

A sound strategy.

"Don't you start, too," I said, before waving my hand. "Never mind."

"I'm sorry," Christy said, throwing a look Sally's way. "If I'd known..."

"Which is why I hurried us along back there while you were distracted managing two bodies," she replied. "Don't get me wrong. I didn't want to, but think about it. Would that Paladin guy have bought it for a single second if half of us looked like we were waiting for a bomb to drop?"

"I thought my quivering microtubules would give us away for certain," Glen added.

All of us stopped to glance his way, but thankfully nobody chose to comment.

Ugh. A part of me *really* wanted to be insulted by what I was hearing.

Sadly, I had to admit she was probably right. We weren't dealing with feral monsters here. Gan wouldn't hire anyone less than the pinnacle of competence. When it was just my own bullshit, I could keep it together, but had I known Christy was out there alone, well, I can't say for certain I wouldn't have screwed it up. As for Tom, we'd have had to staple his mouth shut to keep him from spilling the beans.

"It has nothing to do with trust." Sally said after a moment, her tone turning conciliatory. "Believe me, I do trust you."

"Both of us?" Tom asked.

"Yeah, something like that. It's just..."

"We suck at acting?"

"Speak for yourself," I said. "Don't forget one of us was in the NJIT drama society."

"Yeah, for one semester."

"Ooh," Glen replied. "I would love to see you on stage, Freewill."

Tom shook his head. "Trust me, you really don't."

"All right, enough of this shit for now," Sally interrupted. "What's done is done. The important thing is it worked."

I raised an eyebrow. "But what if it hadn't?"

She grinned at me. "Remember what I told you about the difference between good ideas and cataclysmically bad ones?"

"Hindsight," I grumbled.

"It's always twenty-twenty, and right now it's telling us this was a sound strategy."

"Barely," Christy said. "I'll admit I was kind of worried after they drugged you. Wasn't sure if you were going to start dancing or not."

"Dancing?" I asked.

"That was our signal to get this party started," Sally replied.

"It was?"

"You didn't think I was out there playing ballerina for shits and giggles, did you? Fortunately for us, that concoction they shot me up with wore off as quickly as it hit. Guess they just don't make drugs like they used to."

Either that or it was her. After all, she'd recovered minutes after her bracelet had run dry, despite it being filled with magical happy juice.

"All right then," she added after another beat, as bullets continued to bounce off the force dome. "If that's all settled, we need to..."

"Not so fast." I turned and met Christy's gaze. "We can talk about the rest later, but I have one more question for now."

"What is it?"

"We're kinda deep in the shit here when I thought the whole point was to take the fight to Gan."

She nodded. "It is. That's exactly what we're doing."

"How?"

"By showing her that she isn't as invulnerable as she thinks. We don't need to kill her to hurt her."

"Just for the record," Sally replied as the hail of gunfire finally trailed off. "I'd be okay with killing her, too."

"Yes, and we will ... eventually. But what we're doing tonight will shake her confidence, put her on the defensive."

"This is Gan we're talking about, right?" I raised an eyebrow. "I mean, is that even possible?"

"I think so, yes. But in order to do that, we need to get into that house and down to the basement."

"Why? What's in the basement?"

"Probably the leather gimp dungeon she has waiting for you," Tom replied.

"Aside from that."

"Not *in* the basement per se," Christy said. "Below it."

"*This is the only warning you're going to get,*" Paladin interrupted from outside our force dome, his voice amplified by the speaker system of the vehicle he was next to, one of the reinforcements that had arrived while we'd been taking our time out. "*You've had your fun, but now it's over. Surrender or else.*"

Before the rest of us could respond, Tom shouted back, "Or else what, you'll eat my ass?"

Okay then.

"Huh. That sounded so much better in my head."

"What a surprise," Ed replied with a sigh.

"*Have it your way.*" Paladin dropped the receiver then turned to some of his people and whispered something too low for even me to pick up.

Several long seconds passed, making me wonder if he was just blustering, but then I caught sight of what appeared to be distortions in the air from several places around us.

What the?

"We've got magic incoming," Sally warned, a second

before the distortions turned into full on shimmering, like something out of *Predator*.

In the next instant, the glamours all dropped at once, at least half a dozen of them, revealing people wearing tactical armor similar to Paladin's forces.

Their clothing aside, however, their true nature was revealed as each and every one of them lit up with arcane power.

Guess Ed had been more right than I'd hoped about Gan keeping mages on her staff.

If shit hadn't been real before, it sure as hell was about to get that way.

37

THE HOST WITH THE MOST

Not only were we heavily outgunned, but now it was six mages to one. No, wait, make that more as a couple stragglers shimmered into view from the corner of my eye.

It was pretty clear what Paladin had done. He'd called in reinforcements all right. Some had come guns a blazing, but they weren't the real threat, especially since it was obvious by now he planned to take at least some of us alive.

The real problem were the mages who'd simply waltzed into the area under cover of their glamours, positioning themselves so they had us surrounded.

Shit on toast.

Most of this merry magical bunch was lit up bright blue, telling me they meant to subdue us. That was good, at least for those of us who wouldn't be waking up naked handcuffed to Gan's bed.

Far less good was that a few were glowing yellow – mind magic. It painted a picture. Paladin might not want us all dead, but I had a feeling he didn't want us in any position to fight back either.

Either way you looked at it, we were long past shaking hands and writing this off as a misunderstanding.

"All right, so what's the plan *now*?" I asked, fear and annoyance bubbling over into my voice.

"Same as it was before," Sally replied calmly, glancing Christy's way.

Glad someone had their shit together because most of the mages picked that moment to open fire, blue beams of electricity lancing out from them and striking the force dome – causing an annoying crackle of static to rise up around us.

I half expected to see Christy fall to her knees from the strain, but she appeared oddly untroubled for the moment. Either her stamina had recently taken a major uptick, or something else was afoot.

Make that aback – as in the Winx Club backpack she still wore. It began to glow as the onslaught continued, the mages letting loose with enough power to light up a small town.

"Hurry," Sally warned, her calm demeanor starting to crack. "I can feel it coming."

"That's what she said."

Christy ignored Tom's asshole remark, instead dropping to one knee and unzipping her pack to reveal more of those white quartz thingies.

"Those are..."

"Orbs of Amun-Ra," she confirmed. "Matthias told me where to find his."

"Good idea."

She pulled one out and threw me a wink. "I had Tina overcharge them before I left, so they'd have a little extra oomph."

"Even better idea."

"By the way, now would be a good time for everyone to duck again."

Oh shit! She didn't need to tell me twice.

Christy tossed the orb to Sally. In the next instant, she dropped her force dome and hit the deck. Fortunately, this time everyone was up to speed, falling flat as blue energy washed over us. My nerve endings lit up like a Christmas tree ... for about a second anyway.

Then the orb flared up in Sally's grasp, causing her to throw back her head and scream as a wave of pure kinetic force erupted from her – obliterating the crystal and cutting through the enemy magic like the invisible fist of God himself.

Some of the Magi were ready, raising force domes of their own. What they weren't prepared for, though, was their magic shattering like so much glass.

It was insane. So far as I could tell, nothing seemed immune to her strange power. I'd seen it cut through monsters, magic, and even Tom's faith aura. Whatever rules there were for the eldritch energies of the universe, these shockwaves seemed to laugh in their face.

And Christy had apparently figured out how to weaponize them.

The vehicle we'd been hiding behind was torn to shreds as, to our right, more of Gan's mansion took the brunt of the assault, an entire wing of the massive building collapsing in on itself. Suburban renewal at its finest.

All around us, mages were scattered like pine needles in an autumn breeze. Some weren't hit too hard, having braced themselves in time, but others were broken like twigs. Same with Paladin's men, although I couldn't help but notice more of them seemed to have gotten the memo this time around, including the boss man himself who'd hit the ground in the nick of time.

On the upside, the confidence he'd shown earlier had been erased right off his face. He was no doubt beginning to understand what mean motor scooters we could be – some of us anyway.

Unfortunately, unlike the first time Sally had unleashed her power here, the blast wasn't the end of things.

There came a low rumble from the ground below us,

growing in intensity until I was glad I'd fallen prone. Jesus Christ, were we over a fucking fault line or something?

Sally wasn't quite so lucky, losing her balance and falling onto her butt beside me. I turned to make sure she was okay, and maybe mock her lack of grace, but the words died in my throat. Her eyes were glowing brilliant green, as if someone had plugged a sixty watt LED directly into her brain.

Oh no!

The air began to distort around her, as if the very atmosphere were superheating. She raised her lips in a snarl, all sense of humanity gone from her face, just as had happened back at the pier when those fish monsters had gotten too up close and personal with her.

However, before she could inform us how fucked we were thanks to the coming of the Great Beast, she gave her head a shake. A moment later, the light went out of her eyes and she was once again just Sally.

"Woo. That one took a bit out of me."

No shit. "Are you ... okay?"

"Uh huh." She looked around. "Better than the assholes around us anyway."

There was little doubt of that. For now, though, I took stock of the rest of our group, hoping Christy hadn't picked that moment to melt again. Once was more than enough for me.

Fortunately, everyone in our little war party seemed no worse for the...

"That's odd," Glen remarked, several of his eyes aimed skyward. "I don't recall the forecast calling for rain."

I looked up to find he was right. Clouds had rolled in at some point – thick, grey, and hanging low in the sky. Weird. The stars were shining when we'd arrived but, despite it feeling like an eternity since then, in reality it'd only been minutes since Sally's first shockwave had erased about three million dollars from Gan's property values.

We could worry about the weather later, though.

"Now, before they can recover," Christy cried, pushing to her feet and heading toward the mansion. At least there was no need to worry whether the front door was locked, since there wasn't one anymore. Same with the windows, most of the walls, and some of the ceiling. On the upside, we'd almost certainly made some contractor happy with all the work that would need to be done here.

Hopefully Gan was the type who hired local.

So far, we'd mostly made short work of Paladin's defenses, but a lot of that had to do with us bringing a nuclear bomb to a knife fight. His forces were nothing to sneeze at, but Christy and Sally's plan was the sort of thing it was hard to prepare for – whether you knew about it or not. Hell, I doubted even Alex, for all his military prowess, wouldn't have been caught with his pants down.

We just needed to keep it up. Opening gambits could set the tone for a battle but they didn't necessarily mean we'd won, especially when the other party knew what they were doing.

"Don't even think about it," Paladin cried. He pulled something off his belt and held it up for us to see. I couldn't pretend to know the ins and outs of military grade hardware, but I sincerely doubted it was a joy buzzer. "You have to know she would be prepared for something like this."

"That won't destroy it," Christy said, turning to face him.

It?

"No, but it'll sure as hell bury it ... along with all of us."

"Are you prepared to do that?"

"Ma'am, please don't insult me by assuming otherwise."

I had no idea what they were talking about. Guess I shouldn't have been so quick to conclude our little powwow back there.

"I think the more important question is," Sally replied, "do you think that'll stop *us*?"

Paladin smiled in response. "Maybe I don't need to stop you. Maybe all I have to do is slow you down."

Don't ask why? That never ends well in the movies.

"For what?" Christy asked.

Damn it!

Paladin cocked his head just as a buzzing sound began to fill the air. It wasn't very loud, almost like the hum of an electric wire. Heck, judging by the looks on most of my friends' faces, Ed was the only one other than me who'd noticed it.

What the hell?

Hell was exactly what Paladin had in mind, though, as people began to appear from out of nowhere behind him. Worse, they were wearing white robes with a familiar *Hunger Games* rip-off motif on the front.

Falcon's crew, or his aunt's anyway. This wasn't like the last group, however. They weren't decloaking from glamours, not from what I could tell. There'd been empty air behind Paladin one moment, then the next they were simply there, walking toward us – no flash of light, no shimmering, nothing.

Weren't these guys supposed to be in the city? Falcon had even said as much. There was simply no way for them to have gotten here that fast, unless...

But how? The grounds were warded against teleporting. Something like this wasn't supposed to be possible. And yet here they were anyway.

I didn't recognize any of them, just their robes, but that little bit of happiness quickly vanished as a damningly familiar face made her appearance a few steps behind the rest.

Marjorie's smug grin caught my eye as she stepped forth from thin air. She was joined a moment later by Falcon himself, looking none too happy to be there. He wasn't restrained or anything, so hopefully his little secret hadn't been found out. That he might need to join in fighting us to maintain his charade wasn't exactly a plus in our favor, though.

Mind you, I would've taken a thousand magical ass beatings over the final member of their little band – her green eyes sparkling as she appeared from out of nowhere and directed her crazy gaze my way.

"Greetings, beloved. I knew you would seek me out eventually."

Oh, this wasn't good, not by a long stretch.

Gan had come ready for battle, donning body armor with martial arts weapons strapped to her side. Her getup seemed to be a mix of old and new – combining the traditional Mongolian garb I'd seen her wear in years past with more modern tactical trappings. What caught my eye, however, were the sigils and glyphs carved into it, stuff that didn't ring a bell, despite me having seen – and set off – more than my fair share of wards.

"Miss Khan," Paladin said, greeting her.

"Kindly put the detonator away," she replied. "I believe it will prove unnecessary at this stage. Do you concur, Grand Mentor Falcon?"

Marjorie stepped forward as her people began to power up. Interestingly enough, the energy forming around them was different than the normal battle magic greens and reds I expected. This was more a bright magenta, almost pink. Something different was about to happen, although I doubted it would be in our favor.

"Did you really expect this gambit to work?" Marjorie asked, her gaze focused on Christy – the one person in our group she probably thought worthy of her time. "The wards here would keep out a base practitioner such as yourself, true, but I have studied the ways of Kala the

White. I have access to tomes and teachings you couldn't possibly imagine."

Christy had been pretty unflappable through all of this so far and, to give credit where it was due, she was still sporting a pretty good poker face. However, a furrow of worry appeared on her forehead, telling me now might be a good time to consider shitting my pants.

She inclined her head, replying with only three words. "The ley line?"

Ley line?

"Of course, child," Marjorie replied, sounding so full of herself I was half surprised she didn't topple over. "As was once used to reach The Source, so too can a practitioner in the know walk the ley lines as they so choose, bypassing that which keeps others out."

"Hold on," I said. "Are you saying we're above one of those...?"

"Is it not obvious, my darling?" Gan replied, her voice like nails on my mental chalkboard. "One of the thirteen rivers of elemental energy lies beneath our very feet, nourishing this planet with its power." She glanced Christy's way. "But your witch already knows that, doesn't she?"

"I know more than you might think," Christy replied.

"I sincerely doubt that." Gan glanced my way for a moment, then turned her attention back toward Christy, her eyes flashing gold. "Regardless, please know that what comes next is not personal. Time and again, you have survived overwhelming odds and risen above those who've sought to lay you low. I ... *respect* how such strength may have ensnared my beloved's heart."

Oh boy, here it comes.

"In fact, it may surprise you to learn some part of me even understands. After all, you have fought together, survived together, and grieved together. Such things create a strong bond."

"But?" Tom and I simultaneously asked, causing me to glare at him. "Do you mind not helping?"

"But, my beloved," Gan replied, "it is as I have said time and again. You are mine and I am yours. Destiny has bound us together." She drew the sword by her side. "And that means all other ties must eventually be severed ... via whatever means necessary."

38

CHICK FIGHT

C hristy wasn't the type to stand around twiddling her thumbs while someone else pontificated.

She'd retrieved another of those orbs from her backpack, the meaning obvious. Sally was our ace in the hole and everyone here knew it. Though by now they also probably knew to duck and cover before she went off, that still gave us an opening to do ... something.

For me that choice was obvious. It was time to power up. Though I'd sworn not to use Village Coven as my personal battery pack, I wasn't a fucking idiot. Neither were they. Knowing shit was afoot, they'd each donated some blood during our pitstop in Brooklyn. Besides, I could always work on not making this a habit next week, when Gan and Marge were both hopefully little more than unpleasant memories waiting to be repressed.

"Do you honestly think we didn't learn our lesson from last time?" Marjorie asked contemptuously. "That we haven't come up with *alternate* means of containment?"

Means of...

The Falcon Coven, for lack of a better name, turned our way and let loose with the spells they'd been holding. *Oh shit!* I braced myself for whatever was about to fuck up my day, taking small solace in the fact that blowing me to bits would likely cause Sally's power to go off as well.

I was wrong, though. The magic seemingly fell harmless around us, barely causing a tingle on my skin. *What the?*

Apparently these birds of prey were more piss poor pigeons when it came to this shit. They...

Or not, as the ground beneath us began to rumble again, this time far more violently than before.

"Move!" Ed shouted, grabbing Tom and dragging him along for the ride as he dove to the side.

I was hot on their heels, jumping out of the way as something began to rise up from the ground below us.

Turning back, I saw what appeared to be thick columns of ice, or maybe some sort of crystal lattice, erupt from the earth all around Sally. Without her former vampire speed, she was too slow to avoid it. The crystals continued to rise, meeting at the top above her head, penning her inside an almost solid cage, one that almost looked like a miniature version of Superman's Fortress of Solitude.

The walls weren't entirely clear, but it was translucent enough to see through. I could only watch as she touched the inside of the unnatural construct, causing me to instantly tense up as I readied to hit the dirt once again. However, nothing happened.

"A solid conjuring," Marjorie explained. "Harder than diamond and with no ambient magic for her to tap into."

Fortunately, at least one of our number wasn't dumbfounded by this new occurrence.

"Move," Christy commanded me.

I stepped out of the way as she let loose with a bolt of green energy, one of the nastier spells in the Magi arsenal. It hit the crystal prison like a runaway truck, causing even Sally to flinch from inside. She might as well have shot it with a Super Soaker, though, for all the good it did. Her blast didn't even scratch it.

"Non-conductive as well," Marjorie continued, exuding a level of smug that gave Gan a run for her money. "It was developed by a fringe offshoot of our people back in ancient Persia, in a foolish attempt to create a barrier capable of withstanding gods-forged weapons. Suffice to say, some of the gods in question took exception to this hubris. The sect didn't survive. But portions of their teachings did, secreted away from the eyes of the divine."

"This isn't what the Archives are meant for," Falcon snapped, finally growing a set. "It isn't a weapon. It's supposed to be a repository for research and..."

"I'm sure we can all agree these are extraordinary times," Gan interrupted, "requiring extraordinary measures."

"And the Falcon family thanks you for those measures," Marjorie replied.

Falcon's eyes opened wide. "What do you mean?"

"This incantation," his aunt explained. "It was incomplete, missing key sections thought lost to time."

"Not lost," Gan continued. "Merely kept safe by the First Coven ... until recently."

Falcon looked distressed, his focus back on his aunt. "What did you do?"

"I merely requested information aligned with our shared goals, nothing more. Perhaps someday we can truly merge the knowledge of our respective peoples, for the greater good of course. For now, simply consider this a fair exchange for aid rendered."

"What aid?"

I glanced at Ed and he gave me a nod. This was the sort of shit we'd talked about on the ride up. Guess Marjorie was up to her aristocratic eyeballs in Gan-related business.

"Don't act so ignorant, nephew," she continued. "It ill suits you. The Falcon Archives as well as those kept by the vampire nation, both powerful in their own right, containing knowledge mere commoners could not hope to understand." Oh yeah, she threw some side-eye Christy's way as she said that part. "Yet they remain incomplete, the result of thousands of years of mistrust and rivalry between our two people, each side jealously hoarding what they could."

"I don't understand."

"Don't you?" she asked, almost sounding genuinely perplexed. "I'd thought my brother had raised you to be more clever. All we have today, everything that has been returned to us, it is because..."

"She sold you out," Tom said. "I mean, shit, that's obvious even to me."

True enough, even if he could've worded it a bit more diplomatically judging by the way Marjorie glared at him.

"Hardly," she scoffed. "I ensured our future by sharing a fragment of an old ritual that was otherwise useless to us."

"You did *what*? How could you betray...?"

"That and that alone is the reason why our people once again stand tall and proud!" she snapped, cutting her nephew off. "Righting the wrongs that were done to us. Ensuring your parents didn't die in vain. Or have you already forgotten, nephew?"

Falcon turned away from her, from all of us. Call me crazy, but I had a feeling that didn't bode well for him as our inside man. "I haven't."

"Good. I'm glad to hear it. I don't like hiding things from you, Matthias, but sometimes steps must be taken rather than opened up for debate."

"Indeed," Gan said, looking up from where Paladin was whispering something in her ear. "Secure my beloved and his friends. I shall decide what to do with them afterward. The witch, however, is mine." She turned Marjorie's way. "Is that amenable?"

Marjorie gave her a single nod. "Christine Fenton was once deemed a traitor to the Magi. I, as ranking Mentor here, uphold that decision and declare her unbound by either the Humbaba Accord or any other standing truce. You may do with her as you please."

There's a reason why gamers know to take out the spell-casters first. Ranged fighters were dangerous enough with normal weapons. When they could bend the very forces of nature, well, those weren't the folks you wanted to ignore while trying to punch your way through the rest.

Unfortunately, the other side had that in spades now – thanks to Marjorie's coven, who all appeared fresh, as well as any of Gan's remaining magical hit minions.

Add to that what was left of Paladin's team, and we were pretty well fucked when it came to having nowhere to turn.

With spells, guns, and black bladed knives all pointing our way, we had little choice but to put our hands up – especially with our big gun neutralized. Sally was stuck fast in her crystal prison and, sadly, it seemed to be the real deal.

As she pounded on it from the inside, the sound of her cursing muffled but still audible, there came another low rumble from below us. The crystalline shell shuddered in response, sounding like a million rocks grinding together, but it remained standing.

"What the hell was that?" Ed asked.

I had a feeling I knew, being that the situation had just turned extra *stressful* for us all. Before I could answer, though, Falcon gave voice to what I was thinking.

"Her power," he said, turning our way, the look on his face unreadable. "The construct contained it."

"As I suspected it would," Marjorie replied.

If so, then we were truly fucked. Mind you, the alternative was probably us being peppered with a barrage of razor sharp shards that would've cut us to pieces. But still, it didn't bode well that they'd effectively neutered her.

As for Christy, orbs of Amun-Ra or not, she was still one spellcaster against a dozen or more. She powered down, apparently not caring to test those odds.

Gan, for her part, didn't order us cuffed or zip tied or anything. She didn't need to. She pretty much had us right where she wanted us. Although, I noticed, her focus was mostly on Christy.

"I think we both knew this was inevitable," Gan said to her.

Christy simply nodded. "From the day we met."

"I will not dishonor you with lies. The truth is, I have never much cared for you or the cattle you chose to breed with."

"When did Christy own a cow?" Tom asked as Paladin's team lined the rest of us up.

I glanced his way, one eyebrow raised. "About five years back. Now shut up!"

"...And I suspect the same is true of you," Gan continued. "But know I have come to respect you nevertheless. Your power and resourcefulness are both formidable."

"Thank you," Christy replied, her eyes locked on the other woman. "Know that I feel the same."

"Very well then. Despite what the Grand Mentor may have suggested, I offer you the honor of trial by combat under the provisions stipulated within the Humbaba Accord."

"To the death?"

"Of course."

Christy nodded again. "So be it. As the challenged, I await your terms."

Gan looked down at the sword in her hand before tossing it away. "My prowess against yours."

In return, Christy took her backpack off and laid it on the ground. "Done. The rest?"

"Should I win, you will be dead and I will thusly lay claim to my beloved."

"You can stick your claim up your ass!" I cried.

Christy ignored my outburst, inclining her head as if waiting for her opponent to continue.

Gan glanced Tom's way then let out a sigh. "Both the Progenitor and Shining One will be free to go ... for now."

"For now?"

"I offer this boon for your daughter's sake, but know that if the Shining One should raise arms against me again I will not hesitate to strike back. As for your child, I promise she will be well provided for. You need not go to your ancestors worrying about her future."

"She doesn't need anything from you."

"Let's not be hasty here," Tom called out.

I glanced at him. "Really?"

"What? Number one rule of finance – never turn down free money."

"Should you defeat me," Gan continued, "you, my beloved, the Progenitor, and the Shining One will be free, to live your lives however you so choose."

Okay, that wasn't great, but it was better than I'd expected. Gan was a lot of things, but she was also honorable. Of course, that assumed her crew didn't pull the obligatory bad guy double-cross afterward.

"Is that clear?" Gan added a moment later, fixing both Paladin and Marjorie with a stare.

Well, that was something at least. Now to only hope Christy could beat...

"What about Sally? You failed to mention her."

Oh shit, she was right. I'd totally missed that. The thing was, much like a genie's wish in D&D, the devil was in the details. And the three-hundred-year-old nutjob holding the cards was as close to the devil as I cared to imagine.

Gan gave a single shake of her head. "Her life is forfeit no matter the outcome. I'm sorry, but for the good of this world it must be done." Before Christy could tell her to eat a bag of French fried dicks, the not-so-little psycho turned toward Marjorie. "Seal it."

What?!

Her coven reacted almost instantly, having prepared as the rest of us were distracted by the spectacle in front of us. Once again suffused with magenta-hued power, they raised their hands and pointed Sally's way. In the next few seconds, the crystalline shards began to meld together – fusing into one solid mass, filling any cracks in the prison. Sally cried out, slamming her fists into the side, but the sounds she made grew ever fainter before cutting off entirely as the crystal prison became airtight.

Oh God, no! "You can't do this!"

"She'll suffocate in there!" Ed cried.

Gan merely inclined her head as she turned to once again face Christy.

"If we are lucky."

◄────── ⋙ ──────►

I stepped forward, fully intending to pop my claws through the side of Gan's head. After that, well, I didn't know, but I had to do *something*.

Unfortunately, our captors were intent on making sure I wasn't in a position to do anything but eat shit, as my legs were kicked out from beneath me, driving me to my knees.

Paladin grabbed hold of my hair and placed his gun to the back of my head. "Don't. If not for her, then for the rest of them."

The security goons on either side of me did the same to my friends – the one minding Tom, a human judging by the lack of effect his aura was having, holding a black-bladed knife to him instead.

As for Glen, he... Wait. Where the fuck was Glen?

I looked around, not seeing him. He'd been with us

when Christy had made her appearance, but after that I'd lost track of him. In all fairness, there'd been plenty of distractions since then.

Wait a second. Is that...?

I focused on where Sally's silhouetted form continued pounding against the sides of her impenetrable prison. There, down around her feet, something was undulating around, an amorphous yellowish mass.

What the fuck was he doing in there? *Shit!* He must've been next to Sally when Marjorie's pack of harpies summoned those crystals – and the rest of us had been too busy hauling ass to notice. Now he was trapped in there, too.

"Stop!" I cried. "Glen's in there. You have to..."

"Then it's already too late for him," Paladin said. "I'm sorry. I really am."

Sally continued banging on the sides from within, her actions growing ever more frantic.

No!

There came a flash from inside, her eyes blazing green. All at once, the ground below us shook again and there came a sharp crack from the crystalline structure.

She'd unleashed her power once more, her stress levels no doubt off the charts. But it had been for naught. There was barely a spiderweb crack in the side of the cage to show for the effort.

Tears fell from my eyes as the tremor passed and she slumped to her knees – albeit whether from defeat, exhaustion, or lack of air, I couldn't tell.

All I knew was that I couldn't watch her die, not like this.

Thunder rumbled and the skies momentarily lit up above us, the unexpected storm system starting to grow worse. Not that it mattered, not that any of it mattered while her life was hanging in the balance.

Come on, Dr. Death!

Sadly, there came no response from my subconscious,

the beast inside me little more than a frightened kitten when I needed him most.

Fine. Then I'd do it myself.

I ceased struggling and turned back toward the battle to find Christy and Gan circling each other out on the front lawn.

Paladin, in return, eased up on his hold a bit as I let my hands fall to my sides, where I slowly reached for the carabiner still attached to my belt loop.

"Kick her ass, babe!" Tom shouted, drawing some attention his way and giving me a chance to free the travel mug weighing down my pants.

I needed to do this slowly because I was only going to get one shot. Too bad neither of the women in my life had any time to spare.

Almost as if in response to my growing despair, Gan made her move, so fast it was as if she practically teleported across the battlefield.

A purple force dome appeared in the moment before she struck, deflecting the blow. Christy meanwhile let loose with a blast of red killing magic. Alas, it struck nothing but the ground where Gan had been, the crazy cunt-muffin already well clear.

Had a vamp like me been fighting her, I'd have given easy odds to Christy. She was both smart and dangerous. Gan, however, was beyond fast. Not only was it almost impossible to keep track of her movements, but she was using her speed wisely – stopping just long enough for Christy to loose another spell before moving again, slowly wearing her opponent down.

Without those orb thingies to help, Christy was forced to rely on her own reserves. It was a battle of attrition, one she couldn't win in the long term.

Fortunately for us all, I wasn't above a little unsportsmanlike conduct, working to one-handedly unscrew the cap of the travel mug. *Grr! Why did I have to put the fucking lid on so tight?*

Out on the battlefield, Christy, no doubt realizing she was playing a losing game of whack-a-mole, abruptly switched tactics. When Gan next came at her, taking a swipe at her force bubble, she dropped it instead, replacing it almost instantaneously with a shimmering blue cloud of electricity.

Unable to avoid it, Gan stumbled as her body sparked from the stun spell. Unfortunately, she was way too tough a cookie to be put down that easily.

As she quickly shook off the effects, though, Christy vanished.

A moment later, an entire field of Christies appeared, scattered throughout the yard. *Oh yeah, if you build it, I will come.* A glamour, it had to be. Since the direct approach wasn't working, she was going to force Gan on a wild goose chase – hopefully while looking for an opening to take her out.

Speaking of fighting dirty, I managed to get the cap loose. Glancing out the corners of both eyes, I saw that everyone around me seemed fixated on the fight. It was now or never.

I just had to hope that Paladin's kneejerk reaction wasn't to empty a slug into my brainpan. Smart as that would be, though, I couldn't help but think it would piss off his employer something fierce. And if he did shoot me dead, well, at least that saved me from having to play slave Leia to Gan's Jabba the Hutt.

Now! I brought the mug up and ... Paladin's hand clamped down on my wrist before I could even get a drop. *Fuck!*

"Did you really think I wasn't paying attention?"

"One can always hope. But come on, man. I'm just thirsty."

"I know all about you, *Dr. Death*, which, just for the record, doesn't leave you in any position to make fun of my name."

Damn it! It was one thing to be outmaneuvered, but

to be out-snarked, too? Talk about pouring salt in my wounds.

And I saw it was only going to get worse from there.

"Your skills are formidable, witch, but you forgot to hide your scent." Gan spun around so fast she almost left an afterimage. Two Christies were nearby, but she lashed out at the one on the right, catching her by the throat.

Oh no!

Christy's eyes bugged out of her head as all the other illusions simultaneously vanished from the yard.

"You may know all about him," Ed said from my immediate left, not that I was really paying attention to him at that moment. "But don't forget about me."

There came the squelch of blood, followed by a scream.

I turned to find him chomping down on his captor's arm, his metal teeth sawing into the vampire's wrist, letting loose a veritable fountain of blood.

Holy crap!

In that same moment, Paladin loosened his grip on me ever so slightly. Ed raised his eyebrows questioningly as if telling me to move my ass, forcing me from the shock of what he was doing.

Vamps biting other vamps was a big fat no for most. We're talking food poisoning with a capital V for vomit. The blood smoothie in my hands would have quite the opposite effect on me, though, but not if I was idiot enough to waste the opportunity.

I wrenched my arm free and leaned in, hoping the next sensation I felt wasn't that of my brains splattering against the grass. There wasn't time for any decorum. I simply upended the mug into my mouth, gulping what I could while the rest ran down the side of my face.

The blood hit my stomach like a Mortal Kombat finisher, instantly amping up my powers.

It wasn't a second too soon – literally, as I sensed the

gun at the back of my head tremble ever so slightly, telling me what was coming.

I shifted to the side just as the roar of the weapon sounded, ensuring a monster-sized headache for myself as the bullet clipped my ear. Still, it could've been a lot worse. Resting on my laurels was a good way to end up resting in peace, though, so I quickly spun around, using my arm to sweep Paladin's legs out from beneath him – my strength and speed now several times what it had been.

The situation was still shit, don't get me wrong, but at least it was slightly better smelling shit. The only question now being who to help first: Sally or...

"Did you honestly think I'd make such an amateur mistake?" Christy's voice echoed, causing me to waste my advantage by turning back toward the field of battle.

I couldn't help it. I had to know.

The Christy that Gan was choking out vanished into smoke within her grasp, just as I caught the slightest hint of a yellow glow around her head. Mind magic!

She'd used Gan's own arrogance against her, throwing out a magical honeypot while setting a trap for the wannabe world dictator.

Christy reappeared about twenty yards away, decloaking from another glamour, her body aglow with power.

She let loose with another red beam of energy, but it was the space of an instant for me to see it was going to miss by a country mile. There was no way she'd hit Gan with such a sloppy...

But she hadn't been aiming at Gan, though. The beam struck the backpack containing those crystals, the one she'd conveniently dropped close to the crowd of onlookers ... of which I was in the front row.

Fucking A!

Thank goodness my reflexes were amped, because I spun and dove for cover in the split second before the pack exploded like a brick of magical C-4.

39

THE BURNING SKY

U nlike Sally's shockwaves, this was a full on explosion. Hitting the ground didn't mean shit when the ground itself blew apart around me, sending me flying.

All I could do was curl up into a fetal ball as I hurtled through the air, feeling all sorts of unpleasantness as magical feedback tore at my skin like a thousand red hot cheese graters.

One kinda had to wonder what Gan's neighbors were thinking, since this shit wasn't exactly subtle. That was a worry for the local HOA, though.

I slammed into something solid then landed on what felt like hardwood, telling me the explosion had likely hurtled me into the remains of the mansion. Either that, or it had blown me all the way back to my apartment in Brooklyn – a nice fantasy, but unlikely considering the sound of crumbling plaster all around. I needed to move my ass before the rest of this place collapsed atop me.

Thankfully, my recent power boost ensured that was possible, having augmented my endurance and healing to the point where I was able to get back to my feet in seconds.

I looked around, noticing I hadn't been the only one blasted in this direction. Mind you, it wasn't a pretty picture. I spied a dead guard, a Magi with a broken spine, a vamp missing both his legs, and more.

Oh well, too bad so sad.

They weren't my concern so much as those who remained outside.

Amazingly enough, while a good chunk of the crowd had been scattered like bloody bowling pins, several had apparently weathered the storm.

Sally's crystal prison still stood like a monument to it all, but it was now too covered in dirt and debris to see what was going on inside.

"Eat this, ass licker!"

I caught sight of Tom already back in the action, his aura having no doubt protected him from the magical explosion. He'd retrieved his sword, which he was now busy impaling one of Gan's downed guards with, stabbing him in the chest repeatedly until his body immolated from the inside out.

That was one of my friends. Now where was...? There!

Ed was down on his hands and knees, looking scorched to hell as he puked his guts out, the double whammy of being caught in the blast right after ingesting vampire blood. He was alive, though.

So too were the Falcon brigade. I caught sight of Marjorie and her nephew, both ensconced inside a purple force barrier they'd managed to erect in time.

Rather than racing to rejoin the battle, Marge's attention appeared focused on something in front of her, hidden from my sight by a partially collapsed wall.

My own healing had brought me back up to snuff in the time it had taken me to gawk, so I peeked around it to get a better look, my eyes opening wide at what I beheld.

Gan was on her back unmoving about twenty yards from where she'd been when Christy had set off those crystals. She'd obviously eaten a good chunk of it. Sadly, it wasn't enough as evidenced by her not being a pile of ash.

I then caught sight of Christy, seemingly unharmed thank goodness, having likewise raised her own protective dome.

I couldn't quite celebrate her victory yet, though, as I noticed she was floating in midair – hovering, as the ground beneath her had caved in.

The sinkhole the explosion had opened was massive, at least twenty feet across. I couldn't tell how deep it went, the bottom being obscured by dust. Far more interesting than that, however, was the reddish orange glow shining dimly from within.

Call me crazy, but I had a feeling that's what had caught Marjorie's attention.

It was as if Christy had blown open the gates of Hell itself which, considering who owned this place, wasn't something I was so quick to dismiss. *The fuck?*

It's one of them, my subconscious cried.

"Huh? One of what?"

Whatever answer he had would have to wait, though, as Gan kipped up to her feet, suddenly looking far too lively for my liking.

I opened my mouth to shout a warning, but Christy was focused firmly on Marjorie.

"You think you're the only one who has some new tricks?" she cried out, floating forward until she was over solid ground again. "That you're the only witch capable of searching the old manuscripts for how to tap the power of a ley line?"

Oh boy. All at once I found myself wondering if maybe I should've taken her concerns about the Falcon Archives a little more seriously.

Christy cast a spell, although I wasn't able to tell what kind – the power around her shimmering in an array of different hues.

A part of me was hoping to see Marjorie's head explode, or Gan's too for that matter, because that would've been awesome. But I quickly realized neither of them were her target.

Hold on. Was she aiming at...?

Yes!

The ground around Sally's prison began to glow, the air seeming to vibrate from the ground up – the effect slowly encasing the unbreakable crystal.

What the...?

Unfortunately, that was the end of all coherent thought as a high frequency squeal of sound blared out, growing in both volume and frequency.

My ears, juiced up far beyond normal, began to ring painfully in tune with the warbling noise, causing me to cover them with my hands for all the good that did.

I wasn't alone in this either. Further out in the yard, Gan fell to her knees, likewise clutching her head – as did several of her people. I caught sight of Ed doing the same, as he continued puking his guts out while Tom stood over him, an amused smirk on his face.

The fact that he as well as others, including the Magi, didn't seem affected told me the ever increasing pitch, so intense I could feel my teeth rattling, was likely outside the range of human hearing.

Lucky them.

Less so for me as I was driven to my knees, wishing that someone would put me out of my misery. What the fuck was she doing?

Crack!

That's when I realized her gambit. The crystal. It was strong enough to withstand Sally's shockwaves but, where raw power failed, physics still applied. If Christy could produce a sound strong enough to resonate with the latticework...

Crack!

Okay, we were probably already past that point. Worse, I felt the remains of the house shudder below my feet. Christy's ploy was working, but she was also vibrating apart everything solid in the immediate area.

That included the sinkhole. It widened as the rock and stone around its periphery crumbled and collapsed.

But still she kept at it, increasing the intensity until the prison's walls, already covered in spiderweb cracks, began to fracture. There! A small opening appeared in the side, as more of it began to crack from the insane warbling.

At last, Christy dropped her spell – falling to one knee, no doubt exhausted by the effort.

I finally pulled my hands away from my ears, finding the palms covered in blood. *Wonderful.* Just what I needed to complete my day, a brain aneur ... oof!

Something tackled me from behind, sending me stumbling. Before I could recover, my side exploded in lancing pain as if someone had driven a hot poker right through me.

Argh!

Looking down, I saw that wasn't far from the truth, spying a combat knife sticking out of my favorite abdomen.

"Do you think that will change anything?" Marjorie's voice cried out, as I spun back toward the mansion to find Paladin waiting for me.

He looked even worse than I felt, his ears stained red and his eyes bloodshot from having likewise experienced Christy's dog whistle from hell, but he was obviously in good enough shape to impale me with his pig sticker.

Too bad for him, I currently possessed the power of an entire vampire coven.

I ripped the knife out and... Oh fuck, it was serrated.

It was like pulling a fucking harpoon out of my guts. *Goddamn it!*

Unfortunately, those Freewill blood boosts didn't come with any perks when it came to my motherfucking nerve endings.

"I guess we'll see," Christy responded from somewhere behind me. "Now, Glen!"

Glen?

Fuck! I needed to know what the hell was going on. I threw the knife at Paladin, missing by a mile, then dared a glance back toward the yard, trusting in my healing to close the exit wound I'd so gracefully inflicted upon myself.

Christy's banshee impersonation had not only cracked Sally's prison, but it had knocked all the dust and dirt from it, too, leaving the interior once again visible. Talk about a sonic shower.

I spied Glen undulating inside around Sally's feet. A moment later, something popped up out of his body. *What the hell?* Sally reached out and caught it just as the object began to glow – a soft white light not unlike those orbs of...

Oh fuck!

I took shelter behind a stone column in the instant before the already damaged prison blew apart, shards flying in every direction. Some hit Tom's aura, causing it to flare up as it protected him. Others weren't so lucky. Several who'd been spared Christy's explosion were hit – Magi, human, and vamp – instantly dropping to the ground as their bodies were peppered with razor sharp splinters of eldritch Gorilla Glass.

And in the center of it all stood Sally, her eyes blazing with green fury and...

Oof!

I'd gawked for one second too many. Paladin plowed into my backside, sending us both tumbling away from the mansion to the cobblestones outside.

Goddamn, I really needed to work on my focus. The

entire property was a warzone and what was I doing? I was acting like a freaking squirrel, turning toward every shiny object in sight while ignoring the people trying to kick my ass.

Sally was free and my friends were, well, probably not in great fighting shape, minus Tom maybe. Unfortunately, right then I had a pissed off security director with a stupid name to deal with.

I rolled to my feet only for him to be right up there in my grill, throwing a series of punches that all connected, including one to my windpipe, effectively sealing off the one advantage I had – my killer quips.

Fight back!

What do you think I'm doing? I thought, as I raised my hands and tried to block the next flurry of blows as Paladin had obviously multiclassed with a few levels of monk.

Fast as I was, I couldn't figure out any pattern to the blows being rained on me. Oh, and speaking of rain, I felt the pitter patter of it hit my head as Paladin continued to unleash a thunderstorm of brutality to the rest of me.

I was forced back, taking punches and kicks one after the other, my accelerated healing the only thing keeping me on my feet.

Or not, as an uppercut caught me under the chin, making me see stars and sending me flying. I landed at the edge of the sinkhole, feeling the loose dirt shift beneath me.

This close, the red glow from below was unmistakable, making me feel like I was lying next to a volcano – except there was no heat.

Wait ... red glow, no heat...

That train of thought would have to wait for the next station, though, as Paladin leapt atop me to continue his beatdown – proving he was far more adept with the grapple rules than I'd ever hope to be.

Gah! As I covered my face in the hopes of preventing an even worse pummeling, I realized what this all reminded me of.

It was like being back at the edge of The Source five years ago. I'd been all amped up, having finally conquered my inner demon, basically leaving me at the pinnacle of badassdom – or so I'd thought. Then I'd made the mistake of challenging Alex, serving as his punching bag as he took me apart piece by piece, our power equal but his skill far eclipsing mine.

Except this man's power isn't equal to yours.

What? As Paladin continued handing me my ass, I tried to internalize Dr. Death's words, striving to find a split second for my addled brain to think.

All around us more explosions rang out, in addition to myriad cries of pain and whatnot, telling me ours wasn't the only battle going on. Sadly, survival finally trumped taking a look around.

Paladin was hitting me with everything he had, and it definitely hurt – don't get me wrong – but, as Dr. Death's advice sank in, I realized he was working for every shot. That was the key. I didn't need to match him strike for strike. All I needed to do was remember I might be a clumsy hammer to his surgeon's scalpel, but though he might be sharper, I was a lot harder.

Okay, maybe that was a bad analogy, but you get my point.

Rather than try and block him when he came at me next, I simply flailed back. I caught him with a glancing blow at best, but there was a lot behind it – enough to shove him off. I rolled with him, using the momentum to straddle the mercenary asshole and pin him beneath me at the fissure's edge.

The view below us was fairly terrifying – like that scene from *Indiana Jones and the Temple of Doom*. Only in this case, I didn't care to play the part of the hero.

As Paladin continued to battle me with far greater skill, I forced my right hand down to his chest where I sprung my claws and dug into his skin.

That quickly caught his attention.

"Mola Ram, Sudha Ram, bitch!" I clenched my fist, digging through flesh and into his ribcage – finally causing him to cry out.

He grabbed hold of my wrist and ... almost pulled me free, making me remember my blood rush was limited in duration.

Time to remedy that.

With his hands otherwise occupied, I bent low with my teeth, chomping down on his cheek and ripping it wide open, allowing his blood to bolster my rapidly fading rush.

I won't lie. It was pretty gnarly – my claws digging through his chest while I quite literally chewed his face off. I tried not to think of it as the rain came down harder, dark goo dripping onto us as we...

Wait, dark goo?

I sat up, slamming my free hand into Paladin's ruined jaw for good measure, only to find his face covered not just in bloody gore but some kind of thick black runoff as well.

Okay, now this was getting weird.

I backed away from my downed foe, raising my palm and watching as drops of what appeared to be tar hit it from above.

What the fuck kind of freaky weather did they have here in upstate New York?

Wait a second. I'd seen shit like this before, recently as a matter of fact. It was like the muck that had been all over Falcon's pier after that creature attacked it. But we were nowhere near the Hudson. There wasn't any...

"THE TIME OF THE GREAT BEAST DRAWS NEAR!"

Oh, fuck biscuits.

I turned toward the sound of the echoing voice and saw Sally standing about forty feet away, eyes blazing and a look of inhuman rage upon her face. More importantly, I noticed the ground around her – stained, not with whatever shit was falling from the sky but with steaming entrails and bloodied bodies.

Almost as if to confirm the unholy horror of what I was seeing, one of Marjorie's witches, her white robe stained black from the sky muck, approached Sally with battle magic at the ready.

In the moment before she unleashed her spell, though, Sally turned her way. She made the barest gesture with her hand and the witch's body simply exploded, as if an invisible truck had hit her at ninety miles an hour.

What was left fell to the ground deader than dead, her innards painting the grass beneath her.

"TREMBLE," she said, her tone almost casual, "AS ALL YOU HOLD DEAR RETURNS TO THE DUST."

Huh. Dust would've been a hell of a lot cleaner than what she'd just done.

I was less worried about some rando witch, though, than about...

There! As I shielded my eyes from the falling gunk, I caught sight of Tom a ways off, his aura burning brightly as he continued standing guard over Ed – who'd apparently finally managed to stop puking his guts out long enough for the sky to do the same onto him.

Hold on, the rain... I turned back toward Sally, noting the crap from the sky was falling everywhere *but* where she stood. She had plenty of blood marring her outfit, but not a single drop of black ichor on her.

"Oh, this is most exciting!"

I glanced down to find Glen slithering nearby, aiming his fucking camera every which way. Goddamn, we really needed to have a talk at some point.

For now, though, I had more pressing concerns. "What did you do to her?"

"Do?" he asked, sounding as clueless as ever.

"To Sally, when you were in that crystal prison with her."

"Oh that. Before we arrived, Madam Witch asked to borrow one of my eyeballs. She hid a chunk of one of those glowing rocks in it before giving it back."

"You gave her one of your eyes?"

"Why not? I have plenty. Besides, she called me her secret weapon. How awesome is that?"

Not quite the word I'd use for it, but before I could say as much, movement from the corner of my eye reminded me I'd left a fight unfinished.

"Hold that thought."

I stepped away to face Paladin once again, leaving Glen to continue gleefully filming his magnum opus. The security chief glared at me ... for a moment anyway. Then he dropped to the ground twitching, his body enveloped ... in a stun spell?

What the hell?

He hit the crumbling dirt at the edge of the sinkhole, right before it collapsed beneath him, causing him to disappear from sight as he fell toward whatever waited below.

Before I could question what had just happened, a hand fell on my shoulder and I turned to find a sight for the sorest of eyes staring back at me – Christy. *Thank goodness!* She looked absolutely exhausted, but she was alive.

"Are you okay?" she asked after a brief but wonderful hug, stepping back to notice I was kinda splattered in gore.

"It's not mine, most of it anyway. How are...?"

"Don't worry about me," she interrupted. "We need to get Sally out of here. I think we ... *I* may have pushed her too far."

"You don't say."

"It's not just her power," Christy replied. "The proximity to the ley line, to the Source below us. I can't say for certain, but I think it's affecting her, too."

Suddenly it all made sense. The strange glow from below, the lack of heat, what Dr. Death had been trying to tell me. Had I not been getting my ass beat, I'd have maybe put two and two together myself.

Gan had created thirteen Sources to replace the original. We hadn't known where any of them were located, but in retrospect it made perfect sense that she'd have one right beneath her personal fortress.

"You knew, didn't you? That it was down there, I mean."

She shook her head. "I suspected it, but wasn't sure until now. I knew there was a ley line nearby. Then, when I tried to scry the grounds here and failed, even using that blood magic spell, I realized she was using it to super-charge her wards. I figured there was only one reason to do that."

"But how did you know...?"

She put a finger to my lips, no doubt realizing we didn't have much time for exposition, not with Sally busy exploding people like rotten turnips. "I couldn't see inside, but I could scry outside the gates just fine, well enough to know when Gan was here and when she wasn't."

I opened my mouth to reply, but she leaned in and kissed me, freaky tar rain be damned. Oddly enough, whatever I had to say didn't seem all that important in that moment.

"I'm sorry I didn't tell you," she said, pulling away. "I meant to, I really did. But then this morning happened and it all went crazy. Afterward, there wasn't time and..."

"Then Sally remembered I'm a lousy actor?"

She smiled and held up two fingers close together. "I can't say I agree with what she did, but ... I can kind of understand it, a little bit anyway."

Guess it was time to look into the local community theater scene. But first things first. We...

Shit!

I tackled Christy to the ground, pinning her beneath me as I spied something from the corner of my eye. A moment later, a beam of green death magic lanced past where we'd been standing.

I looked up and saw Marjorie stalking our way. Oddly enough, she didn't seem all that pleased.

"Look at you getting all frisky," Christy remarked from under me.

"Really?" I replied. "I thought I was the one who's supposed to be making the ill-timed sex jokes here."

"What can I say, you must be rubbing off on me."

I couldn't help but grin. "I knew there was a reason I loved you."

Time seemed to stop for a moment as my synapses went into overdrive realizing what I'd just said. It didn't matter that we were right above a magical portal to beyond, that a witch was coming to kill us, or that it was raining black muck. No, what mattered were the words that had left my lips, slipping out almost of their own accord.

In the back of my mind, Dr. Death screamed for me to focus but I shushed him, trying to figure out how I was going to backpedal from this one.

But maybe I didn't need to. As I pushed to my feet, heedless of the danger around us, Christy smiled at me – so sweet and pure, despite the mess raining down on us both.

"I ... uh..."

"Later," she said, raising a force dome just as Marjorie let loose with another volley, one that surely would've cooked my inattentive goose had she not been there. "But it's going to be a good talk. I promise you that."

Oh mama!

It was only the sight of her stumbling from exhaustion that forced me to focus on the shit storm going on around us.

They say that love conquers all, but I had a feeling whoever coined that phrase hadn't been facing a pissed off witch at the time.

Behind Marjorie, I saw Sally gak another mage, rendering the poor sap into human spaghetti before turning her gaze on the old hag – her eyes blazing with green fury, as if a part of her was still in there and remembered.

That was the part we needed to reach. But first...

Unfortunately, Falcon picked that moment to race to his aunt's side. My ears caught just enough of his frantic words to understand he was trying to get her to stand down.

"*Matthias*," Christy cried out, amplifying her voice with magic. "*Behind y...*"

As loud as she was, though, it was instantly drowned out by the sound of something much louder – like thunder given form. It was a scream or screech of some sort – like a hundred cars all decided to slam on their brakes at once, yet still low pitched enough for me to feel the air vibrate around us.

What in the ever living fuck?

Though I wasn't sure which direction it had come from, my eyes instinctively turned toward the sky, the cloud cover now lower than ever – hanging over our heads like a dark portent of...

Hold on. That black rain. Yeah, it was like what I'd seen down at the docks, but I also realized what else it reminded me of – that gunk Sally had been covered in when she'd first woken up from her cocoon.

No way could that be a coincidence, or good for that matter.

As the strange cry faded, a hush seemingly fell over the estate – all eyes within looking for whatever could have possibly made it.

Or most of them anyway.

Sally continued stalking toward Marjorie's position.

However, she stopped before she could make it to the witch, turning her head as another voice finally spoke up and broke the eerie silence.

"You will face me instead, whore," Gan said, stepping toward her, sword in hand. "If you so dare."

40

RODANCING IN THE DARK

S ally inclined her head toward Gan, an amused smile playing out across her face as if a part of her was enjoying this.

Knowing her, I couldn't exactly rule that out.

Watching Dave die had hurt, although not as much as I'd thought it would. I realized at least some part of me, a part I wasn't necessarily proud of, understood that he had no one else to blame but himself.

The truth was, Gan deserved the same, albeit a *lot* more.

On some level, however, I think I'd accepted that she'd always be there – lurking in the shadows like a boogeyman, waiting to swoop in with her demented love. And I suppose that was why I'd never seriously put in the effort to stop her. Gan was a survivor. No matter what I did, I assumed she'd still be there waiting to try again.

But nothing lasts forever, not even the daughter of Ögedei Khan.

I realized that now as Sally raised her hand.

Here it comes.

"I am the one who made the covenant with your master," Gan said, her voice just barely audible over the patter of dirty rain. "I am she who offered the tithe and paid it."

"AND YET," Sally replied, "YOU STILL FAILED."

Ooh, sick burn by the evil entity from beyond.

She gestured toward Gan and, though her power was invisible to the naked eye, I saw the grass flatten as she sent death racing toward the love-starved psycho – seeking to end her claims upon both this world and my crotch once and for all.

And then, as I waited for this nightmare to finally end ... nothing fucking happened.

Well, okay, that's not true. It was as if the kinetic energy coalesced around Gan, becoming momentarily visible as a greyish blur of power, then it parted ways and went around her, leaving her standing there with nothing worse to show for it than slightly mussed hair.

"Um, is it me or should she be kinda dead by now?"

"I...," Christy started, but then Sally gestured again.

This time the result was far more dramatic. The ground erupted before her as if she'd set off a series of seismic charges. However, once again, as it reached Gan it was as if it decided to hop step right past her.

"The armor she's wearing," Christy said. "It has to be. The symbols on it. I didn't recognize them, thought they were maybe ancestral crests, but..."

"But Gan came prepared," I finished for her. "Just like she fucking always does." *Goddamn it!*

I wasn't sure what made me angrier, the fact that she was still alive or that she'd been okay with hanging everyone else – including her own people – out to dry while keeping all the good shit for herself.

Hell, even Marjorie seemed to be getting a clue, narrowing her eyes at the little hellion, at least in the second before Gan bolted forward, sword raised.

Oh shit! "Move, Sally!"

I might as well have been screaming in slow motion

for all the good it did. Gan struck before I'd even finished the second syllable of my friend's name. She stepped past, her sword striking true, as blood bloomed across the front of Sally's shirt, falling in a cascade to the ground.

Sally stumbled then fell to her knees. For a moment she stayed that way, head lowered. But then, disemboweled or not, she ... actually smiled, her eyes blazing brighter than ever, like two green beacons in the middle of a storm.

In the next instant, the ground rumbled as another screech came from above, drowning out everything else and somehow sounding both angrier and meaner than before, if that was even possible.

Gan turned, no doubt intent on delivering the killing blow. Sadly, there was no way I'd get there in time. Fast as I was, it wouldn't be nearly fast enough, especially since I had to make it past Marjorie first. Crazy as all of this was, I wouldn't have put it past the old prune to take a cheap shot at me.

That didn't mean I wasn't going to try, though.

"Stay here!"

Though my initial boost had worn off, I'd bolstered it with a chunk of Paladin. Regardless, even though I was halfway there by the time Christy screamed my name, I knew in my unbeating heart I wasn't going to make it.

Too bad I wasn't the only one on the way.

The clouds above Sally swirled into a maelstrom as something immense descended from the sky.

The ground literally exploded from the impact as whatever it was landed atop where she knelt, the shockwave knocking Gan away as well as everyone else within ten yards – Tom and Ed included. Hell, even Marjorie wasn't able to get a force dome up in time, her magic dissipating as she and her nephew were knocked from their feet.

It was all I could do to put on the brakes and veer left

as chunks of earth flew my way and I was engulfed in dust.

The truth was I was acting on instinct alone, my brain pretty much beyond the capacity for rational thought as I'd caught a brief glimpse before all hell had broken loose – the image seared into my mind.

It had looked like the claw of some enormous eagle. The size of a bus and dripping with that black tar, it possessed talons twice the height of a man, all of them aglow from the strange sigils etched into them – each burning a bright electric blue.

There were a lot of questions in my head as I finally skidded to a halt, unable to do much more than gawk skyward, but first and foremost was whether this thing was here to save Sally or destroy her.

Okay fine, figuring out whatever the fuck it was also rated pretty high on the list. However, if I was hoping for an unobstructed view I was in for disappointment. All I could see was a shadow in the clouds of something enormous hanging in the air above us.

Needless to say, at least one thing was crystal clear.

I was in so far over my head, I might as well have been buried at the center of the Earth.

Being slowly torn apart by Alex seemed like a pleasant memory compared to the shit storm I was smackdab in the center of. Less than a day ago I was waking up next to Christy. Now I was starring in *Jurassic World: Upstate New York*.

I remembered as a child watching a stop motion special called *Mad Monster Party*. I didn't remember the plot too well, but it starred classic movie monsters such as Dracula, Frankenstein's Monster, and the Wolfman. It had also featured an appearance by King Kong, who'd proven that size most definitely did matter by scooping up and manhandling the other monsters like they were little more than dogshit.

Safe to say, I was beginning to understand the feeling.

As the dust started to clear, the creature roared again, a shriek like an enraged bird of prey strapped to a stadium-sized amplifier. The claw closed upon the ground beneath it, scooping up a massive amount of dirt, soil, and rocks, before lifting back up through the cloud cover – leaving behind a trench the size of a small swimming pool, but no sign of Sally.

A heavy downdraft of air slammed into me, almost knocking me off my feet – the flap from an enormous pair of wings, unseen but definitely felt.

Holy shit!

I could only stand there stunned, barely comprehending what I'd seen. It was as if someone had finally given Toho the budget and expertise to make a realistic...

"Look out!"

Ed's cry came a moment too late, as something red hot hammered into me from behind.

"ARGH!"

I was sent tumbling, green fire lapping at my backside. That wouldn't have been so bad had most of my left arm not gone flying in the opposite direction, turning to dust a moment after it hit the ground.

Thank goodness the rest of me didn't follow, my power boost likely the only thing saving me from taking the last dirt nap of my life.

Unfortunately, between the shock, pain, and all the burning, I was left too stunned to do anything save look groggily around.

About fifteen yards away, a bunch of Gan's people were rushing to her side. *How thoughtful of them.* I guess good help wasn't so hard to find after all, at least when you were an uber-charismatic mega-millionaire.

That was all well and good, but my immediate concern was Marjorie. She looked ... dirty, which was probably the worst thing an upper crust twat like her could imagine. Mind you, that didn't stop her from bearing down on me, aglow with angry green energy.

"You should not have interfered. Whatever happens next is entirely on your head."

Ironic, considering she was about to blow that same head right off me. At least that didn't leave me a lot of time for regret before...

"Eat a bag of rancid assholes, Queen Pricktoria."

Tom stepped over me protectively, his aura ablaze. His intentions were in the right place. Too bad he was a little close for comfort, setting my legs on fire in the process.

Son of a...

"Oh shit," he cried as I screamed. "Sorry, man."

Fortunately, in the next second, Ed was there to drag me back as Tom tanked Marjorie's spell, his faith shield absorbing the brunt of it.

"T-thanks," I said, trying to force myself to remain conscious. At least my vampiric healing was already staunching the worst of the blood flow. Less good was that I was in agony and pretty much wanted to do nothing more than die.

"Are you okay?"

"On ... a scale of one to ten ... about a negative two," I gasped. "S-Sally?"

"No idea, man. What the fuck was...?"

The creature shrieked again, sounding like a freight train running over my ear drums.

If any of us had thought that was it, that it was over now that it had taken our friend, we were dead wrong.

I turned my head in time to see another massive claw descend from the sky. In my pained daze, I couldn't tell if it was the same one or not. More important was that it had descended right over the sinkhole Christy had created – the one she was still next to.

No!

Exhausted or not, she still managed to raise a force barrier around herself as the titanic claw raked the edge of the crater, shaking the ground hard enough that – combined with another heavy downdraft from above – it sent everyone stumbling, even Tom, forcing me to roll out of the way before I caught another taste of his faith aura.

When I looked back again, it became painfully obvious what the creature was doing – widening the hole, almost as if it were digging for...

The Source! That's what it's after.

"T-the Source," I repeated, not bothering to argue with myself. "It's going for The Source."

"What?" Ed asked.

"One of the thirteen Sources," I explained. "Gan's had it beneath her home this entire time."

"Y'know, somehow that makes sense in a crazy sort of way," he replied, cocking his head. "But what the fuck are we supposed to do about it?"

That was a really good question.

Amazingly enough, though, the answer came in the form of the woman I loved. As a second claw descended through the clouds, likewise bent on widening the hole that had been ripped open in the ground, I saw her clamber to her feet, force dome flickering around her.

A moment later, she dropped it in favor of offense, firing a blast of red hot death at one of the beast's talons.

She might as well have been shooting Nerf bullets for all the good it did.

"We ... need to help her," I said, pushing myself up with my remaining arm.

"What?!" Tom and Ed both cried.

"Help her!" I snapped, forcing strength into my voice that the rest of me didn't feel. I turned toward Marjorie and Falcon. "Please."

"He's right," Falcon said, placing a hand on his aunt's

shoulder, even as she looked more than ready to blast me again. "We need to stop this."

She turned to her nephew, making a face as if he'd just suggested giving her a Dirty Sanchez instead. "It's too late for that."

"No. It's not."

"We will take our leave of this place, nephew," she stated, "but first, you will let me finish what I..."

The only thing that finished was her pontificating, as her body lit up with blue electricity and she collapsed to the ground.

"I'm sorry, Aunt Marjorie, but you're wrong." Falcon paused to take a suck from his vape pen, then turned to the rest of his coven, those who were still functional anyway – probably far fewer than we needed. "All of you with me! We stop this now."

With Marge down, the others looked confused as he turned his attention to the two massive claws still busy excavating. It was apparently time for a bird fight, as he unleashed a bolt of green fire their way.

Too bad it had about the same effect as Christy's spell.

Thankfully, it wasn't just them alone. The remaining Magi joined the assault a few minutes later – pouring it on, even though I had a feeling they were all on their last legs from the protracted battle.

I think on some level everyone present was slowly beginning to realize that, whatever had been their goal here today, this monstrosity was now our common enemy. Hell, even Sally, had she been here, would've been...

That gave me pause, forcing me to wonder what had befallen her – images of her being devoured by this Rodan-sized monster playing out in my mind.

Enough of that! You need to focus!

Dr. Death was right. Worry, regret, all of that would have to wait. For now, I had a job to do, however daunting it might seem.

I stood on shaky legs, turning to my friends.

"Come on. It's time to Pacific Rim this kaiju back to Monster Island."

Now to only hope we could make good on my ridiculously overconfident words.

41

FALLING IN LOVECRAFT

They say the definition of insanity is doing the same thing multiple times and hoping for different outcomes.

I beg to differ.

I'd say pure insanity was more along the lines of facing something so horrendous that you had less than a zero percent chance of winning, yet still running toward it anyway.

If so, then me and my friends were crazy as shithouse rats.

Nevertheless, I'd be damned if I was going to let Christy face this thing alone.

The creature continued to dig. The dust it raised, along with the unnatural cloud cover above, serving to mask its body from sight, giving us nothing more than a hint as to the monstrosity above us.

As it dug, the glow from the sigils adorning its claws began to war with that from below – the blood red illumination of something that was never meant to be unearthed.

I raced toward one of its claws and slashed at it – my talons hitting home with a *clang* as if I'd decided to try my luck at slicing through a steel girder instead.

Beams of magic lanced out from every direction, each of them doing more than me, even if that wasn't saying much.

The harsh retort of gunfire soon joined the Magi's efforts, as Gan's people no doubt did the math and realized it was time for an economy-sized turkey shoot against the beast excavating their boss's front lawn.

I marveled as a few feathers fell from the sky, each of them at least ten feet long and covered in that strange black tar.

Yet, despite the assault, it continued to dig like we were nothing but ants. In short order, it had cleared a massive trench – long and wide enough to give me a clear view below, where I could see an open cavern. Smack dab in the middle of it was one of the thirteen Sources, an Olympic-sized jizz pool of swirling reddish gunk.

It wasn't as large as the original Source, but it was more than big enough to give me the heebie-jeebies. I half-expected to see rock monsters with orange lantern eyes staring balefully up at us, but thankfully there was no sign of anything of the sort.

"Come on!" Ed said, grabbing hold of my good arm and dragging me out of my reverie. "You too," he cried to Tom, who was busy swinging his sword at the other claw – and mostly missing.

He led me over to where Falcon stood by Christy, firing beams of magic at the beast. She was down on one knee, looking on the verge of collapse, while he paused his assault long enough to suck from his pen.

Jesus Christ this guy liked his nicotine.

The same exhaustion on Christy's face appeared true of most of the mages still standing, their spellcasting starting to falter despite doing little more than ruffling a few feathers.

"It's no good," Falcon said, shaking his head. "We'd need an Apollo's Prism just to get this blighter's attention." He glanced my way, his eyes falling on my missing arm –

scabbed over and no longer bleeding at least. "I'm sorry, Freewill."

I shook my head. "Don't be. Nobody could've foreseen this shit."

"Help me up," Christy said.

"Don't," I told her. "You've done enough. There's nothing more..."

"You're wrong." She stopped as she noticed the ruined remains of my arm. "My goddess..."

"It's fine. Nothing that won't grow back ... hopefully."

"I think it's time for us to consider a strategic withdrawal," Falcon offered.

Even Tom agreed with that one. "Fuck yeah. This shit would be a lot easier if we had maser canons."

I gestured toward the Magi still fighting. "We do, but so far they're about as effective as in the movies."

He let out a sigh. "Somebody needs to hurry their ass up and invent the Oxygen Destroyer."

"No!" Christy said, this time more forcibly. "I mean, we can't let it have the Source."

Falcon shook his head. "We don't even know why this bloody thing's after it. We..."

"No, we don't. But we can probably assume it's for nothing good. Tell me otherwise."

On that, Falcon was silent.

"You're gonna ask me to jump in there and try to blow it up, aren't you?" Tom replied, gesturing toward the sinkhole. "Because I will, even if it'll suck balls to die again."

She stepped up, placing her hand on his cheek. "I know you would." She then turned to the rest of us. "I know all of you would." Her gaze finally came to rest on me. "And I love you all for it."

Our eyes lingered on each other for a moment longer, prompting me to open my mouth, but she wasn't finished yet.

"But there's another way."

"There is?" I asked, stumbling as the ground beneath us rumbled.

"What are you getting at, Christine?" Falcon replied, his eyes narrowed.

"The Source, obviously," she said. "We need to use its power."

Wait, what?

He shook his head. "This isn't like drawing from a ley line. Nobody's seen the bloody Source for thousands of years, not until recently anyway, much less figured out how to tap into its..."

"The White Mother did, millennia ago, before she became twisted into that creature we were forced to stop. Her writings, her *original* teachings..."

"Have been lost to time," Falcon said. "The only known copies are under lock and key in..."

"The Falcon Archives," she interrupted. "Yes, I know."

She turned my way again for a moment, her face a mask of determination. Yet beneath it lay all the fear she'd expressed about relying on forbidden texts not meant for mortal eyes. At the same time, if she had a solution for Big Bird here, I'm not sure we were in any position to argue.

"I told you, you weren't the only ones who came prepared," she said to Falcon before stepping to the edge of the rapidly widening crater, the Source – one of thirteen scattered throughout the world – clearly visible below.

His eyes widened with disbelief, fear, and then finally resolve as she began to chant in an unintelligible voice, waving her arms about in what I assumed was more than just sick dance moves.

She pointed one hand downward, continuing to chant.

"Stop this madness," Falcon said. "You have no idea what..."

I stepped in, putting my hand on his shoulder. "I think we're long past don't and can't here. If she's got a spirit bomb to drop on this thing, we have to let her."

"It's not that simple, Freewill. The power she's talking about, it can't be..."

Apparently, it *was* that simple, though, as a tendril of the Source shot up toward her, reaching out like a freaky ass tentacle and touching her outstretched fingers.

In that same instant, Christy lit up as if a spotlight had just been turned on her – prismatic energy dancing off her body. It was the kind of power I'd only seen two other spellcasters harness: Calibra – the White Mother – and Tina.

I felt my hair stand on end, as if the area immediately around us was one giant field of static electricity.

"I think we might want to back up a bit," Ed cautioned, not incorrectly.

"Yeah, kick it in its cloaca, babe!" Tom cried.

We weren't the only ones who'd noticed her, though, not by a long shot. All around the battlefield, spellcasters dropped their incantations to stare her way, as the aura around her grew in intensity.

Falcon shook his head, his eyes betraying disbelief. "I don't understand how!"

"I think you do," Christy replied. "And I know there will be a reckoning, one I will gladly accept. But for now, this is what must be done."

"No! You don't know what you're..."

His warning fell on deaf ears as Christy lifted her other hand and unleashed an attack not dissimilar to one Calibra had made five years earlier, an attack that had been powerful enough to stop a god.

A blast of prismatic lightning erupted from her, a thunderbolt that likely would've made even the Mighty Thor shit himself. It flew upward, slicing through the clouds above us and giving me a momentary glimpse of a massive feathered body. Then it struck home and the skies lit up with a blinding flash of light.

What answered was a shriek of pain and pure rage, loud enough to be heard all the way back in Brooklyn.

The monstrous claws lifted from the ground as a deluge of horror fell from the sky – singed feathers large enough to use as blankets, chunks of scorched flesh, and a cascade of thick black goo that had to be its blood.

"She got it!" Tom cried, echoing the painfully obvious.

"Hell yeah," Ed replied. "Although, if that thing's about to die, now might be a good time to..."

"Start running?" I offered, his words sinking in. Not exactly the worst plan I'd ever heard.

Rather than a thousand ton beast falling on our heads, though, the claws continued to rise, disappearing back into the clouds.

"Hit it again," I said, insane as that sounded. "Before it can escape."

"No!" Falcon cried, pushing past me toward where Christy stood aglow in the primal energies of God knows how many other worlds. "That's enough. You don't know what it will do to you."

She looked at him, her eyes aflame with so much power that even I was tempted to step the fuck back. However, rather than blast us to atoms for daring to question her, she took a deep breath and shook her head. When she blinked again, her eyes were back to their normal beautiful blue. "It's okay. I'm fine."

The rush of watching her kick this thing's ass was rapidly wearing off, bringing with it the clarity of how crazy all this was. "I ... think he might be right."

Christy nodded, the glow around her starting to fade. She began to turn toward us, but then her eyes opened wide in surprise as she was pulled back toward the Source.

The tendril of power she'd called forth had wrapped around her wrist, like the arm of some overly friendly alien octopus. She tried to pull away, but it held on tight.

"Hold on," I told her. "I'll help..."

The rest of whatever I had to say was drowned out, though, by a voice echoing from above – the same we'd heard coming from Sally when she'd faced Gan.

"DID YOU ACTUALLY EXPECT THAT TO WORK?"

Uh oh.

Less than a second later, that threat was proven more than idle as both of the creature's claws emerged from the cloud cover, racing toward us like a pair of runaway locomotives.

⟵————◆————⟶

Tom and I both leapt for Christy – great minds thinking alike. Sadly, it was more like two dumbasses cancelling each other out. His aura activated as one of the massive claws came down, catching me in its periphery and blowing me clear just as the ground caved in, sending up a shower of rocks and dirt.

Screams filled the air as the creature's other foot touched down at the far end of the trench, where Gan's forces had been peppering it with weapons fire. Too bad I didn't give a single flying fuck about them in that moment.

I sat up as the massive talons lifted away, fearing the worst. Bodies lay all around me, Magi who'd been scattered by what had happened.

There!

Christy hung suspended in the air. The Source was still wrapped around one of her arms. Tom, however, had a hold of the other. The only thing keeping them both from falling was ... Glen! The little blob was stretched to his limit – a tendril of slime wrapped around Tom's free hand, while the rest of him held onto the rock face, grasping at any crevice he could get his goopy self into.

Tom's teeth were gritted as his aura sparked around him, flaring up one second then dying down the next. For a moment, I thought he might've been injured, but then I saw smoke rising from Glen's tendril and realized what he was doing – trying his damnedest to keep his powers contained.

"Hold on," I cried. "I'm..."

"Freewill ... Bill!"

I turned to see Falcon. My first instinct was to tell him to take a number, but the words instantly died in my throat as I saw who was lying next to him.

Ed was convulsing – his body, his *face*, a ruined mess of raw flesh and blood.

"He pushed me out of the way," Falcon said, dropping to his knees as if searching for something. Talk about a poor time to lose a contact lens. "He saved my life. You have to help him!"

"Use your magic, I need to..."

"Where in god's name is it?" he cried, desperately looking around before turning back and meeting my eyes. "I ... I can't."

I had no idea what he was talking about, but it was the space of a second to see something needed to be done. Ed's face was missing from the nose down, having been sheared off in the attack, leaving nothing behind but a broken bloody mess of flesh, gristle, and the ruined ends of silvery metal.

His eyes rolled into the back of his head as he gurgled, blood pouring from the horrific wounds.

Oh God no!

It's not too late, the voice in my head cried.

But he's... Dr. Death was right, though. There was one rule of vampires I'd come to know and accept over the years: when a vamp died, they turned to dust. If there was still a body, that meant there was still a chance.

Although not for long, judging by the choking sounds coming from him, growing fainter with each breath.

I glanced back at where Tom continued to hold Christy, the Source refusing to give up its grip on her.

Damn me to hell, but I didn't see any way to help Ed. Not in the condition he was...

There came a groan from nearby. I looked down to see one of the white-robed witches from Falcon's clan, injured but still alive, blood dripping from several minor cuts.

Blood.

Do it, Dr. Death commanded.

But...

If you want to save your friend, do it now!

Fuck it all.

"Don't let go!" I cried out, reaching down and dragging the mage over to where Ed lay.

"What the bloody hell do you think you're doing?" Falcon asked, wide-eyed.

"I'm sorry," I said to them both. Then I grabbed hold of the injured witch with my good arm, unsheathed my claws, and ripped out her throat.

"Dear god! What have you done?"

"God has nothing to do with this place, not anymore."

I dropped the dying witch atop Ed, letting her blood pour into the gaping maw where his mouth used to be. It was all I could do. If it wasn't enough...

Regrettably, I realized in the next instant that it wasn't ... but not for him.

Tom cried out as Christy was ripped from his grasp, the tendril of the Source's power having somehow snaked up her arm and taken an even stronger hold.

"No!"

For a moment I watched in horror as she seemingly hung in midair. Her eyes met mine and in them I saw both terror and sadness, although that might have simply been a reflection of what I felt in that instant.

Then the moment passed and she fell, dragged down below – one hand still reaching up as if hoping to grasp hold of salvation that wasn't there, as if praying that we hadn't failed her.

But we had.

In the next second she was gone, the Source

reclaiming its wayward tendril as well as its new prize, dragging Christy below its surface.

All I could do was stand there and watch, useless as I was. Tom, likewise, seemed to be in shock, hanging there by the thread of Glen's efforts, looking down as if expecting her to surface again and for everything to be all right.

Truth of the matter was I expected it, too – for her to rise again, but not as herself, as something inhuman. But all that remained was the unbroken surface of this strange pool of power.

For a few seconds anyway.

Then the creature struck again, its enormous claw shooting past us, down below toward the Source. And all at once I understood. This was its true prize, what it was really after.

What for, I couldn't begin to know. I didn't care either because she was gone.

Oh God, she's gone!

The nightmare wasn't over yet, though.

The creature's massive talons struck the Source, its strange waters splashing up high, as if it were the world's weirdest bird bath.

The beast wasn't merely there to take a dip, however. The glow of the magical goop began to change. The orange hue was slowly replaced, turning a sickly green wherever the claws touched it.

What in hell?

"Oh yeah? Well, fuck you, asshole!"

It was Tom, still hanging by a goopy thread. His eyes were aglow with fury, no longer able to contain the power within him.

It spread from there, the faith magic around him growing stronger by the second, even as Glen's tendril began to sizzle.

"Eat shit and fucking die already!" he screamed, his aura exploding in intensity.

"Too hot!" Glen cried, the handhold of slime snapping, leaving Tom in freefall.

No! Not again.

Tom wasn't about to go quietly into the night, though. Not this time.

Even as he fell, he held his hands out in front of him ... and then it happened. Back in Pennsylvania, he'd somehow tapped into his powers in a way I'd never seen before – using his faith magic offensively instead of as a shield.

And that had been for no reason other than over some stupid toys.

What we'd both lost today was far more precious, and it showed as the power around him channeled itself into his hands and then flared out below – slowing his descent as surely as if he were riding a rocket booster.

The beam of pure faith struck the Source, now fully corrupted by the creature's touch. It exploded like an atom bomb, causing a cascade of power to erupt forth – green and white, both vying for dominance, until at last it flared up blindingly bright, causing me to cry out as my retinas finally overloaded and all became darkness and shadow.

✦

I wasn't sure what I expected to find when my eyes finally cleared, but this wasn't it. There was no sign of the creature, save the destruction it had left behind. I looked up to see the skies once again clear, the moon and stars visible above.

It spared me, for a moment anyway, from having to deal with the awfulness of what waited below, but I forced myself to look nevertheless.

There was nothing but darkness down there. The Source was gone. The space it left behind was now nothing but fused rock with maybe a few puddles still faintly glowing green. There was no sign of...

No, wait. I spied something below. Trying my best to focus, I caught sight of Tom, the meager starlight glinting off the few spots of his armor not sullied in the fight. For a moment, I feared the worst, but then I saw him move – slowly at first as he touched his leg and his hand started to glow.

"Fuck that hurts."

His voice was barely a whisper to my ears, but he was alive. Sadly, I didn't see any sign of Christy anywhere.

I needed to get down there to see if she...

I left it at that, not wanting to finish that thought. First, I turned to where Ed lay. At some point he'd grabbed hold of the dead witch, grasping her tightly. Though I couldn't see his face, I heard the disturbing sounds of slurping, telling me he at least had a chance.

The question now was what price would have to be paid in saving him.

Falcon stood a few feet from us, pointedly looking away.

He held up a hand as I took a step toward him. "Don't." He let out a deep shuddering breath and said, "What you did ... what she did... I ... I need to leave this place."

"I'm sorry."

"I have to go," he repeated, walking away, toward where he'd left Marjorie.

I watched him for a moment or two, then decided it would probably be best to make myself scarce.

There wasn't anything more I could do for Ed. He'd either be okay or he wouldn't. All I could do was hope for the best.

"Drink up, buddy," I said softly, making my way toward the trench once again.

A familiar blob of eyeballs met me at the edge. "Are you okay?" Glen asked.

"Not really. You?"

"Nothing some proper rehydration won't fix. I

managed to slough off that part of me before I took any serious damage and... Listen, I ... I'm sorry about what happened to Madam Witch."

"So am I."

He slithered up next to me, wrapping a comforting tendril around my ... ankle. "Do you need a hand getting down?"

I glanced at the remains of my left arm and let out a mirthless chuckle. "Yeah. I suppose I do at that."

Tom was okay. He'd suffered a broken leg in the fall, but it wasn't anything he couldn't fix by the time Glen and I got down there.

We took some time silently searching the cavern – Glen slithering beneath rocks we weren't able to move.

There was no sign of her, though. The Source, this one anyway, was likewise gone, leaving behind nothing but cracked earth in its place. I wasn't sure whether that was due to the creature or because of what Tom had done, but I wasn't sure it even mattered at that point.

Though I would've gladly continued searching all night and beyond, eventually we realized our time was up. Searchlights shone down from above, and there came the sounds of voices from further in the cave – albeit none of them the one I wanted to hear. No, it was Gan's people moving to resecure the area, and I was pretty sure I heard Paladin's voice among them, meaning he'd survived and it was definitely time for us to go.

It was only once we'd climbed out that the weariness hit, making me realize how truly spent I was. Hell, it was all I could do to keep from checking whether Ed had left anything of that mage.

He was sitting up, looking far more hale than he had been, with a section of bloodied Magi robe wrapped around his face obscuring his injuries.

The only upside was that the fight seemed to have gone out of everyone, Gan's people included, as they all seemingly paid us little heed.

"Come on," I said. "Let's get out of here."

"But..."

I held up a hand toward Tom, interrupting him. "There's nothing more we can do."

"But she's..."

"I know."

The words fell between us, seeming to linger in the air for far too long.

He nodded without another word, instead turning to give Ed a hand.

"You too, Glen," I said. "Keep up with them. Give Ed something soft to land on in case he falls."

"It will be my pleasure, Freewill," he replied, slithering away.

I stood there for a few more moments, despite knowing I needed to join them.

Finally, I turned to follow, just as my foot caught on something half buried in the dirt. Glancing down, I saw it was Falcon's vape pen. *Figures.* I picked it up and was about to chuck the fucking thing down into the hole, but stopped myself short of being a petty asshole.

Who knew? Maybe I could use it as a sort of peace offering when we got back. Doubtful, but I at least had to try. None of this had been his fault, after all.

I stuffed it into my pocket then decided there was no point in delaying the inevitable.

It was time to go.

I started walking, taking perhaps two steps in the direction my friends had gone when a hand fell on my shoulder.

I'm not sure how, but somehow I knew who was there before I even turned around.

"I'm sorry, Bill," Gan said. "I truly am."

Maybe it was the way she used my name or because I

had no more fight left in me, but all I did was turn and glare at her. "Don't."

"I didn't wish this for her."

"Bullshit! You tried to kill her."

"No," she replied. "I merely intended to incapacitate her, take her out of the fight. Please understand, despite our words to one another, I would have shown mercy ... knowing what she means to you."

"Oh really? You'd have shown her mercy? Why? So you could..."

"Because I knew what would happen if it was allowed to continue."

"Hold on. What the hell does that even mean?"

She lowered her gaze, the expression on her face so ... unGanlike, I didn't know what to make of it. "I warned you she was dangerous."

"Sally?"

She gave a single nod.

"Yeah, you did, and then you threatened Christy's life in the same breath."

"Because I wanted you to take that warning seriously. Do you think it is my wish to see you like this? Of course not. Your happiness is paramount to me. If anything, I had hoped you would take a different path, one that led you elsewhere, anywhere but here. But I underestimated your paramour's resourcefulness. She proved herself as clever as she is formidable."

"You mean she figured out you had one of those Sources in your back pocket."

She nodded. "Yes. And now, because of that, what has been foreseen is coming to pass."

"What's been foreseen?"

"As I've told you, all that once belonged to the First Coven is now mine. Even as we speak my seers continue to plumb the mysteries of what may come. And though the future remains uncertain, the winds of fate grow stronger with every step you take, soon to become an unrelenting typhoon."

"I don't give a shit about..."

"You should. For you will face a great many dangers if you choose to follow in her footsteps. I would spare you that suffering, but I also know you better than that."

I backed away. "You don't know shit. Christy's dea ... *gone*, and it's your fault."

She inclined her head then turned away. "Just know I speak true when I tell you I did not wish for any of this."

"Really?" I replied to her backside. "Why the vague threats then? Why not just come right out and tell me all of this if you were so concerned? Better yet, why not stop it yourself?"

"It's not as simple as that. Once one becomes aware of the future, one becomes entangled by it. Choosing to follow or deny fate matters not once you are set on its path. All roads will eventually lead you where you are meant to be, as I believe you already know." She let out a sigh than added, "But that is not the only reason I didn't tell you."

"Oh? And why's that?"

"It's because you would not have believed me."

As she walked away, leaving me alone with my darkening thoughts, deep down I realized she was right.

42

THE DEATH AFTER LIFE EPILOGUE

There was a car waiting just outside the gates – keys inside and the engine already running.

It was possible Gan had left it for us, or someone might've simply abandoned it the second we turned this place into a remake of *Destroy All Monsters*. Either way, it didn't really matter. This was one gift horse none of us were about to turn down, especially once the strange barrier around this property almost knocked us for another loop on the way out.

As the only member of our party still in one piece and possessing a license, the duty of driving fell to Tom. This didn't make for the most stress-free trip back to the city, but I doubted any of us cared.

We were returning minus two of our best. That was all that mattered.

We'd gambled and lost, perhaps more than any of us realized.

If anything, watching Tom swerve through traffic while Glen cheered him on was a welcome distraction from the reality waiting back home.

Home. Even that had no easy answer. Sally's building was demolished while ours was currently full of vampires and likely under werewolf surveillance.

That left only one place for us to retreat to – a place where I wouldn't be able to escape my failure – Christy's.

If ever there was a day to rue the lack of Village Coven's old properties, it was now.

Regardless, we needed a place to heal and that was all we had left.

It also wasn't nearly as unoccupied as I'd expected.

When Christy said she'd asked Kelly to watch over the tyke, I'd assumed it was at whatever love nest she and Vincent were holed up in.

And even if not, it was pretty damned late by the time we got back to Brooklyn.

So, when we finally unlocked the door and let ourselves in, it was no small surprise to find Tina running our way clad in her pjs.

"Daddy!"

She quickly skidded to a halt as she caught sight of us all, no doubt looking like quite the horror show.

"Hey, you know what, Tina," Kelly said, rising from the couch along with her husband, their eyes wide as saucers, "why don't you go into your bedroom with Uncle Vinny. I'm sure Daddy will be there in a few minutes to tuck you in."

Tina, however, continued staring at us, mostly at Ed and me.

Fortunately, for once anyway, Tom was there to pick up the ball we'd dropped. "It's okay, Cheetara. Me and your uncles just ... err ... finished playing a really tough round of paintball." He lowered his voice to a conspiratorial whisper. "They lost."

Tina appeared dubious, but thankfully she was too young to question the bullshit sandwich she'd been fed. "Where's Mommy?"

"Um ... she got called into work. They're ... having a sleepover."

I glanced sidelong at Ed, his face still wrapped in a

bloody robe. His eyes were enough, though, to convey the same thing I was thinking. We were utterly fucked.

Fortunately, Tina was of an age when such things sounded perfectly feasible, instead of like the plot of a sleazy Cinemax movie.

She took Tom's hand in one of hers and Vincent's in the other, and together they walked to her bedroom.

It was only after the door was shut that I let out a breath. "Why is she still awake?"

"She woke up a little while ago. Had a nightmare about her mom." Kelly was no idiot. Even had we not looked like we'd been run through a meat grinder, she could see the haunted looks on our faces. She took a deep breath then gestured toward the other apartment. "Why don't you two go get cleaned up. I'll put on some coffee."

Thank goodness we hadn't completely emptied Ed's fridge earlier. Even the single pint he had left was enough to sate the hungry beast inside me, for now anyway. We'd both need a lot more before the day was through, but hopefully by then at least one of us would be in shape to make a supply run. So long as it happened before the neighbors started looking tasty.

Killing that Magi had won me no points with Falcon, but there was no doubt Ed had needed it. As I helped him into some proper bandages, I saw his healing was moving along – having already regrown a good chunk of his jaw. However, he wasn't in any condition to hold up his end of the conversation, beyond maybe nodding and flapping his tongue around, so I told him to go to bed while the rest of us brought Kelly up to speed.

When Glen and I finally stepped back in – or slithered in his case – Kelly and Vincent were waiting on the couch, a pot of fresh coffee in front of them as promised.

Couldn't really say I was into threesomes involving ex-Templar, but right then I could've kissed them both.

"Where's Tom?" Glen asked, his eyeballs looking in every direction at once.

Vincent inclined his head toward Tina's room. "He tucked her in then passed out next to her."

I nodded. "Good. Let him sleep. He's earned it."

"Looks like you did, too," Kelly replied, eying the remains of my arm.

"Maybe, but I really don't want to close my eyes right now."

"I'm not surprised," Vincent said. "Have you seen what's been going on out there?"

Kelly put a hand on his leg. "That can wait for now." She then turned back toward me. "What happened?"

I opened my mouth but no words came out. The tears I'd been holding back for the last few hours took their place instead, finally allowed to fall freely.

Falling...

"T-there was no way to stop it," I stammered, "for either of them."

It took me a while to get the story out, sitting there bawling as I was. Glen offered me tissue after tissue, while Kelly tried to comfort me as best she could.

Though I was forced to relive it all, talking helped a bit. It's true what they say about it being cleansing in a way. It probably also didn't hurt that they listened without judgement, even Vincent.

That was okay. I'd be judging myself more than enough for a long time to come.

"There was nothing left," I said as I finished the tale. "When the smoke cleared, the Source was gone and so was she."

Kelly sat back. Her eyes were damp, but I could see

she was deep in thought, too. Maybe she was judging me after all. I sure as hell deserved it.

"What about Sally, or that creature?" Vincent asked.

"No sign of either. They were just gone, like they'd never been there. Hell, if I hadn't seen that thing up close and personal, I'd probably think I'd hallucinated it."

"If you did," he replied, "then so did a lot of other people."

"Huh? What do you mean?"

"What I was trying to tell you earlier. Here, hold on a moment. I managed to DVR it."

He flipped on the TV and called up an earlier recording.

Vincent fast forwarded through the first part of the newscast, some talking head blathering on about something, before letting it play.

"...a source unauthorized to speak on behalf of the airport confirmed that another unidentified radar contact was made earlier this evening. He described it as being the size and speed of a passenger jet before abruptly disappearing from the scope. The military in the meantime has denied conducting any tests in the area. Several eyewitnesses on the ground were quick to deny it was an aircraft of some sort, claiming that what they saw appeared to be a living creature..."

"No doubt in my mind on that one."

"I wish that were all," he interrupted. "It's ... been a busy night." He pressed the remote, fast forwarding to another report.

"Enemy submarines in the Hudson? That's what some are speculating after a New York Waterway ferry went down, claiming the lives of at least forty people aboard it. Though first responders are still calling it an accident, that's now been put into doubt thanks to footage released by one of the first news copters on the scene. I warn you, what you are about to see may be disturbing to some viewers."

The footage cut to an aerial shot of the Hudson. The cameraperson was mostly focused on the rapidly sinking ferry, as people could be seen on deck scrambling away from the water. All at once, the shot became unfocused, jittery, as if whoever was shooting it had caught sight of something else. Then it panned away, growing blurry for a moment before focusing again – showing something beneath the water heading away from the ferry. Whatever it was, it was huge, dwarfing the unlucky boat.

"If you look closely, you can see what appears to be running lights..."

I knew better, though. The blue glow visible beneath the surface weren't portholes, running lights, or anything manmade.

"Not one great beast, but two," I said wearily. "Just what we fucking need."

"What do you mean?"

"It was something Christy was looking into. Whatever Gan made a deal with, the thing that ... possessed Sally, it's called the Great Beast." I shook my head. "I thought it was that thing in the Hudson, but now I'm not so sure. I don't know exactly what I saw, but whatever's in the water didn't look anything like the thing that swooped down and fucked our shit up."

"A shapeshifter, perhaps?" he offered.

"If so, then it's on the same scale as *Godzilla vs. the Smog Monster*..."

I trailed off as the newscast switched to a different story. *What the?* Vincent moved to turn it off, but Glen held up a tendril. "Ooh, what's that?"

"Just some crank story that was next," he said. "Crazy stuff."

"Well, these are crazy times."

"True. Trying ones as well."

"Can we see it?" I asked.

He shrugged then hit the remote again, backing up a few seconds.

The newscast switched to a daytime scene – lush greenery with a mountain range in the background. Then the image shifted, showing a different view of the same range and what had caught my eye in the first place. For a moment, I wasn't sure what I was looking at, but then I saw it. One of the mountains was missing in the second bit of footage.

"This is the scene in the Sudan today, where scientists are puzzling over claims that one of the formations in the Marrah Mountain range disappeared overnight. Outside of a minor earthquake being reported in the region, along with some unusual aurora borealis activity, local authorities insist a volcanic eruption is not to blame for this phenomenon. Perhaps even stranger, a few eyewitnesses are making the somewhat outrageous claim that the mountain, and I quote, *'woke up and walked away'*."

They showed a montage of the area, flipping through multiple images, until I said, "Wait. Pause there!"

Vincent stopped on a photo of the night sky glowing an electric blue, the so-called aurora borealis stuff they'd been talking about. To me, though, it appeared as if something were lighting up the sky from below, somewhere in the jungle.

Staring at it, I couldn't help but fixate on what they'd just said about eyewitnesses claiming it walked away. "Something in the water, something in the sky, and now on the land, too?"

It made no sense. Sally had talked about serving the Great Beast, as in singular. But now it seemed like we had a fucking threesome going on. What the hell was up with that?

I wracked my brain, trying to think of something, *anything* that made sense and, of course, came up blank ... for a moment anyway.

He's here now. Ask him.

Ask who? Did he mean Vincent? And about what? But then, just as I was about to dismiss my inner demon, I remembered. Huh. It somehow seemed unimportant compared to everything that had happened, but it's not like I had much insight into anything else right then. Fuck it. I'd take even a momentary distraction from my misery.

"Does this..." I paused, feeling like an idiot for asking, but nothing ventured... "Is any of this, I dunno, mentioned in the Bible?"

"Excuse me?" he asked.

"Gan. She was talking about this stuff. Then she handed me a Bible and said it made mention of the Great Beast, or something like that."

"Was she speaking of Lucifer?"

I shrugged. "Who knows? I mean, she didn't mention him by name. Probably considers him an underling if anything."

Vincent leaned back, looking thoughtful for a moment. "The serpent in the Garden perhaps?"

"Maybe. Although whatever sunk that ferry was a bit too big to be picking apples. It's... Wait, there was something else she told me. She said something about looking to the sea, the sky, and the land. Any of that make sense in conjunction with the rest?"

He inclined his head for a few minutes before finally nodding. "Perhaps. The Good Book speaks in passing of monstrosities placed upon this Earth, beasts that even the angels trembled before."

I raised my eyebrows. "Okay, that sounds like it has potential. What about them?"

He leaned forward. "There was Leviathan, the great serpent of the oceans. Behemoth, who made the Earth shake with every step. And finally Ziz, king of all birds."

"Huh? Did someone say jizz?"

We turned to find Tom stepping out of Tina's room, looking barely half awake.

"Ziz," I corrected. "And what are you doing up? Thought you were getting some shuteye."

"I was," he said with a yawn, his eyes red – although I

doubted it was entirely from exhaustion, "Cheetara's tossing around and talking in her sleep." He shook his head. "Keeps saying her mom is calling for her. That she's somewhere dark and ... I ... couldn't..."

"It's okay, man," I replied, feeling my own tears welling up again.

"Poor child," Vincent said. "Do you think she knows?"

"I'm not ready to tell her yet. Not until we..."

"What if she does?" Kelly replied, sitting up after being quiet through most of this. "Know, I mean."

"It's just a bad dream. She was probably..."

"Could be mind magic," I interrupted. "She was playing around with it earlier. Maybe she heard what Christy had planned."

Kelly shrugged. "Or ... maybe they're still connected."

I raised an eyebrow. "Not following."

She turned Tom's way. "What exactly did she say?"

"I don't know. It was a bad dream. Kids have them." At Kelly's persistent stare, however, he added, "Like I already said, she was talking about Christy being trapped somewhere, calling for help."

"Trapped," Kelly repeated. "Not walking into danger, or worried whether things will go awry, but stuck somewhere."

"What are you getting at?" I asked.

"I'm not sure, maybe nothing. All I know is that the bond between a mother and child is a strong one, one of the strongest in nature. But in Tina's case we have to consider her power, too. It's beyond anything I've ever seen before."

"But..."

"Hear me out," she said, holding up a hand. "I've been thinking about what you said. How Christy tapped into The Source, how it pulled her in."

"Yeah, but she didn't come out again, not even as..." I paused not wanting to say it. "Not even as a Jahabich."

"Nor would I expect her to. That only happened to

souls who were already dead. We all saw it ourselves." She tapped a finger against the side of her chin. "Then there was Sheila. Remember when she got knocked into it, back before we blew it up the first time? She walked right out again."

"I remember, but Christy didn't..."

"Yes, but Sheila was the Icon. Her powers repelled magic. Well, think about it. What is the Source if not a pool of raw magic, pure, in its most distilled essence?" She held up a hand again. "But that's not all. It's supposedly also a portal, leading to all the myriad worlds we draw our magic from."

"Okay and...?"

"What I'm saying is, it makes perfect sense for it to spit an Icon out, but not Christy. She's a Magi, a magic *user*. You even said it yourself. She was able to tap into its power and use it against that thing."

"Yeah, but then it grabbed hold of her and dragged her in like it was hungry or something."

"Maybe ... or maybe it was simply reacting."

"Reacting? How?" I asked, my attention firmly grabbed by this point.

"She drew power directly from it. Maybe some sort of, I don't know, opposite reaction was required to balance those scales. Like filling a vacuum." I opened my mouth, but she wasn't done yet. "I know what you're going to say, but it's entirely possible this was something the White Mother knew to ground herself against. Y'know, being that she had a few thousand years to figure this shit out."

"Okay, so if that's the case then what happened to her?" Tom asked.

Kelly shook her head. "I have no fucking idea. All I'm offering are possibilities." She gestured toward Tina's bedroom. "I'm just saying, that little girl in there is capable of doing things in ways even *I* don't remotely understand. If *any* other child had said this, I'd be all for stroking her hair and telling her it's going to be all right, even if it's not. But Tina..."

I nodded, not daring to believe it was possible, but finding that seed had already taken root nevertheless. "If there's a chance that she's still out there and Tina's able to sense it..."

"Then we need to fucking figure that shit out and save her," Tom finished for me.

"How?" Glen asked, eyes on us all.

I had no idea on that front, but we'd just been handed a sliver of hope from out of nowhere, which was a lot more than we had a moment ago.

"Are you sure about this?" Ed asked.

"Not even remotely, but some things need to be done. Speaking of which..."

"Okay, enough already. I'll call her."

"You'd better. If I wake up and find another fucking message from Kara, I'm going to drag your ass out into the sunlight and kick the shit out of it. No more excuses now that you have a mouth again. Are we clear?"

I was talking tough despite being scared shitless. But, if there was even the slightest chance Christy had survived and was now lost in some other dimension, then I'd need to be at my very best once we were ready to save her.

My current state, however, served as nothing more than another hindrance we didn't need. Being able to function in daylight wouldn't solve my problems, but it would give us one less to worry about.

Fortunately, that was no longer an issue. After the initial stint of closing his wounds, Ed's healing had taken longer than usual – no doubt thanks to the silver Gan had infused him with. Mind you, it hadn't taken as long as it could have. If one bit of good had come from our adventure in upstate New York, it was that most of the metal fused to his skull had been torn away along with his face.

When at last his jaw had fully grown back, we'd found his mouth to mostly be full of normal vampire teeth. The only aspect of Gan's handiwork that remained were some metal in his molars – no worse than getting fillings at the dentist.

With Ed's fangs restored, there was little reason for me not to upgrade. Sure, I'd lose the ability to compel, but what I stood to gain was far more important. Besides, the last thing the vamps of the new Village Coven needed was me mucking with their minds.

Not to mention, it's not like they couldn't ask for the upgrade now, too.

Ed, of course, was quick to remind me that he wasn't my personal bite-bitch. But it seemed the ideal time to do this, especially with Kelly neck deep in research – having brought in Liz of all people to help out. I still didn't trust her, not after the shit she'd pulled, but Kelly had vouched for her, oddly enough. Besides, we needed all the help we could get since there'd been no word from Falcon, not that I'd really expected there to be.

Now, three days later, we were sitting in a cheap motel room, having decided it would be best to do this far away from Tina, just to be safe – the mini fridge already stocked with a few pints of pig blood.

"What if it doesn't work?" Ed asked, continuing to stall.

"Has it ever not worked before?"

"No."

"Okay, then why the fuck are we worrying about it?"

He shrugged, then finally extended his fangs and took hold of my hand.

"Got your puke bucket ready?" I asked.

"Right here."

"Good, and did you make sure Glen didn't hitch a ride in it?"

"Already checked." He lifted my wrist to his lips.

"Ooh baby, the things you do to me."

"Really?" he snapped. "Do you have to make this any fucking weirder than it already is?"

"Sorry. Couldn't resist. You may bite when ready."

"Fine. Then kindly shut the fuck up."

A moment later I felt pain, a bit more than a pinprick, as Ed bit down – harder than was necessary if you asked me. *Ouch!*

For several long minutes I didn't notice anything different, other than Ed yakking in his pail. Too bad he wasn't a Freewill like me.

A Freewill...

I'll admit, I'd spent the last couple of days ignoring Dr. Death's repeated concerns on the subject. But now, a small part of me realized maybe I should've stopped to consider whether there might be any complications due to me being ... different.

Even so, the simple truth was we wouldn't know for certain until we tried.

Oh well. It was a case of too little too late as a tingle started to creep up my arm. It was like having heartburn, except in the wrong place. My blood suddenly felt too warm for my body, like it was slowly starting to boil inside me.

And that feeling was spreading.

Here we go...

Soon enough, I felt it in my chest, my lungs refusing to work properly. It was a good thing I didn't need to breathe in order to...

Or maybe I did, as my head started to grow woozy, the room spinning around me ... until it all went black.

I shook my head, blinked a few times, and then sat up. Huh. That wasn't so bad.

When I looked around, though, it was the space of a moment or two for me to realize there was no way I could still be awake.

For starters, I was back in the living room of my apartment. More damning, however, was the lone other occupant – me, sitting on the love seat and staring back with soulless black eyes.

"Dr. Death, I presume."

We stared at each other for what felt like a small eternity, neither of us saying a word, until finally the lights blinked for some reason and he let out a sigh.

"I had thought by now you'd know not to call me that."

"Is that so?" I immediately went into defensive mode, knowing how this could play out – standing up and imagining myself wielding a lightsaber.

When I looked down, though, there was nothing in my hand.

"I'm afraid that's not going to work. Our neurons are shutting down one by one. In fact, it's taking everything we have left just to maintain this little space."

Oh yeah. Guess whatever Ed did to me was still going on. "Fine. So what happens now?"

"Your guess is as good as mine, Freewill. I simply thought this might be a good time for us to clear the air."

"Why?"

"Because I'm scared, that's why. I've been through this twice now, both times experiencing my very essence ripped to shreds. And yet, here I am, about to do it all over again."

"Do what?"

"Die of course."

As if to give credence to his words, the kitchen light abruptly went out.

"I don't know what will happen when next I awaken, or even *if* I'll awaken," he continued. "For all I know, my consciousness will be absorbed into yours ... or vice versa."

"Vice versa?" I replied, my eyes opening wide. "I swear, if you're planning to..."

"Please. Enough of that. I would think a child would have been able to figure it out by now, but you can be ... obtuse beyond even what your generation normally aspires to."

"But..."

"Think about it. The lack of threats. The helpful tidbits. Your complete and utter inability to become that *thing*. It's because I'm not him."

And here we were again. I'd almost believed him last time. At the very least, he acted way too ... well-read to be the monster I remembered. At the same time, it's not like I hadn't been fucked over by him before. One couldn't blame a guy for being paranoid. For all I knew, he'd spent the last five years studying up on shit just so he could pounce when I least suspected it.

"If you're not Dr. Death, then how come you look and sound like him?"

He shook his head as the bathroom went dark. "Because even though we now share this mind and body, you still hold sway here. I didn't choose to appear this way. This is how *you* chose to see me."

Wait, I had?

More lights went out, leaving us in a small oasis of illumination with nothing but darkness beyond. There wasn't much time left.

"Are you serious?"

"Quite serious. All I ask is that you take a moment to truly consider it."

Fine. I forced myself to think back to all the times he'd spoken to me – offering up bits of information that I couldn't have possibly known, talking about people he'd met who I had no recollection of, forcing me to focus when my brain was busy playing squirrel, but ... never once trying to take over.

Those weren't the actions of the monster Dr. Death had been.

"I already told you what to call me," he said. "Albeit I'll forgive it if you were too busy, how did you put it, *tripping balls* to remember."

Realization hit like a hammer to the back of my skull. Oh God, was it actually him? "James? Is that you?"

"Close." He shook his head. "He's gone I'm afraid, but I was a part of him for a great many years, long enough that I'm still not entirely certain where he ended and I began."

"The Wanderer."

"Yes. And now I'm a part of you, my friend. How about you try it on for size before..." He gestured at the rapidly encroaching darkness. "All you need to do is accept it."

Closing my eyes, I took a deep metaphorical breath, trying to do as he asked. I can't say I was expecting anything to happen, but when I opened them again the man before me had changed. It was growing dark, leaving him barely visible, but it was enough for me to see his familiar outline – the brown hair, fashion model physique, and overly handsome yet still friendly smile.

He looked down at himself and grinned. "Much better."

I couldn't disagree. Still... "So, what now?"

"As I said, I don't know. But I can tell you one thing. Gansetseg was right."

Oh shit! "You mean about her and I...?"

"No. But I do fear a great many trials likely await you in the days ahead, ones which may test you in ways the First Coven was never able to."

I nodded grimly, meeting his eyes. "If that's the case I ... might be able use some help, if you're willing to let bygones be bygones."

He smiled in return. "Might? I dare say you'll *need* it if

we're to have any hope of saving Christine and stopping whatever is coming."

"Do you think we have a chance?"

"I think there's only one way to find out." He offered his hand to me.

I took it as the darkness finally closed around us. "Together."

"Together it is then, forever if fate so wills it." I felt his hand grow intangible within my grasp. "Oh, there is one more thing, Freewill."

"What's that?"

As his voice faded, he let out a chuckle. "Perhaps at some point you can indulge me by stopping for an espresso. I think you'll find you have quite the taste for them now."

And then he was gone, along with everything else. My little sense of self was the last piece of me left, and I could feel that rapidly fading, too. But somehow the darkness, along with whatever else lay ahead, seemed a little less terrifying knowing I wouldn't have to face it alone.

THE END

◄———————►

Bill Ryder will return in
THE LICHING HOUR (Bill of the Dead – 4)
Read on for a sneak preview.

BONUS CHAPTER

Bill of the Dead, Part 4

Ugh, someone get the number of that metaphysical bus.

I swear, it felt like that time Tom and I went to the Fireman's Fair, got hammered on cheap dixie cup beer, then decided riding the Gravitron would be a good idea.

I'd have called that one lesson learned, except we did the same thing again the following year, this time on the tilt-a-whirl.

Hey, at least we're predictable that way.

Regardless, as the world stopped spinning around me, I began to remember what I was supposed to be doing. Hint: it had nothing to do with puking on shitty carnival rides.

Of course, it was still possible that might all change in a hot second, depending on what I saw once I finally cracked open my eyes.

For now, I took a breath, noting the air smelled clean and fresh — a far cry from the garbage and exhaust fumes of Brooklyn.

I waited a moment to see if there would be any ill effects, like me getting high or exploding. No luck on the former, but good deal on the latter as my lungs seemed to be processing everything normally in this new atmosphere.

Sensation started returning to my limbs, telling me I was either lying on soft grass or some really funky carpeting. Considering how my journey into the world of the weird first started five years ago – with SoHo, shag carpet, and dicks drawn on my face – I found myself really hoping for the former.

My nose was already telling me the answer, though, which meant it was time to get this show on the road.

I opened my eyes and saw ... grass, disturbingly normal looking grass at that.

Pushing myself to my knees, I adjusted my glasses, and took a look around.

I was in a forest, surrounded by trees and vegetation on all sides – the boring kind of forest I could've gone camping in as a child in New Jersey had I the slightest interest.

Well, this is pretty fucking basic.

I wasn't sure what I'd expected, but it wasn't this. I mean, hell, years spent watching sci-fi and fantasy movies had left me anticipating either some bleak horrorscape, leaving me surrounded by acid-drooling vegetation, or a Willy Wonka-esque magical garden full of candy and topless nymphs.

Anything but ... *this*.

I swear, as batshit insane as the supernatural could be, there were some parts that would've had to strive to reach mediocrity.

Looking up, I saw it was daytime, however, the sunlight – assuming such a thing applied here – was thankfully filtered through a thick canopy of leaves and tree branches far above my head.

That was a plus I suppose.

"What do you say we get moving?" I called out once I'd finally clambered to my feet.

Silence greeted my entreaty. Well, not total silence. My

sharp ears picked up the faint sound of wind through the trees, the light rustling of branches above, and a few piercing whistles that sounded not entirely dissimilar to birds.

"Hello?"

I turned and scanned my surroundings, seeing nobody else in the area.

Crap!

Before panic could set in, I started searching – stepping around trees, looking in bushes and low hanging branches, even checking the ground for footprints – as if I were some Army Ranger. All to no avail.

Damnit! Why the fuck hadn't I insisted on bringing Thundersmite with me? I mean, shit, being alone in a strange new land sucked, but I can guarantee it would've sucked a lot less with a giant magical war hammer by my side. Think of it like an ... adult teddy bear of sorts, except more smashy.

Just as I was about to lose it and freak out, though, the last of the fog cleared from my head and I remembered what I'd been told. They'd said it was possible, likely even, that we'd be separated upon transit. I'd also specifically been told not to panic if that happened. That so long as we had our tethers, we'd be okay. All we needed to do was follow them back to...

Shit ... my tether!

I searched the ground again, once more seeing nothing but grass, leaves, and dirt. The fuck? It was supposed to be visible to me. Without it, I'd likely be lost forever, destined to wander the Abyss for all eternity as a...

Wait a second.

I took a deep breath and focused, willing it to appear ... just as I'd been instructed. I knew I should've written all this shit down first. But no, I had to be all gung-ho about there not being a second to waste.

Oh well. What was done was done.

Speaking of which, I envisioned my tether then

opened my eyes to see ... more nothing! *Son of a...* Or at least that was the case until I glanced over my shoulder.

Duh!

Of course it made sense that it would be behind me. I spied a glowing silvery strand of energy leading away from my body, off into the distance.

Hold on a second.

I followed the astral tether back to my body, seeing it snake up the back of my leg, only to disappear inside my pants, making it look like I was taking an infinitely long silver shit.

"You've gotta be fucking kidding me."

Good thing I was the only one who could see it. The last thing I needed was to be mistaken for trying to get a world record for world's longest dump.

As I spun to get a better look, the strand of light shifted, moving with me, so it always appeared behind my body. *What the?* How the fuck was I supposed to follow it back if it was constantly...?

However, in the same instant that thought hit my head, the tether suddenly appeared in front of me.

Huh.

Wait. Hadn't they said something about that too – that the tether wasn't a physical thing so much as a concept, my mental connection back home? If so, then maybe I was only able to follow it when I wanted to – the rest of the time leaving it to trail behind me like I was constantly shitting magical Silly Putty.

That said, a part of me was tempted to follow it now, especially since I didn't like the thought of being alone wherever I was. The problem there was I had no idea how long I could follow it before it simply snapped me back to where I'd started.

And if that happened, well, I'd be at square one again without having even tried. No fucking way was that happening. There was simply no way I could look Tina in the eye knowing I'd given up so easily.

Mind you, that didn't mean I couldn't hope for the best.

I cupped my hands over my mouth and shouted, "Christy, are you out there?!"

My own voice echoed back, as well as the sound of scampering from the underbrush – away from me fortunately – but that was all.

Still, it had to be done, even if there was no way it could ever be that easy.

Guess it was the old fashioned way then.

"So what do you say, Wanderer? Any direction look better to you than the rest?"

My subconscious, however, was apparently in the mood to be as quiet as the surrounding forest.

I rapped a knuckle against my forehead. "Yoo hoo, Wanderer. You awake in there?"

Again there came no answer. *Great.* Not only was I physically alone, but apparently the spirit residing inside my mind was taking a siesta, leaving me with nobody but myself to rely on.

Just fucking wonderful.

Nevertheless, I wasn't going to get anything accomplished by standing around. So I turned in a circle and then picked a direction, using the scientific method of stopping at random and deciding that way looked as good as any other.

The hard work finished, it was time to get walking.

I'd never been much of a survivalist. I had no interest in being a Boy Scout. Hell, as a child I'd treated any and all entreaties about camping as fully hostile. Needless to say, that hadn't changed much once I became an adult.

That said, I wasn't a fucking idiot. I'd watched enough wilderness-based horror movies to know how easy it was to end up walking in circles. So I popped the talons on my right hand and used them to mark each tree that I passed – a horizontal slash followed by a vertical one, making it look like a tic-tac-toe board. That way there was no mistaking it.

It slowed me down a little, but not by much. I mean, it's not like I was sprinting mindlessly through here at top speed to begin with.

Much as I normally didn't like the wilderness, I had to admit it was peaceful – a far cry from the hellish landscapes I'm sure I could've appeared in had luck dictated it.

Every so often I stopped to call out Christy's name, each time to no avail. If she was playing Snow White in this enchanted forest, then I had to assume she'd found somewhere to hole up – hopefully without seven horny dwarves to keep her company. I swear, it almost made me sorry I'd downloaded that porno years back because now I couldn't get it out of my head.

I continued onward for what felt like a good hour or more – it was hard to tell in this place – seeing nothing but trees, bushes, and more trees.

Finally, I spotted something up ahead – a break in the trees if I wasn't mistaken.

Double-timing it that way, I realized I'd found a clearing, a large one by the looks of it. Inside, the canopy of trees gave way to open sky – with what appeared to be bright sunlight streaming down upon it, giving it an almost magical quality compared to the relative gloom of the forest.

I stopped just inside the tree line, still protected by the shadows.

Craning my neck to look up, I spied my first hint that I wasn't in Kansas anymore, or anywhere else on Earth for that matter. The sky above was a clear blue with only a few clouds visible, but they weren't the normal fluffy white one might expect. They were bright pink, as if made of giant bales of cotton candy. There was nothing ominous about them, but it grounded me in the reality of needing to remember that the normal rules didn't necessarily apply here.

Looking at where the sunlight hit the ground just a few feet in front of me, I took a deep breath. It was time to test just *how* different the rules of this land were.

I tentatively reached out, feeling the ambient warmth as my hand started to leave the protective cover of the...

And then I quickly pulled back as the most godawful stench hit me from out of nowhere, causing me to double over coughing. It utterly disrupted the pristine smells of the forest like a shit covered baseball bat to the forehead.

What the fuck?

Worse yet, it seemed to come from everywhere at once. The hell? Had I somehow found the diarrhea fairy's invisible summer palace or something?

As my eyes watered, the disgusting odor continued to assault me. Even breathing through my mouth didn't help as I could fucking taste it, too. *Ugh!*

I swear, I hadn't smelled anything this bad in ... over five years.

No way!

In the next instant there came the crunch of leaves from behind me, as if something heavy had just taken a footstep.

It's not possible. I have to be imagining it. There's no way it can be a...

"*T'lunta*," a throaty voice growled, sounding as if it's owner were gargling with broken glass.

Fuck, fuck, fuck!

I turned, praying to whatever gods existed that I was hallucinating on shroom dust. However, the creature looming above me, cutting off my escape back into the forest, was both way too solid as well as far too ripe to be my imagination running wild.

It was titanic in stature – a nightmare given form – ten feet tall if an inch, and covered in rippling muscle beneath matted brown fur. I was tempted to shit my pants then and there, knowing at least nobody would be able to tell with Sasquatch stink dirtying the air.

Oh, this was definitely not good.

But then the beast opened its mouth to speak, and it was an instant for me to realize it was so much worse than I thought.

"Turd remembers you! Turd hates you! And now Turd will finally have his revenge!"

To be continued in...

THE LICHING HOUR
Bill of the Dead – Book 4

Coming soon!

AUTHOR'S NOTE

I guess the first thing I should do is apologize. No, not for
this story's ending or what happened to certain characters.
Alas, their fates were sealed the moment I started writing.
However, what I do feel the need to ask forgiveness for is
how long it's taken me to get this book out.

The bottom line is 2020 was a terrible year for many
of us, and I'm no exception. I'm not sure whether that's an
excuse or not, but it is the reality of the situation. Due to a
series of less than fortunate circumstances, I found myself
in a bad place writing-wise. As a result, the nearly bottom-
less well of story ideas that normally sits inside my head
simply ran dry.

Fortunately, I had a few outlines already finished,
giving me stuff to work on so the year wasn't a complete
waste. Sadly, this book was not among them. I knew full
well I wouldn't be able to do it justice until something
jumpstarted my creative circuits again.

The thing was, I knew where I wanted this story to go,
but the problem turned out to be I was unsure how to
navigate all the roads leading toward the big finale.

I was able to keep a bit of momentum in Bill's world
going thanks to the Bill of the Dead Adventures novella

series, but Bill himself mostly sat in relative silence for the duration.

Thankfully, this year has proven to be much kinder. I felt the well of ideas slowly starting to fill again late in 2020, which meant I was able to hit the new year running.

Obviously we're a wee bit past that point. But what can I say? Writing this story was actually a relatively easy affair, but polishing it ... well, that's why they say the devil is in the details.

Nevertheless, here we are at long last. And, while I'd love to laud this story's happy ending, let's be realistic. We're dealing with an Empire Strikes Back moment for Bill – facing an uncertain future as he, quite literally, dies again. Poor guy just can't catch a break, especially with me at the helm.

That said, Bill's path forward might be murky, but mine isn't. This story leaves off exactly where I wanted it to, meaning I'm already brainstorming all the fun stuff I want to see in his next adventure.

The good thing is I'm in a much better headspace right now, so my hope is that you won't have to wait nearly as long.

Until then, I hope you enjoyed this roller coaster ride of murder, mayhem, and lovestruck monsters. I know I did.

Rick G

ABOUT THE AUTHOR

Rick Gualtieri lives alone in central New Jersey with only his wife, three kids, and countless pets to both keep him company and constantly plot against him. When he's not busy monkey-clicking words, he can typically be found jealously guarding his collection of vintage Transformers from all who would seek to defile them.

Defilers beware!

THE TOME OF BILL UNIVERSE
THE TOME OF BILL
Bill the Vampire
Scary Dead Things
The Mourning Woods
Holier Than Thou
Sunset Strip
Goddamned Freaky Monsters
Half A Prayer
The Wicked Dead
Shining Fury
The Last Coven

BILL OF THE DEAD
Strange Days
Everyday Horrors
Carnage À Trois

FALSE ICONS
Second String Savior

Wannabe Wizard
Halfhearted Hunter

BILL OF THE DEAD ADVENTURES
Bottom Feeders
Wandering Spirit
The New Order
Blinding Justice

Join Rick on Facebook: www.facebook.com/Rick-GualtieriAuthor

CPSIA information can be obtained
at www.ICGtesting.com
Printed in the USA
LVHW040157070222
710423LV00010B/288